I0612774

Friends, Lovers, and Roses

V. B. Clay

Brick Publishing Company®
Chicago, Il, 60620

Chapter 1

— I —

"Girlfriend! Now listen here. Your ass has been ghost for the past two weeks, and you still trying to get me off the phone!"

David raised a furry eyebrow. "Damien. Honey, baby, *papi,* you know I gotta cook dinner for my sweetie. So what's the deal?"

"The deal? I'll tell you what the deal is," Damien started, his Puerto Rican accent getting heavier. "You and that man of yours. I think you trying to get me off the phone so he don't see you talking to me. You know that fucker ain't hardly fond of me."

Damien was about to protest, but the truth held him back. "Okay. You got a point, but that is my man, girl, so try to recognize. I gotta have this dinner fuckin' ready for his ass, and you know that. Chicken takes awhile to cook."

"It also takes awhile to choke," Damien laughed. "Which is what you should be doing, instead of dealing with that wildebeest you call a husband."

David sighed. Friends could be so brutally honest. "Listen, girl. I don't have time to hear how you dislike Allen. I still have a dinner to cook."

"Okay, Betty Crocker, do what you will. Neglect your friends, put them aside, cast them to the—"

"Stop the drama, will you? I swear you Latins are just all about creating a stage show, aren't you?" David said, as he transferred the phone to his other ear. Damien could not only be trying at times, but very long-winded.

"Well, I wouldn't be bothering you so much if you weren't so busy playing matchmaker with Stephen. He's not at home like he used to be since you started setting him up on dates."

Acclaim for
Friends, Lovers, and Roses

"Friends, Lovers, and Roses takes you on a realistic, sensual, fun journey of black culture and life that we rarely see in writing today. This is an inside window to the much-discussed 'down low' phenomenon, with a whimsical, serious, and sometimes hysterical approach. It's the African-American *Friends* shown with naked truth.

Author V. B. Clay knows the talk, writes the walk, and brings to life a world of friends who love, hate, and bicker with one another amid the struggles of family, prejudice, economics, AIDS, homophobia, and generational differences. He can get into the mind of a young gay man and a wizened elderly woman with equal realism and sensitivity.

Here is an unpredictable combination of diverse characters thrown together in a world filled with love and danger. It's as if Clay has peeled open a neighborhood and transcribed the thoughts and dialogue of the colorful characters he finds there."

—Mike Szymanski
Entertainment Writer, Film Critic, and Author;
Regular contributor to *The Los Angeles Times*

"V B. Clay magically weaves the lives and romances of gay African Americans together in his groundbreaking debut novel. A master of lyrical dialogue, Clay has created living, breathing characters who suffer through domestic violence, untrusting relationships, the illness of friends, and being true to oneself. The reader feels their pain and roots them on to a happy finish.

This is a happy novel, for Clay is able to show the power and the magic of friendship, how it heals, how it allows one to overcome troubles. Friendship is the root of every tale in *Friends, Lovers, and Roses*. It is through friendship that Clay captures the glory of living life to its fullness."

—Dan Boyle
Author of *Huddle*

"I only set him up on one date," David said, looking briefly at his watch. "It's not like he's married already."

"He might as well be, since I know you set him up with Jamal Warren. I know that mutha to be as fine as hell."

"And where did you hear that?"

"Don't worry about it, child," Damien said. "Don't you know? Four-one-one calls *me* when it needs information."

"I have no doubt," David said without any reservations. "Guess you can't keep anything from a diva."

David heard Damien snap his fingers loudly, as if he had placed them against the receiver. "And this information line is telling you that that mutha'fucker Allen, is bad news," Damien warned.

David was not willing to hear anymore. He shook his head in frustration. "I don't need to hear any of this, Damien. What do you have planned for tonight? Maybe I should have fixed you up on a date too."

Damien raked his fingers through his fine hair. "Girl, I am not in the need of charity work, okay? And from looking at the husband you have chosen for yourself, I think I am better off with my own devices."

"I can only imagine what those devices are, and the batteries you need to turn them on."

"Funny, bitch. Well, you just dismiss your friend, okay. I'm gonna call up Dominique and then watch some movies I rented. Me and Bette Davis got us some ol'time religion to overcome tonight."

David heard a car pull up in the driveway. "Fine, you just have a good time. Listen, I have to go."

"All right, already! Bye!" Damien said, and then hung up the phone.

David set the phone on its receiver, pressing it down with both hands. *That girl can be soon trying,* he thought. Just then the door opened, and David felt a sheen of sweat steal across his brow.

"Damn key!" Allen shouted, as he wrestled with the door, attempting to free the key from the lock.

"That happened to me earlier today," David said, as he began to stroll toward the kitchen to check the baked chicken.

Allen looked at his spouse oddly, and then looked down at the phone as if steam were rising from it. "And who was on the phone?" He asked, as he finally pulled the keys from the door, then casually tossed them on the coffee table. He took off his coat, casually placing it on the coat rack.

David began to wring his hands. "Oh, that was Damien."

"What did that faggot want? I don't know why you stay friends with such a queer."

"Oh, he's all right," David said, waving a hand dismissively.

Allen walked to the coffee table and leaned his tall, thick frame forward to retrieve the mail that was stacked neatly on it. He examined the envelopes, and then suspiciously peered up at David as he headed back through the kitchen door. "Is dinner ready?"

David stopped in the archway. *That is a calculated question,* he thought. He thought it would be best to ignore it, and continued through the door.

It didn't work.

"Fuck, David! Dinner isn't ready, is it?" Allen asked, tossing the mail back on the coffee table. It scattered like confetti across the rug.

David turned around, keeping the kitchen door open with an extended foot. "By the time you finish taking your shower things will be warmed up and ready for you, baby," he said, as a trail of goose pimples raced along the dark flesh of his arms.

Allen did not reply. He twisted around abruptly, walked toward the front door, reached for his suit coat on the coat rack, and snatched it off so forcefully that the wooden post rocked back and forth on the very brink of teetering to the shag carpet below. He snatched his keys off the coffee table.

"Where are you going?" David asked, stepping cautiously back into the living room. Allen merely looked at him, brow furrowed, nostrils flaring like a charging bull, and hands trembling, formed into fists.

"You had plenty of time to talk to that fuckin' flame of a friend of yours," Allen began as he drove his arm through the sleeve of his jacket. "But no time to get dinner prepared for your man. It's Friday, and you know the DMV gets crazy as hell today. I said I would be going to the gym, and you know I like to have dinner waiting for me when I get here."

David spread his arms out in defeat. "I had to run to the store today, and only got back a little while—"

"Friday!" Allen continued, as if David's explanation went on unheard. "People bitching about personalized license plates, parking tickets, registration fees, extensions—just utter bullshit. I have never been cursed out in so many languages in all my life."

David took a bold step forward, just inches away from Allen. "Just calm down a bit. Maybe I should be running you a bath while I get this dinner ready. Would that help?" he asked, placing a comforting hand on Allen's backside.

The jolt came swiftly and unexpectedly. Allen thrust his hand mightily against David's shoulder, knocking him blindly into the corner of the sofa. He fell against it and tumbled to the floor, his body hitting the edge of the coffee table. He lay there, breathing heavily, not sure what had just transpired.

Allen, with half-closed eyes, gave him a look of disappointment—a declaration of outrage. He quickly turned and headed for the door.

"Don't do this again, David. You promised dinner would be ready when I got home, and you let me down. You lied. Now I'm forced to go out and find something to eat." Allen said all this without once turning to look at David.

The door opened and closed with such swiftness that David could feel its cool breeze slap him in the face. He remained on the floor, eyes shut, as he heard the sound of a car door slam shut, its engine soon fading. Silence commanded the room once more. Then suddenly, as if to mock him, the smell of dinner faintly drifted through the room.

— II—

As he lay upon the sofa, the phone's cry reached into Stephen's sea of dreams, pulling him out of unconsciousness and catapulting him into reality. He cracked open one paste-filled eye and cursed under his breath. He knew that ring anywhere. It was a shrill tone, a siren of a sound that had followed him from Chicago to this very condo in Los Angeles. Eight hundred miles across a thin strand of telephone wire, destined to reach his ears. He wondered if he were working off some sort of bad karma, to be still dealing with what was on the other end of that line.

He reached out to pick up the receiver and shouted into the phone, *"Hello...Hello!"*

"Damn! What's that tone for?" asked the woman on the other end. "You don't sound like you miss me at all."

"And to think, I thought you former models weren't all that bright," he said sarcastically. What do you want, Felicia?"

"Do I always have to want something to call your tired ass? Can't I just call to say hello, Steff?"

"Don't call me Steff. You know how I feel about that name. Listen, I don't have time for this." Stephen said, placing his other hand on his forehead. He looked up to stare at the empty shot glass on the coffee table before picking it up and standing on his feet.

"Okay, *Steff*, I won't call you that anymore."

Two years, and still this nightmare was not coming to its last act. Two years and Felicia was still calling, still trying to force her way into his life. Two years and she was yet to realize that he had made a mistake in choosing her. His desires had changed, and she was not a part of the equation. No woman ever would be.

Stephen could hear the muffled cry of a child on the other end of the line.

"You hear that crying?" Felicia asked, the squeal becoming more audible, as if she were holding the phone near the child's face. Her voice returned. "You hear that, Macho Man? That is your son, our creation, crying out for a man in his life."

Stephen walked over to the wet bar, and placed the shot glass on it with such force he thought it would chip the marble countertop. "Yes, I can hear Tumali. What is it I can help you with, Felicia? I have a very busy day," he pleaded, then reached for the bottle of Glenfiddich and brought it closer to his glass.

"I want the baby's father back in his life, and not some fuckin' faggot! That's what I want. Do you hear me, *Steff?* I want a fuckin' *man* back in his life."

That crazy girl has been drinking, Stephen thought, and he was not far from joining her. He reached out toward the ice bucket on the counter. A pair of steel tongs stood erect in it like a saluting soldier. He pulled it out, gripping a few cubes in its jagged teeth, and dropped them into his glass. He almost sighed in ecstasy as he poured the liquor over the ice. .

"I just know you did not call all the way from Chicago to tell me this news. I just know you are not standing there yelling at me while my son is crying." He reached toward a cluster of lemon wedges arranged in a crystal bowl, lifted two with his carefully manicured fingers, and began to squeeze their juice into his concoction. Are you drunk or something?"

"Maybe I should be asking you the same thing, asshole! I wouldn't be surprised if you had a drink and an ass in front of that useless mug of yours right at this moment."

The only ass I know right now is on the other end of this receiver, he thought. More curses followed under his breath as he stirred the elixir with his finger. He placed the digit between his thick lips and sucked heavily. Perfect. He took a slow drink.

"Are you still there, Steff?" Felicia asked. This was followed by a knocking sound, as if she were tapping the phone against something. "Hellooo! Are you there?"

"Yes!" he said, smacking his lips. "I am still here, and I am on the verge of ending this phone call. I don't have time for this."

"And why not? You got some sort of hot date or something waiting for you?" .

Silence.

She picked up on his sudden hesitation, and he could hear her breathing suddenly become choppy, heavy, rapid. He let the silence stand. It was too late to quell her thoughts now.

"Why are you doing this, Stephen? Why are you doing this to us?" Her tone was suddenly serious.

He said nothing, and took another sip of his drink. She was right. He did have a date—his very first. After twenty-eight years he was.finally going to drop the shroud of fraudulent heterosexuality he had been hiding under all this time. But the evidence of this past relationship was still there for him to deal with. He knew that Felicia thought things would change, that he was going through a phase, that he would return and they could be the perfect nuclear family she had once had. She couldn't be more wrong. The power of the penis was strong.

"This isn't fair, Stephen! Your family needs you here. I'm sorry about whatever I did to make you this way."

"You have nothing to do with this, Felicia. We have gone through this too many times to tally."

"But you haven't given us a fair chance. You don't have to be this way. You can still be normal like—"

"And what do you mean by normal? Are you saying that I'm not normal because I don't want to be in your life, to have sex with you, to desire you? That sort of thinking is what's not normal."

"I didn't mean to offend you, Stephen."

"You could never do that, Felicia. I wouldn't give you the chance."

"I'm sorry. I'm just stressed. The modeling agency has not been able to find me any substantial work lately. It would be so much easier if you were here. That's all I am saying."

"Easier? Have you forgotten what drove us apart? Have you forgotten what you came home to see? I know it's been more than a year, but have you forgotten so soon about—"

"Shut up! You bastard! How dare you mention that again. No. No, I have not forgotten what happened that night. Every time I change our son's diapers, I think about the shit you caused ... about the shit you are." He could always tell when Felicia was about to rant.

"Listen," he said, "I know Tumali is a handful, but I can't deal with that right now. We'll work something out soon, but right now. . . I need to work on myself."

"It's not all about Tumali, Stephen. I just want ... oh, I don't know. He misses you, that's all."

"I know what it's all about. Believe me, I do, and I am sorry, but I'm sure a lot will be missed. Good-bye, Felicia." He slowly hung up the phone.

Stephen took a deep breath. Talking with Felicia could be so exhausting. He walked back to the sofa and fell on it in silence. Across the expanse of his living room, he could see the large oval mirror placed there, and he admired the man he saw reflected in its smooth glass: a man that was once in love with a woman of great quality, a queen of high heels and legs that reached her neck. A former model that chose to give up that life once their child was born. He often saw her face in his dreams: golden brown skin, thick eyelashes, dark hair that reached down to the small of her back. She had a smile that could brighten the darkest room. He hated hurting a face like that, to see that smile turned upside down, to see the eyes clouded with tears, to watch those legs run away from him in horror ... in hatred. What else was he to do? Before he could love Felicia, he had to love himself. It was only fair.

The doorbell rang.

Stephen could feel his heart quicken. He stared at the door as if it were a stranger in his home, an intruder, something he had only noticed at this very moment. Slowly he stood, with doubt weighing him down. Was he doing the right thing? He had admired many men in his life, talked to them with desire, gone to bars to see them, be near them ... but never did he take it to the next level. Tonight, all that would change.

Stephen reached for the doorknob and released the deadbolt. As the door opened, he stood flabbergasted, and tried to hold back the smile that was brimming on the inside of him. His best friend had set him up on this blind date, and by the looks of things. . . he had chosen very well.

"Hey there, I'm Jamal. Are you Stephen?" asked the tall gentleman in his doorway.

Stephen looked at the brother before him, with smooth complexion and thin lips hidden behind his neatly trimmed mustache. His eyes were a deep brown that reflected like tiny marbles in the overhead lighting of the hallway. A pretty face, hair cut short with a slight curl at the top. Two gold-studded earrings hung from his lobes—very attractive.

"Yes, I'm Stephen. Glad to meet you, Jamal," he said, reaching out to shake his date's hand. The grip was solid. Stephen watched the long fingers wrap around his own. His eyes traveled up the bare forearm to the rolled-up sleeves of a deep blue denim shirt. It was a muscular arm, swathed in a light covering of hair. His chest showed the same trace of hair, peeking out from beyond three unfastened buttons. Black jeans hugged his thick legs, and leather boots encased his feet. Only things missing were the cowboy hat and steer.

"May I come in?" Jamal asked, pulling away from the handshake that had gone on a bit too long.

"Oh, I'm sorry," Stephen apologized, taking a step back, and holding out his arm. "Come in and have a seat."

Jamal reached out to place his fingers along Stephen's collar, pulling lightly at his silk tie. "I thought I mentioned that this would be a casual dinner."

Stephen could smell Jamal's sweet cologne as he walked by. He looked down at his own apparel. "This *is* my casual look," he said as he closed the door.

"Maybe we could do without the tie," Jamal said, walking over to the sofa. He began to examine the place: the large area rugs on the floor, the plush sofa with an overabundance of pillows, the selection of framed pictures that hung on the strikingly white walls, illuminated by a row of track lights, the china plates that lined the top of the archway leading into the kitchen, the crystal chandelier that hung modestly at the center of the room. Clean came to mind. "You don't spend much time in this room, do you?"

Stephen was silent.

"It seems so virgin*est*... but it looks great," Jamal said, turning to finally take in the comfort of the sofa. "Like an untouched masterpiece."

"Thanks," Stephen replied, as he walked over to the coffee table and picked up his drink, taking a sip. "Would you like something to drink before heading out?"

"A glass of water would be fine."

"I can handle that," Stephen said, as he walked into the kitchen.

Jamal continued to look at the place. He especially noticed the Chinese bench, and the collection of framed photographs placed on them. Some were of Stephen in different parts of the world, but others showed a child of no more than two, eyes sparked with happiness and a smile to match. One photo showed a very beautiful woman holding this same child, her hair caught in a wind that carried it across her and the child's face as they laughed. Jamal leaned forward, seeing the image of the Sears Tower in the background. Chicago.

"Here's your drink," Stephen suddenly said, thrusting the glass before his guest. He hoped to distract Jamal before he could ask questions about Felicia and Tumali.

"Thanks." Jamal took the cool drink and examined the photos once more over the rim of his glass. His gulps were loud and swift; he was thirsty. Then he stood up. "I think we should be leaving. You don't mind if I drive, do you?"

"No, of course not," Stephen said. He wondered what sort of pickup truck this man would be driving. His friend had already told him that Jamal was not an overly wealthy man, but he *was* a man. His friend thought Stephen needed to get away from the set of people that was holding him back.

As they headed for the door, Jamal turned to face Stephen. "And oh, there is one more thing," Jamal said, reaching out to take hold of Stephen's collar. He made a few twists and adjustments and finally tossed the tie onto the sofa. He unhooked a few of Stephen's buttons, then reached up to touch his own chin. "Hmm, that should do just fine. You are now officially casual." He turned and opened the door.

Stephen felt quite naked. A wisp of air caressed his uncovered chest, and he shivered. He was going to play it cool tonight. It was only a first date, and he was going to let the cards fall where they may.

Just then Jamal turned around once more and said, "Oh, and by the way ... I'm driving a Bronco."

Stephen smiled.

— III—

Dominique placed the phone back on the receiver and rubbed at her ear. *Damien would talk my ear off if I let him,* she thought. The living room was cold, and a chill crawled up her bare arms. She dashed back to the warm bedroom.

She tiptoed carefully over her Siamese cat, as it slept in her doorway, and crawled under the covers next to her "other half." The laundry from the dryer lay on the bed, unfolded but clean. The scent of mountain freshness filled the room. She cuddled up to Sarafina, feeling her lover's round thick frame warm her thin bones.

Sarafina ran one heavy hand through Dominique's hair. "Was that Damien on the phone again?" Sarafina asked, pulling the joint away from her lips.

"Yeah. That was him. The moment I leave to get some water, he catches me en route. You know how he can ramble. He said David set Stephen up on a blind date."

"Figures," Sarafina chided, as she brought the joint to her thick lips. "He is always keeping you guys abreast of the latest gossip *he* creates.

"Let me get some of that," Dominique said, reaching for the smoke. "Don't be getting greedy with the grass."

"Just don't drop that ash on the bed. You know how shaky your hands get after a few hits," Sarafina said, handing Dominique the weed and reaching for the remote on the bed. She turned the volume up on the television—an *I Love Lucy* marathon was playing. "And make sure you don't get ash on my tits this time too."

"Girl, those are *my* tits. You're just carrying them around for me. I get more use out of them than you," Dominique said, inhaling deeply.

"Doesn't Damien know that when *Lucy* marathons are on television we are not to be disturbed?"

"I told him that," Dominique replied, "and he got off the phone real quick, as if someone stole his Abercrombie. I told him it was the one where Lucy goes to the club."

"She's always going to the club. You might as well have said that it's the episode where she wails, or she lets a perfect stranger in the house, or there's some mistaken identity. The girl is oh so predictable - but funny as hell. Too bad you weren't back in that time to hook that club up with your design skills."

"Could have hooked up her last name too, while I was at it," Dominique said, as she reached over Sarafina to place the joint back in the ashtray. "Lucille Ball. What's with that Ball name? That brings to mind some real hairy ugliness. Should have been Lucille Clit. Now that's a name."

"Good point, baby, 'cause then she could have married some Puerto Rican dyke queen named Chi-Chi, or something. Then Ethel and Fred could be the upstairs drag queen and king."

"Baby, that's what Ethel was!"

They both started laughing uncontrollably.

Their laughter died as Sarafina watched the covers slip from Dominique's small frame, like the unwrapping of a chocolate bar. Sarafina watched the covers slip past Dominique's tight stomach, and how she managed to kick them even further down, exposing her short and curlies every now and then. She could smell Dominique's hair, her body, her womanhood; it was the smell of mangoes and vanilla rolled into one. She kissed the top of Dominique's head, the hairs tickling her lips. Dominique looked up, her brown eyes very sexy, very inviting. She inched herself up, until they faced each other. Their lips soon touched, tongues intertwined, breath became one.

Dominique pulled back, placed two fingers in her mouth, and pulled them out, wet and glossy. She began to rub them on Sarafina's dark nipples. Soon, her lips and tongue followed.

Sarafina laid her head back and gently placed her hand atop Dominique's head, feeling her movements as her mouth gave her pleasure. "You know we have to get these towels off the bed sometime."

Dominique pulled back from the tit, licking her lips. "I don't think we're going to have to worry too much about those towels, considering they will soon come in handy," she said, eyes focused on her lover's breasts.

"Oh, is that so?"

"Yes, that is very much so. They will be used to wipe up the sweat we are about to produce," Dominique said, moving her hand under the covers, until it reached Sarafina's briar patch below. She could feel the heat escaping from it.

Sarafina looked up at the ceiling, watching the blades of the fan. It cooled her, washing over her face and shoulders like a crisp ocean breeze. It reminded her of when she first met Dominique, many moons ago, at Venice Beach; the coolness was almost the same.

As she remembered this, Dominique entered her cavern, and her womanhood pulsated. she could now remember another breeze; the wind whipping across her face as she rode into Los Angeles on the seat of her Harley-Davidson, which was crusted with miles of dirt and sand; the freedom she felt in leaving San Francisco behind; the memories it wrought.

She remembered the last time she saw Gerri Moore, her former lover—a woman who was wealthy beyond anyone else Sarafina had met. She owned a prosperous cosmetics firm. A beautiful woman, an older woman—a white woman: a woman who loved her career more than she loved her partner. Sarafina had questioned whether she had ever really fallen in or out of love with Gerri.

Until she met Dominique.

Dominique was at Venice Beach, diligently reading a book called *Crossing the Border,* by a Kim Chernin. Sarafina remembered that the story had to do with a journey, a leaving behind of what was once familiar, and going into the unfamiliar. . . then finding paradise by surprise. It was something that reminded Sarafina of her own journey. They had talked about that book over lunch at the Promenade. Then there was dinner at Marina Del Rey. A year later, Gerri was long-forgotten, a relationship whose intricacies she could no longer recall. Sarafina and Gerri had continued to talk, and a friendship had developed between them, despite Dominique's jealousy.

Sarafina let out a moan as Dominique's warm fingers went deeper insider her, and kisses dampened her neck. The phone suddenly began to ring, and it startled them both.

"Thank goodness I have the answering machine on, baby," Dominique muttered softly.

On the machine came a voice and Dominique cringed when she recognized it. She tried to please Sarafina more, thrusting deeper, but Sarafina had stopped moaning. Then she moved, crawling across the bed toward the waiting phone. Dominique looked at her fingers, still sticky from her lover's jelly, alone and cold now from the absence of flesh departed.

Dominique watched scornfully as Sarafina talked on the phone as if the conversation could last a lifetime. She could feel her anger augment, like heat trapped within a popcorn kernel, ready to burst. She could not believe Sarafina had answered the phone; could not believe she had leapt through the air like a superhero off to save the world. Dominique could not believe she had been making love to this woman, and she had been dismissed like she was a fly disturbing her meal. Talk about a mood killer. Talk about betrayal.

Dominique knew who was on the other line; she knew all her enemies by name. She was beginning to think that Sarafina was getting pretty close to entering that category herself. Imagine, leaving to talk on the phone with her ex, to talk to that bitch with a million-dollar bank account ... Gerri Moore. Despite the coolness of the fan, it was about to get mighty hot in that room.

Chapter 2

— I —

Stephen was drunk.

Jamal had seen that look before on many of his flights. It didn't matter how much turbulence there was, how they had turned off their overhead lights, how they buried their eyes in some glamour magazine or bobbed their heads to the latest beats on their headsets. He knew when passengers were on the verge of having a few too many. Stephen was almost there. He could only hazard a guess when the man had actually started drinking, but Jamal could sense that it had started early. And now, after three or more beers, it was very clear that they were going right to Stephen's head. Jamal could also tell that Stephen was a little bit nervous, and trying to hide it behind each beer he ordered was not working.

"Are you gentlemen ready for me to take your orders?" asked the young waiter who had arrived at their table. He was very young, and his forehead was riddled with the acne that Noxzema missed. He looked curiously at Stephen, who sat staring at his menu, his body slowly swaying from side to side. He was holding the edge of the table in an attempt to cease the motion, which only helped slightly. The waiter shook his head; his pre-drunk skills too were sharp.

"Give us a few minutes, Charles," Jamal said, staring at the young man's name tag.

The waiter understood, nodded, and then placed his pad back into his pocket.

"Are you okay, Stephen?" Jamal whispered. He took a close look at his date, trying to determine his height, weight, and build. It was only appropriate, considering he might have to carry this man home in a few minutes.

Stephen delivered a broad smile. "Sure I am." It was all he could say. He began to look around the restaurant. "This *Aunt Kizzy's* seems like a nice place."

Jamal looked around too. "I thought you would like it. I can't believe you haven't been here before."

"I can't either," Stephen responded, as his stomach began to react to the thick scents of fried chicken, fish, barbecue, and sweets wafting through the air. He took in the mostly black establishment, hearing the light but steady chatter, and noting the walls, which were covered with photos of black entertainers, past and present. "It's a very pleasant place. And by the smell of it, the food is going to be a sensation I think I will enjoy."

"How about I order for the both of us? I would hate for the waiter to make a third trip over here without you deciding. Sometimes too many choices can leave you without making one at all."

"Third time ... has the waiter been over here that much? I haven't seen him since I sat down."

"I'm not surprised," Jamal muttered. He decided to cut to the meat of their conversation, before Stephen fell off the chair to the tiled floor. "How long you been married, Stephen?"

Stephen coughed loudly and patted his chest. He looked up at Jamal in surprise. "I never said I was married."

"Well, you do have a family, don't you?"

"Did David tell you that?" Stephen asked, as he began to look around. "Where is that waiter when you need him?"

"No, David didn't have to tell me that. I saw the photos in your place. There was one with a baby and a beautiful woman. She looked very familiar."

"Yeah, that's Felicia. She's done some modeling in the past. You may have seen her in a few print ads," he explained, as he took a sip from his water glass. "We never married, just lived together for two years."

"How was the breakup?"

"She's still getting over it. She's still in denial about the whole thing."

"And when did you realize you liked dick?"

As Stephen sat there with his mouth open, the waiter arrived, and placed a basket of cornbread in the center of their table then pulled out his pad. He focused his attention upon Jamal. "And have we decided?" he sighed.

Jamal slapped his hand on the table. "Why yes, Charles, we have. We'll both have smothered porkchops, macaroni and cheese, collards, and yams. I'll have a lemonade, and my friend here will—"

"I'll have another beer," Stephen interrupted.

"Fine," Charles said hesitantly, then returned his attention hack to Jamal. "Enjoy the cornbread, and if you need anything just raise your hand. I'll be right over."

As the waiter left, Jamal stared in silence at Stephen. The last question was still on the table.

Stephen smirked, placed his elbow on the table, and rested his chin in the palm of his hand. "You are a bold one, aren't you?"

I'm a flight attendant, for God's sake. I have to be."

"Well, why don't I start with Chicago, where I grew up? My first job was at a place called Happy Chicken, where I met my friend David."

"Hmm, I guess that was the first indication of your love of poultry."

They shared a laugh.

"Perhaps so," Stephen said, taking in a deep breath. "When I first met David I hated him because he could be so arrogant, but later I learned to love that part of him. He was so short and dark-skinned, and he looked so angry all the time, like a black cloud — but as with me, first appearances were deceiving. He didn't know I played around on the side; I kept up my straight appearance quite well, until he saw me at a club downtown called the Rialto. We started talking about men, women, sissies, tops, and bottoms, all the time getting stoned and drunk.

"At the time I was going to this hole in the wall, I was also going to other straight clubs like the Illusions and the Copperbox. That's where I met Felicia. A year later Tumali was born. I had never been with a man in Chicago, but I was turned on by many of them. I was a bit confused at that time. Do you have a child?"

"No," Jamal said, reaching over to take a piece of cornbread. "I don't live in the Land of Confusion. How did it all end?"

Stephen took another sip of water. "Well, she kinda caught me in bed with another man."

Jamal's eyes widened, as he spoke though masticated cornbread. "Guess that ended the confusion."

"That, and the fact that she was seven months' pregnant at the time didn't help either."

"Maybe I should have ordered the beer."

Stephen grinned, but his eyes stared into the distance, as if the scene he was describing was happening directly on the Wall of Fame in front of him. "Well, to say the least, she couldn't deal with the cheating, the homosexuality, or being a new mother, after giving up a career to start what she thought would be her dream family. She moved in with her mother. David had since moved to Los Angeles, and I talked with him about moving there with him."

Charles returned with their drinks, and Stephen swallowed half his glass before it hit the table. Jamal pushed the basket of cornbread in Stephen's direction, wanting something to soak up that liquor. "Try the cornbread. It's great," he said.

Stephen took a piece and slowly pulled at its yellowness. He tucked the warm morsel into his mouth as he continued. "So right now she has support from her mother, and her big-assed brother to help her deal with this. She still thinks I'll change and come back to her," he said, and grabbed another piece of his bread, stuffing it quickly into his mouth. "You're right—this cornbread is great."

"Thought you would like it," Jamal said. "It's a shame that some women think that their pussy is some magic lamp, and that if a man rubs it enough times her dreams about him will come true."

"Well, it's making dreams come true all right, but not on her end. I guess the one who rubs it is the one who gets the wishes."

"Looks like dinner has arrived," Jamal announced, as he noticed Charles heading their way with an armload of plates. Jamal could feel the saliva eject from the corners of his mouth as the fare was placed before them in such quantity that it hid most of the table.

They attacked their food like dogs going in for the kill. During their meal, Jamal spoke a little of himself. He told Stephen about his mother and stepfather living in Indianapolis. His real father lived in Sterling, Virginia. He had run away from home at sixteen because of his stepfather's homophobic diatribe. He found his way to Los Angeles, where he had lived with an older gentleman for his first year, before getting a job with American Airlines as a flight attendant. His introduction to the gay lifestyle came at a young age. In that time, he had never had a lover or boyfriend— just escapades that ended in emptiness and anger. Love at home was what he wanted the most, and all other admissions of love seemed fake to him.

By the time dessert rolled around, Stephen had had quite a few drinks. He could feel a slight throbbing in his temples, and the floor seemed to be moving. He looked around the room and began to notice some strange things happening. Other things began to move on their own accord too.

"How is your dessert?" Jamal asked, as he placed another piece of sweet potato pie in his mouth. He looked at Stephen and his peach cobbler, awaiting a response.

None came.

Stephen was noticing something very odd occurring in this restaurant, something bizarre in the people around him, something peculiar happening to him. He watched the patrons at the table across from him. Both were men, and both were glancing his way. One pointed at him, and the nails were pristine, manicured, and there was a tiny ring dangling from its tip. Gay! If the nail was not a giveaway, then surely the sequined coin pouch hanging from his red-checkered belt was.

He closed his eyes, but it was too late. He could feel the laughter begin to tickle his throat. He opened one eye and saw Jamal staring at him as he continued to eat his dessert. The way the man's jaw seemed to be in perpetual slow motion as he spoke caused a *giggle* to escape Stephen. He didn't know what was amusing him so, but he was like a capped volcano about to burst. Suddenly visions danced in his now throbbing head in a kaleidoscope of images. He could hear Jamal asking for the check, and then it began.

He burst into uncontrollable laughter.

"Your friend seems to be having the time of his life."

Stephen looked up to see Charles at their table. He tried to calm down, until he felt the pressure of a small belch vibrate in his throat. Then he was off laughing again.

"Yeah, looks like there's a better party going on in his head. I do apologize for this."

It is Jamal speaking, Stephen thought, his eyes slowly beginning to cross. *But why are there two of them at the table? Did his twin show up?* Stephen could feel hands grabbing him, and his feet were somehow moving, because the people staring in the restaurant were receding from his view. He could feel the comfort of a car seat on his ass. Jamal was beside him, and even without a smile on his face, he looked pretty damned good. Stephen, however, had the feeling that this date was not going too well. Stephen could hear himself saying, *damn, damn, damn!* But they were only voices in his head. Soon he joined them in that darkness, which was soon followed by what sounded like the tranquil reverberation of saws sawing.

Jamal slowly lowered Stephen to the sofa, and watched as this man folded himself into a fetal position. He shook his head and smiled. *He has first-date willies, no doubt,* he thought. Suddenly a small dog peeked around the sofa to stare at him, and he reached down to rub the collie's soft fur. "Where did you come from? Stephen been hiding you in his room all this time?" he asked, as the animal licked his fingers.

Jamal left the house keys on the glass end table, grabbed the sports coat that hung on the arm,' and nonchalantly placed it across Stephen's shoulders. He looked up at the clock on the wall. Ten o'clock. *The quickest date I've had in some time,* he thought. He ran his fingers across Stephen's wet brow, patted him on the shoulder, and left.

The dog sniffed the door for a moment until the footsteps faded, and returned to his master. For the next half hour, he tasted a bit of soul food on a pair of lips that could laugh no more.

– II –

David heard the lock on the front door release, the rattling of keys, then the same door slamming so hard that the walls shook. Allen was finally home, and drunk as ever.

David rolled over to take a quick glance at the clock on the nightstand. Midnight. *Well, that's pretty early for him,* David thought. He closed his eyes and could feel his heart beating so loudly that he believed at any moment it would discharge through his ribcage. He listened. *Clop! Clop!* The sound of Allen's shoes hitting the floor, followed by the *k'shhh k'shhh* of his feet dragging along the carpet. *Yeah, he's pretty fucked up this time,* David concluded.

He turned back around to face the wall and hugged the pillow closer to his head. Why was he putting up with this? This constant routine was getting very old: the fighting, the walking out, the late returns, the quietness, the apologies . . . the fucking. *We make up to break up; that's all we do.*

It had not always been like this.

He'd met Allen a little more than five years ago, after he had walked into the Cartwright Insurance Company. David knew it was kismet the moment this handsome stranger, with skin like honeydew and eyes like sand dollars, sat in front of him, propping his wet umbrella between his legs. He had brushed back his moist mane of curly locks and pulled those delicious pink lips into the warmest grin David had seen all day. Two hundred ten pounds of six-foot-four goodness was sitting right at his desk, and David had felt like a boy let loose in a room filled with balloons and asked to pick his favorite.

They discussed business. Allen wanted some information on acquiring new homeowner's insurance for property he had had in the Torrance area for a year. Filled with an unusual boldness, David had casually mentioned his familiarity with the area and dropped the names of a few gay establishments in the vicinity. Allen once again had smiled, and, in his own unabashed fashion, asked David to join him in seeing the opening of *Phantom of the Opera.*

David had accepted.

It was their first date, with Michael Crawford as the centerpiece on stage, playing the phantom with exquisite finesse. During the second act, Allen had placed a hand upon David's, and he could feel the electricity pass through them. His memories of the play began to fade from that point.

Many dates later, David discovered that Allen's father had died while he was a teenager. But he had been a very wealthy man, leaving Allen a trust fund and controlling interest in a very lucrative plastics coating firm. On his twenty-second birthday,

Allen had sold the company and invested the monies in quite a few successful ventures.

As their relationship progressed, David followed Allen's suggestion of leaving his insurance job to go to school and study landscaping, which had been David's original passion. After receiving his license, David worked at a number of construction firms on a temporary basis. During this time, Allen accepted a job at the DMV just to keep his time occupied. Although to David this seemed strange, it had been Allen's dream as a child to someday work there.

Two and a half years into the relationship, things began to change. Allen began to change. A union built on kismet was now becoming a walk on broken glass. The dishes were not done on time, laundry wasn't finished by the end of the week, David came home late from work or was sleeping too much. . . dinner wasn't done. David felt his self-worth slipping, like a torpedoed ship sinking into the sea. Nothing was ever good enough, and when the verbal abuse abated, the physical abuse escalated.

It began as a shoving rage. Allen would push David out of the bathroom for taking too long, elbowing him aside as he tried to answer the door first, shouldering him out of the way and storming into the bedroom when he could not make a valid point during an argument. Then the bedroom became too immediate, and soon he formed the habit of leaving the house altogether, going to the liquor store, and coming back with a little something to drink. Later he would leave and not come back all that night, showing up the next morning with skin that smelled like raw sewage.

Still, David blamed himself. He cried himself to sleep. He tried to work things out with gifts, kind words, and sometimes silence. He didn't pursue contracting work any longer, and he dedicated his time to their home life. He thought it was his mission to find out where this anger was coming from. This man loved him. Maybe being Allen's punching bag was a way for his lover to heal. It had to be.

But tonight, David began to think differently. He tried to evaluate what was going on in a house where the only sounds were that of a drunken man's feet sliding against the tiles of the kitchen floor. He could hear the microwave oven come to life and the clang of silverware chiming against each other. A chair was pulled out. Anita Baker flowed through the CD player. A fresh can of soda hissed open. Ice cubes crashed against the sides of a glass. *After all that fuckin' commotion,* David thought, *this man is still going to eat!*

David was pissed. He could feel his body tighten as if his skin were made of stone. Something had to stop. They had to discuss what it was to be in a relationship. They had to determine what future this union held. Was this a marriage or martyrdom?

The music stopped. The dishwasher began to rumble. Dinner was over. Then a chill covered David as the door to the bedroom was slowly opened, and the light from the hallway burned against David's closed eyelids.

"I'm sorry, David."

The words had come to his ears with such care that David thought he'd imagined them. Then he heard the customary tone of shifting clothes as Allen undressed. Soon the bed sagged as his so-called lover slid under the covers beside him.

"You're always sorry," David quietly uttered, not wishing to feign sleep any longer. "You're the sorriest individual I know."

Silence.

David could smell the beer seeping through Allen's pores as he inched closer. He could feel the heat from this man pull the very coolness from beneath the sheets. David moved away, striving to widen the space between himself and this he-devil. "Dinner was very good, sweetheart. Thank you very much."

Damn him for this fuckin' politeness! David cursed under his breath. It was tearing through his skin, breaking through his wall. Allen reached out his icy hands to David's shoulder. David tried lurching himself away, but the grip was tight, the palms sweaty.

David hated himself at that moment—not for the weakness he felt, but for the arousal he was *beginning* to feel.

"I was wrong, David. I overreacted. You know I'll always admit when I'm wrong, and this time I was. Can we try and forget this, and move on?" The stench of his breath was filling the clean air around David.

Protest! That was the plan. That's what David wanted to do. Unfortunately, it didn't happen. He could feel his lips parting on the fringe of objection, but surprisingly, Allen met that objection with a kiss.

His walls were breaking.

David could feel those lips touch the sides of his cheeks, the curve of his jaw, the flesh of his earlobe, and all muscle tension began to relax. He wanted the right words to come to him, to stop this advancement, this ultimate violation, but they would not come. They melted away as Allen edged closer, his manhood throbbing strong and hard against David. David's own manhood was stirring too. He could feel a pair of sturdy hands explore his hips, his thighs, his butt ... his sex.

The walls were breaking.

David's organ jumped to life. He didn't want this to happen. He tried to remember the fight, the pushing, the dinner, the disrespect. He tried. But as he was trying to picture all this anger, make it tangible, Allen gently pushed his shoulder, turning him smoothly onto his back. David opened his eyes to see Allen's smiling face as he looked between David's thighs, to see the miniature pyramid rising from beneath the sheets. That smile caused all the resentment David had been feeling to knot in his throat, choking him. He swallowed thickly.

"I love you, David," Allen said, as he pulled David's underwear down and maneuvered himself to cover David's erectness with his open maw.

David found himself gripping the pillows around his head, venturing to rip them asunder. Quivering skin, short sporadic panting, a ticklish chill through his flesh—David felt it all. He began thrusting his hips upward, forcing his sex into Allen's mouth. Warm breath surrounded his member until even his stomach burned from the gift. At that point, he knew his walls had crumbled, crushed under the weight of uninhibited desire.

Allen paused for a moment, catching his breath. He twisted his blissful face toward David, grinning in all his contented delight. Allen pulled David's underwear the rest of the way off and tossed them across the room. He then shifted his body until they lay chest to chest. He kissed David again. His thick member pulsated against David's own. His movements were hard, deliberate, erotic, the sweat between them causing their flesh to slide in various directions, the gyrations frantic.

David could feel his orgasm pass through him, and Allen was close behind, as his gestures heightened, became more quickened, intense. Then David could feel a blast of liquid heat erupt against his stomach, slide across his torso, and fall against the bedraggled sheets.

Then nothing.

David reached up to this heavy-breathing dragon, feeling the sticky glue of their love juices bond them, and hugged him, and then whispered words into his ear that would forever doom him.

"I love you too, Allen."

– III –

Dominique pressed PLAY on the CD player, and the soft soothing sounds of Ella Fitzgerald floated from the speakers: 'The Lady Is a Tramp.' she was pissed.

With her knees drawn up to her chin and her arms wrapped around her legs, she closed her eyes tightly in an effort to hold back tears. She could feel the coolness from the ceiling fan spiral down her back, relieving her of some of the heat and anger she was feeling. Her resentment was like a loose bull in her belly.

Dominique had never met this woman known as Gerri Moore, but her name was synonymous with just about everything that had come into Dominique's existence. Gerri Moore was Sarafina's ex-lover, her present-day friend, and a thorn in Dominique's side, like some clandestine mosquito that had just taken a bite from her. She turned her head to look at the closed bedroom door, thinking about the argument that had occurred only moments ago.

"I'm sorry about that, Dominique," Sarafina had said, as she'd placed the phone back on the cradle. "Letting my mouth run off like that wasn't cool. I should've let that fuckin' answering machine grab it."

It was too late. Dominique had already slid out from beneath the covers. She had run her tongue across her lips, still tasting the salt from Sarafina's tits. It served only to anger her even more.

"I don't know what to say about you," Dominique had replied, shaking her head in disbelief.

"You're not angry, are you?" Sarafina had risked, her voice trailing off, as if she'd wanted to take back the words.

Dominique had stood near the bed, naked, her hair falling across her exposed breasts. She had run her fingers across her scalp, stopping there to scratch, as if she were lost for words. "I just know you didn't ask me, am I angry. Those words could not have come out of your mouth."

"Well, I guess you are, with that tone. I was trying to apologize for-"

"What were you thinking?" Dominique had interrupted. "We were laying here in this bed, making love, and you have the nerve to pick up the phone for your ex-lover. Where is the sense in that?"

"It was just a habit. I just hadn't talked to her in a while, with all the traveling she does, and I had ..."

"A habit? You calling that white woman a habit? What is she, some cigarette you have to puff on every now and then? You her nigga girl that's gotta jump every time she calls? I thought she lost ownership of you." Dominique had sniffed at her fingers. "Maybe I've been smelling her cunt all this time. You must have given yours up when you met her."

"Fuck! Is it that serious? Me and Gerri are just friends. I don't trip when your friends call here. Why you gotta trip just because Gerri is my ex?"

"Because she *is* your ex, and she is calling you at some eleven o'clock at night. My friends know the meaning of respect."

Sarafina had remained quiet. She had watched as Dominique's chest heaved and her nostrils flared. There would be no compromising this night. She had remained quiet even as she watched Dominique reach for her pillow. "It was only a phone call, baby, nothing else. Nothing else."

"It was that nothing that had you answering the phone. You shot my fingers from your pussy like a stream of hot piss for a fucking phone call you call nothing. You might as well have left me for her."

Sarafina had quickly motioned toward the edge of the bed and reached out to grab Dominique's arm. "It was nothing like that, Dominique. I swear it wasn't. Come back to bed, baby, and let's talk about this in the morning."

Dominique had stared at Sarafina's hand intensely, then slowly pulled at those fingers one by one with her other hand, until Sarafina's grip let go. "Yeah, we will be talking tomorrow, but there will be little sleeping tonight. Somehow it is becoming hard to believe that the relationship you and Gerri shared, the one that began all those years ago in San Francisco, is completely over." She then reached out to grab an extra sheet from the edge of the rumpled bed, and scooped up a pillow. "I think I'll go listen to a little jazz for a while."

Dominique had seen the look on Sarafina's face, and the room had gone silent. Jazz was Dominique's way of calming down from a mass of frustrations. It was what she did when she knew the next word out of her mouth would be an accumulation of verbs and adjectives that she might regret in the morning. She had said nothing as she turned to walk out the bedroom door, slamming it shut as she did.

And now she lay on the sofa, her back pressing deeper into the cushions, her arms crossed over her face as she hugged herself. She could feel the music seep into her pores, calming her, telling her that she was doing the right thing. She continued to relax, until the sounds of Billie Holiday's, "Aint Nobody's Business if I Do" pulled her into uncomplicated slumber.

Chapter 3
— I —

The top to the yellow Mustang convertible was down, and the cool air whipped Damien's face. He adjusted his Ray-Bans slightly, leaned quickly to his side to observe himself in the rearview mirror, smiled, then returned his attention back to the road.

David continued to stare at Damien, then at the road, and then back at the speedometer. Are you trying to reach cruising altitude, or warp speed, Captain?" he asked, tugging at his seat belt, testing its strength.

Damien shook his head as if in pity, and reached over to turn the radio up a few more decibels. "Girl, this is L.A. What's speed got to do with anything?"

David nodded, as if he understood it all now. "Oh, I see. I was just wondering if it was time to store my tray table and return my seat to an upright position before we land."

"Not before you finish your beverage, and turn off all electronic devices ... vibrators too, bitch." Damien laughed.

"I thought we were supposed to be picking up Stephen. San Diego is more than two hours away, if you remember."

Damien waved his hand at David as if he were a pestering fly in his ear. "Quiet, lady! We're taking the scenic route. I has to make a pit stop, okay? Besides, this is a Mustang, sweetheart, and a good hour is all we gonna need."

David pulled down the passenger-side sun visor to smooth his eyebrows with the tip of his finger as he looked in the mirror. "I can see the headlines now: DIVAS KILLED IN A MANGLED YELLOW TRICK-MOBILE. How dramatic."

"You're a smart-ass this morning, huh? I know what that means,"Damien said, taking a quick sidelong glimpse at David.

"And what does your crystal ball tell you?" David asked, raising the visor and reaching into his breast pocket to pull out a pair of Armani shades.

"Honey, I smell Allen all in your attitude. What's going on at home, David? And don't tell me nothing, cause yo' nose can't get any bigger."

David sighed and rested his head back in his seat, defeated. "We had a little fight last night. He was upset that I was on the phone with you, and dinner wasn't ready."

Damn, girl, I'm sorry. Did he walk out of the house again?"
David nodded. "I guess he went to the Annex or something. He smelled like a liquor store when he came back."

David," Damien began, his voice slow, as if he were choosing his next words with caution. "I'm sorry about talking yo' ear off and making trouble for you, but I think Allen is using it as an excuse to start shit."

Yeah, I think that too sometimes," David said.

Damien sighed; they'd gone this route a thousand times before. Damien knew this relationship was all wrong, but the boy was in some sorry state of L-O-V-E. Damien decided the best advice he could give right now was no advice at all. He swiftly careened along Santa Monica Boulevard, twisting the car at a breakneck speed along Hollyway Drive, pulling into the parking lot of the International Male.

"Now what're we stopping here for?" David asked, sitting up in his seat.

"Don't you worry about it, sweet-cakes. I just need to pick up a few things."

David looked at the large rectangular building and then back at Damien as he stepped from the car. 'Honey, I hate to break this to you, but this is the Queen store, and you are not going to find anything here that hasn't been cloned all across West Hollywood."

"Don't you know it's not what you wear, but how you work it?" Damien educated, snapped his fingers, and placed his keys in the fanny bag he had casually slung across his shoulder.

"Whatever. Just leave me the keys so I can listen to the radio," David suggested, leaning his elbow on the door and resting his head on his palm.

Damien could see the faraway look in David's eyes. He pulled the keys from his pouch and tossed them in David's lap. "You need to stop thinking about that fool, is what I think."

David clutched the keys. "What're you talking about? I'm not thinking about anyone."

"Don't lie to me. I've known you too long. Now, I'll be a minute, Johnny is just holding a few things for me that I have to pick up."

"Allen's not really a bad person," David said to himself. Damien looked back at the hushed statement and shook his head. The boy was sprung.

"Damien!" Johnny's loud voice greeted him as he stepped into the store.

Damien held his arms out to share a long hug with his friend. They both pulled away, and Johnny held Damien out at arm's length, looking at him from head to toe. "How you doin', Johnny? Haven't seen you in too long."

"I can see that, sweetheart," Johnny replied, sweeping his hand up, and down in front of Damien. "What you been wearing out there in the big bad world? This look is so last season."

Damien looked down at himself, sticking his leg out to take notice of his work boots and thick blue socks, and he tugged at the midriff T-shirt he was wearing. "What you talkin' about, *papi?* I got it going on.

Johnny waved his hands at Damien. "Then keep it going, girl-friend, 'cause *it* don't need to be caught. This is what's going on, baby," Johnny said, stretching his short arms out and standing with his feet together, crossed in front of each other.

Damien cupped his hands under his chin, contemplating the clothes Johnny wore: a large and loose-fitting black pinstriped jacket, baggy slacks, a yellow form-fitting nylon T-shirt, and matching yellow socks. Damien thought it wasn't bad for a white boy; even the square-toed shoes were pretty stylish. "It's fine, I guess," Damien commented.

"You guess?" Johnny repeated, and then reached for Damien's wrist. "Bring your big butt this way, honey, and let me save you from fashion hell." Johnny pulled Damien to a nearby rack of clothes, pulling a bright red collarless shirt from the rack, pressing it against Damien's chest.

"I didn't come here to buy nothing, Johnny," Damien said, hands on his hips.

"Who said you had to buy anything? I didn't say that. I must have mistaken you for someone I thought was a grander diva, that's all—but if you want to stay with this ... this, oh, I don't know. . . this *straight* look, then more power to you."

Damien pressed his palms against his stomach. "Ohhh, now that hurt. You cut deep with that one, Johnny, and I thought you was my friend."

"I am, baby," Johnny replied, plucking another shirt from the rack and holding it against Damien. "That's why I'm trying to save you. Can't you see the big *S* on my chest? Now come over here," Johnny demanded, throwing the chosen shirt over Damien's shoulder and pulling him to the back of the store near a row of pants.

"Who said I need saving?"

"Honey, it's obvious your friends haven't been doing it. Speaking of which, where is that clan you hang out with?" Johnny asked, holding a pair of deep brown slacks against Damien's legs.

"Well, David's in the car, and we're going to Stephen's place this afternoon, then drive up to San Diego to see my moms."

Johnny clutched his chest through the rumpled jeans he held. "You girls are going to Momma C's? Damn! I haven't seen her in two years. That was the best eating I ever had. How I wish I were going with you guys. And why isn't that girl coming out the car to see me? She a fashion disaster too?" Johnny asked, directing his finger through the window at David.

Damien held his hand up. "That dizzy girl got marriage problems."

"Poor princess. I tell you, husbands are just overrated Roto-Rooters. For thirty bucks I can get a blow-up doll at the Pleasure Chest," Johnny said, laughing.

"I understand," Damien said, placing a hand on Johnny's shoulder, It's all about having options, honey."

Johnny quickly spun Damien around and shoved him into a dressing room. "Now you try those clothes on Dear and tell me what you think," he said, leaning against the door.

"Now how'd you get me trapped in here, you whore! I just came to pick up my other stuff, Johnny," Damien said, pushing at the door.

"I'm not asking you to buy anything, sweets. I just want you to simply take a look at them, that's all. No harm, no foul."

"All right," Damien submitted, "but I could swear I smell something foul regardless."

Johnny listened to the door. A dead silence came from within. "You still alive in there?"

After a moment, Damien came through the door, the clothes he'd tried on draped across his shoulder. "You know, I hate yo' ass."

Johnny threw his hands in the air. "We have a sale!" he shouted. "So you want that added to your bill?"

Damien grinned. "Yeah, bitch."

"Stop with the compliments already," Johnny said, latching hold of Damien's wrist and dragging him to the register. "And here's your other order," he said, pulling a small bag from beneath the counter.

"Child, I don't know why I come here and let you talk me into buying stuff all the time."

Johnny reached up to pull playfully at Damien's cheeks. "Commission, Mother, commission. And I thank you for every penny." He then blew Damien a kiss.

"Mother? I must have adopted your white ass."

Johnny smirked. "That's not what my daddy say. He say you got the sweetest chocolate kitty cat he's tasted in a long time. I hear it purrs."

"Why don't you just ring up my accessories, before I scratch your ass," Damien said, reaching into his shoulder bag for his wallet. As he did he heard laughter in the back of the store. He looked up to see a couple kissing playfully near a rack of coats. They hugged and smiled at each other as if they'd just met. They were both rather tall, the darkest one, whom Damien could see, was mildly handsome. The other's back was to Damien, and he couldn't recognize who this large man was. But as they spun around in their frivolity, Damien dropped his bag in shock.

It was Allen!

"Your card, Queen!" Johnny voiced, getting Damien's attention. "I know this place got some fine boys in here, but get out your trance, girl, and take this plastic."

Damien blinked, and slowly reached for his Visa card. "Thanks," he replied mechanically. He looked up again at Allen. *He's supposed to be at work. It couldn't be him*, Damien thought. But as he contemplated this, Allen casually looked his way, and his face froze.

Damien looked back at Johnny, smiled nervously, and seized his bag. "Okay, dawww-ling, I'll talk with ya later. I've got to get out of here. Momma doesn't like it when I'm late. You understand," Damien said, waving at Johnny as he began rushing out the door.

Damien rushed past the automatic doors, directly into another problem: David had left the car, and was heading his way. "Where you goin', baby? I'm through in there."

David motioned his hand in the direction of the store. "I should go in and say hi to Johnny. It's kinda rude to be sitting out here and not even give my dear fashion consultant any acknowledgement."

Damien looped his arm around David's, spinning him back in the direction of the car. "Girlfriend, don't even bother. Johnny-lina has got pure a-ti-tude today."

"Really?" David questioned. "What's going on with her?" "Men, girlfriend ... just men."

"Humph, I can understand that. Poor baby. The single life can be so unsure," David replied, as he opened the door to the passenger side.

Damien sat down, immediately revving the engine. He backed up so quickly that David hastily reached for the comfort of his seat belt. "Damn girl, you act like you parked in the handicap zone and Ms. Lisa was coming to give you a ticket."

"I would rather the police give me a ticket than for Momma to be mad that we late."

"I guess," David said, leaning back in the seat. "That's the third one I've seen today."

"What's that?" Damien asked.

"A Honda Del Sol, parked around the corner. It looks just like the one Allen has. Been seeing quite a few of those in the last couple of days all around town."

Damien saw an opening and sped out into traffic. As he did, he looked into his rearview mirror, back at the store. In the door's glass entrance, he could see Allen, watching him as his Mustang raced along the road. "I'm sure you have," Damien replied, as he extended his arm to turn on the radio. He said nothing more as Aretha Franklin sang "Chain of Fools."

– II –

"Baby girl, I think you should leave that man alone," Margaret said, as she sipped smoothly from her cup of herbal tea.

Felicia looked back at her mother as she hefted Tumali from his playpen. "Mama, please don't give me any more headaches," she replied, holding her son in her arms, as he delighted in pulling his mother's shoulder-length hair.

"I'm just saying that Stephen can be nothing but trouble for you. He's caused you nothing but misery since you two met. I saw his eyes, honey, and I knew they meant nothing but problems."

"Who told you that ... a Psychic Friend?" Felicia sat at the table directly across from her mother. She placed Tumali on her lap; giving him a bottle of apple juice she had waiting for him on the table. He pushed it away, his brow knitted together in annoyance.

"Why don't you give that child a glass to drink out of? He's trying to be grown up, and you won't let him," Margaret said, shaking her head at her daughter.

Felicia looked at the digital clock above the television: **3:00** stood out in bright orange numbers. Her mother had been here only a few minutes and somehow it felt like hours. "Don't worry about Tumali, Mama. Tumali will be grown enough, soon enough. The bottle was just handy. All right?" Felicia sighed. She loved her mother, but since the death of her father, her mother has been trying to get in as much grandmother time with Tumali as possible…sometimes too much.

Felicia's mother was a strong woman, and the death of her husband, by that brain tumor –which killed him within weeks – didn't bring her crashing down. The insurance money was good, paying all her expenses, and leaving her a fairly wealthy widow.

At fifty, she could now have and do all she couldn't when she had children to raise. She still looked good; her hair a salt-and-pepper blend of thinning strands that stood curled tightly above her head, teeth that were still hers, nails that were always manicured to perfection, and only slight pockets of flesh under her eyes that did nothing to hamper her radiant beauty. If not for the Virginia Slims she constantly smoked, Margaret would be the model of fitness. She was also spoiled in her world of aerobics classes, a new BMW, fine dining, and her Friday night bridge games. Imagine, bridge! Felicia thought only white folks played that.

Felicia glared at her mother. Tiny crow's feet were etched at the outer corners of her eyes; a minute double chin was also evolving, and a noticeable little tummy was swelling around her midsection. She sat with her legs carefully crossed and at an angle, the perfect lady. Felicia wondered if this would be a reflection of herself when the years took their toll on her. Her shoulders shook at this thought, and the idea of being that parvenu.

"I called Stephen yesterday," Felicia mentioned, as she steadied Tumali on her knee.

"Now what possessed you to do something like that?" Margaret asked, blowing steam from her tea.

"Just to ask for a little money for me and the baby."

"I thought you were making good money at that taxi company the temp agency set you up with."

"I am, but he doesn't have to know that."

"Mmm-hmmm," Margaret lamented.

"Now what was that supposed to mean?" Felicia asked.

"Oh, nothing," Margaret said, shaking her head, "You're just still wrapped in that man, and it's not getting you anywhere. Calling him up for no reason—that's what you were doing. That child is doing all right. And if it weren't for Tumali, Stephen might not have given you the time of day. I tell you, niggas and flies."

"Am I going to be in for another lecture?"

Margaret placed her cup on the table and reached out for her grandchild. Tumali instantly smiled and leaned over to touch his grandmother's outstretched fingers. "Hey, Grandma's baby!" she looked up at Felicia, seemingly ignoring the last question and answering it all the same. "Why don't you give me this child and go get me some of that lemon pound cake I baked for you?"

"You're gonna spoil this one, Mama," Felicia commented, as she guided Tumali across the table. She stood, brushing at her wrinkled knee-length nightshirt.

"Don't you worry about me spoiling my grandbaby. What you need to worry about is trying to cut this child's wild hair," she said, pulling at the dark billowy tufts.

Felicia ran her fingers through Tumali's hair as she passed him. "Don't let Grandma talk about your head, baby. You just tell her you just need your little Afro trimmed out, 'cause Afros are back in style this year."

Margaret looked down at her grandchild's face. "And you just tell your mommy that you ain't no fashion statement." she began bouncing Tumli on her knee. "Girl! What you feeding this boy? I know his hair ain't making him this heavy."

Felicia went to the kitchen, retrieving the fresh pound cake from atop the refrigerator. "You know that child likes to eat. He's got a manly appetite, just like his father."

"What that man has an appetite for I'd rather not mention," Margaret expressed.

"Be nice. Whether you like it or not, Tumali does have a father."

Margaret swung her legs around until she could see her daughter in the kitchen. "Baby, he's gay! What makes you think he could be any kind of father to this child?"

"What has that got to do with his being a father? He was man enough to make Tumali."

"It don't take much to do that, my dear. How can you stand there and think that he knows what a man is supposed to be about when he's sleeping with them?"

Felicia turned, glaring at her mother, irritated. "Maybe that makes him even more knowledgeable about manhood than any other man out there. At least he didn't just vanish from his child's life. Black men these days just like to drop the seed and leave the fieldwork for the women. Then when the crop is ready for harvest, they pop back in the field to lay claim to the bounty. Would you rather Tumali had no father to speak of?"

"I didn't say that. But you can't keep expecting him to come back as your man or your husband, Felicia. You act like you can accept him as Tumali's father, but you won't accept him as never being your husband. You just need to leave him out there with his sissy life and his sissy friends."

"He'll still be Tumali's father."

"If you ask me, I think Tumali inherited two mothers."

"Well, I didn't ask you," Felicia expressed, returning to the cake, where she violently pulled open a counter drawer, and brought out a knife.

Margaret swung back around in her seat, rolling her eyes in her head, as if certain her daughter was just not listening. "I don't know why you find you have to defend that boy."

"I'm not defending him," Felicia responded, reaching into one of the overhead cabinets to bring down two small plates.

"Then what are you doing? You need to stop carrying that torch, 'cause I don't see any men knocking this door down to get your attention these days."

3:15. *Damn that clock is slow,* Felicia thought. "Oh, here we go again," Felicia said. It was the famous Invisible Man in My Daughter's Life speech. *Why does that woman think I need a man to bring me fresh air in the morning?* Felicia wondered. Was there some unwritten Mother's Act that mandated she look down on her daughter when the father of her baby was absent? Hell, the working class, educated, sensitive black man was on the endangered species list. Stephen at least wanted to be there for Tumali in some way.

"Mama, I don't need the extra dilemma of having a new man in my," she said, slicing the dessert.

"You need somebody, so you can get that boy-girl out your space." Felicia held her breath. "I just don't see why I should hate him, like you seem to want me to do."

"No reason? Girl, that boy slept with someone right in your bedroom, and you mean—"

"Ma!" Felicia shouted, dropping the knife to the floor, the slice she cut plummeting to the tile. "I don't want to talk about that!"

"Mommy!" Tumali bellowed, as he pulled up on his grandmother's shoulder to see into the kitchen. His mouth was contorted, as he stood on the verge of crying.

"It's okay, Tutu darling," Felicia assured, looking out to wave at her baby, an exaggerated smile on her face.

"Don't worry, sweetie," Margaret cooed to the child, rubbing his cheeks with the palm of her hand as a tear drifted across his fat orbs. "I didn't mean to upset you, Felicia," Margaret apologized.

"Yeah, I know," Felicia remarked, as she bent to the floor to toss out the spilled piece of cake. After slicing a new one, she brought both plates to the table. "I'll make some more tea," she said, retrieving Margaret's empty cup from the table and carrying it back to the kitchen. She took a second cup, filled them both with bottled water and new tea bags, then put them in the microwave. She pressed the START button and listened to the soft hum coming from the machine.

She shook her head as a deluge of memories quickened through her mind with the alacrity of lightning through a cluster of clouds. She'd tried so hard to forget those past events—that afternoon she had come home to discover Stephen in their bed with another man. She had heard the sounds of low grunts, heavy moans, and deep sighs coming from beyond the bedroom door. At first she had thought it a prowler—funny how the mind immediately journeys to the safer hermitage. Perhaps it was another woman? She never imagined it would be another man. How could a woman deal with that?

She remembered tapping on the door. The noises had stopped. She had twisted the doorknob slowly. She had heard bedsprings rebounding at an erratic pace. Then she had eased the door open and was stunned to see a strange man sitting on her bed, *their* bed, and would have screamed if not for the bizarre fact that this intruder was trying frantically to pull his pants over his naked legs. He had looked at her for only a moment, both caught in a mild tunnel vision, and it all seemed to happen in slow motion. To this day she could not remember that face hidden in the dim light and dark shadows. But adjacent to him, sitting at the opposite corner of the bed, the table lamp illuminating his dismayed features, had been Stephen.

Images. Clothes strewn across the floor. Unrecognizable items. The scent of cigarette smoke had filled the air; Stephen hadn't smoked. Her stomach had twisted into a wretched cramp. *Could our child come two months early?* She'd worried. Why had she gone to the doctor's office that day, absently forgetting that he was on vacation for two weeks and she'd changed her appointment to the next week? At least two hours she should have been occupied away from home. Instead she had come home to this. The sheets had been askew on the bed, and in the large mirror she had seen the television reflected: some porno of two men doing God knows what to each other was playing! The blinds had been drawn tight. There were two tiny bottles on the nightstand, both dark in color, and a rumpled towel slung over the headboard. She hadn't been able to interpret what she was seeing, what was going on. Two men? Naked... Sex? She was absolutely mystified, and thrust into denial.

She had sensed the bile rising in her throat, and if she had not moved she surely would have retched right where she stood. She had run quickly from the room, pretending not to see, pretending not to be seen. she had run from the scene filling her brain, she had Hung open the door and stumbled down the stairs in her haste, and it had been by the grace of God that she was able to grab onto the railing in time, or she would have surely fallen down the stairs and tumbled to the bottom. She had bolted out into the rain-slicked streets, the soles of her shoes spraying water as her feet clapped against the pavement. It was mid-September, and the cool winds of fall pressed against her face, causing her tears to stream back along her jaw and into her numb ears. She could faintly hear Stephen's voice beckoning to her, calling her name in the quiet neighborhood, begging that she return, she hadn't wanted to hear him. She hadn't wanted to know he existed, for to have him exist meant what she saw was real.

She had rested five blocks later at a corner bus stop that stood directly in front of the looming structure of Comiskey stadium. She had placed a hand over her heart, feeling the swift beating of the muscle throb under her fingertips. Then she had placed a hand on her plump belly. *It will be all right,* she had told herself. The coldness in the air had dried her mouth like sand, and a chill fluctuated through her flesh as her head pulsed on the perimeter of fainting. Soon she had stood, regaining her composure, and walked to a nearby phone booth to call her mother. Margaret had sent a cab, and the ten minutes it took to arrive had been the longest ten minutes Felicia ever felt in her life- time. As she sat in the back of the cab, she had cried, oblivious to the verbal concerns coming from the cab driver. She had cried and cried and cried.

The beeping from the microwave roused her, and she realized she was in her kitchen. A shiver erupted throughout her skin. She wasn't outside, on a cold afternoon, but in the secure confines of her home. Felicia took the two cups from the oven and placed them on the table. She wiped away a tear that had skulked down her cheek.

Margaret placed Tumali on the floor to play with his scattered toys. "Honey, I just don't want you to stop living. You just want that man to change, and he's not."

"What's wrong with wanting us to be a family?" Felicia asked, hope in her voice.

Margaret slipped a piece of cake into her mouth swiftly, stopping a forthcoming comment.

"What ever happened to that Emmanuel fellow you were seeing?" she finally returned, avoiding the predictable pattern of the previous conversation. "He was a good churchgoing boy. Good dresser too."

Felicia carefully sipped her tea. "He has three kids. And he was bent on telling me how I should raise my own."

"There you go!" Margaret said, slapping the table as if coming to a point. "That's his fatherly instinct emerging. He's ready to start a family with the right woman. Why don't you call that fine young man? I could watch Tumali for you while—"

"Oh please! Just stop it. I have no intention of seeing a man that still isn't over the death of his wife. That first date, she was all he talked about. The boating accident, and how the storm took them off guard, and she fell over the edge, and how she looked once they pulled her out. It gave me the creeps."

"Picky, picky, picky. That was the perfect opportunity to kiss his wounded soul, be there for him, and help him to forget. Instead of kissing the wound, you pour salt on it," Margaret cited, waving her hand over the table, and sliding her fingers together as if she were sprinkling salt upon the table.

"Can we change the subject? I'm doing just fine by myself," Felicia remarked.

Margaret looked to the ceiling. "Jason, did you hear that? Your daughter said she's doing fine. The girl doesn't have a steady job yet. She's single with a child to feed. No ring on any of those dishpan fingers. The father's actually a mother. And the child's hair is brimming with naps, like mini Afro explosions."

"Mama, will you stop that! Goodness!" Felicia said, stuffing a piece of cake into her mouth, her teeth clashing against the silver of the fork in her vexation.

Margaret rolled her eyes slowly from the ceiling and lifted her mug to her mouth, very condescendingly, conciliated in her point being made. "Well, be glad your lovely father can't see how this man has dragged you down. To see his child so confused. You *are* in a state of confusion, you know," Margaret said, more statement than question.

"I am not in a state of confusion. I have my life organized or at least organized the way I like it."

"What you need is a good man in your bed, and that's all. I will give Stephen credit for at least deciding that himself, and not wanting to marry you because of it."

"I thought I said I didn't want to talk about this? Maybe he was just scared to make that kind of commitment. Maybe the idea of being a father frightened him," Felicia said, sipping her tea loudly, as if trying to drown out any response Margaret had to offer.

The effort proved futile. "Child, he wasn't too scared to trade in some tit for a dick."

"Ma!" Felicia shouted, choking on her drink.

"Well, it's true ... and don't give me that tone of voice either. It took some wingdinger to get you into this world, so don't act like I ain't never seen one," Margaret said, licking crumbs from her fork, which to Felicia suddenly became offensively phallic.

Felicia glanced at her son, as if eye contact with her mother was now too much to bear. "Tumali can hear you," she said as an afterthought.

"If that child don't know what dick is by now, then I suggest you send him to his father for a little direction in penile affairs," Margaret said in a burst of laughter.

Felicia found no humor in the statement. "Momma, quit talking like that about this boy's father. He's two years old, so he can pick up on anything."

"Damn! You still in love with him, ain't you? Just as the day you two met. Two years and some odd weeks, and you still pining over this fool."

Felicia slammed her cup on the table. "And so what if I am? He was a good man. He never beat me, never raised his voice in a demanding nature, never acted selfish. He just made a mistake, and he needed some space. That's all he needed."

Margaret kept silent; Felicia was on the verge of crying, as tears danced on the rims of her eyelids. Margaret reached across the table to place her hand sympathetically upon Felicia's. She spoke with more care this time.

"Felicia. He's gay. I'm sure he didn't just wake up in the morning and decide he was going to be that way. It must have been with him for a while, so that means he tried to deny himself that. He was hiding. Now he isn't, at least to you, which makes the decision very important to him. He must have loved you a great deal to trust you with such a thing, such a secret. And despite you, despite Tumali, he decided this is what he wants. And now you must decide what you want, without compromising the beliefs or life of anyone else. You say Emmanuel is still mourning ... well, so are you."

Felicia looked up at her mother, letting the tears that showed themselves fall across her face. Why attempt to wipe them? Margaret had seen many tears fall from her eyes. This was nothing new. She just couldn't believe this was the same woman spouting such wisdom. But she'd said it, and it calmed the fire that had been blistering inside her.

"But how can he be gay? He made such a beautiful child. He was made for the both of us to share."

Margaret looked at Tumali. Her grin was instinctive. "True, Tumali is beautiful, but it had nothing to do with being gay or straight. It had to do with love. And above all, I believe Stephen loved you."

"Then he could change. You see that he—"

"Hey, stop that," Margaret said, slightly raising her voice for emphasis, like a gentle slap on the wrist. "He will never change. How could he, when he's come so far to accept himself? Stop looking for him to make your life complete. He was never there when the puzzle started to fall apart, so why should he be the one to put the pieces together? You were the only player in the beginning, so you have to end the game and put the puzzle together yourself."

Damn! Who was this woman? Had her situation become so bad that a genuine mother had somehow emerged in place of the old one, to do the job the former was incapable of? She wanted to protest, but this old lady knew what she was talking about. Her life would have to change, but in truth, Felicia didn't know if she were strong enough to do it. She didn't know if she wanted to even try. It was just hard looking into Tumali's eyes and not seeing Stephen there. Through all the bad memories, through all the muck, through all the illusions, it was his face she'd see. She liked that. And now her mother was becoming the devil's advocate, and doing a mighty good job at it. Damn good.

4:00… Boy! How time flies.

—III—

"Are you feeling better, Stephen?" David asked, as he craned his neck to take notice of Stephen in the backseat of Damien's Mustang. He was sprawled out, with one hand to his forehead, the other holding on for dear life.

"Hell, can this Puerto Rican fool drive any faster?" Stephen commented, as he slid across the backseat.

"Don't make requests like that from Damien, 'cause you know he will oblige. As for you, what are you doing getting sloshed on the first date anyway? Isn't that considered bad etiquette in some parts of the country?" David asked, unable to hide his amusement.

And then you didn't get any! That fine-ass man walked out of your place without sharing any of the goodies. Honey, I'm gonna have to take back your diploma in the Playa-Playa club."

"Oh, both of you cease!" Stephen said, annoyed. He took a deep sigh, and let the wind that barreled in his face reel him back to sobriety. He felt a little better now than he did two hours ago, when Damien dragged him from the couch and forced him on this journey to San Diego.

"Get yo' lazy butt up, girlfriend!" he had begun. "My momma don't like to wait on drunk black boys from Chicago, okay?"

All Stephen could remember from last night was Jamal placing him on the sofa, then kissing him softly (although very sloppily), and quietly leaving. "Damn! Those speakers are right in my ear, Damien," Stephen complained, placing his palm against his ear as the house music thrummed.

"Oh quiet, you drunk bitch. This isn't loud," Damien replied spiritedly.

"How long before we reach our destination?" Stephen asked. "I thought it only took two hours to get to San Diego."

"Child, it's only been an hour and a half. Stop trippin'. Besides," he suddenly turned onto the off ramp with a sharp right turn, "We almost there."

"Whoa!" David exclaimed, gripping his armrest. "This ain't no racetrack, Miss Indy Five Hundred. I know this is a Mustang, but hold those horses."

"Boy! Didn't know I was in a car with a bunch of sissies."

"You pull this car over and I'll show you a sissy, or at least a sissy with a black eye," Stephen retorted.

Damien disregarded the comment, and continued to dash through the streets, his yellow horse only recognized as a blur to pedestrians. Soon he approached a cobblestone driveway, and there was a collective sigh of relief from all.

The car stopped in front of a beautiful four-bedroom colonial style home. It was a soft cream color with white picket fence, surrounded by yellow tulips, and had a grand front porch from which hung a bench swing. A flower garden blossomed under bay windows, with efflorescent displays of lilies, gardenias, and magnolias. At that moment, the curtains pulled back, revealing a stout little woman who was busily untying her apron. She rushed from the window to the door, trotting downstairs in tiny rhythmic leaps. She wore a generous pink floral dress that hugged her girth and pulled at her breasts; the buttons appeared to be under great stress. She nervously tugged at her long curly hair, patting the top to alleviate any loose strands, and then held out both arms, fingers beckoning in a come-to-me action. This was Momma C.

Damien stepped up to this woman who was all cheeks and dimples. Sweat dotted her forehead and a large pair of glasses rested on the tip of her shiny nose. "Oh, it's so good to see ju boys," she said, running up to meet Damien, her furry slippers clapping against the soles of her feet.

"Mama, como estas?" Damien greeted, and reached out to hug his mother as they clashed into each other's welcome arms.

"Miho, mucho tiempo ha pasado, " she replied, squeezing Damien a bit tighter. Her head rested right under his chin, and she pressed her face firmly against his chest in adoration.

"Yeah, it's been awhile," he whispered.

Lola Cockota then leaned over to take a look at Damien's friends behind him. *"Que pasa? Tus amigos estan actuando como forasteros. Digales venir aqui,"* she said, extending her arm, gesturing toward them.

Damien turned around. "Momma say ju boys actin' like strangers."

"Yeah, get over here and give ju Momma C a hugs," Lola said, her arms out to her sides now, waiting.

David stepped forward, kissing Momma C on her cheeks. "How you doin', Momma C?" he asked, noticing the scent of rich spices coming from her skin. *She must've been cooking up a storm,* David thought.

"Been goods, been goods," she replied happily, tapping David on the back. "Glad ju boys could come." She looked over at Stephen, noticing the way he squinted at her, and his slightly chapped lips. "What's wrong with this one, a little too much tequila?"

"You can say that," David replied, unable to hide his amusement at Momma C's fortitude.

Stephen sauntered over to Lola and reached down to give her a powerful squeeze, then braced his legs to pick her up, happily spinning her around. "How you doing, sexy lady?"

"Oh boy! Stop that!" Lola laughed, pushing Stephen away, as she smoothed out the hem of her dress. *"El es loco,"* she replied, placing her hand at her chest as her normal breathing resumed.

"Yeah, she's a crazy ol' fag," Damien replied.

"Come on, everyone inside," Lola beckoned, as she began to walk towards the house.

Inside, Damien looked around at his mother's home and noticed how nothing ever changed here. Family pictures remained cluttered atop the fireplace mantle just as they had for many years before, depicting his siblings, which consisted of his two brothers and three sisters, their wedding photos, the children, and a few aunts and uncles. These were typical of the whole house, this gallery of photos showing her strong love of family. Two large paintings of the Virgin Mary hung opposite the fireplace, with rosary beads swinging from the corners. Numerous depictions of Jesus in figurines, paintings, and a plaque were placed around the room. Under the coffee table there sat a large Bible and a scatter of magazines.

He could see a barrage of foil-covered dishes in the kitchen. She had been cooking all morning. The scent of food saturated the air.

Suddenly someone lightly tapped his shoulder. He looked down to see Momma, hand cupped to her mouth, trying to get his attention. *"Andrew esta aqui!"* she whispered, craning her neck to be heard.

"Andrew is here," he repeated, looking back at his friends as they rummaged through photo albums.

His mother joined the men on the sofa, as Damien repeated that name in his head. *Andrew, Andrew, Andrew.* It had been at least two or three months since he'd last spoken to Andrew. It had been almost six months since he'd seen him in person. It had been a long five years since they'd broken up as lovers. It had been as little as two years since Andrew hit him with the news of being HIV positive; and only one since he'd been afflicted with AIDS. He was only twenty-eight.

Damien began to head for the back room to see him.

— IV—

The door to the patio was open and the shades were drawn. The soft light that filtered into the room gave a warm glow to the area. A melody of soft instrumentals playing some unfamiliar song came wafting to Damien's ear. The patio was moderately furnished with a floor model color television, a small radio sitting atop it with CD player, a two-tier bookshelf, a card table with a linen cloth thrown atop, supporting a small candy dish that was presently filled with M&M's, and a sofa where Andrew was sprawled out, eyes closed, hand waving back and forth through the air to the soft sounds of music.

Damien leaned against the doorway, thinking about the better times they had. He was twenty when he first met Andrew at a house party given by his friend George. Andrew had been such a handsome young man, with dimples as deep as a fingertip, a perky "white boy' nose that sat straight and sharp on his face, delicious thin ups, and smooth brown skin. He had entered the party with a top hat and cane, leopard-print stretch pants, Doc Martens boots, and a black suede vest with tails. The boy was givin' you fierce wardrobe, and Damien just loved it. "Who is that fine muther-sumpthin'?" Damien had asked.

George had replied, "That's Queen Andrew, honey."

Damien had approached him, and there was an instant chemistry. Numbers were exchanged, and soon they were on that dating train, heading nonstop into love. But they had been young and both very independent, so after two years they had outgrown each other. Andrew had called it quits over a sloppy meal at Fatburger. He had stated that the arguing was becoming too frequent, and he didn't want to be with anyone when the relationship had dwindled down to nothing but a good fuck. Damien looked at Andrew, a bright smear of ketchup on his cheek and bits of fries in his teeth, and agreed with a simple nod of his head.

Looking down at Andrew now, he wondered if things would have been different if they had stayed together. Andrew was still a dashing man, but he'd drastically changed. Damien could see that he was much thinner, with his clothes hanging on him in folds, hiding any form beneath. His cheeks were sunk a bit, the dimples were much more pronounced, and the skin around his eyes appeared to be pulled down, dark. His face was dry, ashy-looking. Even his Adam's apple poked forward like a ripe walnut. With so many drugs not working for him and his constant visits to the doctor, Andrew had decided to allow the disease to take its course.

Damien still found him attractive, and he grinned as he walked over to his friend, bent over, and kissed him lightly on the lips. *"Lo que pasa, mi amigo?"* he asked, rubbing his fingers through Andrew's thinning hair.

Andrew quickly sat up, elated. "Damien! Your mother didn't tell me you were coming here today, you Puerto Rican faggot. That explains all that food in the kitchen."

Damien playfully pushed Andrew on the shoulder, and was momentarily stunned at the sharpness of his collarbone through his shirt. "Stephen and David are here too, baby," he added.

"Really? That's wonderful. It's so good seeing you. I thought Momma C. was just inviting me over for another little lunch. That woman can burn some food, and I'm glad my mother lives right down the street, and since I am staying with her, it made it that much easier to visit."

"Momma's great. I know, considering I *am* the favorite daughter," Damien said with a snap of his finger.

"That's right girl! You are the reigning sibling."

Damien sat beside Andrew, sinking deeply into the sofa. "So how's it going, *papa?* The last time we spoke you was in the hospital."

Andrew waved his hand, "Oh, you mean my little vacation spot. Yeah, I guess that was the last time. I was just getting over my second battle with that pneumonia demon, but it's over now."

Damien sighed. "Well, I'm glad you're okay."

Andrew jabbed Damien in the rib. "Cut that out," he said.

"What?" Damien questioned, rubbing his side.

"Sweetness, quit sounding soooo sad. I'm not going anywhere, so save those soap opera tears for Erica and her girlfriends."

"Well, excuse me for not putting on my Butch Aura before coming in here."

"That is less Butch Aura, and more Bitch Aura if you ask me."

Damien quickly raised a pointed finger. "Watch it, Miss Thang, cause you ain't too old for a nine inch heel up yo' Ass Aura!"

"Watch it! It won't take much for me to snatch that ponytail weave from your head."

"Oh, baby, now you ain't said nuthin but a word," Damien said, standing to his feet, and pretending to take earrings from his ears, as he thrust his feet forward as if kicking off his shoes. "Ain't nuthin on me fake, or used."

Andrew pointed toward Damien's midsection. "Nothin' used? Child, you better check that cootie catcher, 'cause you done used the hell out of that."

Damien stood. "Don't be jealous cause this milkshake is in demand," Damien said, slapping his hips.

Andrew reached out to grab Damien's hand, pulling him back to the sofa. He spoke condescendingly. "It may be in demand, but what was once homogenized is now soy, girl."

Damien burst into laughter for a moment, but stopped when he noticed a cane leaning against the arm of the sofa. "Is that yours?" he asked.

Andrew looked back. "Yeah, that's mine. It's for the neuropathy in my legs."

"Neuro-what?" Damien questioned.

Andrew explained. "It's a pain caused by my medication, like the feeling you get when you hit your funny bone—except this ain't funny."

Concern registered in Damien's eyes. "I don't think I could be as brave as you," Damien expressed.

"Sure you would, honey," Andrew said. "I just think of it as a cold with an attitude."

Damien leaned his head back on the couch, the silence in the room mounting. He wondered once again what it would have been like had he and Andrew remained lovers.

"What you thinking about?" Andrew asked, swinging his thin legs across Damien's lap, and then placing a reassuring hand on his friend's shoulder.

"Just thinking about life," he responded. "Do you ever think you'll fall in love again, Andrew?"

This time Andrew leaned his head back to look at the ceiling. "I used to, Damien, and sometimes in the back of my mind I still do. But I have other things on my mind lately. It takes a lot of time and energy to be in a relationship, and if I were already in one I would be used to the drain, but I just don't have that kind of energy right now. I have been through two bouts with pneumonia. They say I have CMV in my left eye. Of course there is MAC in my blood. And there is a host of medications to take for all this. I can't even have any of these new cocktail drugs because of the side effects."

"I don't know why you would consider taking any of it," Damien said.

Andrew squeezed Damien's shoulder warmly. "A lot of people ask the same question, Damien, and I have to admit I sometimes ask it myself. Some people think that it's the medication that's making us sick, if not sicker—the side effects, the toll on the liver, the immune system, and our lives. But when I first heard this news, I was not about to take any medications to impede my lifestyle. My mistake, 'cause it wasn't long after, that pneumonia caught the better of me. But I still continued to take pills when I felt like it. By that time, some years into it, I was catching all sorts of other illnesses, so now I take my medications on time because I have no other choice."

"I just hope it can work for you, Andrew," Damien said.

"It's a full-time job, baby. That's why I don't worry about a man. I got Larry and Charley to help me every now and then. You remember them, don't you?"

Damien cocked his lips to the side, but nothing came to his recollection. "No, I don't think so. Have you introduced them to me before?" he asked.

"I guess I should have," Andrew said, holding up one palm. "Well, this is Larry," then he held up the other, "and this is Charley." He laughed, and in seconds they were both rolling with amusement. "When I was younger, I would go to the spas," he mentioned.

Damien was visibly shocked. "You mean the bathhouses!" The gaiety was gone.

Andrew reeled back. "Don't look at me like that. If you don't have the energy to play the dating games, you—"

"But those places are filthy. They are unsafe and dangerous," Damien interrupted.

"Unsafe? Unsafe isn't denoted by the building you're in." "Well, I think it's a major contributor to this epidemic."

"But who do you think goes in those places?" Andrew questioned. "The popular ones? The fine motherfuckers you see on the street? The really healthy ones? Perhaps once in a while, when they get too damned horny, and they've fucked everyone in town, but it's the ones who can't get a date in this town that go there, baby—the ones that have had a little too much bullshit thrown at them."

"But there are places you can find dates. They have a lot of services in San Francisco you could have used while living there. HIV/AIDS dating programs, group counseling, classifieds. L.A. also has a bunch of—

"No, they don't, Damien," Andrew interrupted again. "When you want some dick, baby, you look for something you're attracted to."

"Well, I just don't know. I just can't see it being right; I can't see it being safe," Damien said, shaken for words.

"No, you wouldn't, but you've never been there. Sometimes it's not about sex. It's not about being safe or unsafe sometimes, because truthfully there are some men out there that don't believe in the plastic, sometimes it's about companionship. I was there to have a man hold me in his arms, look seductively at me, lie to me with words of adoration, and just allow his flesh to touch mine; sometimes that's what it was all about."

Damien let the silence stand. He was quite disturbed and didn't know why. Perhaps this whole disregard for sex in a lifestyle where it was the norm upset him. It was a lifestyle without legal commitments. The gay lifestyle was always in search for Mr. Right. Yet there was no Mr. Right, only a mate you loved that *made* everything right.

Andrew blew his nose. "I hope I didn't upset you, Damien, but that's the way things are."

Damien began rubbing Andrew's legs, noticing the hardness of his bones through his jeans. "No, baby. I understand what you're saying. People play by their own rules, what they consider responsible. It's just disturbing, that's all. And I . . . well .....

Andrew swung his legs to the floor, then leaned in closer to Damien and kissed him on the cheek. Before any words could be exchanged, they could hear Lola walking down the hall, and they sat up against the back of the couch at full attention. She peered around the doorway. "Ju two better gets in here. Andrew must share with everyone. Come on, before dinner get cold."

Damien stood and began to follow Lola. Suddenly Andrew gripped the back of his belt, pulling him back. "Honey, this is a Gucci belt! Bitch, be careful with the tugging!" Damien protested.

Andrew only smiled and said, "I love you too ... you big flame."

They both smiled as Damien held Andrew's waist a bit tighter and they both trotted from the patio toward the wonderful aromas wafting from the kitchen.

– V –

In Pacific Heights, among the many hilled streets and colonial homes of San Francisco, there sits Tony's, near Sixth Street in Knob Hill. It's a modest little eatery; containing a bar, live four-piece band, and outdoor patio. It's known for its Italian cuisine, and the pasta Primavera with marinara wine sauce is to die for. It is most popular among the elite of the Bay, the famous, and the who's who. It has two dining rooms. One is large and opulent, with a grand crystal chandelier suspended from the ceiling, exquisite lithographs by Monet donning the walls; his lilies giving the place a sense of placidness. There are bottles of rare vintage wines at each table, and crystal flatware wrapped in silk napkins.

The adjacent room, connected by a redwood-lined hallway with torches jutting from the walls, is the second dining room, often called the Cellar. It has more private booths, with low lighting and candles at each table, fresh cut roses as centerpieces. Small oval mirrors line the booths, reflecting just enough light to complement any flaws in beauty and still enhance the splendor of the victuals. The patio has a spacious atmosphere, with looming oak trees, a mini banana tree, hanging lanterns, and umbrellas covering each table. The floors are the smoothest Spanish tile, vented for heat, with the center fountain made to resemble a large mountainous waterfall. It is calm from front to back.

Tony's is known for its solitude, its seclusion, its ability to take you away, let you escape. On Saturday the live band plays, in full tuxedos, covering a litany of classics from Bach to Beethoven.

Gerri always made it a point to be here on Saturday afternoons; she needed the escape. The cosmetics industry was not without its adversity, its competition, and its debts. When coming to Tony's, she often asked her best friend, Cyan Kai, to join her. After all, misery loves company.

They were both enjoying the flavorful scents of their hazelnut cappuccinos this day. Cyan realized she drank such concoctions only when at Tony's with Gerri; she loved her Asian teas. Of course, being Asian herself, it went with her upbringing. She was now wrapping her hands around the cup, letting the warmth soothe her fingers. She tossed a thatch of hair from her shoulder, and looked up indifferently at Gerri. "You know, Darlene has a showing today at her gallery. She asked me if you would be interested in attending."

Gerri shifted in her seat, pulling her attention away from a very attractive waitress across the room, and focused on Cyan. "Why does that woman think I have the time to entertain her? We both know what she really wants to accomplish, don't we?"

Cyan looked down at her drink. "We both know she has affection for you. Of course that seems to be par for the course when it comes to you," Cyan answered.

Gerri sipped her coffee, letting the silence command their space. "They only have affection for my money, and what I can do for them. You want the same thing too."

Cyan turned her eyes up at Gerri, in disbelief of her last statement. "Yeah, you're real funny, aren't you, Ms. Moore. I am surely not as impressed as the press seems to be by your rise to fame and fortune. All I know is that Darlene is a wonderful person, a successful art dealer, and she has other interests besides your yearly profit margin. Anyway, the showing is in celebration of her newly acquired Wiesenthal collection. His oils are fabulous," Cyan said, tasting her drink.

Gerri wrinkled her nose. "Nope. She's too much into herself. Her high horse is too elevated for me."

"Hmm, sounds like someone I know very well myself," Cyan pronounced, with arched brows. Her eyes burned a hole through Gerri.

"Are you saying I'm like that, Miss Squinty Eyes?" Gerri asked, leaning forward and placing her elbow on the table.

Cyan's only reply was a loud sipping from her upturned cup.

"Stop that! I am not *that* cocky."

Cyan raised her hand. "Don't act like it isn't true. I think you are filled with just too much overconfidence."

"Oh, and has overconfidence become a crime in this U.S. of A.?" "No, and that's why you two are made for each other. You and Darlene are like clones. I could give her a call and—"

"What's that I hear?" Gerri interjected, placing a cupped hand behind her ear. "Is that the sound of a matchmaker? A nosy body? An instigator?"

Cyan spun her coffee cup in circles on the table, as if she were thinking about what words she would speak. "If you want to know the truth, Gerri—and I really don't think you do—you are becoming an old maid real fast." She then looked intently at Gerri.

"Quit looking at me like that. Those eyes make me think you're trying to read into my soul."

"Perhaps I am," Cyan responded, moving her eyes back to her cup. "And what, pray tell, have you foreseen, All Great and Powerful Gypsy Guru?" Gerri asked mockingly.

"I see a forty-year-old woman who has become just a little too busy. You were a bit more spontaneous a few years back. I see what's happening to you, Gerri, and you're going to have to rise from that rut you've dug for yourself."

"Are you trying to give me some of that overpriced therapy you charge your clients? I am not one of those people, Cyan, so ease off."

Cyan closed her eyes and shook her head in overt pity. "Maybe you need to be," Cyan said. "You've immersed yourself in your work so you don't have the time to date, and thus you don't have to worry about finding a replacement for Sarafina, which frankly, you'll never find, because she is her own person. You're not over her departing, and you're going to have to get over it so that you can move on, Gerri." Cyan leaned back, folding her arms. "So there, you've been counseled, and this one is on the house. Now, I'm really starving. Where is that waitress?"

Gerri looked at Cyan with an open mouth of surprise. To her, this conversation was far from over. "Is that what you've been thinking?" Gerri asked, and suddenly began to laugh. Cyan stared at her as if she'd finally gone insane. Is that what you thought?" Gerri continued, grabbing a napkin from the table to dab at the corners of her eyes. "Sarafina hasn't gone anywhere."

Cyan was perplexed. "What are you talking about? She's living with someone in Los Angeles, Gerri. When you guys broke up, it was—"

"We didn't break up!" Gerri interrupted. "We came to an understanding, which caused us to separate for a while."

"What? Okay, fine. You both came to this *understanding*. Whatever! Just know you're going to have to change your attitude if you ever plan to meet someone else. Sarafina felt abandoned and lonely because you took her for grafted. She needed a full-time lover, which you weren't, and when that occurs—"

"Oh, shut up, Cyan! I don't need any of your psycho mumbo-jumbo. Quite honestly, I think you're committing a crime, charging people to sleep with their eyes open. Sarafina is only out having a little fun, that's all."

"A little fun? I think it was a permanent stress leave. She's got a new life now."

Gerri grinned, placing her napkin across her lap. "No, she'll be back. This is the vacation she needed, that's all," she explained, as she looked across the room for the waitress, she hated conversations like this, when Cyan acted as her shrink. .

"A year is mighty long for a vacation. You really think she's going to return? You think she's just going to drop her present lover when it's convenient, so you two can get back together?"

"Of course she will," Gerri smiled. "You better than anyone should know I hold on to my possessions. Before the summer is over she will be back in my house, back in my arms, back in my bed." The grin became wider, and Cyan knew it meant trouble. "Sarafina just doesn't know it yet, but she will. Believe me, she will." Gerri thrust her hand in the air, signaling the stunning white waitress over to her table. She was quite ravenous now with hunger; best laid plans did that to her sometimes.

Chapter 4

– I–

Dominique chopped the onions into the pot, wiping away a line of sweat across her forehead with the back of her hand. She looked up at the Garfield clock that hung in the kitchen and noticed it was well past six o'clock. She knew the gang was at Momma C's now, eating and having a good ol' time. This beef stew would be a sorry replacement for the spread that woman would have created. Damien had invited her a week ago, and she had said that she would call him if she'd decided to go—but considering last night's episode, she thought it better to stay home and deal with this matter. The anger had subsided, but the conversation was yet to begin. One thing she hated discussing was Sarafina's ex-lover, but it was inevitable.

"How's dinner coming?" Sarafina asked, as she entered the kitchen.

Dominique jumped as she suddenly felt a strong pair of hands wrap around her waist. Dominique slapped Sarafina's thick black knuckles. "Girl, you startled me. Just hold that big stomach of yours in place, and I'll be through in a minute, or I'll be throwing you in the pot."

Sarafina reached up to run her finger across Dominique's sweat covered neck. "You want me to get that small fan from the closet, sweetheart? It's hot as shit in here."

Dominique nodded her head. "Yeah, I haven't been over this stove in a while. I forgot how hot it gets in here."

Sarafina pecked her full lips against the nape of Dominique's neck then dashed from the kitchen. She returned with a small desk fan and placed it on the counter beside Dominique. "Thanks, Tina," Dominique said, continuing to cut her vegetables.

Sarafina sat at the small table at the far end of the kitchen. She leaned back against the wooden chair until the tips of her feet barely touched the floor, and the chair creaked from the strain. "You know, babe, I am truly sorry about last night. I was in the wrong, and I will never do that again."

Here we go, Dominique thought. "I know, you told me this morning. As far as I'm concerned, it's yesterday's news."

"I know I would still be pissed at me. I don't think my friendship with Gerri should come between us. I hope you can come to grips with that."

"Hey, I did say it was all over. Now, why don't you get me a glass of wine from the refrigerator. There should still be some Chablis in there," Dominique suggested. "You can get some clean glasses out of the dishwasher."

"Oh, and I wanted to thank you again for that slammin' breakfast this morning. I should've been the one to throw down for you, but I do thank you," Sarafina said, as she slid two wine glasses from the machine then placed them on the table.

"You gave thanks enough this morning with that freak fest you put on. My crotch will be steaming for days," Dominique replied, fanning her pubic area. "For a minute I thought you were going to rub my clit off."

Sarafina retrieved the carafe of wine and poured each glass to mid-center.

"Woman, fill that thing up! I'm looking to really relax, okay?" Dominique said, walking over to the table and flopping down in a chair. Sarafina leaned over to place a gentle kiss on Dominique's cheek, and then passed her the full glass. "I really apologize," she said, almost at a whisper.

Dominique took a swift gulp, immediately feeling the burn of the alcohol in her throat. "Let's forget it, shall we?" Dominique suggested. "I just want you and me to forget the whole incident, *comprende?*"

Sarafina placed a hand on Dominique's knee. *"Comprende. I* just want you to know that it won't happen again."

"I hope not, Sarafina."

"You think I'm going to forget this whole thing and do it again, don't you?"

Dominique raised her shoulders, unsure. She took another sip then cleared her throat. "Sarafina, to tell you the truth, I think you're still in love with Gerri, and I'm just going to have to figure out how to deal with that."

Sarafina was stupefied. "Why do you say that?"

"I can't be sure, but you two broke up for no other reason than to get away from each other. There was no betrayal, no anger, no major blowup. You just left town, but that doesn't mean you've really left her."

"But that was more than a year—"

"Let me finish," Dominique continued, taking another sip of her wine. She was beginning to feel its effect. "I guess what puzzles me is how you could so easily give up the lifestyle you had with her. She was, damn, still is, a wealthy sonofabitch. Vacations, fabulous parties, shopping at all the boutiques, eating in the finest restaurants, and a whole bunch of other things you had, where I would think you insane to give up. What I make at Shelby's D'zines is a million-dollar mile from what she can acquire. Don't you miss all that, Sarafina? 'Cause you aren't getting it here."

Sarafina shook her head. She had explained this before, but knew she would have to explain it for the rest of their relationship. Sure, she had millions of dollars at her fingertips. Who wouldn't want that? Sure, she missed it. She'd admitted that to herself a long time ago. But she only really missed the charm in it all, in knowing that it was there from the start.

"No, I don't miss that," Sarafina replied, "and I'll tell you why." She began, telling once more of her life with Gerri and the reality behind the glamour.

In the beginning, life with Gerri had been grand, with the wonderful home, in Pacific Heights, the expense account that was set up for her, the Platinum American Express card in her name, the precious Porsche 968 she was allowed to drive, and so much more. But where was her lover in all this? Where was Gerri if not attending meeting after meeting, taking phone calls of great urgency that interrupted their quiet time at home? There were only very lonely dinners, messages left on the answering machine of hellos and how are you's, and the nights that the bed seemed so very, very big. It felt like a long-distance relationship in the same house.

She tried fitting into Gerri's world of corporate parties and Broadway plays. But Gerri's friends always seemed to get in the way. They made her feel invisible. They wouldn't speak to her past a hello and a handshake. Her friends Darlene McKnight and Cyan Kai were the only ones that carried on a bit of conversation.

It was not at all easy dealing with the overt stereotypes. She remembered a time she'd gone shopping with Gerri in Knob Hill to one of her favorite boutiques. Sarafina had parked the car while Gerri went ahead to have some alterations done on an evening gown she'd purchased there. As Sarafina entered the store, she was met by a young woman who asked if she had an appointment.

"No, I don't have an appointment. I'm here with—"

The tall skinny white girl had quickly interrupted. "Well, I'm so very sorry," she had begun, pulling a strand of bleach blonde hair back from her pale forehead, as she looked at a large book that lay on the glass countertop. "You can only come in here to either honor an appointment or to make one, and as I see, we are quite booked right now till the end of June. So why don't you call back." She then closed the book with such force, such finality, that the flurry of air from the pages caused Sarafina to blink her eyes.

Sarafina had placed her palms calmly on the countertop, as if a sudden shift in the foundation of this building would be the only thing that could move her. "I am here with someone, young lady."

"That's funny, I saw you come in here alone. Do you mean you're with someone already here?" She looked down and opened her appointment book once more. "Hmm, let me see here. The only one I have scheduled here is a Miss Gerri Moore. You know, the *wealthy* cosmetics woman. Would that happen to be you? I think not. Not with that attire," she had said sarcastically.

Sarafina had bit her tongue; she knew what this child was implying. Had Sarafina been younger, she would have snatched the blue from this girl's eyes. "That's who I'm with. I was just parking the car while she came in to—"

The young lady quickly held up her hand. "Oh, I see," she said suddenly with a smile. "If you'll just wait here, I'm sure Miss Moore will be only a minute conducting her business and then—"

"What do you mean, wait here? I've never just waited out here for Gerri."

The white girl turned up her lips, placing more wild hair behind her pink ear. "I very much doubt that," she quickly said in a low voice. "But she won't be but a moment."

Sarafina had opened her mouth, on the verge of cursing this bitch, but decided not to waste her time, and charged for the swing door that led behind the counter, when suddenly the small waif stuck her broomstick of an arm out across Sarafina, blocking her path like the post at a railroad crossing.

"*You* are not welcome back there, okay?" she said, quite adamantly.

Sarafina had looked up at her, and then stared back at her tiny little arm. *I could easily break it like a twig,* she had thought. "What the hell are you talking about?"

The little girl took a cautionary step back, placing a hand on her bony hip, eyes closed, and finger pointing stiffly at the curtain that separated them from the back room. "I'm sure Miss Moore would not wish for her driver to be charging in here, using that profane language, and upsetting—"

"Driver!" Sarafina found her head swimming. She reached down to grab the girl's other hand, which had been holding the swing door, and gripped it tightly between her thick dark fingers. "You better take your tired skeleton ass out of my way before I—"

"What's going on out here?" a voice said, accompanied by an older white woman who charged through the curtains. Her hair was rolled atop her head in great massive curls of tumbling red circles, and her face was caked with makeup at an obvious attempt to hide a crater full of wrinkles. She spoke almost without moving her lips, a trait Sarafina had seen more and more in older white women, as if trying not to allow any further flaws in their skin to manifest. "What in the world is going on here?" she asked, looking at the grip Sarafina had on her employee.

Sarafina quickly released her hold, and addressed the older woman, who she knew as Karen Rothschild. "Karen, there seems to be a problem with the *help* around here," she informed, glaring at the girl who was rubbing her injured wrist.

She quickly brought her hand to her chest as if clutching a string of pearls. "*Me?* I would have you know, Ms. Rothschild, that this insulting woman came in here demanding to see Miss Moore. I went on to explain to her that an employee of Miss Moore's was not permitted to—"

"What?" Karen shouted, her eyes darting back and forth between Sarafina and her employee. "Tasha, this is no employee of Miss Moore's, but a very close friend." She turned to look at Sarafina; the grin on her face seemed forced.

"I'm sorry about this, Miss Chandler. She's new here, and it would seem I need to have a small talk with her."

"But I—"

"No questions, Tasha. Miss Chandler has waited out here long enough. We've been expecting her, and I had hoped you would at least inform me of any persons not scheduled, instead of creating your own conclusions," she finished, stepping back against the curtain, and parting it with one slow hand gesture. "If you would like to join us, Miss Chandler, Miss Moore is waiting," she invited.

With one final glare at Tasha, Sarafina entered the back room.

It was always like that: the accusations, the silent rejections, the reserved prejudice that felt like a hand around her throat, choking her to the point of tears. Gerri never exhibited these hidden vices—but then again, Gerri was rarely there. She was a very busy woman. It reminded her so much of her mother, working as a schoolteacher, never having any time for her youngest daughter. Her life went from Jamaica, to New York, to San Francisco, to finally Los Angeles; where she met this wonderful woman named Dominique Devaroe. She hadn't felt a cold bed since then—cool maybe, but never cold. She could be at home alone, but knew Dominique would be there within hours, and not days. It was one reason why she hadn't gone back to work yet, because she felt so at home now; the other reason was because Gerri had wired her a good sum of "settling down" money. She was in love now with a wonderful woman, and she wanted to soak up that feeling like a sponge to water.

Dominique listened to all this, and didn't know what to say. She knew she loved Sarafina too, but the story was far from over. Gerri was a conflict, and Dominique appeared to be the only one to see it. Friendship, lovers, it was all still a relationship. How do you go from being lovers for three years plus to being friends overnight? You don't. *There is so much left undone,* Dominique thought, *and it scares me. It scares me a lot.*

– II –

"Hey!" David squealed. "Watch those bumps."

"David, baby, you are being a backseat driver, so stop it," replied Damien, as he glanced over his shoulder at his friend in the backseat.

"Yeah, cut out all that quibbling. It was bad enough we spent most of this trip waiting for you in the hospital," Stephen said, reaching behind his seat to backhand David on the forehead.

"Stop playing, Stephen. I'm here in pain," David replied, holding up his hand to feign another attack.

Stephen waved at David, and turned back around. "Oh, please. You're not a cripple yet," he said, looking back once more to stick out his tongue and wrinkle his nose. "But you sure do have some of the stankiest and ugliest feet God ever bestowed upon a man."

"Leave my feet out of this. I sit here in dire agony, and all you can do is critique my toes. Some friend you are."

"If I weren't your friend I would have let that stingray have you for lunch, instead of pulling you back on the lovely shores of Black's Beach," Stephen reminded, turning around once more, and taking a huge bite out of his cheeseburger.

David stuck his tongue out at the back of Stephen's head, and took a discreet glimpse at his foot. It throbbed like nothing he'd ever felt.

The dressing was wrapped tightly, and his pulse pounded with a dagger of pain every time Damien passed over the tiniest deviation in the road. Besides that, he noticed he was overdue for a pedicure.

Black's Beach was a nude gay beach on the outskirts of San Diego. It was Damien's bright idea to buy bathing suits for everyone at the International Male and have a relaxing afternoon. The trail to get to the beach was no bigger than a few inches in width, made up of a twisting surface that was both uneven as well as winding. It ran along the side of an embankment that was at times too steep to travel on without sliding. The entrance to the trail was strewn with signs warning DANGER! ENTER AT YOUR OWN RISK! Sissies always were drawn to drama.

Once at the bottom David noticed it wasn't one of the cleanest beaches around, with seaweed scattered on the darkened sand that marked off the rise of last night's tide. Paper was tossed about in small amounts, as were pieces of clothing and other unidentified objects. No glass, thank God.

There was a nice crowd, and lots of flesh about. Tits, cock, and ass swung in all its glory. The limp-wrist children were here, clacking in tiny groups, shades on their faces, and attitude in their walk. The lovers were here, welded together as if sunlight itself was forbidden to pass between them. The modest were here, wearing jeans, hooded sweatshirts, and gym shoes. The regulars were here, sitting in their lawn chairs with umbrella hats and binoculars. The older men were here—in droves it seemed—who's bright wrinkled asses were begging for sunlight. The young were here, skin fresh and tighter than a box of rubber bands.

Then there was Damien, making a spectacle of himself, commenting on every man that passed within his view. *"Damn!* That boy has got it goin' on. Oh, yes, girlfriend, *yes* ... Good Lord! Is that a dagger I see before me . . . Child, pass me a napkin, Momma is droolin' Snap that, and that, and *that!"* Soon he threw off his trunks and bared more than any friend should be witness to. He trotted off into the water, a mermaid reborn. "Now you two had better get into the water. I didn't spend money on everyone's trunks for nothing," Damien said with a snap of his fingers.

"Boy, nobody asked you ..." Stephen began.

Damien swiftly held up his hand. "Hey! Save it, baby. Either you a fish or seaweed, and fish play in the water. Decide what you are." Then off Damien went into the water, buns flapping in the sun.

After a short hesitation, both Stephen and David decided to take to the ocean. Stephen remained close to the shore while David ventured out into deeper water. David found the freedom of the ocean thrilling. He'd plunged into the water head first; the crispness of it slapped against his face and filled his ears and hair with its cool liquid fingers. He swam further out, the saltiness of the water brushing against his lips, the waves flowing along his body, becoming one with him.

David could see Stephen wading back to the beach, then turning back to wave at him.

As Stephen waved at David, he saw David dip beneath the ocean's surface but didn't see him rise again. When he finally did, there was a look of horror on his face, and his mouth pulled wide in a scream, which was quickly stifled when he dipped below again; and the ocean filled his throat.

David's heart was racing. What the hell did he step on? He fell beneath the icy grip of the water again, losing his footing, the motion of the water pushing him about like a rag doll, salt filled his eyes and mouth, his muscles became numb and fatigued, his breath snatched from him in a foam of bubbles.

My *God! I'm drowning!* He thought

It was the pain that pierced his foot which caused him to forget his surroundings. He'd reached down to take hold of his ankle, when he suddenly realized he was not on land; the rules were different here. The ocean quickly swelled in around him, and he was forced to pull his head back out of the water, but with one foot disabled, he was lost to the current. He was totally in shock and out of any control.

"David!" came the faint voice to his ears, followed by a pair of strong hands clasping his shoulder. He could feel himself being pulled back to the shores, sand grating the bottoms of his feet. He looked up to see Stephen staring with morbid concern down at him. "What happened?" he asked, towing him away from the water.

David gritted his teeth and tried to speak, but his lungs ached and his words only spewed forth in a violent spasm of coughing and spit. Tears filled his eyes.

"Something bit me!" he finally said past an exhausted breath, as they both looked down at his foot and noticed a ring of blood trailing with each step.

"Was it some glass?" Stephen asked, trying to pull him back to their spot on the sand.

"Wait! Don't move me. Let me stand on it for a while so the pressure will slow the bleeding," he demanded, bracing his arm around Stephen's waist. "I think it was a stingray. I must have stepped on it by accident."

Once the bleeding subsided, they returned to camp, to find Damien lying back on the blanket. He sat up about to greet his friends, but quickly saw the thin trail of blood at David's foot. "Good Lord! What happened?" he shrieked.

"We're leaving, that's what's happening," Stephen informed. "We have to get him to the hospital. He stepped on a stingray."

Damien reached out to grab hold of David's leg, lifting it slightly to see the thick gash that ran midway up the sole of his foot, blood continuing to trickle. "I'll page Momma C to see if she's at work, and the doctor can look at it."

The hospital stay was short, and the doctor confirmed that it was indeed a stingray that had bit him. They concluded he must've stepped on it real good, because stingrays aren't creatures that attack unless provoked. It would be at least two weeks before the wound healed enough to walk comfortably. David was also instructed to see his doctor first chance he got. Because of its depth, the wound would require no stitches: a precaution against internal infections—it had to heal from the inside out. He thanked Momma C, and soon they were all heading back to Los Angeles.

The wind was cold in the open convertible, and it roused David back to consciousness.

"Are you still alive back there? You mighty quiet," Stephen commented, flashing his hand across David's vision. "Your ass still in shock or something?"

"Naw, just thinking about that fucked-up beach. I just want to rest my pretty ass, that's all."

"Well, we should be home in another hour or so. You can rest then. Allen will be home to take care of you."

"Humph," Damien said under his breath.

David looked at the back of his friend's head. He could see what Damien was thinking, and both knew the pain would be far from over once he reached home.

— III —

David stood at his front door, watching the rear lights of Damien's car as it sped along the darkened street. He balanced himself on his crutches, as they pinched under his arms. The neighborhood noises suddenly came to his ears: dogs barking down the street, leaves rustling along the block, salsa music charging through the air from a party across the way, where balloons, streamers, and big long cars covered the yard.

Then there was the sound of his nervous breathing.

David slowly closed the door as he walked in. The smell of liquor and smoke filled the air. Looking at the coffee table, he could see it was littered with butt-filled ashtrays and empty beer bottles, one of which stood on an empty tray, obviously mistaken for a coaster of some kind. A thunderous belch rocked the air, and David looked to see Allen sitting on the arm of the couch, a beer clutched in his hand. He sipped on it while looking directly at the stereo before him, not bothering to notice David in the slightest.

"So what happened to you?" he asked, continuing to face the stereo.

David's eyes widened. Allen hadn't even bothered to see him hoisted up on crutches, but somehow he knew of his injury. He must've seen him through the window as he stepped from Damien's car. *That has to be it,* David thought. However, Allen was eerie in this sense. "A little accident at the beach," David replied. "A stingray got the better of me."

Allen slowly turned his neck as if it were on a cog, clicking like the sweep hand on a clock ....*click, click, click;* He just stared at David, glaring into his eyes. "So, are you okay?" he asked.

David tried to smile at his concern, but it was strained, because the attention seemed somehow fabricated. "Sure. I'm having it looked at on Monday by Dr. Peterson," he said, as he walked near Allen, leaning his crutches near the sofa. "Why are you drinking so much today? You aren't drunk, are you?" He leaned forward to pick up the discarded bottles from the table and began stacking them neatly together.

Allen leaned forward, placing his now empty bottle on the table, and he pushed it toward David. It slid across, clattering against the set David was arranging, and David swiftly grabbed it before it rolled from the table to the floor. He gave Allen a cross look that was quickly ignored.

"No, I am not drunk, David," he said, rising to his feet.

"Well, you're soon on your way with all these bottles laying everywhere."

Allen dismissed him with a sweep of his hand, and walked to the stereo to turn up the music. An old cut played: RuPaul's "House of Love." David was surprised he hadn't heard the music as he came into the house. Had the beating of his heart been that strong? Allen flopped down in the La-Z-Boy that sat opposite the stereo and reached down to pluck out another beer from a case of six-packs. His eyes were vacant as he took off the twist cap and brought the long-neck bottle to his bright pink lips.

David wasn't stupid.

This fool was drunk!

Allen leaned his head back, eyes closed, and all David could do was stare at him, and wonder what this night was going to turn out to be like. Here he was with a mangled foot (at least it felt mangled), and Allen hadn't registered any genuine concern regarding it. David didn't let that bother him; perhaps it was a good sign. The less said from Allen, the better.

The room was bathed in RuPaul, and David had almost managed to forget Allen was in the room until he spoke. "So, what beach was this?" he asked, not bothering to open his eyes.

"Black's Beach," he replied. "It was some silly idea of—"

"That's that nude fag beach, isn't it?" Allen asked, hastily, opening one eye.

"Yeah, I guess. There's a straight beach right next to—
" "Figures."

He is being sarcastic, David thought. His foot throbbed more, and he wished he'd just gone straight to bed when he came in, but nooo, he had to start cleaning it up. Allen was looking for a confrontation, and David could almost hear its countdown.

"And why didn't you bother to call me? I've been waiting to hear from you all day," Allen asked, as he opened his other eye, batting his lashes, trying to focus.

"What do you mean?"

Taking another sip from his beer, Allen continued to gaze at David. "It's a simple question, that's all. Why didn't you call me?"

"I did call you, as soon as I was at Momma C's, and there was no answer. The phone just kept ringing."

"There wasn't any message on the machine."

"If the phone kept ringing, that means the answering machine wasn't on, dear." David could feel the tension build in the room. The countdown had started.

"And you couldn't call again? I was in the house waiting for your call, David. I thought you said you were going to call me when you got to San Diego."

David exhaled. "I am not going to get into this with you, Allen. I had a nice time in San Diego, despite this little accident, and you're trying to ruin it. I don't know why you get like this."

Allen threw his hands up, beer still fixed in his grasp, and liquid went flying from the lip of the bottle onto the carpet. David flinched as he watched the carpet soak up the beer in tiny dark circles. It reminded him of too much: the building anger, the beer, the carpet. It reminded him too much of his past. "What am I getting like, David? I only asked a simple question."

"Would you look at what're you're doing to the carpet, Allen? We just had that cleaned last month."

"Don't you go telling me what to do about my carpet, in my house," Allen stated, his voice rising. "I paid for it! I should have *you* clean it up!"

David was taken to a past event again. *My God! What is happening?*

"I only want to know what you were doing in San Diego for so long that you couldn't even bother to pick up the phone and call somebody."

David could feel his muscles tighten, and his foot beat with a tiny rhythm of pain; it matched the pain starting in his head. "You're drunk, Allen! So, honey, I am not gonna argue with you any longer. You always want to get into an argument when you're like this," David said, reaching for his crutches. "I'm going to bed. I am very tired." David pulled himself up, braced his crutches under him, and began to hobble from the room.

Allen suddenly jumped to his feet and stood in David's path. David could feel his heart thud in his chest as if it were trying to climb out of his throat. He stood flush with Allen, staring at his chest, refusing to look up at him. The stench of beer and bad breath rained down upon him like a toxic cloud. Allen's chest was rising and falling rapidly. He was most angry now.

"What is your problem, Allen? I need to get some sleep. We'll talk about this tomorrow."

"You can't just walk out on somebody when they're talking to you," Allen raged. "I just want to know why you didn't call. Did you forget the number or something? Maybe that was it."

"This is ridiculous. I am going to bed, damn!" he said, attempting to walk past Allen, when he suddenly felt a hand grasp his shoulder.

"What's our phone number, David?" Allen asked, lightly squeezing David's shoulder.

David twisted his shoulder from Allen and then continued to walk past him into the dining room, heading quickly for a bedroom that seemed miles away. Just then he felt a tug at his shirt, and before he knew it he was being dragged back, nearly losing his footing as the crutches slid from his fingers.

"What are you doing?" David asked angrily.

"I didn't hear you repeat our phone number!" Allen shouted through slurred speech.

David was frightened. Allen began to breathe loudly past flaring nostrils, glossy eyes, and a forehead riddled with pockets of moisture. David swallowed loudly, then said as calmly as he could, "Five-five-five, six-five-two-one."

Countdown.

Allen pushed David's shoulder. "I knew you remembered it, beach faggot!" Allen pushed his shoulder once again, this time a bit harder, taunting, him. "And why didn't you use it?"

"I did," David said, frantically, "but you were not home. If you expect someone to call then you at least turn the answering machine on, or at least be home until they do."

"So what were you doing out there with your sissy friends? Who were you with all this time? Huh? Do you hear me?"

"What the hell are you trying to get at? You think I was out doing something like fuckin' around or something? You just need to let me get to bed and stop all this nonsense," David said, as he continued to head for the bedroom.

Allen thrust his open palm forward, hitting David squarely in the chest, reeling him back against the china cabinet; dishes rattled violently. Then Allen reached out to take hold of his shirt, pulling David back into the living room and thrusting him on the sofa, his crutches flying from his hands as he landed hard on his back, three buttons ripping from his clothes.

"What the fuck!" David shouted, as Allen walked toward him. "You must be the one doing shit if you can't be at home to answer the phone. Where was your ass? Doing some more window shopping at the International Male?" David was no fool. He knew the car he'd seen that day at the store with Damien looked too familiar. The look on Allen's face told him that too.

Then, as if he'd vanished in a charging blur, Allen rose up and swung his hand down at David so quickly that the lightning flash of pain that ripped through his jaw had erupted before he knew that Allen had actually struck him, and a stream of tears shot out his eyes from the momentum alone. When his vision cleared, he could see Allen standing over him, a smirk across his face. In a fit of rage, David surged forward, forgetting his handicap, and attacked Allen, fists bared, arms swinging. Allen took a cautionary step back, and then swung out his leg, kicking David, and causing an explosive amount of agony to plow through his ankle. David plummeted to the floor, writhing in torment.

"Who do you think you are, accusing me?" Allen said, pointing at his chest. "I got something for your ass!" he said, leaving the room.

David could hear the footsteps fade as he lay there waiting for his pain to diminish. He prayed this fool had gone to bed and fallen asleep. But the footsteps returned. David remained still, his chest to the floor, his eyes closed. He heard a thud near his head, opened his eyes, and saw an object on the floor beside him; something Allen had tossed down. He was shocked.

It was a tube of K-Y jelly!

David swung himself around on his back, his head aching as he did, and looked up at Allen, who was now in a T-shirt and boxers. "You must be out of your mind!"

Allen dropped the fistful of condoms from his shaky hands to the floor. "Shut the fuck up! I want some ass, brother, and you're gonna give that shit up!"

David reached out for one of his fallen crutches and attempted to swing it at Allen. Allen effortlessly snatched it away from David and brought the heavy aluminum back down upon David's shoulder, beating him with hard, powerful pelts. He then rammed the end of the crutch into David's chest, forcing him back onto the floor.

Allen tossed the crutch behind him and then stepped over David, who could look directly up and into Allen's boxer shorts to witness the instant swelling of his manhood. Allen fell to his knees, his huge butt pressing into David's own crotch. David tried once again to swing at Alien, his fingers bared, his teeth clenched. His hand brushed against Allen's thick jaw, but it did him no good as Allen keenly dodged each attempt, and then delivered one himself, with a hard blow to David's ribs.

David coughed as his chest ignited, and he could feel utter anguish charge through all his major muscle groups. He did nothing more. "You need to learn to call someone," Allen advised, as he rose a bit to turn David onto his stomach. With little effort and even less resistance, Allen was able to slip David's pants and underwear from him. This was soon followed by the sticky coolness of the K-Y, and the sound of a condom wrapper being torn open. Soon there was the feeling of pain, sometimes associated with pleasure; it was not the case today.

As the pounding continued, David cursed himself; his own manhood was betraying him again as it pushed itself along his belly. Deeper and deeper came the sting, and David wondered: Was he being raped? Was he too shocked to know? Was he wrong in not calling periodically? Was he wrong in going to that stupid beach? The man had worried about him. There was no crime in that. There was no need to mention his assumptions about his car being at the International Male, none at all. David was wondering if he'd been just a little selfish.

"Oh yes, David! You feel so good, baby! Damn! I just love you! Love you!"

The words echoed in David's ear as if he were at the far end of a tunnel. This was not happening to him. This was happening to someone else. It was all about the intangibles. Everything felt intangible, disconnected, not a part of this world. The friction across the rug that ran along his thighs, his pelvis, his chest; the constant throbbing he felt as Allen filled him with his thickness, fingers digging deep into his hips, the heaviness placed fully on his back. It was unreal. This whole relationship felt intangible.

"Oh yes, that's it! I'm getting there! I'm getting there!" Allen shouted as he shook, drawing blood under his nails as he held David tighter with his fingers, his orgasm tearing through him.

Allen pulled himself up, tied the plastic that held his essence, and dropped it on the rug in view of David, who just remained still, his body a human drum, slowing in its beat. There was a sudden chill, as his sweat-covered back sucked the warmth from his skin ... the warmth Allen had provided. Then came the sounds he prayed for; Allen's footsteps as he walked down the hallway and the groan of springs as he fell upon the bed. The giant was finally in his slumber.

David remained in the living room, the carpet his mattress. He looked at the condom that lay plump before him, and he laughed, in spite of himself. All their love, expressed in a tablespoon of ejaculate, trapped in a plastic sheath. The irony of it all was he felt trapped in a house with only a little bit of love in it. Life was such a tragic comedy.

David laughed once again, this time to keep from crying.

Chapter 5

— I—

Sarafina sat in the pew watching Pastor Daniels wreak havoc upon the stage with his pastoral antics. He was yelling something about Jesus and a boat, and how Jesus was trying to get some sleep, but his friends kept nagging him about some storm brewing and what they should do. Jesus just rolled over, and was forced to get up, walk on some water, quiet the storm, amaze his friends, and save the day... Yadda, yadda, yadda.

Sarafina barely understood anything the preacher was saying through an earful of flying spittle, amen's, and hallelujahs. It was also hot, and someone had forgotten to wear deodorant. Someone needed to open a door, window, or even lift the roof, if anyone was to survive this olfactory assault. She thumbed her fingers through the hymnal's worn out pages, her mind wandering, traveling, venturing into dangerous territory. She was thinking about Gerri, and the last time they saw each other. It had been one year ago, in San Francisco...

"That thought was just going through my head, Gerri. Just a thought," Sarafina remembered saying as she sat on the edge of Gerri's king sized canopy bed.

Gerri had been sitting on the ottoman across from the bed, her legs crossed, her body leaning to the side, elbow resting on the edge of the seat. She was a beautiful woman with olive skin, full hair, and thick lips. "I understand completely, Sara," she had agreed.

Sarafina had lowered her head, keeping her focus on the beige rug underneath her bare feet, as she ran her toes between the thick fibers. "I just can't compete with your career anymore."

"I guess I should apologize because my career has gotten between us. I've seen this coming for some time, Sara," Gerri had said, running her fingers through her hair, pulling at the short ends.

Sarafina had gripped the edge of the bed, finding it harder and harder to enter into this conversation. "I know you can give me a lot, Gerri, and I must look like a straight up fool for dismissing all you've done for a sister," Sarafina had said, patting her chest. "And I really do appreciate it all, but I—"

Gerri held up her hand. "I know, girl. I know. You want some time to think for yourself, to set your mind clear. You need your own space, correct?" Gerri had asked.

Sarafina had looked up, and a knot suddenly rose in her throat. "Yes, Gerri ... Yes, I need some space. I can't exist like this anymore, single and married all at the same time."

"And where will you go, Sara? What will—" she had stopped as a tear showed itself at the edge of her eyelashes. Casually, she wiped it with the back of her hand. "I'm sorry about that, Sara. Excuse me."

"Don't think that I don't still love you, Gerri, because I still do," Sarafina had quickly said, as if her words could stop the tears from flowing. "I just don't feel like I belong in your world."

"Are you referring to the gay lifestyle, dear?" Gerri had said in jest, a tender grin on her face.

Sarafina had tried to smile too, joining in her mirth, but the situation at present seemed inappropriate for such behavior. "You know what I mean."

Gerri had looked away, as she quickly spoke. "So this is it? You want to leave all of this, all I can give you, because you feel lonely sometimes?"

"It's more than that, Gerri, and you know it."

"I thought I did," Gerri had replied, turning to look back at Sarafina. "I really did, but I keep thinking all this is transpiring because you think of me as some white woman and you can't get beyond that."

Sarafina had almost stood. *Where did that come from?* She thought. She was too shocked to be appalled at a white woman sitting here and having the nerve to ring the bells of injustice at her. "What in the world would have you thinking that I care anything about your color after three years?"

"Maybe it's my *lack* of color that's the real issue here. Do you think your life would be less problematic with a black woman, someone who might have a better idea of where you're coming from?"

"You talkin' real whack now, Gerri. It's got nothing to do with that. It's just that I'm all up in your bed and we got your job sleeping right between us. I don't need that shit, okay?

"Would you rather I be some poor, white trash? Is that it? You want me to sell my company to keep you company?"

"No, I don't."

"Well, I wouldn't anyway," Gerri had said, almost as an afterthought.

Sarafina had refused to reply to the very flippant comment. She knew it came out of anger.

"You're just pissed at my decision, aren't you? Even after you said you saw it coming," Sarafina had pushed.

Gerri had shifted defensively in her seat. "No, Sara, I'm not. Right now your mind is made up, so it doesn't matter what I think. The pleasant breakups are always the worst."

"At least I'm coming to grips and telling you, trying to be honest."

"Honesty after three years. I'm so overjoyed that you can come to such quick resolutions. Took you that long, although shy of three months, to tell me about these feelings you have. How diplomatic," Gerri had said.

"Gerri, don't make this any harder than it already is," Sarafina had said, slowly standing. She had walked across the room to the vanity dresser opposite the bed. She placed her hands atop its mahogany surface, staring at Gerri through the reflection. Three years and she had never seen hurt in this woman's eyes as she did today. Three years that swept by in a dash, hardly noticed. Three years of dealing with a woman she loved, trying to understand her elite group of friends who still remained a mystery to her. Three years of being a black woman and constantly being reminded of that fact; that was the hardest.

The world of the highbrow and sophisticate treated her so very different when she was out shopping with money she knew wasn't really hers; and they seemed to know it as well. She'd walk into a jewelry store and was immediately ignored; or if it were a boutique, constantly watched or followed. Even when she could show she had the funds to purchase anything in the store, the attitude changed only slightly. She was a stranger in their world, a parasite, an unwanted. It opened her eyes to the world, and she wondered why she, or any black person, would search for validation in a nation that distrusted them. She could dress immaculately in her Versace originals, or she could shine in her blue diamond accessories. It all was done to try and be accepted, and still she could not erase the color of her skin. Gerri's world of the Rich and the Bitch was not for her, and trying to fit in it made her stand out that much more.

Sarafina had watched as Gerri stood and walked toward the mirror Sarafina was occupied with. "I do understand all of this, Sara. I've been through this too many times not to know," Gerri said, her voice melancholy. "I've just never lasted this long with anyone else. My lovers have always said it's my job, or the people associated with it, or the loneliness, or my indifferent attitude about the whole circumstance. They say I'm a selfish bitch to my back, but accept me wholeheartedly when I'm paying the bills. I like your honesty, Sara, even though it has a bit of hidden prejudice behind it."

Sarafina was astonished. "What're you trying to get at?"

Gerri had placed a warm hand on Sarafina's shoulder, squeezing it tenderly. "Don't act surprised, Sara. You let a simple few anger you. When we went to one of Darlene's openings and you stepped into the room, I could see that you had formed an opinion about all the white faces you saw there. You were cold to those that reached out to you, very distant. You expected something from them before you'd even spoken to them. It's the same with some of the whites there; they assumed your blackness was an attitude, not a color. That's why I left the party early, and you know how I've loved Arnold Gray and his oils."

"I thought you said you weren't feeling well."

Gerri had kissed Sarafina lightly on the lips. "Silly girl." She then walked back to a love seat that sat near the ottoman, and perched herself on its arm. "Hey, I didn't reach thirty-eight by looking through the curtains; I always pull back the shades. I know what you were going through, because in a way I've lived it with you. You know you are not my first black lover, so I'll always have my share of racism just because I'm with you. It has made me strong, and able to deal with people and their remarks. That's where the loneliness comes from, Sara, because I am not there to always remind you that you are a person beneath your dark skin. So maybe you do need your space, and we'll let fate take its course. There is an underlying prejudice that we all face at one time or another, and there is one that we unknowingly send out."

Sarafina had wondered if it were true. She had become untrusting of whites because of all the phony hellos and centered conversations. She never thought she could develop a bias against whites, because it all eventually became *a* direct attack upon Gerri, her *white* lover.

"Come here," Gerri had directed, holding her hand out toward Sarafina, beckoning her. When she did, Gerri had gripped Sarafina's hand within her own. "You see that bed over there?" she had directed with a tilt of her head and a seductive sweep of her eyes.

Sarafina had looked at that bed, its four gold posts just inches from the ceiling, its canopy draped smoothly across its top, silk sheets glimmering upon the mattress. "Yes," Sarafina had responded.

"Before you leave here to start life anew, I want to make love to you. I will not stop you from growing, from attaining the desires you feel you need. I was twenty-five before, and I know how important growth can be. But I know you'll be back, because love is a powerful magnet. So with every touch tonight, every kiss, every caress, every movement, I'll make you remember, believe me."

And she did.

The collection plate was coming past her row, after it passed, Sarafina decided to take the opportunity to leave. Her thoughts were too occupied to stay, and she felt the fresh air would do her good. Perhaps Dominique was right, and there were still things left unfinished between her and Gerri.

— II —

David dreamed.

He found himself in bed, in his old room as a child. The stars were out in bright unison, and the moon flickered through the window blinds. It was very late. He was wearing his Snoopy pajamas, and he slept in a bed shaped like a racing car.

He was ten.

He looked around the room, pulling his Spider-Man sheets close to his neck, and could see the eyes of his Superman poster staring back at him from above his headboard, as if alive. His collection of Micronauts sat on his bookshelf, along with his great collection of Archie and X-Men comics, and Encyclopedia Brown mysteries. An assortment of Chicago Bulls pennants was tacked to his closet door, along with a poster of Michael Jordan. Hot Wheels lined his windowsill, illuminated by his lightning bug collection, which he kept in a mason jar. All was quiet in the Attik's home, and that caused David's heart to beat a bit louder—because in this house, silence was treasured but very short-lived.

Through the door, he could hear *Late Night with David Letterman* coming from his parents' room. He rushed to it, trying to peer past the slightly opened door to catch the television bit *Stupid Pet Tricks*. He thought it was funny, but his parents thought him too young to watch such shows. However, his mother would let him stay up sometimes if his father wasn't home.

David loved his mother.

He could barely see the television beyond his father's favorite chair—a huge La-Z-Boy, tattered and frayed. He could see his father's arm hanging over the side. David swallowed his laughter when something funny came over the television.

Harvey Attik's was a large man, well over six feet, of stocky build, and he had a look of stone most of the time. He was a massive man who had played football but never pursued the sport past high school because of his drinking problem. So his strength and violent tendencies, so useful on the field, was transferred to the field at home.

David hated his father.

Looking out into the dining room, David could see his mother, Brenda Attiks, cut through the room and enter the kitchen. She'd been married to Harvey for a good twelve years, and she looked worn from the journey. David always liked it when his mother would dress up on Mother's Day or Easter, because she was a beautiful woman, everyone looking twice at her, admiring her big fluffy hats or her sexy clothes, and the figure that wore them. He remembered when she was working as a waitress— happy, filled with such amazing energy, that David, at seven years old, wished she would have that look forever. Tragically, Harvey disliked that job. When Brenda was two months' pregnant, Harvey demanded she stop working and stay home to take care of their son. She wouldn't hear of it. Then Harvey began questioning her need to be down at the restaurant working, with all those men gawking at her and making passes, and he accused her of carrying a child that was not his.

They had had a huge fight that ended with his mother screaming in pain and a baby brother that had never been born. Later, David had learned a new word: *miscarriage.*

His mother said that God had taken him because there was so much work to do in heaven. David couldn't understand what good a little baby would be in heaven—he could barely hold a hammer—but he thought God had taken him for a reason. He looked at his father and concluded that God knew what he was doing. That baby was the lucky one.

"Brenda, bring me another beer!" Harvey bellowed across the room.

David knew the word *beer* very well. He also knew the words *vodka, gin,* and *whiskey.* He learned those words when he was five. He also knew that these words were making his father a very bad person, so he hated those drinks more than he hated the man. His mother emerged from the living room, hair a cascade of loose strands that surrounded her head like some dark halo; herself a tormented angel.

"Sure thing, Harvey," she said as she trotted off to the kitchen. "Hurry it up!" he yelled back.

That voice always made David's skin crawl. It was so deep, so hollow, and reminded him of a man yelling from an open grave. His mother returned with a glass filled with some dark brown liquid, ice floating near the top—the beer. She stood in front of Harvey, hand shaking, frightened.

Harvey pointed to the glass. "What the hell is this?"

Brenda hesitated to respond. She began nervously licking her lips as she spoke. "It's your beer. There wasn't any in the fridge, so I put it in a glass with some ice to make it cool for you, honey."

"You put my *beer* in a glass ... with ice? It's gonna taste watered down, woman. I bought two whole cases, and you mean to tell me that you could not put one of those in the refrigerator?"

"You told me to never touch your beers, or your liquor."

"I just can't believe you couldn't put a beer in—"

"But you said that I shouldn't—"

"Are you interrupting me?" Harvey said, rising from his seat.

Brenda took a step back. He looked at the glass she held, and slapped it from her hand. The tumbler fell to the floor, spilling beer and ice to the outdated carpet. David stared at the stain, watching the fibers of the carpet drink the liquid, turning it a shade darker.

He couldn't have known then that in his future he would see that occur again, as an adult, in another home, by another man he too would learn to hate.

"Now look what you've done," Harvey said, running his foot through the stain. "You clean this up, now!" He smacked her against the head.

David flinched at the familiar sound. In his dream, the door suddenly became transparent, glasslike. He ran back to bed, pulling the sheets up to his neck.

"You didn't have to do that. I was gettin' a rag."

Harvey raised his hand. "I didn't have to do what?" he said, keeping his open palm wavering above Brenda's head. "Forget that damn rag, and clean it up now," he commanded, reaching out to grab a tuft of her hair.

Brenda let out a stifled cry of pain as Harvey pulled her closer to him. He pushed her to the floor. She stumbled to her knees, reaching up to hold her aching scalp. "I want you to use that pink assed robe you're wearing to clean up this mess. That rug cost me hard earned money and I don't need you spilling beer on it."

Defeated, Brenda quickly pulled up the hem of her robe to dab at the moist spot in the rug. Her breathing was like an infant who was caught in a crying fit and couldn't inhale. David felt frozen as he watched these events unfold. His mother was frantic, pulling her robe up so tight that David could see the lining of her white panties; ashamed, he closed his eyes.

Harvey looked at David's door, glancing back at his wife again, then back at the door. A smile crept across his face. "Maybe we should get that lazy child in here to help you," he said, motioning in the direction of David's room.

"No, Harvey! Let the child sleep," Brenda shouted, as she grabbed Harvey's ankle.

Harvey thrust his foot back, and then brought it down on Brenda's arm. "You just worry about that floor!" he ordered, walking toward David's room.

David quickly slid under the covers, heart racing, body a tremulous bundle of dread. He pretended to sleep, but couldn't stop shaking.

"Get up, boy!" his father roared, entering the room. Suddenly David felt a great pain rivet through his skull.

He cringed, gripping his head as the lights in his eyes diminished. He could feel a rush of cool air as the sheets were ripped from his body. He was afraid to open his eyes, but he could tell that his father was within inches of his face, looking at him with an intensity he could feel; the smell of him bitter, vomit-like. He'd been drinking quite a bit.

"Boy, I said get up! Yo' momma needs some help in the living room."

David could feel his shoulders being clutched so tightly that he thought they would break free from the sockets. Harvey hoisted him up and flung him down. Pain surged through his hip as he crashed to the floor.

"I said get the fuck in the living room!" spoke that horrid voice again.

David couldn't move. He was too afraid. Opening one eye, he could see his father standing above him. His eyes were angry slits, hands on hips, fists clenched, and breathing rapid. A comb was sticking out of his Afro, teeth bared, face hard with deep bags and pockmarks on his skin. He was a menace.

Suddenly the whole room grew colder. David's fingers became numb, his breath came out in thick folds of white vapor, the edges of his ears tingled from the unexplained chill in the air. Strange. Then his father knelt beside him, craning his neck so close that David could feel the old man's breath brush against his cheek. "I love you," he said, as one fist came crashing down upon his arm. "I love you." Then another fist was buried into his rib cage. "I love you." Another against his stomach. He thought he would retch. The strokes rained down upon him until it was like a thousand pebbles pelting his naked flesh, leaving him doubled over in pain. This is what he knew as tough love.

The nightmare ended.

David woke. Sweat coated the sofa pillow. His heart thrashed against his chest. He looked at the television to see Pastor Rice waving his Bible in the air as he continued on with his sermon. David could remember a time when his religious roots were more grounded, when daily prayer was so much a part of his routine. Then he met Allen: Satan with a nice ass.

Damn dream! Once more of his life with his father and the abuse he tried to forget. He cried. Cried for the abuse of a father that he thought he'd escaped from, only to find the same spirit in the man that he now called his lover.

— III —

Sunday night. Felicia placed her purse on the sofa and glanced at her watch. Her mother was keeping Tumali for a few days, and the silence made her nervous at times. She looked back at the door to her bathroom, hearing the slow trickle splash against the commode, as her recent dinner date relieved his bladder.

She could see her mother grinning somewhere at this very moment, ecstatic that her daughter was finally going on a date, thrilled that she was finally getting Stephen out of her system, overjoyed that her daughter was finally gettin' some dick. Felicia just wanted to puke thinking about the whole affair, and her mother's overripe concern about her personal business.

Brian Jones was his name. Tammy Fae Russle, her good friend, found this man for her. Tammy had spoken to Margaret. Big mistake! She had told Tammy never to speak or listen to her mother, but for Tammy, that was an incentive to do just that.

Margaret informed Tammy that Felicia was digging herself a grave of solitude and destruction, needing a good virile man to come along. The way Tammy described it, you would have thought Felicia's uterus would burst from lack of use. To please them both, she had accepted this blind date.

Brian Jones was a nice enough guy—a fairly handsome, five- o'clock-shadow kind of man. He was tall and dark-skinned, had good sized love handles, his nails and teeth were in order, and, best of all, he was a lawyer. Financial security was just around the corner.

During dinner, she casually mentioned her son and watched as Brian's face went through what she called "the twitch": a wide-eyed, mouth gaping, hand shaking, foot twitching, conversation stopper. Of course, some men thought of this as an easy pussy-catching opportunity, or that they had found an instant mother for their out of control kids from a previous marriage, or some just simply ran for the hills.

"So, where is the father?" Brian had asked, as she choked on her Caesar salad. It was a question that usually followed the main course, never before the appetizer! Brian was not going with routine. She had to dig deep within her pocket of rebuttle. . .

... *"Oh, him . . . I eliminated all that. Tumali is a proud test-tube child."*

... *"His father?" she grabs a napkin to wipe her eyes for effect.*

'Wonderful man, saving all those men's lives in his unit before those bullets rained down upon him."

... *"Father! That man had been married to two other women while being to me. Imagine my surprise. Biggest bigamist I've known."*

. . . *"Would you believe that Immaculate Conception could happen twice?"*

... *"Oh, his father. The biggest faggot queer homo that ever walked God's green earth!"*

Sometimes the truth was the best answer.

Then their conversation would veer toward themselves, as if a woman with a child had nothing more to contribute to an adult discussion besides laundry tips, soap operas, and diaper brands. You would think a woman had given birth to her intellect instead of a child.

Men could be so much like ... men!

Brian seemed just the type of man that was fit to be groomed into Mr. Right. He didn't drink, he knew how to cook, he even called his mother twice a week... and he had a pedicure once a month. All this possibility, all this potential, and yet Felicia waited for the bottom to fall out. It always happened.

Felicia looked at the bathroom door again and wondered if Brian wasn't speaking the truth when he told her he really had to use it; maybe it wasn't a line just to get into her apartment.

When the door finally opened, Brian walked out with a huge grin of relief on his face.

"Are you feeling well, Brian?" Felicia asked, stepping aside as he walked past her. He removed his leather jacket and placed it on a nearby chair.

"Must've been those oysters on the half shell," he said, slumping on the sofa.

Felicia stared at him as if he were from Mars, because he was suddenly making himself comfortable without so much as an invitation from her.

"Why don't you sit down and rest those pretty little feet," Brian suggested, patting the space next to him. "We can chat awhile."

Felicia folded her arms. "Brian, I don't want to seem rude, because I had a wonderful time, but I have so much housework to do before my mother brings my son back," she lied. "I would hate for them to suddenly see a strange man here in my apartment. I'm sure you understand."

Brian smiled coyly, scratching his nose with the back of his hand, as he calmly crossed his legs. "I only wanted to have a little conversation. You look so worried."

"Believe me, I'm not. But I thought you came in here to use the washroom, and would be ready to go."

"Why are you acting so defensive?" Brian asked, sitting up. Felicia took a deep breath. "I'm just not used to entertaining men at this late hour."

Brian looked at his watch. "Entertain? My God, it's only ten-thirty, and I'm not asking you to do magic tricks, unless you feel a need to pull a rabbit out your purse or something," he said, giving Felicia a warm smile.

Felicia returned the gesture with a smile, and suddenly felt a wave of embarrassment for her lack of hospitality for a man who had just spent a small fortune to fill her belly. "Okay, I apologize for my manners. I guess we could talk a bit, but I do prefer to sit over here," she informed him, pulling out a chair near her dinner table.

"Well, that would be fine," he said, leaning back once again. "So why don't you tell me a little about yourself? I don't think we talked too much about you."

Talk about her? At dinner, that conversation took as long as it took for the waiter to take the menu order. Now he suddenly found an interest in her verbal skills? Her instinct said he was hiding something. He was just too attentive, too nice, too perfect. "I love riding my bicycle, watching the Bulls kick some butt. Fashion design is a little hobby of mine which I hope to get back into once Tumali begins first grade."

"Fashion design—that's an exciting field. Too many women with children forget about their goals in favor of their child's."

"I hope that I will be able to do both, and for that very reason. I have given up a lot already in my life."

"Be true to yourself, I always say. Sometimes parents, because of self-sacrifice, are actually putting the responsibility of their dreams on their children."

Felicia nodded and was also a bit bewildered. Brian had not talked this much and wasn't this focused during dinner. "Don't I know that, but it is never too late to start over."

"My mother used to call it Mirrored Reflections. It means holding up a mirror to your life to see who's in control. She told me for many years she looked back on her life and realized that her husband was in control and was reflected in *her* mirror. She had tended to his needs most of her life, and restrained hers.

"When you look in your mirror, Felicia, I'm sure you see someone wonderful, and your life is not covered in a cloud of baby formulas and broken hearts."

What? Felicia thought. *Where was this man at dinner?* This was a change. They were talking like adults, and she realized for the first time that maybe there was hope in men after all.

"Could you get me a glass of water, Felicia? I'm getting just a tad thirsty," Brian asked, pointing to his throat.

"Sure," Felicia responded. She was beginning to appreciate this night out created by her mother and best friend. The thought of having to actually thank them was scary. Brian had inched closer to the edge of the sofa when Felicia returned. "Here you go. It's iced tea."

"Thanks," Brian acknowledged, reaching for the glass, taking it from Felicia's gentle fingers. He quickly reached up with his remaining hand to take hold of Felicia's wrist. "Why don't you sit down with me?"

She was a bit startled at the sudden action, but was calm in her response. "Brian, it's only a glass of iced tea, not an invitation. It is getting late and I have—"

He tugged her wrist a bit—nothing too threatening, but very intentional. "You've been alienating yourself on that island of a chair over there, and all I'm asking is to not having to pay a toll charge to talk to you."

Felicia was feeling her calm demeanor slipping. "Oh Brian, I don't think it's that serious, so why don't you—"

"I thought you wanted to come out to have a good time, Felicia," Brian cut it, his grin becoming wider, until his gums peeked past his teeth.

Oh shit! Felicia thought. Brian had that look. It was an "I want your panties" look! This date was starting to head along a steep downgrade.

"Brian, you're going to have to let go of my hand," she said, trying to slowly pull her hand back.

Brian only mocked her by gripping her wrist tighter. "Hmm, I wonder how many men before me have had the pleasure of holding this wrist."

"Excuse me," Felicia challenged.

"I was only asking you how many men have—"

"I heard you the first time," Felicia voiced, yanking her arm back, freeing her hand. She rubbed at her bruised wrist. She stepped back. "Please, Brian, I think you should leave now."

Slowly, Brian began to stand; his movements seemed very calculated, as if at any moment he would lunge in Felicia's direction. His gaze was very strange, very lustful—eyes hypnotic, piercing, accompanied by a wry grin. Felicia quickly turned on her heels, heart throbbing wildly in her chest. She didn't know what to expect, but she moved to the chair that held his coat and hastily lifted it up and over her arm.

Something fell from the pocket.

Felicia glanced down at the small plastic bag, squinted her eyes at the contents, let her brain do a quick evaluation, and felt reality jolt her understanding like a charge of gunpowder. A small rectangular mirror, a razor blade, a pixie straw shaved down to a few inches, and light traces of flour (that's what it looked like, but Felicia knew better—she used to be a high fashion model. . . of course she knew). She looked back into the bathroom, back at Brian (who stood stunned), then back at the plastic bag.

"What the hell were you doing in my bathroom, Brian?" she asked, backing up toward the kitchen.

Brian's grin was so wide now that he could taste his own earwax. He held up his hand. "Now, Felicia, don't start jumping to any conclusions just—"

Brian nodded, his eyes still on the knife. He managed to open the door and step into the hallway. "I still had a wonderful time despite the—"

"Goodbye, Brian. I wonder who you see in the mirror these days. The pusher, perhaps," she finished, slamming the door.

She leaned against the wall, hearing Brian's footsteps fade down the corridor. She raked her fingers through her hair, looking down at the knife in her hand. How had it come to this? Did she think she needed a man this bad? Did she need to forget Stephen so much to go through this?

Her tears trailed down her face without hindrance, without the slightest cessation. She felt light headed; her breathing swept through her as if she'd been running a marathon. Her legs felt weak, and soon she was sliding down the wall, falling toward the floor, the knife dropping from her hand, clattering to the tile below. A calendar, which had hung just behind her head, was ripped and tumbled along with Felicia, landing squarely atop her. She looked down at it as it fell in her lap, the dates blurred by her tears. *I still love him,* she thought. She had to go to him, that's all there was to it. She knew he missed her, their son, their love for each other, and their lovemaking.

She ran her fingers across the dates of the calendar. She was going to go to California. She had to. She had to lay claim to what belonged to her. Stephen had to still love her ... And didn't love conquer all?

— IV —

The music coming in over the jukebox was blaring Missy Elliot's "Hot Boyz," and Damien could hardly hear it over the chatter filling this bar, the Study, the Sunday hangout, where there was more reading going on than any bookstore in Hollywood.

The Study was the essence of meat market. Men, packed from one wall to the next. You didn't come here to find marriage material.

The Roughnecks were here in droves; those manly looking men, construction types, hiking types, dirt-and-gravel types; tops that knew how to use the equipment that hung between their thighs. The dark skinned Mandingos were here, and the light-skinned Tarzans; men of raw muscle, shirts ripped at the sleeves, clothes that hugged their chiseled features like the skin covering a plump hotdog. Jaws covered in a cloud of stubble, unlit cigarettes hanging from their lips, faces hard and serious, eyes seductive, and bodies huge and imposing. Lips that stood out large and generous in their Vaseline covered moistness, producing a beguiling sheen that brought to mind images very phallic in nature. Their sex was a sex of sweat, pounding after pounding, tight grips and numerous flips that went beyond the screw and into the psyche. It was hard sex, never wavering. It was long sex, thick sex, vein-swelled sex, crooked sex, sheathed sex, cheesy sex, never-want-to-go-down sex, with pink heads that pulsated, and heavy sacks filled with love juices covered in perspiration. It was a scribbled beeper number and cold handshake. Roughnecks, Ghetto Boys, *Papi Chulos,* Mo-Fos, Rough Trade, Banjees, Tricks.

Nope, you didn't come here to find a husband at all.

"Child, you gonna stare that man's clothes right off his body," said Arnell, the bartender, as he wiped the bar with a moist cloth.

Damien waved his hand dismissively, pushing his empty glass forward with the tips of his fingers. "Sugar, why don't you get me another margarita."

Gary, who sat next to Damien, reached out to place his hand on Damien's shoulder. "Why don't you go on over there, Damien? The way he's hitting those pool balls should let you know something about that man. His name is Sean, if you didn't know."

Damien glared at Gary; his large mustache resembled a rat that was chewing its way up his nose. Damien rolled his eyes. "I know who he is."

Yeah, Damien knew just who Sean Dillister was, but didn't everyone? The name alone evoked images of cowboys and stallions. He was at the pool table knocking out opponents in a game of eight ball, chalking his cue stick, sizing up the table, and looking ever so yummy. His chest muscles seemed on the verge of ripping out the only three buttons on the black silk vest he wore. Damien watched as that chest surged forward, nipples leaving faint impressions across the material as the light danced on it. He was twirling the cue stick in his hand like a miniature propeller, watching his opponent's game with intense concentration. Those long heavy fingers, nails manicured just right, hypnotized Damien, and he could suddenly feel his butt muscles twitch. Sean suddenly looked at Damien, flashing a quick, friendly smile. Damien nearly fainted.

It was known that Sean could work a boy till the sun came up, and could shoot each time like the Mississippi River. He knew the power of the tongue. He was wearing baggy shorts that swung down to his knees, with thick calves protruding from beneath, and bare feet covered in a cute pair of Nike sandals. He had a thick neck and wide shoulders. Damien knew this brother would wear him out and, as he smiled back, he hoped his dream would come true.

Arnell returned with Damien's margarita, waving it under his nose. "Come on, baby. Snap out of it. Maybe this will help you talk to Lover Man."

Damien pulled the drink from Arnell's hands. "Who said I was looking at him?"

"Girl, please!" Arnell said, twirling around and heading off to the other end of the bar to take more orders.

"Look who's here, look who's here," said a voice behind Damien. He turned to see his Caucasian brother, Peter, walking through the crowd. "Do you see what I see? Sean, Sean, Sean," he said, pinching Damien's ass and taking the empty stool next to him.

"Oh, there you go. You guys need to quit it," Damien said, taking a sip of his drink, running his tongue across his lips at the tartness of it.

Peter spun his pencil-thin self around to take a look at Sean then returned his attention back to the bar. "I don't know why you haven't wrapped your thighs around that back yet," he said, batting his beautifully large eyelashes. "Acting shady is not going to get you the goods, lovely."

"Shady? Child, you should talk, actin' all bourgeois, standing against the wall at the Circus," said Damien.

"Don't even go there. You know it was my first time at a Latino club, so I was a bit nervous seeing all that *papi* cake crammed into one place," Peter explained.

"Don't change the subject, bitch," interrupted Gary. "We know you all hung up on that Sean, and the only one that doesn't know it is Sean. You know he's a big whore, so get it while it's cheap, baby."

"That's what I say," Peter said, rapping his knuckles on the bar, trying to get Arnell's attention.

Arnell looked over his shoulder as if Peter had lost his mind. "This is not the Hilton, honey, and that bar is not a pager," he said, sauntering over to the three gentlemen. "I'm gonna have to take it out of your change, Miss Lilly," Arnell said.

"Don't get too fussy, dear, it's bad for the complexion," Peter said, grabbing Arnell's chin. "I just want a Long Island, okay?"

"Whatever," Arnell replied, grabbing Peter's fingers with the tips of his own, and depositing them back on the counter. "You just keep those hands right there, cause I don't know where they've been." He then swung around, purposely lashing his long hair across Peter's face.

Peter brushed at his mouth, "She did that on purpose."

"You act like you've never had hair in your mouth," Gary said, bringing his beer to his lips.

"Not from a fish, I haven't."

"That's gonna be six dollars, Miss Lilly," Arnell said, returning with the drink.

"What? I don't get any kind of family discount?" Peter replied, slapping a ten-dollar bill on the bar.

Arnell picked up the money. "Family? Boy, my momma only pops wheat bread through her cunt, not Wonderbread." He turned to look at Damien. "And you need to slow down on that drink, sweetheart. That ain't no cock."

"Shiiiit! If it was, the glass would he gone too," Damien said, snapping his fingers.

Peter leaned in closer to Damien. "Hey, I heard you went down to San Diego on Saturday. Did you get a chance to see Andrew? I hear he's sick."

Damien's grin fell. He remembered when the word *sick* was not associated with disease.

"It's as if twenty can be considered midlife these days," Peter added, as Arnell returned with his drink. "I guess there's this great T-dance going on in heaven right now."

Damien quickly finished his drink. It kept him from adding to a conversation he found uninspiring. Can I gets another one, *papi?"* he asked of the bartender.

Arnell grabbed the empty glass in one hand and cupped Damien's chin with the other. "Cheer up, sweetness. Reality is a bitter cake, but we all get a slice to deal with sooner or later."

Damien tried to smile, but it only came out as a lopsided grin. Arnell knew there was a soft spot in his heart where Andrew was concerned.

With all those so-called cocktails out there, Andrew was still in bad shape. Between drugs, barebacking, being on the DL, and the cybersociety, the whole world was in bad shape. Everyone was trying to find happiness in other forms of sweets, instead of dealing with the cake in front of them.

Damien shook his head; he hated dwelling on such things. He looked back at Sean. Damn, he was fine! Someone walked past his view, interrupting his eye candy for a moment. His eyes veered off and landed on someone he'd just as soon see dead.

At the back of the club, within the corridor that led to the bathroom, the same hallway that led out to the parking lot, he saw them. His heart raced, his head swam, and his breathing stopped.

"... and if I can get to New York for Pride next month, I could stay with my sister," Gary was saying, but Damien could not hear him.

Damien excused himself from his friends, and walked over to this pair of kissing men only a few feet from him. One he could not recognize, but the other he knew very well. It was Allen.

Damien could not believe this man, in public, like this. David was most likely at home cooking and cleaning for this whore. Damien wanted to dig his clear coated nails into Allen's skull to look for any sign of a brain; but he was afraid of finding only packed feces.

Before he knew it he was standing before this lip locked pair of canines.

Damien got a good look at the concubine: a light brown brother who had the misfortune of unknowingly being in the clutches of a madman. He was as tall as Allen, smooth features, pretty lips, high cheeks, slightly slanted eyes, at least twenty-four to twenty-six in age, nice build behind a gray tank top and baggy cargo pants. Hair was so silky straight that Damien knew only a rampage of chemicals and a mixed marriage produced it. He was good looking but obviously insane. He was, after all, with Allen. He must have sensed Damien's presence, because he turned to face him.

"Do I know you?" he asked in a high pitched voice caught somewhere between masculinity and childhood. He held a drink and brought the long straw to his thick lips as he seemed to wait for an answer.

Allen looked in Damien's direction and drew in a quick breath, but, like Houdini, the expression of surprise suddenly vanished. "Oh, hey there, Damien, what's going on?" he asked.

Damien threw on his best mock smile. "Why hello, Allen," he began, tossing his neck to the side like a schoolgirl. "I thought I'd seen you over here. So how are ya?"

Allen produced a menacing glare. "Just minding my own. I'm sure you can relate."

Damien placed his hands on his hips, and whispered, almost as if to himself, "You seems to own so much lately."

"Excuse me?" Allen asked.

Damien held up his hand. "Oh, I'm sorry. You know how my mouth gets sometimes. I apologize if I bothered you, Allen, and…umm…" he said, waving his index finger at Allen's companion as if trying to recall the young man's name between them.

"What do you need, Damien?" Allen asked shortly.

Damien's demeanor became serious. "I was wondering if I could have a word with you, Allen. It's about that registration problem I'm having with my car."

Allen appeared to be contemplating a response. He slowly turned to his friend. "I'll be right back, babe."

His friend looked strangely at Allen. "Who's this clown?" he whispered.

Damien placed his hand on the guy's shoulder. "Look here, Beauty, I'm bringing your Beast back, but the next time I hear you call me a clown we—"

"Let's go!" Allen interrupted, pushing Damien back along the corridor until they were outside near the parking lot. "Now, what's with this registration bullshit?"

Damien peered over Allen's shoulder, looking back at Allen's forlorn friend. "Nice boyfriend you has there. Been together long?" "What business is that of yours?" Allen asked, obviously brooding.

"I just thought I knew all of David's friends."

Allen's chest swelled beneath his plaid shirt, and Damien could almost see his words caught there, the curses he wanted to spew out, as if his torso were glass. Instead, he whispered, "Listen, you are a friend of David's, not mine. So I advise you to stay out of my business and carry your hot ass back to where you came from."

Damien was flabbergasted. How could David have been with this man for five years? Impossible. This man was more than crazy, and he truly had shit for brains. At this moment, looking in to Allen's eyes, watching his face, hearing his voice ... Damien wanted to vomit.

"This *is* my business," Damien said, trying to control his anger, as well as his English. "Ju es fuckin' over me best friend. What do you think you are doing? I don't think you know caca!"

Allen stepped in closer, waving an accusatory finger. "Listen here, wetback! I don't give a fuck what you like or dislike. You have no idea what David and me are going through. This has got nothing to do with you, so just keep it that way. He don't have to tell you everything, and I don't have to explain anything. Now get out of my face."

Damien mocked Allen's finger gesture with his own. "David is part of my business, fucker. I don't need him to tell me nothing, 'cause I can see it for myself," Damien looked at Allen's friend. "Maybe it's David that should be seeing... and hearing."

Allen grabbed Damien's ridiculing finger. "Don't fuck with me, you butt screwed queen!"

Damien snatched his finger back. The word *queen* was socially acceptable among his friends, but this was no friend of his. Damien was becoming a ball of fury. He wanted to lash out at this Goliath, and considering he was on the lip of drunkenness, it gave him the valor to perform the task. He tried to find a soul deep within those brown orbs, but saw nothing.

Damien felt the need to vomit once more.

"Ju know something, Allen," he began, stepping closer himself, defiantly invading the space between them. His accent was becoming thicker. "Ju make me sick, just fucking sick. Somebody needs to start puttin' a whuppin' on yo ass. So why don't you take yo' high yellow wannabe black ass back over to your charming, smart, bright-as-a-Christmas-tree trick, 'cause I have a best friend to call. Oh, and have a nice day."

Allen furiously reached out to seize Damien's silk shirt, pulling him closer. Damien stumbled forward, smelling the rank vodka on Allen's breath so deeply that it burned his eyes. "Maybe I should just kick your ass right here. Is that what I should do, Damien, you little bitch?"

"Then do it, *puto!*" Darien blurted out, fists clenched for any sudden confrontation.

Allen smiled. "You'd like that, huh? For me to put a foot up your ass, and then deal with all the shit on my shoes. I suggest you just get the hell out of my face, 'cause I am not the one to be playing your little faggot games. When you want to come back and handle this shit like a real man, bring one with you, 'cause I don't fight women." He then pushed Damien away from him.

Damien fell against the railing leading to the stairs, and swiftly lunged for it to prevent himself from tumbling. They were starting to garner some unwanted attention from within the bar and a few onlookers in the parking lot. Damien regained his balance, clenched his fist, and began to charge in Allen's direction. He was ready to pull off a handful of face and hair.

Just then Peter walked into the scene, grabbing Damien by the arm and stepping between the two men. "What's going on here, sweets?" he asked, looking back at Allen, sizing him up.

"He's about to get mopped, that's what's up. I think you better look after your friend," Allen warned.

Peter turned and looked at Allen. Instantly there was a feeling of hate.

"You should find someone to look after you," he said, stepping protectively in front of Damien, shoulders pulled back.

"Oh, the white bread wants some of this too?" Allen said, patting his chest with his open palm.

"Will you guys get back inside? I am not the drink valet." It was Gary, walking toward the trio. He purposefully kept his gaze away from Allen, away from further confrontation, and waited silently, arms crossed, until his friends were walking safely back to the bar, then he too followed.

Allen looked at the three men and shook his head in sorrow. Without a word he headed back into the bar.

As Damien sat at the bar, he thought about David. Allen looked angry and most likely would take out that anger at home, on David. He would have preferred to have had Allen take it out on him, or at least try to. Looking again, after a few minutes, he could see Allen and his friend leaving. Good and bad. He worried about David, but this bar did not need that bad karma. The atmosphere suddenly felt more invigorating. Damien chugged down the rest of his margarita and stood back from his bar stool.

"Where do you think you're going now, Sugar Ray Lavender?" asked Peter. "Off to spar with another ruffian?"

"Jea! You has a lot of splainin' to do, my Ricky Ricardo wannabe," Gary teased.

"Excuse me, but Ricky was Cuban. Now Ricky Martin, we can certainly talk about that comparison. But if you must know, I'm gonna drain the trunk."

"Well, that could really take long, trying to get those stockings of yours down," Gary laughed.

"True, but I borrowed them from you, Grandma," Damien said, looking back at the pool table. "And when I'm done, I'm gonna work Mr. Sean Dillister. Since he likes to use balls and sticks so much, I need to show him how to play a real game of pool." He then staggered to the rest room, ass shaking like loose change.

Gary and Peter both looked at each other, then, at their sister. They both yelled. "You better go, bitch!"

Chapter 6

— I —

Stephen walked into the conference room just in time to see the clock display 9:00. The meeting was scheduled for 9:10, so by Gordon's standards, he was late.

Gordon Hodges rose from his seat. "I do hope that everything is okay, Stephen?"

Stephen looked up at Gordon, pausing before sitting while looking carefully at those seated around the table; as they too observed him. The silence was so thick you could hear a roach fart.

"Yes Gordon. I had some car trouble, but I managed to take care of it," Stephen said, waiting for his boss to sit, after which, Stephen followed suit.

Stephen reached for a writing pad on the spacious oak table and gripped an adjacent pencil tightly in his hand. His breathing was slowing down since running from the elevator, to and from his office, then to this conference room. He knew Gordon was not in the least concerned with his car troubles (which was really a lie—he'd just forgotten about this meeting and was out walking his dog), but mentioned it as a warning to Stephen not to do it again. It was necessary to arrive at a Gordon Hodges meeting at least fifteen minutes early—so Stephen was late by five.

They were here to discuss the $10 million account for the Andes campaign; a Southern cuisine restaurant that was now opening in the ski resorts of Big Bear and Mammoth. They were known throughout Southern California and wanted to head in a new direction. Three months would be the turnaround time for this campaign; it would be a hectic time for all involved, so this was no time to actually be only "on time" for a meeting.

Gordon interlocked his wide fingers, and from behind his round rimmed glasses his bulbous eyes scanned the table. He could be very intimidating. He had to be to run this very successful black owned ad agency. His girth took up all the space his chair granted. The wooden frame of the seat creaked lightly with strains of tension. Gordon had a broad face, round nose, and large teeth that took up his whole mouth when he smiled; salesmen teeth, they called it. His voice was loud, even at a whisper, and very demanding.

The Andes was white owned, by a Mr. Jason Lynn. Gordon was said to have swept into Lynn's office, demographics and stat sheet in hand, revealing the percentage of blacks that stayed at these ski resorts throughout the year. The spiel had lasted a full ten minutes, and then Gordon had brought in the finale: Niles Austin, the only white staff member, and the one Jason Lynn would be dealing directly with.

Lynn was sold.

Stephen looked over at Niles Austin. He brushed the lapels of his Ralph Lauren and sat flush with the table, his elbow leaning ostentatiously on it. He was a tall thin fellow that worked as the account supervisor. At thirty, he was very cocksure of his position of being the resident token cracker of the firm. Jason Lynn was known as a closeted bigot, so it had behooved Gordon to bring him to that first fateful meeting. Niles made sure Jason knew where his money was being spent. Like in a restaurant, Niles was the hostess, while everyone else actually worked in the kitchen preparing the meals; the reputation that the company was built upon.

Jennifer Nickles was one of those cooks. She worked as a buyer, a salesperson of sorts, learning the trait of haggling. She was a dark, average looking sister with huge doe eyes and a pair of rather outstanding breasts. She knew how to work with the budget Jason offered, and gave Niles the reasons for its eventual increase.

Jennifer, as well as all present, kept in constant contact with the research department. Research was headed by Trenton Smith, a thirty-two-year-old balding brother from St. Croix whose blue eyes and high cheeks made him the envy of all the women in the firm. His presence wasn't needed at this meeting, but he was always privy to certain details: the latest polls, charts, figures, growth percentages of any company or product anywhere, and how the advertising dollars were used.

Barbara Jackson worked as the copywriter, Stephen's right-hand woman. She worked on the words that lured people into spending their cash, so the Jasons of this world had money to pay the advertising agencies that began the cycle in the first place. Stephen worked well with Barbara, and since finding out about his bisexuality, the office conversations became that more interesting.

Gordon cleared his throat, and it didn't come across as something he did for effect; it sounded as if something was actually lodged up that fat windpipe, and it caught everyone's attention. "Okay, I'll make this simple. Our contract with the Andes is coming to an end, and he's being swamped with deals from other ad agencies. As you know, marketing to the black community has shown to be positive, and now he wants to branch off into the children's market, giving the resorts more of a family atmosphere. I need a presentation readied for him and a meeting set up by next week. We won this contract. Now let's keep it."

At that moment, Niles cleared his throat; this, however, *was* for effect. "I spoke with Jason over cocktails last weekend and sold him on the children's campaign. Of course, Jennifer helped me with some of the research, although I have—"

"It was pretty interesting," Jennifer interrupted, knowing Niles could talk into a tangent at any given moment. "We discovered that ski resorts were becoming the vacation getaway, and families were shown to be traveling together more than ever, and that—"

"Thanks, Jen," Niles said, raising his hand. "So I relayed this information to my client and—"

"The client!" Barbara emphasized, giving Niles a cross look. "We are all in this together, Niles."

Unwarrantedly, he stood and bowed in Barbara's direction. "Why, I do apologize for that, Mrs. Jackson," he said, and in his vainglorious way, he remained standing, "As Barbara so kindly pointed out, *our* client would like to start off with some menu designs for their upcoming children's menu. I think the radio spots can feature children, but the print ads could be more family oriented. Oh, and thank you," he finished, sitting back in his seat to resume his pose.

"And he wants the layouts and copy by Friday?" Stephen asked.

Niles grinned wryly. "Um, I do believe the winter season is but five months away. I think getting them out before then is rather advantageous."

Stephen sat back, gripping the edge of the table. *Niles can be such a bitch,* he thought. "We'll have the layouts by tomorrow morning," he spat out.

Gordon rapped his knuckles against his 'writing pad. "Try by noonish today." He turned to Barbara. "You should know this account like the back of your hand by now, Barbara, so I don't—"

"It will be no problem, Gordon," Barbara quickly said, as she began scribbling on her paper. "We'll work on the copy and storyboards if you intend to go with television ads. The designs for the menu shouldn't be a problem as long as we know the age range we're trying to reach. With the contract ending in December, I know a lot is riding on keeping our old

Jason Lynn happy, and making sure the plantation's profitable for da Massa."

"You don't have to speak about him like that," Niles defended.

"Oh, cut the compassion, Niles. Remember he's *your* client, as you like to think."

"It's his money we're spending, so the least you can do is treat him with a little respect. Just a little."

"Whatever, Niles," Barbara said, knowing full well that Jason Lynn remained with this agency only because of Niles's presence. It seemed so charitable to help the little black agency with some big white dollars.

"I don't care what your personal feelings may be, Barbara. You don't have to like your client to do the job expected of you. We are in fact working for him right now, so keep the attitude in your head, and your talent on paper," Gordon added.

"Yessir, I sho' is gonna ack right dis time," Barbara replied, pouting her big amber colored lips and crossing her arms defiantly.

Stephen saw that Gordon was about to respond, very unkindly, and quickly interjected. "Don't worry about it, Gordon. We'll see you at around noonish." He looked at Barbara pouting like a child. She winked at Stephen, playfully. Barbara had many adolescent qualities about her, which made her such a joy to work with.

After a few final announcements, the meeting was over, and Stephen and Barbara returned to their office more exhausted than if they'd done a full day's work. Gordon's little briefings could wear on a person. They began work right away, conversation at a minimum. When Stephen eventually looked up from his drafting table, he saw that it was nearing 11:30. Time was becoming the beast at the door.

"So how was your blind date?" Barbara asked unexpectedly. Stephen smiled, offering nothing. "You actin' shady on me now?"

He spun around in his swivel chair, coloring pencil clenched between his teeth, through which he still managed to speak. *"Shady?* Where did you learn that word from? You've been sneaking around North Hollywood un-chaperoned?"

"Never mind that," she said, standing. "Get to the details. It's been quiet enough in here with all this shop talk. The menu copy is almost done, so get to blabbing about this blind date and stop keeping me in suspense."

"What if I don't feel like it?" Stephen asked, twisting back toward his desk.

She smacked the back of his head. "Boy, don't play with me." "Damn, okay, okay, I'll confess all," Stephen pleaded, turning back to face her. "You sure you're not a dyke?"

"Oh shut up and get with the gossip."

Stephen began telling her about this fine man he met and the fiasco at Aunt Kizzy's, and he also managed to mention his trip to San Diego in addition to David's stingray mishap.

"Damn! All this on the weekend? All me and Spunky did was go to Red Lobster and do the Venice Beach thing. Shoot! That ain't fair," she said, stomping her feet. "You girly boys have all the fun."

"I can fully understand, but as my friend Damien would say, don't hate—just celebrate," Stephen commented. He then leaned in closer to Barbara. "I have something else to talk to you about…a little favor you can say."

Barbara leaned back, wrinkling her nose, squinting her eyes, and trying to guess what was on Stephen's mind. "I don't like that tone, Stephen. A woman knows when something risky is about to be asked of her." She looked back at the clock. "We have to see Gordon in about thirty minutes and you're asking for favors."

The only item remaining is the copy. Just find a typestyle Gordon can debate about and show him the rough drafts. He's not looking for finished comps yet," Stephen explained.

Barbara shook her hands in the air. "Whatever, Stephen. I can smell the shit rising from your shoes. Why don't you just tell me what you—"

"I need to leave and take care of some things, Barbara," Stephen interrupted, and then quickly added, "and I need you to present these to Gordon yourself."

Barbara flung her hands above her head. "I just know I'm hearing things. You want me to face the Grand Dragon alone? You must be on some new kinda crack to be thinking some shit like that." She sat back in her seat, staring intensely at Stephen, as if he were crazy.

"This is really important, Barbara. You know I wouldn't ask if it wasn't."

"And what am I supposed to tell Gordon, as he's blowing fire at me through his nose?"

Stephen shrugged his shoulders. "Hell! Tell him I'm finishing some additional storyboards, or I had an important call, or I spilled some turpentine on the floor. I'm sure you'll think of something."

Barbara held up her index finger, pointing it accusingly at Stephen. "Now you know this is quite unprofessional."

"Now you're beginning to sound like Niles."

"Oh, and now you insult me, by comparing me to that lily-white kiss ass. I don't think I should do anything for . . ." and before Barbara could finish, Stephen was on his feet, at her chair, and gripping his hands to her shoulders. He eased forward to kiss her on the forehead.

"Thank you," he said softly.

She shoved him in the chest, and then swung herself around in her chair, facing her computer console. "Now cut that out. I don't need you slobbering on me and having my man finding your brand of perfume and lipstick on my forehead."

"It might turn him on," Stephen said, returning to the back of his chair to lift his sports coat.

"And where do you have to be that I have to cover for your sorry butt?"

"Well, my dear . . . I have a plane to catch."

– II –

Dominique stuffed a corner of the meatloaf sandwich into her mouth, quickly forgetting her manners. Hell, she was starving! Angela could only look at her in an open-mouthed daze.

"Um ... Dominique, I think the practice of chewing your food is still in vogue. I'm sure Emily Post would be highly ashamed," Angela commented.

Dominique exposed a sheepish grin, quickly reducing her eating speed. "Please excuse me, Angela. I had to skip breakfast this morning."

Angela continued to enjoy her onion soup. "I've always said, 'the first meal of the day is the most detrimental to the rest of your night.'"

Dominique nodded in agreement. "Yes, I know. It's hard to run a train of thought if there is no coal in the furnace," she said.

"I said that to you at one point," Angela said, smiling. "How sweet you remembered that." She was obviously flattered.

That should hold her, Dominique thought, as she returned to her sandwich with as much force as before. With the clatter and activity in this lunchroom, Angela would pay her little mind; Shelby's D'Zines was always awash in the sounds of soft conversations, the pecking of fingers on laptop keyboards, high heels, and the constant rustle of papers as portfolios snapped open to reveal blueprints, fabric samples, sketches, contracts, or checks exchanging hands.

Dominique glanced at her boss, who mirrored the cookie-cutter image that was carried throughout all the project managers: the pointed, perky nose, the high heeled shoes, the bleached hair, the wide-rimmed glasses that hung at the edge of the nose, the conservative silk blouse with complementary cashmere jacket and skirt. She also wore a huge solitaire diamond on her finger to signify a wealthy husband or boyfriend. And then there was the skin color: white.

It was the color that commanded this firm, but that wasn't out of the ordinary. Minorities had their place, met the demands asked of them, in an industry bombarded with the harshness of deadlines, contract disputes, personal feelings, dealings with many and their many attitudes. Many people stepping into a design house just as quickly departed, opting to try related careers in the design field such as set designers, curators, private interior design, or working within a building development firm. For blacks, it proved even tougher. Your skill level was often determined by your melanin levels. Dominique, however, had survived. She'd also been waiting for three years for the opportunity to become a senior designer. Her white counterparts had made it in two.

Angela was good at what she did, and she let you know it herself, if by chance you hadn't heard of her through the gossip mill. To be under her wing was a gift sent down from heaven. If you prayed, then it was to her and her incredible knowledge that you gave thanks. Many regarded her as too bossy, demanding, and sometimes just plain bitchy. Dominique thought of her as a closeted, pussy depleted dyke; she knew how to deal with that type of personality.

"So how was your weekend, Dominique?" Angela asked, pushing her glasses up on her nose.

"All right, I guess. I stayed at home and relaxed, listened to some jazz. Nothing special," Dominique answered. She always kept her conversations with Angela very cut-and-dry.

Angela lifted an eyebrow, as if she actually wanted Dominique to expound. "Well, honey, I was talking with Connie Tishman over lunch this past weekend. We were at her fabulous home in Malibu," she said, rather proudly, and you happened to come up in conversation."

This caught her attention. Connie was a partner within Shelby's.

"Me? That's surprising."

"Indeed," Angela agreed. "But, nonetheless, you were being discussed. We were discussing your work on the Hadley site last spring, and of course the Corbell account we billed two weeks ago. Stanley Askew just loved the idea of centering a fountain within the library. They organize story time around that structure. The colors you suggested were perfect also." She stopped to wipe the edges of her mouth ever so softly with her napkin.

"Why, thank you."

Angela pushed her soup back and swung herself around to cross her legs more comfortably. "And Connie was also telling me of this new client we just received last week—Gerri Cosmetics. Have you heard of them?"

Dominique almost fell out of her chair, her last bit of food threatening to choke her. She coughed violently, reaching for the relief of her water glass.

Angela sat up, concerned. "Are you okay?"

Dominique let out a series of small coughs. "I'll be all right," she replied, taking a few deep breaths. "Now what was this you said about a cosmetics contract?"

"Yes, Gerri Moore owns it. She may be a bit out of your price range, but she owns a very big line of cosmetics. I'm sure you've seen her product," Angela said, almost as a question.

"Yes, I've heard of her quite extensively," Dominique assured.

"Great," Angela said, with a sigh of relief. "Her headquarters are in San Francisco and New York, but she's planning on bringing a corporate building to Los Angeles for her shows. We managed to wrestle this account from Pinkin & Coles, because we handled the designs for the old Hewlett-Packard building in Inglewood, which is the building she wants to use now."

"That's very interesting," Dominique said nonchalantly. She had no idea what this had to do with her.

Angela looked on, perplexed, as if she'd expected a much different reaction. She continued. "And we already have the blueprints of the building, so building codes and zoning permits should be no problem." Angela quickly went silent, staring at Dominique once again. "I would think you'd be a little more excited, Dominique," she finally said.

Dominique leaned back in her seat. "This firm is known for landing big accounts like this almost every day, Angela."

"No, no," Angela said, patting the table with the palm of her hand. "Can't you see what I'm saying? I will be giving you full reign of this new project. You will be formatting the design of the parking lot and the interiors, choosing the contractors, supervising, deciding the budget for the furniture, installation, and labor costs. My sweet, we were thinking of advancing you to senior designer, and to he considered so quickly is nothing less than a miracle," she proclaimed.

Dominique could see where Angela was headed now; her imminent promotion hinged on her success in handling this account. The account, she added, of a woman who was her nemesis. It would be the talk of the firm if Dominique proved herself; it would be quite disastrous if she didn't. She felt a tinge of horror. "Will you be there?" she asked.

Angela reached over to tap Dominique lightly on the hand. "Of course I will. You will get written recognition of this one, but I'll be there to help you with structuring the contracts, assist in billing, making sure you have skilled staff nearby. We also have an interview with Gerri Moore and her representatives on Wednesday."

Dominique reached for a napkin and pressed it against her moist forehead. "Yeah, this is pretty exciting, Angela. I don't know what to say. I don't know where to start, to tell you the truth."

Angela grinned. "That's all right. We'll start off by going over the blueprints this afternoon."

Dominique's mind was now as blank as her expression. Technically, she was now working for Gerri Moore, Sarafina's ex-lover. What was this world coming to? She didn't like Sarafina communicating with the woman, and now she was in both their lives.

Angela noticed Dominique's silence and cold stare. "You're too excited to speak. Understandable," she said almost giddily, and returned to her soup.

"Yeah, I'm just bubbling over with joy," she whispered.

– III –

Flight 1 from JFK came into Los Angeles International Airport smoothly and effortlessly. Jamal sighed as the plane taxied to the gate and he leaned his head back against his jump seat. Ten years he'd been fascinated with planes, ever since his father took him on his first trip in a DC10. All he could remember thinking was that this was a *big* plane. Terrance Warren was his real father and, although unable to care for him, had always managed to take him on a plane to fly off on a father-son jaunt. Planes held a great joy for Jamal, and being a flight attendant made it that much better.

Jamal had lived with his mother, half-sister, and half-brother, not to mention his stepfather. He spent his childhood growing up in Gary, Indiana, while Terrance lived in Washington, DC, and the bulk of his relatives resided in Nashville. Jamal could remember his father: a tall thin man, wonderful dark features, deep brown eyes with thick brows. He had a smile that could melt butter and a laugh that could warm hearts. Unfortunately, Terrance Warren was just not a settling down man.

Terrance Warren was a great lover of women, but eventually he met one that managed to put up with his wandering eye—over nine years, and still going strong. Aunt Sylvia was the best, and there had been seven different "aunts" before her. Terrance was in his early sixties; Sylvia would be the last of his "aunts."

Jamal's best memories involved his father. Most of their trips together were to family socials. He could picture his father's people crowded around barbecue grills, laughing deeply from their full bellies, drinking and cussing under a shady tree, or spitting tobacco across a freshly mowed yard. He remembered plates heavy with food, plump faces buried in succulent watermelons, sweet potato pie smeared across satisfied lips, fresh lemonade dripping from eager mouths. He remembered it all. He wished he could have created a bond with those relatives, but he hadn't. He was just glad to be with his father, and even though he was surrounded by aunts and cousins and grandparents, they all seemed like strangers he simply saw once or twice a year.

Terrance had a great memory. He knew all the names and faces at these reunions, and he also knew everyone's birthday, who married, single, divorced, or undecided; what they had been doing with their lives, who had produced new rug rats, and who would be expecting some. On the phone, Terrance could always recall their last conversation, what homework assignment Jamal had had trouble with, his teachers' names, classes, schoolmates: His father helped him deal with the difficulties of school, his nightmares, his loneliness, and his stepfamily, who treated him like the plague.

His mother always said Terrance was a bum, a cheap sonofabitch, a hustler, and a bastard that knocked her up and ran the streets. He later found out that his father, although a smart man, could not read, and had dropped out of school in the tenth grade. He ran the streets looking for work, but with no education he was only able to get under-the-table labor jobs. When Terrance's mother moved in (Grandma Wren), she put an immediate wedge in the household. Jamal's parents divorced, and his mother ran back to her ex-lover, already pregnant at this point. When Jamal was born, his stepfather appeared to accept him into the fold—until years later, when Jamal told them he was gay.

"Boy, get your head out of the clouds," said the number one officer on the flight, Gale Martins. She pushed Jamal's shoulder, rousing him back into reality.

"So, are you going to get something to eat?" Gale asked, after the aircraft had landed and they began to deplane.

He looked back at Gale, and her face had suddenly turned into a giant pepperoni pizza with anchovies. He shook his head, and big lipped, wide-eyed, Afro wearing, hooped-earring-clad Gale stood in front of him again. "I think I'll be getting me a pizza."

"You still haven't told me all about your blind date, Jamal," Gale replied, her rouge colored lips twisted disappointingly. "I want to hear the *gooood* stuff."

Gale was the first one he had told about his sexual preference. There were so many single female attendants that it was quite dangerous to remain in the closet. Gale had quickly become his fag hag. "I can't tell you all my secrets, Gale"

"Oh, please. I've been with you to the Sound Factory in New York, and I have seen you in some pretty compromising positions . . . *in the Sound Factory!* So start talking."

"We have an hour-and-a-half layover, so I'll tell you more on the way back, okay?"

"I guess. So will you be going out tonight? I have my black mini in my bag."

"I don't know why you be trying to cruise the boys in the New York clubs, when you know they don't do tuna salad."

"Hey, you can't blame a girl for trying. All they need is a little sample of the Gale platter, and they'll be chewing on the plate. You should try a sampling yourself, Jamal."

"I'd rather have the pizza, 'dearie," Jamal replied as they walked out onto the jet bridge.

"That was cold, Jamal," Gale said, pinching Jamal in his rib.

He laughed slightly. "Stop that," he said. "Don't play with a hungry man."

As they entered the terminal, she pinched him again. "Come on, Gale, that hurts!"

"Never you mind that, Jamal, I think someone is here to see you," she said, raising her hand slightly, pointing to a smartly dressed limo driver holding a sign:

JAMAL WARREN-FLIGHT ATTENDANT

Gale whispered in Jamal's ear. "Go and see what he wants. I bet it's from that new man of yours. I think you hit pay dirt with this one."

Jamal stepped up to the tall Latin driver, with stone cold features etched into his skin. He was beginning to think there had to be another Jamal Warren somewhere, 'cause this guy looked like he wanted to kick someone's ass. "I'm Jamal Warren," he stated.

The driver reached into his breast pocket, pulling out a business card. He handed it to Jamal. It was a card from Aunt Kizzy's Back Porch, and written on the back was: Follow Him. *Stephen.*

"See—I told you," Gale said, directly over his shoulder. "A woman knows these things."

"Goodness, girl, you are the nosy one, aren't you?" Jamal commented, stepping away from Gale, while placing the card in his pocket. He began to follow the driver.

Remember, bring back the details,' Gale shouted, as she stood there like a mother watching her son on his first night of prom.

The driver led them to the outside parking lot where there sat a Lincoln Continental stretch limo that was so long it spanned six parking spaces. They walked to the rear door, and there Jamal waited, letting the gentleman open the door.

It was very dark inside, the tinted windows offering no outside light. Jamal bent forward slightly, peering into the car. He was surprised to see Stephen looking back at him.

"Hello there, Jamal. I thought I would meet you for a little lunch today," Stephen said, motioning for him to enter.

Jamal was taken aback. He slid into the limo and slowly closed the door. Although the windows were tinted, he began to see his surroundings clearly. It was amazing. The seats had been taken out and a blanket spread across the floor. An assortment of foods were laid out before Stephen, who was also laid out in a beautiful double-breasted suit. A fruit bowl was the centerpiece, and it was surrounded by smaller bowls filled with cheese, bread, sour cream, sliced carrot and cucumber, and caviar and watercress. On two separate trays were selections of hors d'oeuvres. A hidden compartment inside the door revealed two chilled wine bottles. At the corners of the blanket long stemmed candles in exquisitely carved golden candleholders. Jamal held his breath as he heard the soft croon of Sade bellowing "Smooth Operator." He was speechless.

"What's all this?" he asked, mostly to keep from fainting. He crossed his legs to sit on the floor.

"I just thought it was time that I showed you what I can do on a real date," he replied, pulling one of the bottles from the ice. He wiped the wetness from the bottom and reached for one of the wine glasses near him.

"I guess when you want to prove a point, you go all out," Jamal said, as he picked up a finger sandwich from the silver tray. "I can't have any wine, though. I still have one more leg to do."

Stephen continued to pour. "Don't worry. It's only grape juice. I think you can handle that."

"I can handle more than that," Jamal said, with a grin.

"Why don't we just see how you handle this food first?" Stephen commented, handing Jamal his glass.

"I guess we can start there ... for now."

– IV –

"Felicia, I swear to God, had I known that creep, Brian, was a crackhead, I never would have suggested you go out with him," Tammy said, leaning back on the couch, clenching her fists.

Felicia pushed back her unkempt hair; the scarf wrapping it refused to keep the loose strands at bay. "You're lucky I've had a chance to sleep, so I'm not as upset as I should be, or you would still be prying my hands from your throat."

Tammy unwittingly touched her throat. "Believe me, sugar, I am truly sorry. I'm glad that boy was mellowed out and didn't get violent or anything, 'cause I would hate to have to seek his ass out and mop him all across Chicago."

Felicia could only smile at her best friend because she knew the truth behind that statement. The girl could get street in a New York minute. She also had the look that could carry her threats. Her skin was as dark as day-old molasses, her nails so thick and long that they curved at the ends, her makeup dark and hinged on being loud—but even with her massively broad body, she knew her look, and worked it well. Heavy braids fell to her shoulders, their flow interrupted only by the two large hooped earrings that swung from her lobes. She was chewing gum as if it had been served to her on a platter, and Felicia wondered how she could complete entire sentences with all that action going on between her molars. But after two years, Felicia was used to everything about Tammy Fae Russle.

"This whole dating scene is becoming too much for me. I think life in general is too much for anyone," Felicia said, looking at Tammy's nails, then her own, and reaching for a fingernail file that sat on the end table.

"Honey, tell me about it," Tammy began, squirming to a comfortable position in her chair. "I hear that Erica is thinking about having some affair with this twenty-year-old. That woman must be crazy, the way that boy has messed up so many lives."

Felicia stopped mid-file. "Who the hell is Erica?"

Tammy pushed Felicia's shoulder. "On *All My Children!* Where you been?"

"Girl, you talking about some corny soap opera? Shit! I'm talking about life here. I tell you, Tammy, you amaze me sometimes." "What'chu talking about, Felicia? That is life."

"Whatever," Felicia replied, returning to her nails.

"So, you gonna give up on dating for a while? I wouldn't blame you though. I hate that this man caused you to lose a day's work."

"I called in sick because I was just tired, that's all. It had nothing to do with Brian," Felicia assured, as she blew on her nails.

"Yeah, right. You should've called the police on his sorry butt, bringing drugs in your place. That fool has got some nerve," Tammy fumed.

"It's not like he attacked me or anything. What would I go running to the police for? Because Mr. Wonderful turned out to be Mr. Wonder-What-the-Fuck? No, maybe I'm not meant to meet anyone in my life. Being alone isn't bad when—"

"Gimmie that!" Tammy said, snatching the fingernail file from Felicia's hand. "You always file your damn nails when you're thinking too much. Now don't let that fuckhead Brian mess with your head. He was rotten meat, smellin' up everything. Don't have him make you start to feel sorry about yourself," she said, taking the fingernail file to her own nails.

Felicia sighed. *This dating is more of a problem than it's worth. All I need is a good pair of rechargeable batteries.* "Maybe going back to Stephen would solve my problems," she uttered, not realizing she was speaking aloud.

"What was that you said under your morning breath? I thought I heard the name *Stephen.* The man that cheated on you in your own bed with another woman? Was that his name I hear tell you mention?"

Felicia pulled her scarf nervously down upon her scalp. She had not told Tammy, or any of her friends, about Stephen's sexuality. It was tough enough dealing with her own feelings about it. "I've been thinking about him, that's all. It's tough taking care of Tumali. Besides, I've been thinking about putting a plaque above my bedroom saying LIBRARY, it being so quiet in there lately."

"Girl, you'll get used to the chilly sheets. You should be used to that by now. I'm sure you've had a little dipstick in your tank every now and then."

"It's only been a year and a half," Felicia said hesitantly.

Tammy remained quiet. She watched Felicia's body language: the shifting feet, the wringing hands, the avoidance of direct eye contact. "You haven't had dick since that man left, have you?"

Felicia stared, stunned. "What're you talking about?"

Tammy placed a hand on her hip. "Now, you ain't that off, so don't even play it. You ain't had a man up in here, have you?"

"I was dating Emmanuel and Alex, if you remember, and—"

"Girl, please! I mean you ain't *had* a man in here. You talking about Emmanuel and Alex, shit! That's only pussy popcorn. They were the snack, not the meal. You don't need nobody in here just teasing you if you ready for a real dinner. Your mother was right ... you are sprung."

"Now how did my mother get into this, Miss All-Up-in-My-Clit?"

"Miss Felicia, if I was in your clit, at least something would be keeping it busy, and you could get your mind off that man. The nigga done fucked you over, and you still want him."

"Well, I am just sorry that you and my mother think that Stephen is the enemy. I know he was a very good man who treated me right."

"Not with some bitch in the same bed you two were in. If'n it was me, I'da whupped him and this girlfriend of his all up and down State Street," Tammy said, slamming the file on the coffee table. "I should smack some sense into you with these nails, girl."

"Then smack me!" Felicia stated, with more emphasis than intended. She had to face the truth that she was still in love with Stephen. He was just going through some gay phase, and she had to be there when he emerged.

Tammy was still a bit shaken at Felicia's outburst, and she tenderly leaned across the sofa to place a warm hand across her friend's knee. "I don't need to ruin my nails on your face, okay? Hey, if Stephen is all you think about, then who am I to judge? He doesn't have any woman in his life, so maybe you two can still talk things out. I'm only making a suggestion. I still think he doesn't deserve anything you have to give him."

If only she had never gotten off the phone when they'd talked a few days ago. He'd said he was going on a date, and it scared her. She'd never felt so out of control in all her life. Was she not enough woman for him? Was there something wrong with her? She'd thought about that for a long time, and still she wasn't sure. "I wish it were that easy to talk things through, Tammy."

"I don't see why not. Maybe he's sorry. You did say it was the first time. He loves his son, and I guess he's still got something of an affection for you. Hell, I don't know. Just get together and work this mess out if that's what you want."

Felicia remained silent, and instinctively reached for the fingernail file.

Tammy watched her slowly fade out, her mind heavy. "What's going on, Felicia? There's something more going on between you two, isn't there?"

"What? Oh, there's nothing between us."

"Uh-huh, sure. Don't try and faze me out, Felicia. This is Tammy Fae Russle you talking to. There is something more, and I know it."

"I didn't say anything," Felicia said.

"I know you didn't, and that's what I'm talking about. Girl, you are trippin' bad, and I've known you long enough to tell. But if you don't want to share your feelings with your best friend, then I guess I have to understand."

Felicia couldn't look at Tammy. She wanted to tell Tammy the truth about Stephen, but didn't know how she would react.

"Damn girl, this is serious, huh? ' ain't never got the silent treatment from your ass this bad. What the hell? Is this really about Stephen?" she asked, blowing a bubble.

"Kinda. I mean...oh, I don't know. How did we get on this subject, anyway?"

"Your love-struck ass, that's how. I want to know why you would want this man back after he done did the pussy sneak. Is he like some fuckin' mass murderer who threatened your life or something?"

"I wish it were that simple," Felicia replied, rubbing her hands together once again.

Now Tammy's curiosity was piqued. "Damn! Am I gonna see your ass on Ricki Lake or some shit? I'm not starting to like this conversation, Felicia. We've been through a lot of crazy stuff together, and I hope that this nigga ain't holding anything on you or something. You know I got your back in anything, Felicia. You don't have to—"

"He's gay, Tammy!" Felicia spat out.

Tammy said nothing. She blinked rapidly, as if rising from a dream. It was as if Felicia's words came at her too fast.

"Yes, you heard me right," Felicia reassured. "Stephen wasn't in bed with a woman. He was in bed with a man."

Tammy closed her eyes then swung her arm through the air as if keeping some astral image at bay. "Hell naw! Hell, muthafuckin' naw! That man is a fairy? Is that what you're telling me?"

"I don't like that word, Tammy," Felicia said, flatly.

"You don't like ... Are you crazy?" Tammy stood, placing her hand firmly on her hips. "You caught this man in bed with another man while you were pregnant? All this shit was going on and you couldn't even tell me?"

"I thought—"

"Maybe it was better you didn't, 'cause I would have sent that punk packing myself," she took a deep breath, then spoke again. "And you act like you're still in love with him."

"I know he can change, Tammy," was all she offered.

"Change?" she questioned, standing there glaring at Felicia. The girl remained quiet. "You are still in love with him, aren't you?" Tammy responded, as if she'd just had a revelation. "You truly are, and you can't let him go. Before you know it, you'll be telling me you're on your way to California."

Nothing.

The conversation had suddenly ceased. Tammy could see a cocked grin, slight yet noticeable, ease its way upon Felicia's face. It was eerie and yet prophetic; Felicia was thinking just that. Tammy knew it!

— III —

Dominique flung the door open and stood in the center of the living room, arms outstretched. She exhaled, dropping her briefcase to the floor and raising her head toward the ceiling. She was one tired bitch, and if she'd had enough air in her lungs she would have shouted it to the world.

She was also one frazzled lipstick dyke too, with the added pressure and utter disbelief that her present lover's ex was now her boss. She was also what could be considered a senior designer in training, and that too would become a great responsibility. The work on the Gerri account didn't appear too demanding, but in the world of interior design it was all about appearances.

Dominique turned to shut the door and noticed the keys were still in the lock. She laughed. It had to be a stressful day when she started doing forgetful things like that. She took the keys out of the lock, closed the door, and then flung herself on the couch. Bootie came into the room and jumped on the sofa, looking at Dominique with her deep gray feline eyes.

"So how you doing, my little precious?" she cooed to the Siamese, while running the back of her fingers along its spine. "Where's your other mother, and what has she been doing all day?" Dominique didn't need the cat to relay that answer; it only nibbled at her fingers affectionately while purring deeply. Dominique was fully aware that Sarafina spent most of her time at home, calling her friends, cruising the streets, doing whatever came to mind since she quit working part-time at her father's bookstore. But why should she work? Gerri had given her upwards of about $10,000 to squander. Dominique had tried to explain that ex-lovers do not hand over parting gifts without wanting something in return, but Sarafina would not listen.

"Damn! I need a joint," Dominique said, as she headed for the bedroom, disrobing along the way—her suit jacket, panties, bra, stockings, pumps, earrings, watch—everything, and then she reached for her terrycloth robe hanging behind the closet door. She flung herself on the bed, reached across the rumpled down pillows, and pulled open the nightstand drawer. There she was, Mary J, and she was never happier to see her friend this day.

Dominique watched the smoke from the bud rise to intertwine with the blades of the ceiling fan above. Ella Fitzgerald was belting on the CD player as Dominique played back the messages on the answering machine. A message from Sarafina was there. She had gone to Jewel's Room. It was Monday, and that club was known for its bid whist card action today. It would be hours before she returned home.

How, she continued to ponder, could Sarafina have rushed to the phone just because her ex had called? Dominique also wondered about herself, and what sort of hell she was in to be appointed to work with this woman. Were there any more surprises that could fill this day?

Dominique walked to the living room, falling sharply against the doorpost and stumbling to the sofa. She leaned forward to grab a bundle of mail left on the coffee table. There was a subscription renewal form from *Ebony,* a notice announcing that she MAY ALREADY BE A MILLIONAIRE!, and a manila envelope. It was the envelope that caught her attention, because it contained no return address, and the postmark indicated it came from San Francisco. She also noticed the sender's name: Gerri.

She drew in on the joint again then tapped its tip against the edge of the ashtray, watching as if in slow motion, as the ash plummeted and scattered. She twisted the envelope in her hand, examining it closely. She placed it back on the table. *Should I open it?* She asked herself. She stared at the deep piss-yellow color of the packet. The conversation began in her head again. *Should I open it?* Her hands shook, and she tried to think about something else entirely.

Open it, said her inner voice. She tapped the spliff against the ashtray once again.

Sara Chandler. It was the name on the envelope. It was no secret that Gerri called her Sara as a nickname. What was it doing here? Before she knew *it,* she was sliding her fingernail under the tiny aluminum clasp securing the flap. She pulled at it, testing its endurance, slowly unfastening it.

How easily it opened.

Dominique slid her fingers within, examining the contents, feeling the roughness of paper against her flesh. She tugged at it and slowly pulled out a newspaper. The classifieds section. It contained listings for apartment rentals. The *San Francisco Chronicle* stood out in bright red newsprint, and below the headline there were highlighted sections displaying certain apartments for rent. Dominique was confused, and looked in the envelope again.

There was a note inside. It read:

Hey there, Sara,

Got that list together we talked about. I tried to keep within the price range you suggested, but don't be afraid to splurge a little. Remember, I'll be there to help you. I am so glad you decided to come back home, although I know it will be tough to leave so much behind. But I think you deserve better than what you're getting.

Love you, always. . . Gerri

"That whore!" Dominique yelled. She could plainly see what was happening; Sarafina was moving out on her! She rammed her fist into the arm of the sofa. Bootie ran from the room. She threw the package on the table and stood, walked to the stereo, and put in a Sarah Vaughn CD, closed her eyes, and took a deep breath. She had some thinking to do.

The phone suddenly rang, startling her. She seized it from its base. "Hello!" she bellowed into the receiver.

"Damn. Calm down, baby," came the voice of Sarafina. Dominique could hear music in the background. She was still at Jewel's Room.

"Hello? Dominique? You still there?" Sarafina asked - her voice just above a shout.

"Yeah, I'm still here," Dominique replied dryly.

"Just callin' to let you know I'm still here waiting for the drag show to start. Did you get my message?"

"Yeah."

"Are you okay? Did you have a rough day at work?" Sarafina questioned, sensing something was amiss from Dominique's terse remarks.

"You could say that."

"What's up, baby? You wanna come down here and kick it a bit?" "No, thanks, Sarafina. I'm gonna call *it* a night."

"You feeling tired, huh?"

"Of a great many things," Dominique said, twisting the phone cord between her fingers.

"What?" Sarafina questioned. Suddenly she heard music playing in the receiver. Jazz! Something was wrong. "Are you fine with me hanging out here? I can get back there if you want."

"No, Sarafina, you just do what you want."

That's an odd remark, Sarafina thought. "I won't be long, okay? We'll talk when I get home."

"Whatever you say. I'm exhausted, so I'll see you whenever," Dominique replied, gently dropping the phone back on the cradle. She then returned to her bedroom and fell on the bed. She quickly fell asleep. Funny how frustration can be a great method of sedation.

Chapter 7

— I —

The sex was good.

Four days and nights of high energy passion and lusts that felt as if it lasted a lifetime. All David knew was that when Allen returned from the Study Monday night, he was a changed man. He had a hunger in his eyes that night, almost radiating anger somehow, as if he'd had some altercation at the club. David could remember him charging into the bedroom and standing at the foot of the bed, staring at him. David could almost feel Allen's uninhibited craving for flesh, as he lay there feigning sleep.

Allen had let him sleep that night, but in the morning....

Allen had slid next to David and pulled him closer as he went through the motions of lovemaking—not lust making, mind you, but deliberate, unhurried, raw, lovemaking. It was as if he'd forgotten he had a job to go to. And the next day there were flowers in his arms, and a surprise trip to Malibu, strolls along the beach. Four days! My God, and they had been amazing.

David lay in his bed, the pillow swallowing his head as he looked toward the ceiling. The smile was still on his face. He was remembering this morning—Allen looking over him, just inches away from his brow, small billows of air pelting his face.

They had been naked. Allen lay atop him, his manhood pressed firmly between them. The movements, the gyrations, were a symphony, a melding of sweat and sin. Allen rose to his knees, releasing his load of love across David's chest in a massive display of cream-colored spray that coalesced with David's own perspiration.

"I love you, baby," Allen had said, as he leaned forward to press his soft lips upon David's.

"I love you too," David had acknowledged.

Allen had reached down to pinch David's nipples, kneading them between his strong fingers; it was just the way David liked it. It began to stir his arousal once more. Allen too had become excited again, his massive pendulum swinging back and forth, its erectness becoming more and more pronounced with every swaying motion; he knew they were ready to go at it again.

And they had. It was majestic!

Yes ... the sex had been very good.

David sat up and stretched his arms. His whole body was alive. He could rest no longer. He felt revived. The clock on the nightstand displayed 1:00. *Allen should be going to lunch right about now,* David thought. Although Allen had warned him about calling him at his job, David was tempted just to say hello. Surely the DMV took hundreds of calls per day; they wouldn't notice just one more.

He reached over to the nightstand and grabbed the phone with the tips of his fingers. His heart was fluttering like a child reaching for his favorite dessert on a tray of hundreds. He dialed.

"Hello, this is the Department of Motor Vehicles. Debbie Sinclair speaking," said the high pitched voice on the other end, bringing David back to the present.

"Oh, I'm sorry," David apologized after a moment's hesitation. "I was wondering if you could connect me to Allen Morrison."

"Hold on, please," she responded, followed by a short silence. She returned, "Hmm, Sir?"

"Yes," David replied, wondering why Allen hadn't been the one to answer the phone.

"You said Allen Morrison, correct?"

"Yes, that is correct. Is there something wrong?"

"Well ... I don't think he came to work this morning."

David wasn't sure he heard her correctly. "He didn't come in today?"

"You know, it has been busy here and I start later than he does. I'll just connect you with my supervisor, okay? He'll be able to help you a little more," she said, as the line quickly became silent once again.

David didn't know what to think about the woman's assumption. If Allen didn't make it to work this morning then something must have happened to him while he was on his way. He prayed there had been no accident or crime of any sort.

"Yes, Terry Jones," came the husky voice. From the tone, David could sense this man did not like being disturbed.

"Excuse me, but I was calling for Allen Morrison, and I—" "He's out sick," replied the man hurriedly.

"What?" David asked, knowing this man was mistaken.

"I said he is still sick, been so for the past two days; the flu or something.

"Are you sure?"

"Hey, I only go by what they tell me. Is there something else I can help you with?"

David wanted to question him further, but he realized this man was not the one he should be questioning. "No, I guess that was all I needed to know. Thank you."

"No problem," said the rushed gentleman as he quickly broke the connection.

David could hear the dial tone of the receiver as he cradled it in his hand, afraid to place it back on its base, afraid to accept any of what he'd just heard. Allen had called in sick for the past two days. But he had left each morning the picture of perfect health. Was there something going on with Allen physically that he was afraid to talk about? David wondered if he was just making more excuses for a guilty man. It seemed to come so naturally for him lately.

David needed answers. He clicked the phone with his thumb, the dial tone blared again. He punched in Allen's work pager.

Five minutes later the phone rang. "Hello!"

David answered tensely. "Hey baby, it's me. You must've been right by the phone."

"The phone just startled me, that's all."

"I was calling to see how your day is going. You're not working too hard, are you?"

"Not right now," Allen said, his voice a bit muffled. "I'm having lunch at the California Pizza Kitchen, with the gang. We'll be heading back to work in a few minutes."

David strung the conversation along, his mind reeling. "I'd thought about calling you at work, because I considered you might be going to lunch soon and that we could meet up. Hope calling was okay."

"Oh no," Allen quickly exclaimed. "My supervisor just suspended a girl for taking too many personal calls. I don't need any more hassles at work than the ones I already have. I usually work through lunch and get off early so I can get to the gym."

"Then it was good I paged you," David said, his hands clenching the phone.

"Well, I am glad to hear from you. I had a wonderful time this morning."

David hesitated. "Yeah, I had a wonderful time too."

"I'll be at the gym after work, so I'll be home a little late. You gonna wait up for me, baby?"

"Sure. You know I will," David could feel himself getting flush. He could not believe the deceit transpiring here.

"See you tonight. David," Allen replied, blowing a kiss through the phone.

"Bye," David spat out, then quickly hung up.

California Pizza Kitchen, California Pizza Kitchen . . . the name reverberated in his head; the legitimacy also came to mind. David seized the phone again, this time dialing star 69.

"Hello," said the young, perky female voice on the other end. David took a deep breath. "Hello, could I speak to Eric?" "Eric?" the young woman questioned.

"Yes, Eric Matheson. Is he there?"

"I'm sorry, but do you realize this is a pay phone, mister?" "Really? I must have dialed the wrong number."

"It happens to the best of us. I do hate to end our little conversation, but I was hoping to use this phone."

"Of course you were. I was wondering if you could tell me where this phone is located."

"It's in the French Market. It's a restaurant on Santa Monica. Now, If you'll excuse me, this is an emergency call I am trying to make," she informed, her timbre becoming a bit less patient.

Before he had a chance to thank her, she hung up. David threw the phone on the nightstand, knocking over the clock. How could he have been such a fool? How could he have been so trusting? How? How? How? David rushed to the dresser drawer and flung open the bottom one, tossing his clothes out like a madman. If Allen was at the French Market, then that is where he would go. It was time for some much needed answers.

– II –

"You want what?" Sarafina asked, as she brought the coffee cups to the sink.

"I want you to have the phone number changed this afternoon," Dominique said, chewing casually on a piece of toast.

"Now what brought this craziness on?" Sarafina asked.

"Don't worry about it, Tina. There have been just too many strangers calling this house, and I want it to stop. I don't know what is going on with our phone—crossed wires, bad reception—but I am still getting those crank calls."

"I haven't heard any crank calls, and I'm here most of the day," Sarafina said, as she walked back to the table, moist rag in hand.

"Well, somebody keeps calling me!" Dominique said, agitated.

Sarafina looked at Dominique doubtfully. She glided the wet rag across the breakfast table. She figured it was stress, and it wasn't coming from a crank caller.

"So what kind of shit are these folks talking about? If it's some sexual shit, then just tell 'em you're a lesbo, baby," Sarafina joked.

This isn't funny, Sarafina!" Dominique said, rising from her seat and wiping her mouth with her napkin. She walked out of the kitchen.

Sarafina tossed the rag into the sink and trailed Dominique into the living room. "What in the world is up your hairs?" she asked, folding her arms. Dominique sat on the sofa and reached down to retrieve her portfolio from the floor. She opened it without a word, thumbing through a set of color patterns.

This is one pissed lipstick, Sarafina thought, as she walked toward the sofa. "All right, we'll change the phone number. Is there anything else you want?" Sarafina asked hurriedly, wanting this drama over.

"Oh, I don't want to overburden you," Dominique mocked.

Sarafina placed a hand on her hip. "Now you're being a smart-ass. I guess I don't get an opinion whenever you get that I-wanna-change-the-phone feeling."

Dominique sighed as she flipped through a set of blueprints. She looked up at Sarafina, giving her a momentary glance, and then returned to her portfolio. She spoke calmly, but it was visibly forced. "No, my dear, that is not the case. Are you trying to start an argument, 'Fina?"

Sarafina instinctively held her breath, keeping herself in check. "I just think it's a lot of trouble: calling up all our friends, family, and even people you and I do business with, to let them know that our number changed."

"Are you saying that you just don't want to do it?"

"I didn't say that, but I—"

"Then what's the problem?" Dominique expressed.

Check again. "I didn't say there was a problem, Dominique. I was just wondering where all this was coming from."

"Damn!" Dominique voiced, closing her portfolio. "I just want the phone changed, and you act like I asked you to kill somebody. Can't I make a simple request here without you coming up with all these questions?"

"Now wait a minute. I said I would take care of the phone, okay? You don't have to get bent out of shape. I'll get right to calling up everyone we know to give them the new number, if that's all right with you.

"Well, for starters, you can leave one number off your roster."

"Who are you talking about?" Sarafina asked.

"Well, don't bother calling your friend Gerri."

Checkmate! *So that's it,* Sarafina thought. *This shit with Gerri is never going to end. Crank calls. Bullshit!* "Is that what this is all about? You still upset over Gerri calling while we were in the bed fucking."

"Fucking—ha!" Dominique said with a scowl. "We never got that far, remember?"

"Whatever! The point is you want the phones changed because of that? What kinda sense does that make?"

Dominique zipped up her portfolio. "You know, I don't have time to discuss this with you, Sarafina. I have to go to the design center today and order some fabrics."

"I'm not doing it," Sarafina said, overtly.

"What?" Dominique said.

"I am not changing the phone just because one woman called and pissed you off. You must be trippin' to let this get to your head."

Dominique stood to her feet. "Fine," she said, her nose flaring, breathing heavy. "I am not going to sit here and argue with you about your girlfriend. I don't know why I bother to compete with her, when it's obvious who the winner is."

"What the hell are you talking about? There's no competition going on here. Me and Gerri are just friends, and that's it," Sarafina explained.

"Yeah, I wonder about that."

"What do you mean by that?" Sarafina asked.

Dominique placed her case on the floor, closed her eyes, and took a deep breath. "When were you going to tell me about you moving back to San Francisco? Was I going to return home one day and just find you gone? Is that how you do things? Why couldn't you just tell me you were thinking of going back into a relationship with Gerri?"

"What?" Sarafina was totally perplexed. "Where did you get that information? I haven't thought about going back anywhere. You must be—"

"Listen!" Dominique blurted. "I saw the envelope. I saw the newspaper ad. I saw the apartments that were highlighted for you. I know you two have been talking behind my back, and she has probably even told you that she is now my new client at work. She's establishing another sales office out here."

"What?" Sarafina was trying to clear her head of all this rushed information. "She's your new client? You never told me this."

"And you're going to deny getting that package from her too?"

Sarafina thought about it. That was five days ago. It had slipped her mind. That was the night she returned from Jewel's Room. Dominique must've opened it before they talked on the phone that night. That would explain the attitude in her voice. And to think, Gerri was now her client—and her boss. *It's no wonder she's acting the way she is,* Sarafina thought.

"Yeah, I got a package, but it didn't have my name on it. I called Gerri about it, and she said it was a mistake. She sent it to the wrong address. It was to go to a Sara *Fletcher* and she wrote my name and address by mistake."

"I know what it had on it!" Dominique uttered. "I saw the mail when I came in. I don't know what to believe, Sarafina. The late phone calls, the package, the letter inside, the fact that this bitch is now my client. All this is coming at me from nowhere. I can't take this woman's intrusion into our lives, and sooner or later you're gonna have to decide."

"Decide? Are you saying I have to make a choice between you and Gerri? I have to choose to have friends or a lover?"

Dominique slapped a fist against her head. "News Flash, Sarafina! Gerri is not your friend. She has been disrupting our lives just a little too much to keep her friend membership valid. And I can't stand here while you seem to want to always defend this woman, *your* woman."

"My woman! Where did you get—"

"Oh, I am so sorry. Should I be saying your lover? Is that more politically correct?"

"What the fuck! Your ass is off the deep end or something! I only have one lover, and unfortunately I'm arguing with her right now. Me and Gerri are just friends, and I would hate to think I gotta clear all my friends through you first. I live with you, not her."

"Your choice should be easy then," Dominique said, and reached down to grip the handle of her case. "I have to get to work, and I just don't have the time to go over your love affairs."

Sarafina bit her tongue, she wanted to grab this woman by the throat and shake some sense into her. She was on the verge of pushing her out the door, and getting her to work as soon as possible and out of her face. Instead, she fell back upon the couch, defeated. "All right, Dominique, I'll get the phone changed. I see that this is really bothering you," Sarafina said, exhausted.

Dominique nodded. "And. . ." she prodded.

"And I won't give the number to Gerri," Sarafina finished.

"Good," Dominique said, walking out and slamming the door shut.

Sarafina just placed her head in the palm of her hand. Things were not looking good these days.

– III –

Stephen kicked at the ground playfully, as he stuffed his hands into his pockets. Griffith Park. He never thought he would be taking a romantic stroll through this place, considering its tainted reputation by the gay populace that frequented its bushes on sweltering nights. Jamal walked beside him, dressed in baggy jeans, a turtleneck, and boots. Stephen was dressed in a sweat suit and windbreaker.

"It's funny seeing you looking so casual," Jamal commented. "You look so different when you're not all creased up."

"Hey, I gotta send those clothes to the cleaners sometimes," Stephen joked. "And I even have gym shoes on," he added, stopping to lift one of his feet.

"Yeah, the latest Jordan's. Very impressive."

They continued to walk. The park was scattered with visitors this afternoon: a couple in the distance was spread out on a thick blanket eating sandwiches; an old man chatted away while feeding the squirrels; a vagrant sat in a tattered makeshift tent created from a car cover and rope; a few children tossed pebbles at dead tree trunks; and just a few yards away were hustlers giving their come-hither stares in cutoff jeans and ripped tank tops.

"What made you want to come out here?" Jamal asked.

Stephen continued to look around. "Oh, nothing. I just wanted to show you a nice time, that's all. I still feel bad about Aunt Kizzy's."

Jamal looked surprised. "I think that lunch in the limo was quite enough."

"I know, but this day felt special—don't ask me why."

"Funny you say that, because this is a kinda special day for me, being my birthday n' all."

"It's your birthday?" Stephen said. "I didn't know that. If I had known I would have gotten you something."

"Please. We haven't known each other long enough to have shared that conversation."

"Wait! I think I may have something I could give you ..." Stephen began to fish in his pockets. He stopped and pulled out a bulky white napkin. "This should do."

The weight of it was heavy. Jamal began to unravel the napkin. Inside the silk cloth sat a silver fork and spoon, their edges inlaid in gold trim. "What a strange thing to have in your pocket," Jamal commented.

"So ... do you like it?" Stephen asked.

Jamal gave a withdrawn smile, unsure of how exactly to respond. "Sure," was all he could think of saying.

Stephen continued to walk again. "So, you're twenty-nine now? You still looking good, Mr. Jamal, sir. If I had a gin and tonic, I could make a toast to this occasion," he said, smiling.

"We'll keep the drinking to a minimum on this second venture."

"Perhaps. Maybe you've extinguished my need for a drink. Of course I'm sure you've extinguished the thirsts of a lot of men," Stephen said, smiling.

"It depends on what they're thirsty for," Jamal replied.

"Might depend on how bad they want a drink. I've been a thirsty man for quite some time, and a cool glass of Jamal might be just the thing."

"I don't do glassware." Jamal, said, as he playfully pushed Stephen's shoulder. "I'm glad to see you so relaxed today. That in itself is refreshing."

Stephen kicked at the dirt trail before him. "Do you speak to your father much?"

Jamal looked at him oddly. It was such a strange question to ask. "I try to call him at least three times a month. It's hard communicating with him with the Alzheimer's, but I try. He has Aunt Sylvia there taking really good care of him. Most likely I'll be going out there for Father's Day."

"You two seem very close.... I like that. I hope to have that with my child when he's older, but the world has such a negative opinion about the gay lifestyle. That makes it hard for a child to form his own opinion. That very opinion will affect his opinion of me."

Jamal nodded. "True, but you can't control the way the world thinks. You just have to show your son what a good father is like— one who just happens to be gay."

"Yep, I agree, but let's not dwell on that, especially today. So what did you have planned for your birthday?"

Jamal shrugged. "Nothing really. I've passed that birthday-celebrating phase."

"Is that so?" Stephen remarked.

Jamal noticed they were walking toward a couple of teenagers, kissing beside a tree. Beyond them was a festive looking table covered with balloons. A tablecloth was scattered with what looked like red petals, two covered plates, and what appeared to be a pitcher of lemonade and two champagne flutes. *Beautiful,* he thought. *That is the way gay lovers should be—out in the open, no shame.*

Jamal began to veer away from the couple, but Stephen continued toward them.

"Where are you going?"

"What are you talking about?" Stephen answered, just as the two teenagers walked away.

"Happy birthday, Jamal," Stephen said, stretching out his hand toward the table.

Jamal looked closer at the arrangement. He thought he saw something resembling a stone, but soon realized it was a white cake, and on its surface was written HAPPY B-DAY, JAMAL. He was speechless. He turned to look at Stephen, words caught somewhere between his teeth and tongue.

"I've never wanted to kiss a man so much as I want to kiss you right now," he finally managed to say.

Stephen stepped closer to him. "And I never wanted to let a man kiss me as I do you, right now."

And they kissed, and it felt as real and looked as wonderful as two teenagers leaning against a tree in their first embrace.

Jamal pulled back and looked at the table again, seeing everything: the crystal serving dish filled with chips and dip, a small bowl of ice cream sitting on a bed of dry ice, and vegetable sticks resting in a tin receptacle of dressing. "So where is the silverware so we can dig in?" Jamal asked.

"Why, they're in your pocket," Stephen said with a sly grin.

Jamal felt flushed with embarrassment, as he pulled out the napkin and eating utensils Stephen had only just given him. It warmed his heart to think Stephen had known about his birthday all along.

– IV –

David dashed through traffic so fast that he was barely able to avoid a rear-end collision with a Jeep. He almost sideswiped a cat, nearly hit an old lady pushing her grocery cart across the intersection, and sprayed a homeless man with a water pistol he had in his glove compartment (the man had been trying to wash his windows).

He stopped across from the French Market. His heart thudded. Allen was there, eating with someone he could not recognize.

They could be friends, or co-workers, or maybe they just met and decided to have innocent conversation, David tried to reason. But Allen had lied to him on the phone. He lied each morning he pretended to go to work. So many thoughts filled David's mind. He didn't want to think anything worse, but it was too late.

A wooden partition concealed all but their heads, and David wondered if they were holding hands, touching feet, exchanging gifts, eating from one plate, swapping terms of endearment. He wanted to know who this ebony brother was, talking to his man. How long had they known each other? How many lunches had they shared?

His questions soon found an answer, as he witnessed Allen paying the check with cash. They walked to the outside parking lot. It was here they embraced, gazed, smiled, and then finally kissed. More like chewed each other's lips off.

David was disgusted.

He wanted to die. He felt faint, his head seeming to swell to twice its size. Breathing became difficult. The pin pricks of a thousand needles were nothing to the pain he was beginning to feel now. Even as they drove away together, David continued to stare at the empty parking spot they'd occupied.

Suddenly he snapped, and slammed his fists against the steering wheel, pounding and pounding until the very car shook from the impacts. He stopped when he could feel his stomach cramp and his bottom lip began to quiver uncontrollably. He wanted to cry.

"Why?" he shouted to the roof of the car. "Why, goddammit! You bastard!" He placed his head on the steering wheel. "I loved you, Allen. Damn! I loved you."

He soon found he was crying, despite himself.

What to do? Anger, confusion, and exhaustion seemed to immediately overwhelm him. When his father beat him, the pain had felt external. Allen produced internal pain the likes he had not experienced. He would rather have had the former.

Fresh air—that's what he decided upon as he stepped from the car, slamming the door so hard that the windows rattled. He stumbled aimlessly along Santa Monica Boulevard, stopping only when he found a bus stop bench to sit on. A bus suddenly pulled up, the driver staring at him as the door opened. He weakly waved him away. He choked a bit in the passing exhaust. This was not his day.

"You miss your bus, dude?"

David turned, and behind him stood an almond skinned brother smiling at him. He had a Walkman in his hand, and pulled the earphones away from his head. He had large, pretty brown eyes and long lashes, thick eyebrows, and a goatee. Two large diamond earrings hung from his rather large ears. His body appeared sculpted in his tight fitting shirt, with Janet Jackson's portrait smiling at him. He wore below-the-knee oversized FUBU shorts that hung loosely from his waist, white thermal socks that rested below his massive calves, and black Rollerblades. He was truly a part of all that was West Holly-wood. He adjusted the backpack that hung across his shoulder, as he awaited David's reply.

"No, I wasn't waiting for a bus. It's just been a long day, and I needed a seat," David answered.

"Would you like a piece of gum?" this handsome stranger offered.

"No thanks. I'm fine," David said indifferently.

The young man looked at his watch. "I'm sorry, bro, but I usually don't talk to strangers for more than five minutes without finding out at least their name." He extended his hand. "My name is Malcolm."

David hesitated, then slowly shook Malcolm's hand. "My name is David. Is that Malcolm, like in X?"

"Not quite. It's Malcolm, like in Steward."

"Well, it's nice meeting you, Malcolm Steward," David said, turning back to face the daily rush of traffic. He was not in the mood to have a pointless conversation.

Malcolm bent forward to rest his elbows on the back of the bench. His face was close to David's, who could sense the presence. "Could I make a guess that you're getting over some man-type issues?"

"You a mind reader, or just nosy?"

Malcolm smiled at the remark. "No, I'm not a mind reader, but I do know a lot about this bench. I've sat here before, looking as you do now. And back then, I wished for someone to walk by, and offer me something as simple as a cup of coffee…anything, really, to take my mind away if only for a moment."

"Is that what you're offering, Malcolm?" David asked, intrigued.

Malcolm reached down to grab his earphones. "As a matter of fact ... I am. I'm heading to Buzz Coffee, and I would really like you to join me if you get a chance."

Malcolm placed his earphones in his ear and pushed himself away from the bench. He was soon gliding along the street toward his destination.

David watched, and a pang of fear swept through his body. What if Allen had seen *him* talking to this man—an attractive man at that? But then again, Allen was supposed to be at work, and David was supposed to be in bed sleeping. David stood. His legs had somehow become stronger. Funny how a cup of coffee sounded really good right now.

Chapter 8

— I —

Dominique dropped her portfolio on the ground and opened the brown paper bag as if it were filled with diamonds instead of a barbecued chicken sandwich. She looked up at Damien, smiling shyly, before she bit down on her lunch like a wolf on its prey, sauce squeezing out to land on the patio table.

"Honey, slow down! You realize my arm is only a few inches from that maw," said Damien, holding up his hands. He began to wonder if he should have taken time away from the beauty shop to cater to this dangerous liaison.

"You'll have to excuse my etiquette this afternoon, baby. Hell was my welcome mat this morning," said Dominique, wiping the corners of her mouth. She closed her eyes, trying to block out the troubles she'd already had with landscapers at the site, pricing issues on certain items she wanted in the hallway, losing her phone book, getting a flat tire, and then trying to call home to see if Sarafina could fix it for her, but instead being stunned to hear that the phone number had changed, and she had not called her on her cell to give her the new number.

"So what's the matter, Dominique? Girl, you sounded like it was the end of the world. I know this has to do with Sarafina, so spill the muthafuckin' frijoles, child."

"I think Sarafina is planning to go back to San Francisco," said Dominique quickly, taking another large bite of her sandwich.

Damien leaned forward in his seat. "What? Isn't that where her ex lives?"

"Yep, and I think she wants to get back with her."

Damien scooted his seat closer to the patio table. They were in the back of the shop, a small outdoor area, and he could clearly see into the shop from here. There were only five beauticians working today, and he could see them all cut their eyes toward him. Bitches were doing some Bionic Woman shit 'cause they could read lips through cement if they had to. He leaned in closer to Dominique, covering his mouth slightly just in case. "Oh no, baby. What happen?"

Dominique stared at the table as if the words she wanted to choose were stitched into the cover. "Well, that Gerri woman sent Sarafina a newspaper highlighted with some places for rent that Sarafina could look at when she got to San Francisco. It was in an envelope that I know I shouldn't have opened, but I did, and there was a letter in there saying that Gerri couldn't wait to see her."

"Goodness, Dominique, what Sarafina say about this?"

"That she had called Gerri and it was a mistake. The envelope was addressed to our place by mistake. It was for a Sara Fletcher, and I have to admit that the envelope did have Sara on the front ... but the wrong address? I can't believe that."

Damien leaned back in his seat, crossed his legs, and placed his hands on his knee. "I don't know, Dominique. You might be jumping to a conclusion, honey."

Dominique nearly choked on her juice. "What? You think I'm being a jealous bitch or something?"

"This is sounding so like that Christy love drama you went through years ago," reminded Damien.

Dominique ceased chewing, ceased drinking, ceased moving. She hadn't heard that name in years. Christy McMadden—a pretty young girl that Dominique dated for six months, and one she broke up with because their friends had clashed. Dominique had thought Christy was sleeping with all of them, when in truth it was really only half. The other half just never liked her.

"That was different," said Dominique. "Christy was a selfish whore."

"But it was all about jealousy, girl—that ugly monster with the olive complexion," said Damien, shaking his empty cup, the ice knocking against the sides.

"But I wasn't dealing with anyone that Christy had fucked—at least I didn't know it. This was Sarafina's lover!"

"Ex-lover, baby. Sarafina has done nothin', and you need to trust her, Dominique, before you do something crazy."

"Well, I did have the phone changed, and I told her not to give the number to Gerri."

Darien waved both his hand in the air. "Whoa! Child, what's gotten in you?" Darien held up his palm. "Don't answer that. I don't need you taking me there."

"Hey, I couldn't help it. She agreed to have the phone changed." "Knowing you, honey, you prob'ly threatened to close that cherry bush if she didn't do as you say," Damien said.

Dominique smiled. "But really, it's hard enough trying to keep a relationship these days without all this drama of former girlfriends in the way."

"I think you should give Sarafina the benefit of the doubt. You two have been together a good while."

"It's only been a year, Damien. I don't think we're breaking any records," Dominique said, leaning back in her chair.

Child, for us boys, a yearlong gay relationship is like five in the straight."

Suddenly, a short stout woman, hair weaved into a beehive upon her head, stepped out into the patio. She looked worn out as she pushed a wad of gum to the inside of her jaw. She glanced at Dominique, then Damien, unsure of what she may have been interrupting.

"Damien, sweetheart," she strolled over to the table, slapping her palm on the top. "Myisha's done with the dryer, and now Kishana wants to dye her hair some god-awful copper color that is gonna take hours." She then threw her hands in the air. "And Latti just came back and said you did her perm all wrong!"

"Drama, drama, and more drama," said Damien, placing his hand on his forehead. "Don't worry about it, Mo Mo baby. I'll be there in a minute. And you tell that Latti, I told her that she don't looks nothin' like Halle Berry. . . more like Crunch Berry, and it is gonna take more than hair color to change that. She needs to drop some more coins and get the whole makeover." He patted Mo Mo's hand affectionately.

Mo Mo took a deep breath, holding her chest, and closed her eyes, calming herself. She then walked back into the shop.

Damien turned to Dominique. "Looks like my lunch is over, honey."

Dominique began to gather her empty trash. "Yeah, I understand. I have to get back to Shelby's before Angela wonders if I am coming back at all. With Gerri as my new client I should take a leave of absence."

"What was that? *Gerri* is your new boss?" Damien's eyes were wide with disbelief.

Dominique stood up, shrugging her shoulders. "Damien baby, that's only the half of it. I tell you, this friendship Sarafina's having with Gerri is going to drive a wedge between us."

Damien shook his head. "I'm so sorry to hear that, Dominique. I think you both should talk this over some more and quit with all the fighting. You two are too good with each other for this mess."

"You're so sweet, Damien," Dominique said, bending forward to kiss Damien on the forehead.

"Watch that, girl! It's gonna take me all day to get that fish smell off."

Dominique pushed Damien playfully on the shoulder. "You can be a real bitch sometimes."

"You really think so? I've been trying for my bitchology degree." Dominique snapped her fingers. "Well, let me tell you, honey: You have graduated."

— II —

The crowd at the Buzz Coffee was modest. David held his cup of hazelnut crëme coffee with both hands; it was all he could do to keep from shaking. Malcolm sat across from him staring off into the crowd, holding a cup of espresso, a ham and cheese on rye on a plate below. It had been so long since David had been social, even on this small of a scale, that he felt as if he were not a part of it all but watching everything as a bystander. The low rumble of the crowd, the sipping of drinks, the door as it slid open across the tile floor, the sound of papers, computer keys, and cell phone conversations. It was as if he had entered a whole new world, or at least a world that had been passing him by.

"So tell me, David. How long were you guys together?" Malcolm asked.

David hesitated and took a sip of his coffee. "Five years." Malcolm rubbed his chin. "Hmm, that's a good long time."

"Long time perhaps—the good is debatable at this point."

"I made it to four years before I hopped out of my foolishness. My best friend is into the eight-year stretch."

"Yeah ... I am sure," said David, as he looked out the large windows, not really listening.

Malcolm nibbled on his sandwich. "You're nervous, huh?"

David didn't answer.

"It's going to be hard to stop thinking about him and whatever happened. It's probably hard for you to sit here talking with a complete stranger."

"No, I'm fine. Maybe at this point I'm not sure what to think. I could swear I was waking up to good dreams only hours ago."

Malcolm leaned forward, placing his elbows on the table. "Maybe you need a soul cleansing, and you can do that by telling me what made you sit at that bus stop in the first place."

David shook his head, as if the attempt at speaking about it was worse than knowing it happened.

Malcolm nodded. "Hmm, my guess is he was cheating. I am no gypsy, but it is the most common denominator. Or he could be doing that bisexual thing, and decided on women...but we're talking reality here. Now, the last scenario is that he is a great guy, but not the one for you, and you were thinking about how to end it all."

David laughed. "It is definitely not that one."

Malcolm smiled. "Sounds like what I like to call a *wannabe man*. Got the genitals in place, but nothing else is flowing. A wannabe man is no good to no one. You can be assured, it has nothing to do with you, and—"

"Listen, Malcolm, I appreciate what you are trying to say," he interrupted, "but I still—"

Malcolm rapped his knuckles against the table. "Stop right there!" he said in a strong whisper. "I know you don't want to hear this, or even talk about it, especially from someone you just met. I have been there, and it is not a fun place to be. Maybe I should tell you about my little wannabe man. Maybe you need to hear another story besides the one you're replaying in your head right now."

Malcolm took another quick bite from his sandwich then shared his tale. He told David about a man he thought the world of, who worked as a lawyer, traipsing about the country to take the world on his shoulders. A superhero who had spoiled him, listened to him, catered to his every whim. He told him about the fantasy shadowing the reality, and like all shadows, it began to shift. Financial troubles arose. The spoiling stopped. The trips were less frequent. Malcolm thought it his duty to now become the superhero. So Malcolm shared what he had with this man, this angel, this promise of a better tomorrow wrapped in skin of butterscotch brown. He shared so much: his bank account, his credit card numbers, his cell phone, his house key, his whole life. This is what superheroes did.

But soon the shadow shifted greatly, and Malcolm began to see what it had covered. That revelation came with a simple plane ride some months later to Malcolm's hometown. It came as he sat next to someone who also had a superhero. They laughed, shared, and compared. The experiences were not only similar—they were the same. It was even more shocking when this newfound friend opened his wallet and Malcolm found himself staring at a picture . . . of his own man. .

"What?" David placed a hand over his mouth.

Malcolm nodded. "Yeah child, my man had been busy traveling, all right—busy traveling to be with his mistress, or would that have been me? Without the shadow, baby, many things came into the light. I realized then why the sex with him had been so good: 'cause his dick must have been getting bigger with each fabrication that came out of his mouth. So I excused myself from my guest, went to the bathroom, and shed tears in a basin that was not my own. I took his picture out of my wallet, wiped my face with his image, and sent that portrait out into the friendly skies with a piss and a flush.

"When we landed, I met our friend, the bus stop, and I am still pulling splinters out of my ass for sitting there so long."

"Damn, Malcolm," David uttered.

"We had a little confrontation when I got back home, but the cocksucker didn't deny shit, and before I knew it, he stepped out the door and I fell into a black hole of regrets. It was the hardest time of my life, David."

"I bet it was. Like a trip down to hell."

Malcolm downed the last of his drink. "With the devil as my tour guide. Maybe that can give you the courage to tell your story and release it from yourself—which is the first step, my friend."

David took a deep breath. He should have seen so much, but Allen's shadow was long reaching and hid a whole world of shit, it seemed.

It was at this point that David shared with Malcolm and, for a moment, he could feel a pinprick of sorrow lift away.

Malcolm gathered the empty cups. "He's a wannabe man, all right. I could choke him myself. Why don't I freshen up these cups, and I'll be back. I feel this is far from our last conversation."

David reached up to grab Malcolm's wrist. "Thanks, Malcolm. I guess I did need a good cup of coffee."

Malcolm smiled. "Hey, anything is better than splinters in your ass."

Dominique moaned seductively as she watched Sarafina nibble at the chocolate between her thighs.

They were both as high as their libidos. This was a celebration of sorts: Sarafina was taking a job at her uncle's bookstore in the Beverly Hills area. It made Dominique so happy that she started to get moist just from the thought of it. It meant that Sarafina was finally starting to rely on her own resources, and not those of her ex-lover Gerri.

Dominique pushed down on Sarafina's head, letting that tongue carve a new name into her juicy walls. The orgasm came quickly.

"Fuck, girl, you trying to drown a sister?" asked Sarafina, wiping the sweat from her brow, as she watched Dominique's essence flow from her pulsing cavern.

Dominique caught her breath, and then said, "I guess I'm relieving a little stress."

"As long as I get to relieve my jaws in the process, it's all good," she said, crawling upon Dominique's body, their noses warming each other.

The kiss was nice and slow.

"Why don't you tell me what happened at work that's put you in such a cheery mood?"

Dominique smiled as she pondered what she was about to say. "I know I haven't talked too much about work, but I didn't want to jinx myself. But I might be getting a promotion to senior designer at the firm."

"Wow, that's wonderful!" Sarafina said, reaching out to hug her companion.

Dominique threw her head back, spreading her arms out over her head. "Yes, you may touch greatness now."

"So when will you know for sure?" Sarafina asked.

"Well, that's when the script gets flipped. First I have to prove myself to a particular client," she said, and looked away.

Sarafina pulled herself back to look into Dominique's eyes. They both knew who it was. Dominique had mentioned it in the heat of their last argument.

"You know this means I'll have to meet Gerri soon. Angela, my immediate supervisor, will be setting it up. I really don't know how I am going to react to this, Sarafina."

Sarafina could only imagine, and she didn't like the thought of it. "Let's try and not think about that right now. Why don't you turn over and let me give you a good old-fashioned massage?"

"Sounds good to me," Dominique agreed, lying face down on the sheets.

Sarafina kneaded her knuckles into Dominique's back, gliding her hands along her spine, toward the curve of her butt. She pressed the tiny dimple there with her thumbs, as if it were a magic button that could cause unpleasant thoughts to pour from her like juice through a strainer.

Dominique knew Sarafina was trying to make her forget. But Gerri's presence would not leave this home, her relationship, or her work environment.

Dominique could feel Sarafina's lips examine the span of flesh between her shoulder blades. The warmth of those lips made Dominique's depth dew up again. A tongue, heavy and smooth, licked her spine, causing her to quiver just a bit. Teeth, nibbling gently at her trunk, caused her to curl her toes. She could feel those thoughts of old fall away like the peeled hull of dead snake skin, and finally, it seemed as if they were once again alone in the room; their unwanted ghost was gone ... a hand exploring her thighs, another vibration pulling open every pore like electricity. She slowly turned around, and met a face that was smiling, that was beautiful, that belonged to her. She smiled back, feeling large hands tickling the hairs around her fruit, making its meat riper, so much more ready...and for the next two hours, she allowed her fruit to be savored, and put the outside world on a permanent hold.

– IV –

It was late. David knew it before looking at the clock on his dashboard... *one o'clock*. He didn't give a damn. It could be three o'clock in the fuckin' morning and he still wouldn't care. He'd hung out with Malcolm and his friend, Jesse, as they had lunch at the Greenery, did a little window shopping along Melrose, and as afternoon became early evening, they stopped off at Micky's for a little drinking and dancing. David had had the time of his life, and nothing was going to take that away.

He drove casually along La Brea Boulevard, until it became Hawthorne Boulevard, until the cities went from Hollywood, to Baldwin Hills, to Inglewood, to Hawthorne, to El Segundo ... and finally to Torrance. The roads were quiet, but the streets seemed to stretch to infinity, as if some unknown force was trying to keep him from going home. He wanted to heed that strange force, because Allen would be home; and with him conflict. But he felt a power within, that maybe this time he would have the upper hand.

As David pulled into the driveway he noticed the lights were still on in the house. He saw no movement at the windows, which could indicate that Allen wasn't home, or was sleeping, or waiting. He hoped it wasn't the latter.

David pulled his keys from the ignition and noticed his hands were shaking. He took a deep breath, prying himself from the car, trying to get a grip on his nerves, to regain his former strength. The plan was to go straight to bed and ignore any attempts at conversation until the morning, when he could think a bit more clearly.

That was supposed to be the plan.

The house was extremely bright. As David stepped in he noticed the television playing at full volume. Allen was sitting in front of it, unmoving, seeming unaware of David's presence. It startled David when the volume of the television was suddenly muted and his movements became more audible.

Allen spoke.

"Where the hell have you been?"

"Just out enjoying myself," David said, courage welling in him, as he looked around the room. He felt a very dangerous vibe. He began to wish he had not spoken, but he had, and in the eerie silence that had now weighed down the air, he began to walk toward his bedroom.

"Don't bother going in there," Allen said.

David started to ignore him, but something caught his eye. He looked over at the far corner of the living room and noticed two large suitcases stacked against the wall. "What are those there for?"

"They're there for you," Allen said, calmly.

"What? What are you talking about, they're there for me?" David asked, while looking at Allen, and noticing a drinking glass between his thighs; he could smell the brandy emanating from it. It sickened him.

"They're yours, goddammit! If you're gonna stay out all night, you might as well stay out! I don't have to put up with your shit, David."

"What the fu—? You've got to be kidding. You come in this house late almost every Friday, and I never react this way."

Allen raised an accusing finger. "I'm out with friends. You know where I'm at, David. I let you know I'm going out by at least giving you a call. You haven't called anyone, have you?"

David stood silent. It was true. He hadn't called, left a message, left a note, nothing. Should he have come home and waited to discuss this situation before strutting off and making his own decisions? *No! No! No!* David thought to himself. This man was a liar, a cheat, and a fool if he thought his little guilt trip was going to work. Maybe he should thank God that those suitcases were packed. It saved him the trouble of doing it himself. With that thought, he headed for the luggage.

"What do you think you're doing?" Allen asked, sitting up in his chair.

"Well, since you've done such a fine job packing, I think maybe it's a good time for me to take a little vacation...at least till you're sober." But when David tried to lift the suitcases, he found them empty. "What is this ...?"

"Oh, so you were going to leave me?" Allen asked, attempting to rise from his seat. He held onto the armrest as he balanced himself. His other hand held the drink.

David turned around. This stuff is empty. What kind of game are you playing?"

"So you gonna leave me now?" Allen asked again, walking in David's direction.

"What the hell are you talking about? I was out enjoying myself, by myself," David explained, letting the empty luggage drop to the floor as he receded from Allen's advance.

"Then why didn't you call? And don't give me any of your shit," Allen said, kicking the suitcases aside as he approached.

David stood his ground. He was tired of backing away from this man, and it reminded him of a conversation he had recently had with

Jesse. It flashed through his mind like a subliminal message...

They had been in the coffee shop, and Malcolm had gotten up to get another cup of coffee. Jesse was a lean, tall, dark-skinned brother, like a pipe with arms. He was also a queen that spoke her mind.

Jesse had asked, "So, how long has Allen had been beating you?" David had been visibly shocked. "What?"

"Listen, David, I know what's going on with you and that man's man. I have been there, but all of us ain't that tough."

Jesse had explained that he was in the same type of relationship, but he had no way out. His man's man was wealthy, and Jesse had become used to the carefree lifestyle.

"Honey, for each slap he makes to my face, I slap his credit card just as hard."

David began to wonder just how many shopping trips Jesse took in one week's time.

"Some of us can take it, David, and some of us are trapped in it. Which are you?"

"Trapped," David had whispered.

He thought about his prison as he looked at Allen, his warden.

"I was at Micky's. I was relaxing, just like you were doing before I came in," David said.

"Micky's! The white bar? Who the fuck did you meet there?"

"Meet? You're not listening. Why don't you talk to me when you're less drunk?" David suggested as he began to walk back to the bedroom, brushing against Allen. He had gone only a few feet when Allen suddenly struck him in the head with his fist. The pain was immediate. His eyes flashed and he became flush, on the brim of fainting. He fell to his knees, and reached for the back of his head. His hair was wet, dampness ran along his neck. He brought his fingers to his face, noticing the blood, but it was the smell of brandy that concerned him most.

"That's for letting someone else fuck that hole of mine!" Allen yelled.

David looked up, his vision seeming to double for a minute. Allen was holding a cracked drinking glass in his hand...the one he had been struck with. David rose to his feet, his head swimming and aching as if every vein was pulsating on the outer edges of his skull. "I'm getting the fuck out of here," he said, staggering to his feet.

Allen dropped the glass, grabbed David by the shoulder, and spun him around. "Get the fuck in that bedroom, David!"

David shook loose from Allen's grip. "What?" David shouted through gritted teeth.

Allen pushed him in the face. David stumbled back into the dining room. Another push and he was in the hallway. Another push to his chest and he was closer to the bedroom. "Tell me the truth, David. Where were you tonight?" Allen demanded. "Who did you fuck?"

David braced his feet. "Fuck that! The question is who are you fuckin'? I called your job today, and you were nowhere to be found. Where were you?"

Allen remained silent for a moment, visibly thinking. "I told you that Suzanne doesn't like personal calls at my job. She was busy, and probably didn't notice me on the floor," his voice was much lower now.

"Suzanne wasn't there, asshole! Was she the one covering up for you all this time?" David asked, holding the back of his head.

"Suzanne wasn't there?" Allen whispered to himself.

"And they said you were out sick today," David said, stepping up to Allen, looking into his eyes with deliberate movements. "You don't look sick to me. Not sick at all."

"Are you spying on me now? Is that it? Is that how you spend your day?" Allen asked.

"It's better than sitting here waiting for your lying ass to come home. And by the way, how was lunch with your new boyfriend at the French Market? Did you enjoy suckin' that dick for dessert?"

Allen slapped him. David could feel his entire neck pop. His whole body traveled with the blow, knocking him into the china cabinet, rattling the plates inside. He stood there, leaning against the glass, trying to catch his breath.

"So the fuck what? That faggot Damien must have told you something. I should've kicked his ass when I saw him at the Study, for sticking his nose in my shit."

"You mutha'fucker!" David shouted, and with one instinctive movement, he punched Allen in the face. Allen stumbled back, and in that instant David ran toward the bedroom, closing the door and grappling with the lock. He was too late, as Allen pushed the door into him, and he fell on the bed.

"You little bitch!" Allen said, holding the side of his face.

David could see that Allen was fully aroused. He stood over David, eyes enraged, and tugged at his belt. With a simple twist, he pulled the thick leather from around his waist. He held it midair.

"What the hell do you think—" was all David could utter before the first lashing rained down upon him. He could not believe what was happening. Allen was striking him with his leather belt. The strokes were wide and broad, the air hissing as the strap sliced through the air to smartly land on David's arm, neck, thigh, and hack. Not since his father took a belt to him had he been beaten like this. Like a child!

David could feel his whole body start to ache. This man was insane. He was an insane monster. David crawled back toward the baseboard of the bed like a cornered canine.

Allen stopped long enough to pull his pants down, exposing his erect sex. David breathed heavily, wondering when he would wake from this nightmare. Allen crawled on the bed, his fists clenched, his brow heavy with sweat, his eyes dark, hazy. Allen seized David's ankles, pulling him closer, spreading him across the bed, like an angry bear clawing at its prey. In that instant, Allen was a man no longer. He was a stranger. David reached back and grabbed the alarm clock that sat on the nightstand, pulled the plug from its socket, and slammed its hard edges directly into Allen's left temple.

"Dammit! Goddammit, you bastard!!" Allen yelled, releasing David's feet and righting himself so that he kneeled over David.

David thrust his foot out, kicking Allen dead center into his stomach. "You're not hitting me anymore!" he screamed, as another kick connected with this madman's groin.

David rolled from the bed, bolted to his feet, then charged from the bedroom. Allen's curses followed him, until they seemed right upon him.

"You don't hit me, faggot!" Allen shouted.

Allen was on his heels. David started to feel more liquid run along his neck; he knew it was his own blood this time. David looked at this charging bull, afraid, but instead of running...he took the bull head-on, rushed toward Allen, arms spinning like pinwheels, fingers spread like eagle claws. He pulled the flesh from Allen's lips, the hardness of his teeth bruising David's fingers. Allen regained his momentum, and took on a boxing stance, lowering himself clear of David's next few attacks as he punched him in the ribs. David could hear his rib cage give way to a pain like nothing he had ever before experienced. Another drunken swing carried Allen, and he stumbled over the coffee table. David decided to run for the door, leaping over Allen's disheveled body, hands reaching out to grip the door latch, struggling to unhook it. It unlatched, and the cool air saturated his face, the sounds of the night met his ears, he began to run toward the car...but was too late. Something gripped his shoulder, a hand, and he was pulled back into the house. Moonlight instantly became room lights, and he could hear the door slamming shut once more, his prison reborn. He was caught in a whirlwind of fists. More swinging, more pain, more flashes of light streaked across his eyes until all began to fade and melded into one dark abyss.

– V –

Men are dogs! Damien concluded. *All they want to do is get in the cookie jar, spread a little cream around, and come back when they get hungry again.*

Damien flipped the clean bedspread in the air, watching it fall back like some enormous feather. Sean Dillister had departed less than half an hour ago, but the scent of his sweat and Axis cologne remained as a testimonial of his recent presence. For months he had been after that man, and as he talked to him that night in the Study (the night of that awful confrontation with Allen), he seemed so together, so refined, so fucking hot. He should have seen the signs of impending doom when he offered his pager number as a way of contacting him. Pager? Whatever happened to a cell, voice mail, a landline, e-mail, a fuckin' PDA?

Whatever happened to the art of conversation? Whatever happened to the act of foreplay? Whatever happened to a little dinner and dancing? What ever happened to romance? The gay lifestyle was so full of men who just wanted a quick nut, a minute orgasm, a thrilla-in-my-vanilla. It had gotten so tired of late.

Damien knew how Sean's mentality was centered when he had stated, "That's a fine ass you have, *Darren.*"

"That's *Damien,* baby," he had replied heatedly. He knew Sean had been drinking a little before he came over, and so he blamed his selective amnesia on the hops and barley blowing past his teeth.

"Yeah, that's what I said, dude," Sean had lied as he sat on the sofa; legs spread wide, hand rubbing his inner thigh. "So wha'zup, *Damien,* you wanna slide over here and give me a kiss? You lookin' mighty tight in those jeans, seriously."

Damien had rolled his eyes toward the ceiling. It wasn't even midnight, and his Cinderella was turning into a pumpkin already. "Hey, why don't I gets you something to drink instead?" Damien had offered, heading for the kitchen.

"All right, that's cool," Sean had said, unbuttoning his shirt. "You don't mind me getting a little comfortable, do you?"

Damien had waved his hands. "Of course not. Make yourself at home."

That was a statement he regretted as soon as he stepped from the kitchen with two lemonades in his hand to see Sean sitting in his boxers. Damien had almost fainted as he looked down to see what he could only describe as two burnt dinner rolls hugging a billy club. He had timidly handed Sean his glass. Sean took a long drink.

"Hey, there's only lemonade in here!" he had shouted, appalled.

"It's to go with what you already drank earlier," Damien had said, and he took a sip. Part of him was regretting this meeting, and another part could not keep his eyes off this fine-assed dark-skinned man sitting before him. He could feel a wave of heat generate from the tips of his toes to the follicles of his hair. The man was flawless. Huge arms and round chest, stocky nipples like two chocolate Kisses pressed into his skin. He wanted to reach into his stomach and pull out a can of Coors. There was a soft mat of hair near his navel that led a trail to his pubic area, very hot and very tasty looking. Damien suddenly looked at his glass and realized he had downed the whole thing.

"Damn!" Sean's grin was very mischievous. "You sho' know how to work that mouth, Damien."

Seconds later, Sean was carrying Damien to the bedroom. Sean had tossed him on the bed, then fell atop him, his sex aroused, its hardness pressing into Damien's stomach. Sean whipped out a condom from thin air like a magician. After that, it was all over, and Damien was thrown into yet another mindless, emotionless, pounding sexual escapade. He had hit notes Mariah Carey would envy.

Then the end came, and came, and came again. Sean had dressed so fast when he was spent of stamina that his wind current alone was enough to dry the sweat from both their bodies. No kiss, no hug, no nothing, except a wink and a smile.

Damien hadn't been surprised. It is what the single life sometimes entailed. Minor trysts to pull the edge of loneliness away for the time being, and still the craving would return, the wanting, the needing, and always the desire lasted longer than the act itself.

As Damien thought about it, there had been a lot of men on the roster of filling his donut hole, but Krispy Kreme they were not...

...Joseph Hilliard: an older, rather stately man who wore a peace sign on a chain around his neck like an heirloom from a lost era. A dark brother who stood well over six feet three inches, and a body that was very easy on the eyes. He was very regal in his appearance. He was always biting on the end of some fancy pipe, but never seemed to light the damned thing. Just striking a pose, giving you face, putting on airs. He gave you all man with his powerful hands and his menacing stare. He had a deep voice and wonderful diction that flowed colorfully, like syrup, from thick lips: "I hate to seem forward, but you are beautiful beyond reproach, and I would love to wake up to you in the morning. All I ask for right now is a simple kiss to start the interlude off in the right direction." Damien loved that shit.

Damien had taken him home. This brother with the football build, large legs, and tall regal stature, had changed from whale to tuna the instant the doors closed. His wrist seemed broken in so many places that Damien thought to find some masking tape to hold it together and keep it from flailing so much. How he turned from top looking to bottom behaving, Damien was never able to understand. He fucked the brother out of anger, pissed that he was not on the receiving end of this bed; that fool had been stalking him ever since.

Then there was Allicanni Jimbodi, a thin brother, with soft brown eyes, pool-sized dimples, and caramel-colored skin that came on sweet as he talked to Damien at a book reading in Santa Monica Boulevard's Different Light Bookstore. His look was casual, his conversation held no hidden innuendoes of sex. They enjoyed a movie one evening at Hollywood's Mann's Chinese, and he treated. So when the dinner invitation followed days later, Damien accepted, excited to finally see how this new potential lived and cooked.

When Damien arrived that next day, however, that so-called innocent brother had turned totally gangsta on him. He came to the door in sagging, oversized jeans that hung on only half his ass as if by magnetism, a plaid shirt unbuttoned to the center of his small tight chest, a thick gold chain around his neck with a pendant of a reefer plant swinging at its center. Snoop Doggy Dogg's "Murder Was the Case" blared from the house, which was filled with the scent of smoke, sweat, dust, and incense. "Wha'zup, killa? I see you set to chillin' wit' me and ma boyz," Allicanni had said as he led him into the house. Boyz? Damien had mused as he walked in and noticed others in the room. Two other guys were there, dressed in their oversized regalia, leaning back on the tattered sofa like a pair of corpses. The huge forty-six inch television displayed a PlayStation game on pause. On the coffee table below, Damien had recognized the white powdery substance scattered on its surface as cocaine. "I thought we'd have a little private party, ya know," Allicanni had said, grabbing Damien's butt with a forceful upsweep n' grope. Damien was not stupid; he didn't know whether to be angry as hell or start a support group. He had come over for dinner, and an orgy was the only meal Allicanni was cooking up.

Damien didn't remember how he had fled that place, but thoughts of bullets hailing after him, or being gang raped, or simply trapped in that house and having to look at the horrid color scheme of the place, were enough to get him out, back to his car, and speeding away.

Then came Carlos Rodriguez, a fine Puerto Rican with bald head, big teeth, and a simple Mickey Mouse tattoo on his chest. Damien thought he could relate to this one. Wrong! The first few weeks were fine until he discovered the fool was married with children—five, to be exact. It began to explain their weekday only meetings, his refusal to display outward affection, his emergency cell calls from his sick grandmother, and the food coupons that filled his glove compartment. He had just wanted to have a little fun and fool around a bit...but he wasn't gay. DL that day meant Dumbass Latino. Damien left him in his twisted world.

And Jeremy Rothchild: a cute white boy with long dark hair, blue eyes, smooth facial features, and wonderful teeth. He was also a Rick James super freak, with enough sexual gadgets to satisfy himself, by himself, until he was well into his seventies. He had an array of dildoes in numerous sizes and colors, blow-up dolls in both sexes, a drawer filled with poppers, fuck beads, butt plugs, jellies and jams, handcuffs, leather straps, and tons of marijuana. The only problem was there were no condoms in sight, except those he had blown up and hung from his bedpost. He said those plastic things stopped his fun, and that Damien could go to the store to get some if he insisted upon them. Damien had been going to that store for six months now.

But so goes the single life in this crazy world. It was heaven for the nymphs and hell for the committed. The Internet wasn't making things any better with the ability to find men at a moment's notice. The world was like a big fucked up house, and all he was looking for was one good roommate to share it with.

As Damien brushed his hands across the bedsheet, pressing out the wrinkles, the doorbell rang. It was most likely someone else to add to the diary of dead weights that have been in his life. He opened the door.

It was a street vagrant. *They're getting kinda bold if they're going door to door these days,* Damien thought. The gentleman was small, hair disheveled; clothes mangy and unkempt, face bruised with scars and dried blood that remained caked to his forehead and beneath his nose. He wore no shoes. His breathing was heavy, as if he'd run the three flights of stairs at a sprint. Damien looked into this man's tired eyes. *Why did I open my door to a perfect stranger,* he thought; it wasn't the safest thing to do in the City of Angels.

Then he looked into those eyes again. He looked at the clothes, which didn't appear that old at all, and then he looked at the size, coming back to the eyes.

This was no stranger.

This was David!

David wrapped his arms slowly around Damien. Nothing was said as they stood in the doorway, David's tiny body shaking uncontrollably. The sound of soft whimpers, hushed cries, soon followed. In that moment Damien realized why he didn't have the need for a permanent man in his life. He had friends that needed him more.

Chapter 9

— I —

Stephen pushed the sheets down and away from his nude body. The morning sun pierced through the vertical blinds, informing him that it was going to be a warm day today. His stomach twisted in angry knots of hunger, and aromas filled him with the thoughts of bacon, eggs, coffee, and biscuits. Then came a voice out of the recesses of his mind, saying, "Breakfast will be ready in a minute, sleepyhead." He thought that had to be a dream too, until he looked in the doorway to see Jamal standing there in nothing but a pair of boxers and a Los Angeles Olympics T-shirt.

Stephen propped himself on his elbows. "It's nine in the morning, and you're cooking breakfast? You're supposed to be my guest."

"Someone had to put that fabulous kitchen to use," Jamal replied, shaking water from his hands. "And we both know it isn't going to be you."

"I only seem to cook popcorn in there."

"I could tell," Jamal said. "And what are you doing in this house without grits in the cabinet? Imagine a black man's house, and no grits. I am not used to waking up to an apartment not my own to put groceries in the refrigerator."

"You didn't have to go through all that, Jamal."

"After that limo ride, you're lucky I didn't buy the whole damn store."

"I sho' does wants to thank ya, then, for all dis here hospitality," Stephen joked, blowing an air kiss Jamal's way.

Jamal caught it, and placed it on his cheek. "Why, thank you. Now you just rest your little head while I finish making these home fries," he said, and then walked back to the kitchen.

Damn, Stephen thought, and fell back on the bed so hard that he bounced a few times before settling among the down-filled pillows. He replayed last night in his head over and over again. The two of them were watching *Sunset Boulevard,* separated by a huge bowl of popcorn, and a pitcher of Hawaiian Punch spiked with 7Up. As the movie was coming to a close, Stephen had decided to broach a subject that was nagging at his thoughts.

"Are you dating anyone these days, Jamal?" Stephen asked, placing the empty popcorn bowl on the floor.

Jamal had looked at him strangely. "You mean besides you?" "Yeah, I guess so," Stephen said with a grin.

Jamal smiled. "Are you trying to ask me to go steady, Stephen?" Stephen let out a laugh at the statement. "Yeah, I guess I am."

"I would love to," Jamal said, leaning over to kiss Stephen on the lips.

"So this makes you my man, huh? Which means I should expect a little breakfast tomorrow as well?"

"Only if you promise to make the dessert," Jamal countered.

That night Stephen became the chef of the bedroom—turning dials, raising the heat, checking the oven time and time again.

He had never felt a need to commit to a man, but this had felt like a natural progression for them. He had had similar feelings for Felicia once upon a time, but this time he didn't feel as if a part of him was living a lie. He realized that this was happiness, and he was beginning to like it.

"Okay," Jamal said, coming into the room. "Breakfast is now served."

Stephen hopped out of bed like a child on the first day at camp. *Yeah, I could get used to this happiness thing,* he thought.

– II –

Stephen finished his delicious breakfast by gliding his biscuit across his plate to soak up every remaining granule. He had been treated to a king's feast of grits, bacon, home fries, buttermilk biscuits and gravy, scrambled eggs with cheese, and a fruit dish, and they had washed it all down with some fresh squeezed orange juice.

"That was exceptional," Stephen commented.

Jamal chewed casually on a piece of bacon as he replied, "Good God Look at the way you wolfed that down. I knew you had some country genes in you."

"The country gene, and the tennis gene, and the skating gene are all there cohabitating and commingling. Do you ice skate, Jamal?" Stephen asked, finishing his orange juice, as he stood to gather the dishes.

Jamal held out a stern hand. "I'm handling dish detail, so sit your narrow butt back down in that chair."

"But it's the least I could do after that spread," Stephen replied.

"Like hell. Why don't you go check your blinking answering machine for messages while I get busy in my kitchen," Jamal said, snatching Stephen's plate away from him. "You might as well tell those past whores there is a new man in town."

"Now when did this become your kitchen?"

"When that first orgasm hit the sheets. I don't give out jelly babies like that to just anyone," Jamal said, carrying the plates to the kitchen.

Stephen walked to his bedroom, his feet feeling light, and his heart skipping beats. The digital display on his answering machine flashed "*10*" in bright orange.

The first few messages were from his parents wondering if he were still alive or had been abducted by aliens. They were hoping for the latter; they loved drama. A few others were friends wondering what he would be doing on Memorial Day. It was only a few days away, and his straight friends in DC wanted to hang out at the annual Black Lesbian and Gay Pride celebration. They knew his preferred lifestyle and saw no problem with it, and liked the cheap drinks and flirting with the lesbians. But most likely, he and Damien would be attending the Black Gay Pride in Malibu. DC would be too much temptation right now - depending on how he and Jamal's relationship developed.

The last three messages were urgent ones from Damien, asking that his calls be returned immediately. One of the last messages was only an hour ago: "Stephen! Pick up the damn line, baby. I got David over here, and the shit done hit the fan blades."

Stephen quickly dialed Damien's number. So quickly, in fact, that he didn't realize he had pressed the numbers until he heard Damien's voice.

"Hola!" came Damien's frantic tone.

"Yeah, baby, it's me. What's going on over there? I got your messages."

"Stephen! Boy, where you been? Caught up in no good, no doubt." "Never mind that. What's happening with David?"

"Girl, he had a fight with Allen, and he looks bad."

"Allen and him had a fight? Is it serious? Is he gonna go back home?"

"Oh no, baby. I'm not lettin' him go back over there again. This been goin' on a little too long for—"

"Too long! What are you talking about, Damien? This has happened before? What's David got himself into with this man, and why didn't he tell anyone anything?"

"Honey, they like Ike and Tina in that house," Damien said. "Well, I'll be right over after I tell Jamal where I'm going and I get some clothes on."

"Jamal? Clothes? I guess I can see why you not answering phones these days," Damien quipped.

"Don't even go there."

"Not when you already have. Now get dressed."

— III —

"So tell me what you think about the dress," Gerri said.

Cyan leaned back against the ottoman, folding her arms across her chest. She looked at the black Giorgio Armani open-backed evening dress, studded along the waist with rubies. It was stunning. It was great for dancing, as well as cocktails, and its rayon/Lycra material shimmering in the overhead lights made it appear even more glamorous.

Cyan didn't like it one bit.

"Why did you buy that outfit, Gerri?" she asked suspiciously.

Gerri thrust her hand on her hip, then stomped her foot on the soft carpet, ruining the intended effect. "Now that wasn't the question, Cyan. I want your fashion opinion."

"I don't know if I should answer on the grounds that it might incriminate me," Cyan replied.

Gerri flung the dress on the bed, irritated, then sat down beside it. She carefully crossed her legs in her silk nightgown and stared intently at her best friend. "All right, my little china doll. Why—"

"Don't call me that, Gerri. You're just mad because I can see right through you," stated Cyan. "Just like that nightgown you're wearing."

"Oh yeah, I forgot you happen to be a psychiatrist. Can't fool you, can I?"

Cyan shook her head with a smile. "No. I'm afraid not, my dear."

Gerri sighed. "Goodness, girl, what is your problem? You act like your American Express Gold card was revoked. Is it a crime to purchase a new outfit?"

"I want to know why you bought that dress in the first place, and don't tell me because it was calling your name from across a crowded boutique."

Gerri sucked on her teeth. "Humph," she voiced, and then reached under the bed to bring out a long gray box. "Well, if you can't find it in your conscience to help me with that six-thousand-dollar dress, then maybe I can get your opinion on these fabulous Manolo sandals I got in New York." Gerri brought out the shoes, holding them out for Cyan to inspect. She then walked over to where Cyan was sitting and placed the shoes in her lap.

Cyan looked at the dark satin footwear, then at Gerri. Hopelessly, she picked them up at arm's length, shaking her head in judgment. She gently placed them on the floor. "Nope. You must answer my question. Just yesterday you tell me you had this weird dream that Sarafina was going to come back in your life, and then today you're showing me a dress and shoes. What's going on with you?"

"Oh, so now dreams are a sign of psychosis?" asked Gerri, strutting back to the bed and plunging upon it face first. "Now you're calling me crazy," she said, her whining voice muffled in the sheets.

"What would you call a woman that buys an outfit based on the signs of a dream? You are not Nostradamus, my love. Hell, you're not even Dionne Warwick! So save the shit for the bull, because I know you better than that."

"You are the bitch today, aren't you?"

Cyan ignored Gerri's retort. "And what's this about a party you're throwing? I'm your best friend and I haven't received my RSVP for this little Memorial Day bash. I thought you never gave parties on holidays."

Gerri turned around and sat up, alarmed. "What are you, *I Spy?* How did you hear about all that?"

"I have my sources, Miss Moore-to-Her-Than-Meets-the-Eye. I want to know what's brought on this unexpected celebration. A retired veteran you are not."

"Okay, okay, stop with the analysis already. I was thinking of having a little housewarming for Sarafina, that's all."

"Hmm. I figured that was it. I was just wondering how you plan to get her out here? I know it isn't her idea."

"She's coming to see me of course. What else? This is still her home."

"But I thought she was already home."

Gerri quickly stood. "Well, she isn't!" she fumed, and began walking toward the vanity, her body rigid. She hadn't meant to sound so angry, but she knew what was best for Sarafina, where she belonged, where her home was. Gerri yanked the top drawer out forcefully, almost pulling it from its rollers. She stood silent for a moment, calming herself, before bringing out the small ivory box. She did know what was best, she reminded herself as she lifted out a striking diamond necklace. She held the jewelry to her neck, admiring it in the mirror. "She has a home here," she said, her tone somber now. "And it's time she quit playing *Rich Man, Poor Man.*"

"Playing? This is no game, Gerri," stated Cyan.

Gerri squinted, looking at Cyan's mirror image. "Don't pull that mess with me, Cyan."

"What mess? I was only trying to explain—"

"That psycho mumbo jumbo mess. I tell you that Sarafina is coming home. Things are going to be back to normal around here, and you can't even sound happy for me."

Cyan contained her laughter. "Happy? Yeah, I'm happy for you. Happy I'm not charging you for this session, because I think you have some deep problems that need a few months on my couch."

Gerri turned her lips down in displeasure. Oh shut up! My baby is coming back to me. I know she is, because I have set the wheels in motion. I know what I'm doing."

"Aha! Now we get to it. I knew you were up to something no good. What in the world have you done, woman? I thought you couldn't even call Sarafina with her number being changed."

Gerri rolled her eyes at Cyan. "Cyan, please! I know people at the phone company," she placed the diamond necklace back in the box, then brought out a gold herringbone with a striking sapphire stone as the centerpiece. "Now what do you think of this one?" she asked, spinning on her heels, cocking her head to one side like a teenager.

Cyan ignored her. "I can't believe you sometimes. I'm surprised you didn't try and get the number through her lover's firm. I can't believe you decided to go there and have the woman do the designs on your new sales office in the first place. I think you are truly loony."

Gerri sighed heavily. She was exhausted with all this mindless chatter. "Well, Shelby's D'Zines didn't have the new number. But it doesn't matter, and I got it, so what. Now tell me what you think of these," Gerri insisted.

Cyan gave in. "Why don't you just go with some basic pearls and stop this nonsense."

"Good idea! And why don't you just stick to your patients, and quit trying to play with my head."

"Why don't you live your own life and quit trying to compete with Dominique to steal Sarafina away?" Cyan countered.

Gerri quickly snatched the necklace away from her neck in the balls of her tightly wound fist. "Steal! Steal? I think it's that Dominique whore that's doing the stealing. We were under a separation, and no sooner did Sara touch the sands of Los Angeles than that woman set her hooks into *my* woman."

Cyan remained silent. There was rage in Gerri's eyes. She was consumed with this insane passion about Sarafina. Gerri was deceiving herself.

Cyan chose her next words carefully. "You're just a slave master, Gerri. You know that."

Gerri turned around, bewilderment exhibited on her face. "What?" she questioned.

"You're a slave master, Gerri. You're trying to control Sarafina, and don't know how to love her. You used to, I think, but you've changed now. You don't care what makes your little slave happy, as long as the cotton is picked."

Gerri walked over and sat on the bed, brushing at the discarded dress that lay upon it. "I don't know what you're talking about. I don't treat Sarafina like a slave. I'm not trying to control her."

"How can you begin to tell me that you love Sarafina when you're controlling her now? She's found her happiness, her free world, and all you can do is think about bringing her back to the Big House."

"I do love her. I know what would make her happy. When she gets here everything will be all right. She's not happy out there and—"

"Bullshit!" Cyan charged. She waited for Gerri's reaction. Mild shock; that was good. "You know Sarafina's happy. You know it, and don't lie to me. I hate to see you bringing young black girls into this house, dating them, loving them, and then tossing them away, waiting for that Sarafina clone. You knew Sarafina felt uncomfortable here with all your white friends treating her like a second-class citizen. You know she left because she got tired of being the house nigger, and you are just repressing it."

Cyan watched Gerri flinch at the accusations. "You can't have Sarafina back when you get ready. You just can't do that. You can't treat people this way, Gerri. She's got feelings, and you're trying to hurt them. How can you do that? You need to put that dress away and forget this party you're supposed to be having. You have to stop trying to control lives that are not yours."

Gerri was silent. Cyan could see the wheels turning, the eyes jumping, the fingers drumming against her thighs. She was thinking. "Then what can I do, Cyan? I've changed. I want to be with her. I can show her the romantic times she wanted. I can give her the attention she said she missed. I just want to make her happy."

"But she is happy. I thought you two were friends at least and—"

"We are friends."

"Well, you sure don't act like it. I'm your friend, and I never get this much drama from you."

Gerri laughed. "Yeah, I guess you're right, Miss Kai, as always." She said nothing. She was thinking again. *Cyan is right, isn't she? What am I doing chasing after this woman? Could things really change? Could they?* "Okay, I'm convinced," Gerri said smiling. Now what do I owe you for this session?"

"Nothing. This one is on the house," Cyan said, leaning back and crossing her legs.

Gerri stood. "Good!" She reached for the dress on the bed and held it in front of her. "Now, tell me what you think of this dress. You think Sarafina will like it?"

Cyan shook her head. The woman was hopeless, and Dominique and Sarafina had better be ready for some serious trouble.

– IV –

"Thank you, sweetness," Dominique purred, as she felt the warm water slide down her bare back.

"You keep looking at me like that and this sponge will be soaking up a pool of me," Sarafina said.

Dominique leaned back. "Shut up and take care of these, will you?" she said pointing to her breasts.

Sarafina dipped the sponge in the water once again and glided it tenderly across Dominique's bare honeydews. "Is that how you want it?"

"That's it." Dominique reached out to grab Sarafina's wrist. She was still clothed, and Dominique pulled her arm. "Why don't you join me?"

"Tempting, but I don't need any excuse for being late, now that I got a job to go to," Sarafina said, gently pulling her arm back from the perimeter of the tub.

"All right, I can allow that, since you are among the working grunts these days," Dominique said, flicking water in Sarafina's direction. "So how is the bookstore business?"

"Watch the water. You know it only takes a little to make straight hair nappy." Sarafina stood patting her hair. "And the bookstore is coming along. I'm only working for my uncle, and half the time it's stocking detail."

Dominique picked up the sponge and rubbed it across her own shoulders. "It's what's expected of you dykes. I know it's not all that exciting, but it can only lead to something better."

"No shit. When you're at the bottom of the well, all you can do is look up." Then she paused, afraid to breach her next question. "So have we been getting any more strange phone calls?"

Dominique nodded. Yes, the phone calls had been continuing. Which she found odd, considering their new number was only three days old. "I don't know what's going on. Nothing comes up on caller ID, and I know I put a block on unrevealed numbers."

Sarafina began to head for the door. "Listen, I have to get out of here. We've got some sort of book signing going on today, so I'll call you later, all right?"

"Sure. I'll be downtown this morning looking at a shipment of drapes I ordered, and then I'll be back here. Call me this afternoon."

"Not a problem," Sarafina said, waving, as she headed out the door.

Dominique looked at the closed door. She smiled. Things were beginning to return to a state of normalcy.

The phone rang.

As soon as she brought the receiver to her ear, the other party disconnected. She slammed the receiver back on its cradle. Something was wrong. She decided that the only way to put an end to this was to call the phone company, in hopes that they could offer a solution.

"Phone Company," answered the dry voice.

"Yes, this is Dominique Devaroe."

"Is everything okay, Miss Devaroe?"

"Well, no. I seem to be receiving these crank calls, someone just called me and hung up, and this has been going on for quite some time now."

"Crank calls? Are they insulting or obscene in nature? Has your life been threatened by any of them?"

"No, not really," Dominique said, feeling this was perhaps a waste of time. "It has just become very disruptive to my everyday routine, and this is a new number, so I just don't understand," Dominique explained.

"Really?" the young lady said, as if she hadn't heard a word Dominique uttered. "Well, I'll tell you what I can do. I can try and see just where they are originating, or perhaps the geographical area of the call. This is not usually done without a police order, but I will see what information I can provide to you, at least about this last call."

It would sure help me sleep a little easier. Thanks."

"Not a problem. Hold on for just a moment," she informed, and the line went silent. She returned rather quickly. "Okay, we have some good news and some bad news. The bad news is that the number isn't in the Los Angeles area, so I can't pinpoint an exact telephone prefix of the area. The good news is that I do have a general location, and it seems to be coming from San Francisco, or very close to it."

Dominique could feel a cold knife plunging into her back. "San Francisco? Are you sure about that?"

"Yes, I am quite sure. Does that help you?"

Dominique didn't know what to say. Her mind was already far removed from the phone conversation. "Yeah, yeah, thanks," she said, then slowly placed the phone on its receiver.

It had to be Gerri calling, Dominique thought, *but how?* The number was brand new. Sarafina had promised not to give the number to her. Had she gone back on that?

The doorbell rang.

Looking through the peephole she could see that it was a young man in a delivery uniform holding a small envelope. "Yes, may I help you?" Dominique said.

The young black man smiled. "I have a package for a Miss Sarafina Chandler. Is she here?"

Dominique closed her robe more tightly, and then slowly opened the door, securing the chain. "No, but she does live here. I can sign for it if you'd like," offered Dominique, her eyes on the parcel.

"That would be fine," replied the fellow, as he brought out an electronic signing device. "You can sign right here," he said, his finger indicating the glass screen on his apparatus.

Dominique reached for the plastic pen affixed to the tablet, wrote her signature, and retrieved the envelope.

She sat beside Bootie, who was on the arm of the couch, and gradually caressed the feline's fur. "This is happening again, Bootie," she said, looking solemnly at the cat. "You think there's another newspaper in here? Why not, huh? This is total dëja vu. Maybe I should strike up a joint to make the day a complete hallucination." She looked at the return address: a P.O. Box number in San Francisco. Why wasn't she surprised? That city had become the unwelcome mistress. She would not be able to wait for the excuses Sarafina would concoct in trying to explain this one.

She peeled back the flap on the envelope and peered inside. There were two objects inside: an airline ticket and a note. She read the note first:

Dear Sarafina:

    I hope this gets to you in time. I have been trying to call you at home, but that other woman keeps picking up the line. I know you're at home today, so you should be receiving this. I asked that you be the only one to sign for it. This is the ticket to San Francisco that I promised you. Monday is Memorial Day and I will be having a grand party in honor of you coming back home. Don't worry about bringing anything. We can always send for your belongings, or I could just buy you all new things for your new beginning.

    Can't wait to see you again.

Love Gerri, xoxoXOxo

Dominique felt a buzzing in her chest, as if mosquitoes were attacking her from within. Her lip trembled; eyes began to tear up with a welling rage. She nervously began wringing her hands, staring out into nothingness, and suddenly realized she was absentmindedly ripping up the note. Just when she thought things were coming together, the glue was melting. How could she have been so stupid? How could she have trusted so blindly?

How could she have allowed so much to transpire? Friends. Such a lie that was.

The phone rang again.

"Gerri, you have got some fuckin' nerve calling here and—" she began yelling before the receiver reached her lips.

"Whoa! Whoa! Dominique, whassup, baby?"

"Damien? Is that you? I'm sorry," Dominique's voice returned to a more tranquil tone. "What's happening?"

Damien took a deep breath before answering. "Honey, it's about. David. He and Allen were in the boxing ring yesterday. It's not a pretty sight. He is all frazzled and I think he's gonna need some sisterly and brotherly love."

"He and Allen had a fight? Damn, how did that happen? David's no match for that behemoth."

"It's a long story, but it boils down to Allen having this thing for violence, and David has this thing about being his punching bag. He's looking pretty bad now."

"Don't worry. I'll be right over," explained Dominique. "I just need to pack a few bags."

"Bags? Where you goin'? Taking a vacation or something?"

"You could say that. It's a long story. Listen, I'll see you later, okay?"

"Yeah, babe, see you soon," said Damien, as he hung up the phone.

Dominique slowly placed the phone back on the receiver and looked around the apartment. She turned on the answering machine, and sat quietly as a wave of exhaustion flushed over her at what she would have to do. She knew she couldn't sleep here tonight...or any other night, for that matter.

– V –

"I don't want to discuss it anymore, Stephen," David said, throwing his hands in the air and walking over to the loveseat. His face winced in pain with every movement.

"I told you he's acting stubborn," replied Damien, tossing his arms in the air.

Stephen waved his hand aside dismissively. "Well, I don't care." He walked over to sit beside David. "So what are you going to do, David?" Stephen asked, looking at the floor.

"I don't know. I don't know—all right?" David roared.

"You're moving out of there, that's what!" Stephen said, turning to look intensely at David. "And quit acting like you frustrated with us here. You should have been frustrated a long time ago dealing with that asshole."

David shook his aching head. He didn't have time to think about his own situation with Damien calling in the cavalry so soon. There was so much to think about, so many decisions to make, so many questions to ask, so much confusion. This was all happening too fast.

"Sweetheart, Stephen's right. You are moving out of that prison as soon as possible. Do I have to grind some beans 'fore you smell the coffee?" Damien said.

"It ain't that easy, *sweetheart,*" David said stubbornly.

"The hell *it* ain't," Stephen said, turning to look at Damien. "How long you say this has been going on?"

Damien looked to the ceiling, lifting his fingers one by one. "Well, let me see ..."

"What'cha askin' him for when I'm right here?" David shouted.

Stephen looked sharply at David. `Because you weren't the first one to tell me, so why should you now? Look at you," Stephen began, raising his hand. "Your eye is fuckin' swollen, your jaw is red and puffy, and if I can see red on your black ass, then I know it's bad, and you walking around with that strained look on your face like someone pushed your face into an oven. I'm your best friend, David. You and I have been friends since Chicago. I don't understand why you think you would have to go through any of this alone. We are friends, David, or have you forgotten what that means?"

Stephen's right, David thought. He was a mess, looking like a mess, caused by a mess of a man. David felt weak from Stephen's stare, seeing questions behind those eyes and answers he could not give. He turned his attention toward Damien. "Could you bring me some of that fruit punch you got in there, Damien?" he asked, his shoulders dropping, his will deflated.

"Girlfriend, I think you could use something a lot stronger than some damn juice. You sure you don't want something with the word *proof* on the label?"

"No, baby. That will be all for now.

"Well, you could bring *me* some of that vodka, if you don't mind," Stephen shouted after Damien.

"So how are you and Jamal doing?" His fingers ran nervously across the back of his head, over the wound left by the impact of the whiskey glass.

"Don't do that, David," Stephen said.

"Do what?"

"Don't change the subject. You didn't tell me anything about the shit you and Allen were going through. He could've had you laid up in a hospital someplace, or in jail for murder. When a relationship starts to get physical these are the things that follow. And here I am thinking that all is roses and sunshine between you two."

"I don't know why I didn't say anything, Stephen. I don't know why all this happened, or how it happened."

"You can't possibly believe that, David," Stephen said through gritted teeth. "You don't let a grown man beat on you.

You are not at home with your father anymore. You can't allow those times to be relived through this man."

Stephen the compromiser, Mr. Rational, David thought. Dominique would have told him to get a gun and blow the bastard's head off. Damien would tell him he was better off single, and to get out there and enjoy. He felt badly for keeping so much from them all... and he was afraid of the responses they would have when more of his secrets rose.

"I don't know why I didn't say anything about Allen. Things happen so slowly that you lose control of a situation before you're aware of it," David explained.

"But I'm here to help."

"You've got your own problems, Stephen. You're right, I am a grown man, and I thought I could handle my own problems independently. Besides, you've also got a new man in your life. Then there is your son, and also Felicia. Hell! Who am I to add to the soap opera?"

"What does that have to—"

David held up his hand. "And besides, I still love Allen. Shit, I said it, and don't look at me that way either. I'm not able to cut off my emotions in twenty-four hours. I gave that man as much love as I could. I didn't want to believe all that happened. It's hard to think about moving out when all I want to do is make things right." He paused. "I still love him."

Stephen wrapped his arm around David's shoulder. "I know you still love him, David." Stephen didn't know what to do about this; David still loved that monster who was going to eat him alive. My *Man Was a Teenage Werewolf* could be the title of this little play.

"Why, David? Why?" Stephen found himself whispering.

"Because he's all I got. All I got."

"Don't think that, David, because there are—"

"What are you two girls hugged up for?" Damien asked, walking into the room with two glasses. He handed one to Stephen, and the other to David.

Stephen caught the drink's pungent aroma. "Mighty strong, Damien." He sipped at it. "Mmm, but mighty tasty,"

"I know what you lush children like." He turned to David. "And how you like your punch, baby?"

"Kinda sweet, girl. You put the whole bag of sugar in it?" David asked, smiling.

"Naw, I jus' stuck my finger in it and swirled it around." "Oh, so it's imitation sugar?" David laughed.

"Be glad I didn't stick my dick in there."

David leaned back and rolled his eyes toward the ceiling. "Well, at least it would have gotten wet before the year was out."

Damien put his hands on his hips. "Be nice to your mother!" David waved his hand. "Well, stop giving me images of your piece.

I got enough ugliness to deal with."

Damien was about to reply, but the doorbell rang. You must have the angels on your side today, bitch. I was about to let you have it," he said, walking toward the door.

"Where is my baby?" Dominique said, charging through the door, and throwing her jacket and bag at Damien.

"Honey, this ain't the valet," Damien said, picking up her discarded items.

"Oh, quiet," Dominique said, walking over to the couch, wedging herself between David and Stephen.

"Woman—and I use the term loosely—what's your problem?" Stephen asked, as he was forced to the edge of the loveseat while Dominique grounded her hips between them.

Dominique pointed to an empty seat. "Boy, why don't you take that drink over there, 'cause you are not going to fall on me."

"I'm not getting drunk yet, girl," Stephen said, standing up from the couch.

Dominique looked at him, eyes upturned. "Can anyone say Aunt Kizzy's? We never know your drink tolerance."

"Evil one, begone!" Stephen said, dipping a finger in his drink, and flicking it at Dominique.

Dominique pushed him. "You lucky I love you and that this outfit is from Ross." She inched closer to David, and addressed him. "And how are you doing, David? I heard what's been going on. Is this what he did?" she asked, reaching out to touch his bruised eye.

David grabbed her hand before she could touch the tender skin around his pupils. "Yeah, yeah. I guess you heard it from the Puerto Rican CNN report."

Damien went to retrieve another chair, makin room for Stephen. "If you would have listened to me in the first place I wouldn't have to bring in the reinforcements."

"Well, screw that. When are we leaving?" Dominique asked. "Leaving?" asked Stephen.

"Leaving to go over to Allen's house. All these men—and I use the term loosely—in this place, and no one has kicked any butt yet? What's the problem?"

"We are not about to drag ourselves out to that man's place and cause another scene," responded Stephen.

Dominique slapped her hand against the arm of the sofa. "Men! Nothing but a bunch of sissies. I thought I had the only pussy in this room."

"Girl, cut the drama. Fuck Allen. He not worth getting my manicure all dirty. David jus' needs to move on," Damien said.

"Shit! He can do that after we string Allen's nuts up," Dominique said, her fists balled in anger.

All the men covered their crotches.

David clapped his hands. "Now wait a minute! You guys act like I'm not sitting here and listening to this crap. I haven't told anyone what I plan to do."

"Then speak up, honey," Damien said.

David stood. "Well, I haven't decided. I need to make my own decision in my own time."

"You are not a child," Dominique said. "He has no right to hit you." She stood to her feet, towering over David, and reached out to touch his shoulder. He winced at the pain. "This is what I'm talking about. Not even a child deserves that."

David spoke harshly. "Everything is all right between me and Harvey ... I mean Allen. Shit! Why don't you guys just go home, okay? Just get out of here while I think," David said, rushing past Dominique and into Damien's spare bedroom.

The roam was silent. Dominique turned to Damien. "What's going on here, Damien? Who is Harvey?"

"I don't know who that is," Damien said.

"I know," Stephen said. "It's his father."

– VI –

David was resting on the queen-sized bed in the guest room, enjoying the silence and counting the leaves in the wallpaper trim that ran around the room near the ceiling. Stephen sat down quietly on the bed. David remained quiet.

"Do you remember when I first came out here?" Stephen asked, not expecting an answer. "I thought the palm trees were the most exciting thing I had seen. You thought I was weird for holding such a fascination with them.

"I felt this was the place for me, just like you told me, this La-La Land. I thought you had found a good place too. You had moved in with this man you were so much in love with. Allen Morrison, Allen Morrison, Allen Morrison—you said the name so much I thought you had changed your own. I also met your friends, Damien and Dominique. We've had some good times, some fantastic getaways. Do you remember Big Bear?"

David nodded his head slowly.

"None of our black asses knew how to ski, but you said that Allen had a cabin up there, and we would have a good time. Damien had been doing his husband hunting and brought a fake cast to put on his ankle just to sit up in the lodge to attract some sympathetic queen."

David began to speak. "And then we all got casts and sat down beside him, including Dominique."

"Then Damien bought that raw fish from the market, and hung it on Dominique's cast, 'You got to use fish to catch fish, honey,' was what he said. He just had me laughing up a storm," Stephen recalled.

They both laughed, and David sat up. "Yeah, those were the good times. Dominique had just met Sarafina then, her Queen Latifah, as she called her then. She'd brought out the adventurer in Dominique. I remember the time we went to gay night at Disneyland and they dressed as a female Laurel and Hardy, with socks stuffed in their pants like they had hard-ons, with spandex tops showing off their tits."

"Oh God, how embarrassed I was. I thought they would kick us out of there. There was Tijuana, Oakland, and Las Vegas, all of us just living life and having fun. It was mostly just us four, taking a getaway from life, from the drama, from the fever that everyone was putting on us. Even that trip to San Diego and Black's Beach was a getaway for me to escape Felicia's phone calls. I was telling Damien that after two years of separation she still wants to change me," Stephen said, with an exhausting sigh.

"Hey, she still loves yo' fine ass. It's hard to let love go sometimes," David explained.

Stephen let the silence stand for a moment, then asked, "Why don't you tell me about it then, David? I thought you had met your soul mate with Allen. What happened?"

David closed his eyes and turned away in shame. "There's just too much to go into right now, Stephen. All I can say is that I've been through the dating mill, and I always come out burned. Allen treated me with respect, and I never felt beneath him. I never felt too short with him, even though he is six-two and I'm five-eight. I never felt too dark, after all the comments I've heard about my chocolate skin complexion. I never felt like I wasn't wanted. I felt that way with you when I first met you and introduced you to the manager at Happy Chicken. I hoped that you would be hired, and I didn't even know you were family. You had that girlfriend, but I just thought you were a good guy. It's hard to meet people that treat you right and not have ulterior motives. There are just too many sissies out there that want to either fuck you or your man and don't give a damn how you feel."

"But you can do so much better than Allen, David. You have to let go before you can find something new. Allen doesn't deserve your love, and you're giving it to him like an act of forgiveness for something you did. He's fucked around on you. He has used your love, and you don't do that to someone you're supposed to be respecting. He doesn't love you, so why should you love him?" Stephen challenged. He reached out to grab David's fingers, massaging them as he spoke. "My Little Sammy Davis Jr. I used to call you that sometimes. I never meant to hurt your feelings by saying that, you know."

"Yeah, I know. I only let you call me that. I didn't take offense at it."

"Then I hope you don't take offense by me saying that your father is dead, David. Allen is not a replacement for him."

David pulled his hand away and gazed at Stephen, baffled. "What's that supposed to mean?"

"That means I know what was going on with your father before he died. I know he was a drunk, and I know he hurt you. I know that you wanted a bond with your father, and that you hated him—not for what he did to you, but because he was not a father. You hoped that if he beat you then he wouldn't have enough energy to hit your mother. You hated him for what he did to her, but never to you. You think that if you could prove Allen loves you, then your father had to love you too. Your father was Harvey Attiks, and he is dead and gone. You can't get his love anymore, David, if you ever had it in the first place. Allen is another man, and he is taking over where your father left off."

"Stephen, you don't know what you're talking about. Allen is not my father and—"

"Well, you could have fooled me. He's a drunk, he's a philanderer, he hits you. Why don't you tell me who this sounds like?"

"From the smell on your breath, it could be you!"

Stephen lowered his head and laughed. "I drink, David, but I am no drunk. Maybe this man has fucked you around so much that you've forgotten who your friends are," Stephen said, stood, and began to walk to the door. "Maybe you don't need any help, David. I'm sorry that I bothered to care."

"No, Stephen," David said. "I'm sorry. The man I have spent five years loving has suddenly become a cheat and now my heart is bruised as well as my body. And to tell you the truth, I can deal with the body part...dammit!" David brushed at his eyes. "Damn tears keep falling. I feel like a woman sometimes with all this water coming out of my face."

Stephen walked back toward the bed. "Well, let me get those for you," Stephen said, bending down to press at David's tears with the pad of his thumb. "Okay, so you don't want to break up with that man right now. Maybe you need time to think. I think you should stay here with Damien for a while longer. We talked, and he said it would be fine, but you have to make that decision."

David nodded. His smile was all the answer Stephen needed. "You're a good friend, Stephen."

"You're not making it any easier," Stephen said, smiling.

Just then the door eased open, and in came Damien. "Okay, babies, we have another emergency trip to take. Andrew is in the hospital and it doesn't look good."

Tragedy again, David thought in disbelief.

"David is good to go, Dominique has her bags, I don't need much, so it looks as if we are off to San Diego again, any time you choose."

Chapter 10

— I —

The smell was clean. Alcohol-soaked rooms, a crispness to the air, as if it were filtered of all germs. The linoleum floors shot back the reflection of the overhead lights without mar and allowed the soft sound of passing shoes as a resident glided smoothly across the unstained surfaces. There was a quietness too that remained unnerving for people used to the chaos viewed on any television hospital drama. Perhaps this was the norm for San Diego Memorial Hospital.

Perhaps it was the sound that death makes. This was the AIDS ward, and to bear witness to such solitude seemed unnatural. There were the hospital sounds of chatting orderlies, and the intercom churning out a barrage of code blue this, or code yellow that. It looked like they were all waiting in their white-on-white gowns, flashing their pseudo-grins most of the time. It worried Damien as he traveled through the halls. It appeared as if everyone was waiting for that shriek or that cry of pain. It seemed everyone was waiting for death.

Andrew was sitting up in bed, three pillows propped in the small of his back, watching some rerun of *The Beverly Hillbillies* with the sound much too low to hear what was being said. Damien could see that a lot had happened in the two weeks since he'd last seen Andrew. The disease was winning the upper hand on his dear friend. His dark skin was pale and ashy; his eyes were sunken and gave the appearance of him being on the losing end of some boxing match. His long wavy hair, a gift from his father's Belizean genes, was thin and wispy on his round head. The bed-sheets fell across his bony frame as if he were composed of nothing more than broom handles. He smiled when Damien, Dominique, and David walked in. At least he still had a great set of teeth, and it redeemed him.

"Yes, girls, it's me," Andrew whispered as he sipped juice through a straw. "No offense, Dominique."

Dominique stood to one side of Darien. "None taken, baby girl."

"So, what'cha in for now, sweet thang?" Darien asked, as he approached, planting a kiss on Andrew's forehead. The feel was very hot.

Andrew settled back on his pillows and turned his eyes toward the television. "Well, what isn't the problem, sista girl? My MAC has been acting tip on me. I was having some serious night sweats and of course can't hold down any food," he explained, facing Darien again.

"MAC? You mean a Big Mac is the cause of all this?" Darien asked, tapping Andrew's stomach. "It must have been all that special sauce."

"I think that's a blood disease. You can get it from pigeon droppings or something like that. It fucks with your white blood count," David spoke, tone serious.

"Hey cutie-pie. Glad you could tear yourself away from that man of yours. Did he release you, or did you have to gnaw your leg off?" Andrew asked, holding his hand out.

David reached for it, that gesture slowly transforming into a hug. "Don't start, heifer."

Andrew pushed David back at arm's length. "And what's up with the black eye, honey? I said you have to take it in the mouth, and not in the face."

David gave a nervous laugh, and the others did the same. He then receded to the back of the room. "That's a long story. We'll talk later."

Dominique walked to the opposite side of the bed, admiring the cornucopia of flowers in vases arranged on his nightstand. "These are beautiful azaleas, Andrew. Who sent these?" she asked, bending forward to smell the soft petals.

Andrew shifted painfully to face Dominique. "Oh, that's from my mother, Martha, and of course the other arrangement is from Momma C. Your mother is always there for me, Damien. I love the orchids she picked."

"They sure do make this room smell fantastic," said Dominique, as she surveyed the room. Lining the edge of the room were other small bouquets: lilies, carnations, and a few spider plants. "You sure have a lot of good friends."

"I guess so," Andrew said, taking another sip from his juice container, the sound loud and forced as if it were hard to draw breath. "Some are from my support group, and one is from my acupuncture therapist. He's a cute brother with hands of gold and skin like Godiva."

"You mean Go, *Diva,* don't you?" joked David.

"Yes, baby, 'cause that's what I yell every time he touches me; Go, Diva! Go, Diva! Go!" He then eased forward and tried to reach the pillows behind him. "Help me a little, Damien darling."

Damien reached behind his friend, feeling something obstructing the path. He pulled out a teddy bear with a rose affixed to its chest. At that same moment the door to his room opened, and in came a huge arrangement of roses and carnations as high as the door frame. From behind them came a familiar voice: "So who is the fairest of them all?"

Andrew clapped his hands and answered, "I am, goddamit, and don't you forget it, because if I weren't in this bed ..."

"But you *are* in the bed, Blanche. You are in the bed," repeated Stephen, as he peeped from behind the floral bouquet and grinned at Andrew. He arranged them on the small dresser near the bathroom.

"Hey, Stephen, thank you. It looks so good," Andrew said.

"It's from all of us. I just pulled the short straw to go pick them up and drag them up here. How are you feeling, boy?" Stephen asked, walking over to hold Andrew under the chin, and kiss him lightly on the lips.

"Hey, Pain is my middle name, but Morphine is my first. You lookin' good though. I hear you been finally gettin' some. That should clear your face right up. You'll be good and pregnant soon enough, and I'll be an uncle."

"Don't start spreading rumors," Stephen warned, shaking an accusing finger at Andrew. "There's no bun in this oven."

"I am sure it depends on the size of the bun."

Stephen reached back to hold his butt. "Unlike you, this bun shop is closed for business," Stephen retorted.

"Hmm, probably closed for renovations," Damien said. "Oh, and now I am getting double-teamed."

"Well, girl, you know how you like to make it a double," Andrew said, smiling.

Dominique broke in. "Will you two stop this silliness? There are just too many X chromosomes in here. Andrew was about to tell us the deal on this bear."

Andrew nodded, suddenly closed his eyes, then erupted in a violent coughing spasm that shook the whole bed. Damien poured him a glass of water.

"Dick phlegm from last week still in there, huh?" Damien asked, handing Andrew the glass.

"That's right," Andrew said with a wink. After drinking, he placed the glass on the nightstand and slumped back on his pillows. "Child! Bitch is tired today, but about the bear.

"The sixth graders from the Catholic school across the street were all visiting patients on this ward and they all gave away teddy bears they had bought. A cute boy named Timothy Reynolds gave me mine. I would have loved to meet his father. That kid's gonna be fierce when he comes of age. But anyway, Timothy gave me the bear. He said the bear would be my friend when I was hurting and that I would have someone to talk to when I was by myself. The rose on its chest represented a rose garden these students were growing. Each rose represented the patient it would be named after," he finished.

"Ah, honey, I'm getting all misty," Damien said, fanning at his eyes.

Dominique reached across the bed to nudge Damien's shoulder. "Oh cut that out, Damien. I think it's sweet. What did you name him, Andrew?"

"Cock Ring," Andrew said, placing the bear's ear in his mouth. "What?" Dominique stated, stepping back.

Andrew smiled. "Just kidding girl, damn! Mention a cock ring, and the fish gets scared, while my other sisters drool over here. But seriously, I named him Kisan: it means longevity.

"And he looks so much like you," Stephen said, reaching out to pull on the bear's ear. "So, who's the father, Yogi or Smokey?"

Andrew stuck his tongue out. "Bitch!"

Stephen laughed. "So where are the playing cards?"

"I thought you would never ask," Andrew replied, reaching for the call button. "I'll have the nurse bring some in. She borrowed my naked-man set this morning."

Suddenly everyone heard a steady beeping in the room. It was Dominique's pager.

"It looks like Dyke checkup time to me," Andrew said.

Dominique looked at the number. "Oh well, it's the little woman." She saw Stephen about to respond, and she held up a fist. "And don't you go there, Stephen."

Stephen held up his hands. "I didn't say a word," he confessed, "But she ain't little." She and gave him the finger. "You need to be saving that middle finger for her."

"Yeah, someday you might actually tell a joke...and be funny at the same time. But I'll be back, gang," she said as she rushed from the room. She had finally thought of a conclusion to this Sarafina and Gerri fiasco moments ago...and it was time to end it.

Sarafina waited impatiently by the phone, drumming her fingers on the end of the coffee table. She had arrived home from work to find an apartment filled with disaster: CDs were scattered on the floor, two phone books lay spread on the couch with pages torn or ripped out and tossed about, Post-it notes were among the pieces of paper with numbers of hotels and motels written down then scratched out. The bedroom hadn't fared any better, with drawers pulled open and clothes hanging over the edges. Clothes were also piled on the bed and the floor. The phone had been off the hook, with the receiver cord tangled around the nightstand lamp for some reason. In the kitchen, Bootie's litter box was filled with a heap of freshener, and her bowl was topped mountain high with dry cat food; the tiny pebbles were falling off like a miniature avalanche. It didn't take long to see that Dominique had been pissed.

Then there was the discovery of the Federal Express package under the table with a San Francisco return address. Sarafina saw that it had been opened. Then she had the shock of seeing the plane ticket inside. She knew Dominique had seen this, and it worried her. She tried to call Gerri and get an explanation to all this, but was only met by her voice mail, and the office secretary kept putting her on hold or saying that her employer was in a meeting, out of the office, not taking any calls at the moment, or had to attend to an emergency. Sarafina could not believe it; in as little as six hours her world had been torn asunder.

"Hey Sarafina, what's up?" Dominique replied, her voice steadfast, and very genial.

Sarafina was slightly caught off guard by her friendly timbre, still she was cautious. "Nothing much. I thought you were off today, and when I didn't see you here, I thought I would give you a call."

"I said I had to go to The Design Center today."

"Yeah, I know, but I thought that was early this morning, so I thought you'd be home when I got off work."

"You obviously see I am not there," Dominique answered, a hint of sarcasm in her voice.

Sarafina took a deep breath to keep from responding in a defensive manner. "So, where are you, then? Still at the design center?"

There was a slight pause, and then Dominique answered, "No. I happen to be in San Diego."

She had replied so quickly, so matter-of-factly, that Sarafina was reluctant to question her further. But she did. "Why? What's up there?"

"Just here with the gang, that's all. David, Stephen, Damien, you know, just hangin' out with the fellas. Damien got a call this morning. Andrew is in the hospital," Dominique explained.

"Andrew? Is everything all right with him?"

Dominique gave a slight laugh, very sarcastic, very condescending. "My God, Sarafina. The boy is sick, of course everything is *not* all right. What did you think? He has a bad case of pneumonia, not to mention stomach pains. His mother said they were doing a blood culture to see what was wrong. So no, he is not all right." Dominique sighed, paused, and rethought her statement. "You know...I'm sorry about that. It's been a hard day, that's all."

Sarafina waited until the unexplained chill left her, then replied, "I understand. So I guess you'll be home a little late this evening. Or are you staying there for the night?"

More silence.

"Sarafina...I'm not coming home tonight, or tomorrow."

The chill returned. "Well, if Andrew is that bad off maybe it would be better for you guys to stay for a few days. I'm sure his pain must be hard to deal with."

"He's on a morphine drip, so he'll probably be out in another hour or so. I'm sure pain is the furthest thing from his mind. Besides, my not coming home tonight has nothing to do with Andrew. I'm not coming home for a while, Sarafina."

"What?" Sarafina questioned.

"You shouldn't act surprised. You know I saw that package you received, and you act like nothing's going on," Dominique said rather coolly.

Sarafina gripped the phone in her hands. "All I know is that this place is a mess, and you're all the way in San Diego without as much as a note to me, and now you're telling me that you don't plan to come home. How do you know who sent that package? I only saw it myself a few minutes ago," she replied, angrily.

"I opened it!" Dominique blared too honestly for Sarafina's taking. "I opened it and I saw the ticket. I saw the note. I even called the phone company to find out that it was her that made all those strange calls, calling then hanging up. I'm no fool, Sarafina. Do you think I'm a fool?" Dominique barked. "I just want to know how that bitch got our number. That's all I need to know right now."

"She called here?" Sarafina asked, more to herself than to her lover. She reached up to press her temples, suppressing an oncoming headache. "I don't know how she got the number, Dominique. I didn't give it to her."

And then came the suppressed laugh again. "Well, well, why aren't I surprised by that answer?"

"Shit! It's the truth. I didn't give it to her," Sarafina insisted.

"Then who did? Did Jesus himself come down in a vision to Gerri and bestow our beloved number upon her? I think not, Miss Chandler."

"Well, don't accuse me of giving it to her," Sarafina answered, her patience uncaged. "She's your boss. Maybe she got the number from your job or something."

"Errrrk—wrong answer! Shelby's doesn't have the new number. I'm having them contact me through my cell phone and pager. Think of another answer, my dear," Dominique's voice raised a few decibels.

°I don't think I have to come up with anything. I said I didn't give Gerri our number, and you sit here calling me a liar. I didn't give her the number!"

"Go tell it on the mountain, 'cause I ain't hearin' you, okay? That woman is not giving you this much attention without you giving her some back. It's just backing up in your face and you can't handle it. Why don't you just pack your bags, get that fuckin' ticket Gerri sent you, and get out of my life? I said that friendship was poison in the beginning, and I guess I have proved myself right once again," Dominique sounded off, her rage becoming uncontrollable.

"What the hell's wrong with you? You know I'm not interested in Gerri anymore. Are you trying to make up a reason to break us up, Dominique?"

The laugh again. "Now that's a good one. It's entirely my fault now. Why don't I just put my friend on the line to talk to you? Her name's Mrs. Tone."

"Mrs. Tone? Who's that?" Sarafina questioned, her voice softened. She was listening now. Was there another woman with her?

"You know Mrs. Tone. Her first name, Dial." That's when Dominique slammed the phone down, cutting communication, and all Sarafina heard was the dial tone blazing back to her.

She slammed her end of the phone down so hard that the table lamp shook, and she could hear Bootie in the kitchen also being startled, the scamper of her little paws ticking across the tile on the kitchen floor and the sound of kibble rolling behind her. All she could do was picture Gerri in her mind, and an inferno erupted in her thoughts that could not be quenched. She stared at the phone as if her gaze would cause it to ring, to cause Dominique to come to her senses, to put her life back in order. But she knew the reality. She knew Dominique, and knew that her stubbornness would never permit her to return in this state of anger. She would learn to adjust without her, accept this lie that Gerri had set up, and forgiveness would be an island never discovered.

Sarafina reached for the ticket. It was dated for Monday, Memorial Day. *This has to end,* she thought. Gerri was going to have to be taught a lesson on respecting relationships. Sarafina wasn't angry at Gerri for loving her, just angry at where that love was guiding her. They had agreed on a separation with the hope of getting back together. Gerri was still waiting for her to return from Los Angeles. Instead, new love had come into the picture, catching everyone off guard.

Sarafina tossed the ticket back on the table, stood to her feet, and walked toward the stereo. She loosely kicked the spill of dispersed CDs, finding one of interest: a selection by Miles Davis, and even though she knew nothing about the artist, she placed it in the player anyway. It was nice. As Sarafina lay back on the couch, her arms behind her head, she thought about Dominique, the images pleasant... then she thought about her impending journey, the ticket waiting for her, and the sight of San Francisco looming below her from behind the small windows of an airplane. She thought about the clothes she would wear—her best attire. Gerri should see her looking her very best when she arrived. It was the least she could do for a friend who may prove foe.

– III –

Dominique made a stop in the bathroom to sit down and think before she headed back to Andrew's room. She had to calm herself, make sure the shaking had diminished. She had to convince herself that this was the right decision. There was no room in her life for a love triangle.

When she neared Andrew's room, she could see a nurse rushing through the door, and once it opened she heard a series of gut-wrenching shouts before the door closed. Fear gripped Dominique and she found herself flying across the hallway. "What's going on?" she asked frantically. The nurse didn't reply, her back toward Dominique, barring the doorway. Over the woman's shoulder Dominique could see chaos erupting within the room as a blur of shapes crossed her eyesight.

"Stephen!" she called out.

Stephen seemed to look in her direction, but was unsure of the origin of her voice. When he finally saw her, he raised his hand, just as a doctor crossed the room. "Dominique! Stay out there! Andrew's experiencing more pain and they may have to prep him for surgery. They are examining him now."

Then she heard it. First a loud deep-throated timbre, like an old man trying to clear his lungs of mucus, then a series of long exhales, and then an alarming moan of discomfort that sent chills up her spine. She leaned in a little more and could see the doctor guiding everyone toward the door, each footstep crushing the scattered playing cards on the floor. Then she was able to steal a glimpse of Andrew, his arms wrapped around his midsection, his face a twisted contortion of haggard flesh, teeth pressed together in a painful grimace so intense that she could see the fibrous muscles in his jaws. Damien was still near him, holding him up as the doctor talked to him in hurried tones. The whole room was caught in a pandemonium. All she could think was, *is this going to be the end?*

"Could everyone please clear out of here?" the tall dark-skinned doctor asked, his accent sounding very North African.

Minutes later, they all sat in the hallway, watching the door as if their stares could melt away the steel and reveal the scene behind. The screaming continued, followed by intense groans and other mysterious sounds.

"What's going to happen?" Dominique asked, arms folded across her chest.

Damien, holding a cup of coffee, paced the floor, steam from his cup followed him like broken thoughts above his head. He took a sip, "I called home, but Momma C and Martha are not there. I left messages, so maybe they got them and are on their way."

"I'm sure everything is fine. If it weren't they would have been out here to let us know," Stephen said.

'Well, if they don't hurry up, I'm gonna knock that door down and demand some answers," Dominique challenged.

"What do you think is causing so much pain? Is his digestion that bad?" Stephen asked, his question directed at anyone.

Damien shook his head. "I don't know. Might be all the medicine he takin'."

"But I thought the medicine was supposed to help," Stephen said. 'That's what everyone thinks," David added, sitting up. "I think it's killing him."

"I think it's just a ruse to make more money," Dominique said. "The drug companies make money, the doctors make money, life insurance companies make money, mortuaries make money, charity organizations, sad to say, are benefiting too, as much as helping. I just don't get it. Someone has the cure, in a lab, someplace, with a sticker on it and a date they plan to unveil it. I just know they do."

"But I hear they have this cocktail stuff now," Damien said, "And people are supposed to be living longer. This is not supposed to be happening like this anymore, where the sickness is supposed to get this bad."

"Cocktails Smocktails. No one knows how this disease really works. They dust off old drugs and call them new, call them a cocktail, combine them like a broken jigsaw puzzle, hoping to get a picture. I think it is just another form of controlled addiction, getting you to buy into this hope without a cure. I think they created the problem, whoever they are, and they will continue to keep it in check until the next thing comes along," David said.

`"But what are the alternatives these days? We all seem to be at the mercy of the physicians," Dominique asked. "Without medical degrees we depend on those who claim they have them."

David waved his hand. "Like hell we are. For Andrew, for us, there are always alternative medications, acupuncture, mental conditioning, and spirituality. These drug companies are so famous for taking natural additives and making them unnatural, making them marketable, profitable, mass-produced. It's all a twisted roulette wheel of steady cash flow, if you ask me."

David was about to comment more, when his attention was diverted by two women rushing along the corridor. Their voices echoed against the walls in a boisterous cadence. As they came closer, the group saw it was Andrew's mother, Martha, and not far behind trotted Momma C.

"What's going on with my baby in there?" Martha asked, looking tensely at the closed door to Andrew's room.

"I don't know, Mrs. Christenson," Damien said, looking at the two women, their faces filled with unanswered questions. He looked at Martha, her dark skin radiating, eyes big like a mirror. Her features so resembled Andrew's that Damien was taken aback. Martha was pulling at her blouse, perspiration gathering between her breasts. "They're looking him over. The doctor was telling me that they think he'll be fine," Damien said.

"They *think* he'll be fine? What, they don't *know* if he will be fine? My baby is in there on a *think*? *I* better be in there just in case...you know...he needs me," Martha said, her voice clogged with emotion. She pushed past Damien, heading for the door.

"Wait," Momma C said, reaching out to grasp Martha's arm. Martha turned to look at her friend, panic in her eyes. "I'll go with you, honey. You don't need to be there by yourself."

Martha's eyes seemed to soften. She looked at Damien, Stephen, Dominique, and David. She grinned. "I wants to thank all you for comin' here to see my son. He talks about nothing but you guys, and it has always made him happy...even when I couldn't do the same."

"We're just as grateful to you, for bringing him in our lives," Stephen said, and they all agreed.

"Now let's get in there, old lady," Momma C said, pulling her friend along and through Andrew's door.

Twenty minutes. Silence became their master and they slaves to it.

"I'm going to the washroom," David announced, standing.

Seconds later, as Stephen paced, he saw David leave the restroom, wipe his eyes, look around, then head in the direction of the elevators. *Something is very wrong,* he thought, as he saw his friend lean heavily against the elevator doors before continuing through them. He stood, speaking softly to Dominique, "I'm going out for a little fresh air." She nodded as he departed.

— III —

David sat on an outside bench in front of the hospital. There was a thin film of clouds circling his head from other visitors smoking around him.

"So what's going on, David?"

David looked up to see Stephen standing before him. He slid over, making room for him on the bench. "Nothin', just doing some thinking."

Stephen sat. "Nothin'? You came all the way out here to think about nothing? You could've done that upstairs."

David laughed quietly. "I guess I was thinking about Andrew and all that he must be going through."

Stephen leaned forward, clasped his hands together, and stared down at the clutter of crushed cigarette butts on the walkway.

"I'm sure he'll be fine," Stephen sighed, then stood. "Come on, let's get away from this chimney factory and take a walk around."

David agreed, and they strolled along the cement trail that traveled around the side of the hospital. The facility was filled with people milling about; from staff, to visitors, to business types – and Stephen thought it slightly eerie, for despite the foot-traffic, there was a meandering silence blanketing the area, as if the hospital forced one to deal silently with their internal pains. Stephen noticed that David too shared in this look of inward-focus, inward pain.

"This situation with Andrew makes me realize just how short life is. I forget how deeply I used to rely on God in my life, and how that created calm in my life where fear and death weren't such a constant thoughts for me," David said.

Stephen looked at David. "You know I am not a religious man, David. But we all have to believe in something higher than ourselves, which allows us to accept the unknown, without fear, because it was not created by us to figure out.'"

"But you believe in God, or at least the idea of a god, I'm sure?"

Stephen looked away. "You know I do. I just don't think I should listen to some preacher or believe in a book that condemns the life I live."

"I've always known you to believe that. You need to evolve in your thinking. You are afraid of religion, not God," explained David.

Stephen shook his head. "Can we not talk about church stuff? You know I have different views about all that."

"I understand. I'm just saying religion, or the Bible, don't try to control your life. It simply teaches guidelines to make your life better."

"And it curses the homosexual lifestyle; an existence already fraught with immense struggle. Life should be enjoyed and not bogged down in the religious trappings of human opinion."

David laughed. "Homosexuality is such a hotbed issue that I can't really listen to what a preacher tells me anymore. They use it to justify their personal prejudice. 'For all have sinned and come short of the Glory of God. Jesus never condemned, he just taught right from wrong. People put roadblocks in their own lives by allowing others to dictate the life they were given. If I buy groceries, I dictate their use; and if I return them to the store, then I turn the ownership back to them — and they will judge if I get a refund or not based on my use for the groceries. When life is over, and we return to God, He makes the decision on our existence based on how we treated the body he gave us. So I think we live, make some good choices, respect our bodies, and try to share ourselves with others — and God will work out the rest. I'm tired of wasting time with situations I can't control."

Stephen patted David on the shoulder, and shook his head. "My, my, this situation with Andrew has scared you this much?"

"Maybe it has. Situations like this make you think about a lot in your own life."

They soon found another bench to sit on, and as they did, they embraced a short moment of silence.

"Has all this deep thinking come about because of what you and Allen are going through?" Stephen finally asked.

"No. Why would you think that?" he questioned.

"Because you could do a lot better than Allen, and maybe that is where you are wasting your time."

"Believe me, my thinking is not because of Allen. He is far from my mind now, and I am in no mood to talk about him."

"Sorry, if it is upsetting, but this is something you're going to have to deal with you know."

"I'm not upset. I just think you're making a big deal about nothing."

Stephen looked at David, taking notice of the dark bruise around his eye, and the slight puffiness of his jaws. He wanted to shake

David. "Nothing? You think Allen killing you someday is not a big deal?"

"Allen is not going to kill me, Stephen. Quit exaggerating."

"You're kidding me, right? You've got a tire for an eye, a limp, pain when anyone touches you, and a balloon for a face, and you tell me that I'm exaggerating," Stephen said, slapping his knees.

"You just don't understand, Stephen," David said, holding up his hand and waving Stephen off.

Stephen held his palms over his ears. "If I have to hear that again I'll just shit right here on the spot. I think you should open your *good eye* and take a look at what's happening."

David twisted his body away from Stephen. "Oh, you become the mother superior since you got yourself a man, and you think you know it all!" David snapped.

"I didn't say I knew it all," Stephen defended.

"Well, you sure act like it. If I say I can't leave Allen, then maybe I have my reasons."

Stephen looked to the sky. "A reason to get your head knocked in, who would've thought." He then gazed intensely at David. "I guess you must like that. I guess it turns you on or something, this S&M shit."

David swiveled to face Stephen, his finger pointing sternly. "Don't go there, brother!"

"Well somebody has to, *brother*. I can't believe you haven't decided to leave that man. Do you need a fuck that bad, David?"

David pushed Stephen on the shoulder, then stood. "Fuck you, Stephen!" He walked away.

Stephen followed him, and to David's surprise Stephen shoved him from behind. It wasn't a forceful push, but it caught David off guard. "No David, fuck you! You can't seem to tell your friends from your enemies."

David spun around and punched Stephen in the shoulder. "What the hell is wrong with you today? This is my business, so keep it that way." He started to walk away from Stephen again.

Stephen shoved him in the back once again. David stumbled, then caught his balance, but before he could fully regain his equilibrium, Stephen pushed him again, and this time David fell to his knees. He looked up at Stephen and then rushed him, driving his palms into his friend's chest, causing Stephen to stumble back a few steps.

"What? You want to fight me, Stephen? Is that what you're trying to do?" David asked, holding his shoulder, his face a canvas of pain.

"Why would I want to do that? What would Allen have to do in his spare time?" Stephen pressed.

David held a tightly wound fist at his side, the tension twisted between his fingers ready to explode. He stared into Stephen's eyes as if he was a stranger—the friend he once knew was lost in a billow of rage. "Stephen, you need to just leave me alone! There are things you don't understand, and I am not about to tell you! Fuck you, fuck your curiosity, and fuck this friendship, do you hear me? Fuck this friendship!"

Before David knew what had happened, Stephen was upon him, seizing his shoulders, shaking him. "Oh, you don't like me hitting you, is that it, David? You seem to like it when Allen does it. I thought you got off on that. You can't tell Allen to fuck that relationship you two have, but you can tell me to fuck this friendship. What kind of bullshit is that? Well, I'm not hearing you. I'm not hearing you!"

"Stop it! Stop it, Stephen!" David shouted, tears welling in his eyes. He backed away from Stephen, his eyes closed, his teeth clenched, his footing unsure, as if the whole world swayed beneath him. "I can't leave Allen! I can't do it! There is no one else for me. We have to take care of each other, Stephen! Who's going to take care of me?"

"Take care? What are you talking about, David? You're a grown man! No one has to—"

"Me and Allen are HIV positive, Stephen! Do you understand?" David shouted, "It's not about a black eye, or me not loving him. It's about me finding someone that will be able to deal with that. It's about my fear of knowing it but not knowing about it. It's about my terror at seeing Andrew and thinking that someday that could be me. It's about..." his voice trailed off into silent sobs.

Stephen strode in his direction, knelt beside him. *My God!* He thought.

"I'm sorry, David," he said, and hugged his friend.

– IV –

Andrew's pain subsided. He was very drowsy and the constant painkillers didn't help. He was relieved when his mother left and his friends returned; he relished a conversation that was less taxing in his mind. His companions lived the same lifestyle as he; understood its trials, its traumas, and its never ending road that sometimes led to an uneventful path.

While the group left to talk in the hallway, David returned to Andrew's room.

"What's up, cute stuff?" David said, as he walked over to Andrew's bed, picking up his bear and rubbing it against his cheek.

"You told Stephen about your situation, didn't you?" Andrew whispered.

David almost dropped the bear.

"Don't be looking surprised, girlfriend. You two have been quiet ever since you came in the room, lookin' like you tryin' *not* to look at each other."

"Yeah, I told him," David admitted, remembering that Andrew was the first person he'd told.

"And how is that crazy thing for a man you got?"

David returned the bear, and sat on the edge of the bed, his back facing Andrew. "We're doing all right," he replied uneasily, folding his arms.

"Child, who you think you fooling? You doin' all right? By the look of your face, you been doin' a couple of lefts too."

"Yeah, I know about my face, I was there," David said, his tone hostile.

"Now don't be gettin' offended, sweetheart."

"Are you gonna tell me that I should be leaving Allen? Are you gonna tell me how much of a monster he is? Are you—?"

"Girlfriend," Andrew quickly interrupted, "Why should I have to say anything when you already said it for me?"

"Everyone thinks the right thing to do is leave. They don't understand," David said.

"Sometimes I think it is you that can't understand. What's keeping you with this man?"

David thought for a moment, and then replied, "There are a lot of good qualities in Allen that only I see."

"Girl, you need to examine a man's resume a little more closely before putting him on the payroll. He's an unreasonable man who lacks communications skills, is out of control, and is selfish. He's a wannabe man who's truly not a team player. You need to hand him his pink slip."

"But people can change, Andrew. I still love him regardless of his actions."

"Honey, of course you do. Nigga been messin' in your life for five years. But you can't tell me that you put up with this because you love him. How much of that is because you think no one will accept you because of your status?"

David didn't have to think long. "Maybe my status does have something to do with what I feel. I don't want to die alone, Andrew. Don't you feel the same sometimes? Don't you wish you had a lover by your side when you hurt your worst?"

"Oh, give me a break! At first I thought that, but let's get real, David. No amount of man is going to take away the pain I feel in this room. Just hours ago, you guys couldn't. We don't know how or when we are going to leave this world, what pain we will have, what control we will have over it all. That is the scary part. You see my pain, and you think you can feel it too. But it's not your pain. It's mine and mine alone. When your time comes, you will be the only one that shares your experience, no matter how many hands hold you, and how many tears fall. This disease is just a part of your life. It doesn't dictate it—you do."

David sighed and silently shook his head.

"Just make sure you live for you, because you'll be the only one to regret it if you don't. You're born into this world alone, and you die alone. Those are the rules.... Shit! Damn tear ducts leaking again. Pass me a tissue, bitch!" Andrew ordered jokingly.

David reached across to the table beside the bed for a box of tissues and handed it to Andrew. "Here you go, hussy."

"Tramp!" Andrew countered.

"Slut!" David retorted.

"Heterosexual!"

David clutched his chest. "Oh, now that one hurt." David fell on the bed beside Andrew. "And you know something else?"

"What's that, sweetness?" Andrew asked, cleaning his eyes.

David grabbed Andrew's hand. "Thanks."

Chapter 11

– I –

The dream was always the same.

David found himself running through a dark and murky swamp. The dampness seemed to suffocate him. The creature that pursued him was gaining ground; he could hear every twig and dead leaf it crushed underfoot. It wasn't long before he could hear the grunts and howls on his trail and smell the scent of bile over his shoulder. The echo in its throat was equal to hundreds of animals all suffering at once.

He caught a glimpse of the creature in the full moonlight: its shadow was huge, covering him like a ghostly blanket, its form mountain-like. It possessed two heads: one was Harvey Attiks, his father—the other, Allen.

He woke from his nap…his nightmare.

"You mighty quiet in there, David darlin'. I hope you still breathin'," Damien yelled from the kitchen.

David stretched his arms. "Don't worry about me, Mother Dearest."

"Hey, I am just checkin' in on you," Damien replied, his head slipping around the kitchen door.

"Is he all right in there, Damien?" Stephen asked when Damien returned to the kitchen.

"Yeah, don't worry 'bout him," Damien said, going back to rinse a large bowl of lettuce under cold water.

"I guess after hearing about his news I've been just worried about him."

"He be all right, Stephen," Damien reassured, draining the leaves and tipping the greens into a bowl.

"I wish there was something I could do," Stephen said.

Damien shrugged. "Nothing we can do besides treat him as we always have. Now why don't you get those ribs and take them to the grill. I told Dominique to invite Sarafina, and David said his new friend Malcolm is coming over."

"All right, okay," Stephen replied, picking up the pan of ribs. "A good barbecue with friends will be good medicine for us all."

Damien held the door open as Stephen walked through carrying the pan of fresh meat. Damien had planned for an evening of food, friends, and dancing. Dominique was the only one yet to confirm her arrival.

"So how you doing, sweet thang?" Damien asked, strolling over to David and sitting beside him.

'I'm doing fine—still fine since the last time you asked me."

"I jus' concerned 'bout my sista is all. Am I asking about you too much?"

David leaned forward to pluck a vegetable appetizer from the serving dish on the coffee table. "Hell yeah, which also makes me wonder if you are worrying about more than just me. What else is on your mind?" David asked, chewing on a celery stick.

Damien turned to the patio. "How's that chicken comin' along?" he called out to Stephen.

Stephen looked back, fanning a thick film of smoke away from his view. "It's looking pretty good so far. I'll get the ribs on here in a minute," he said, his head lost in the thick cloud of smoked meat. He waved his hand through the plumes.

"Good. Let me know if you needs help, sweetheart," Damien offered.

"Help!" Stephen shouted jokingly, and returned to the grill. "Girlfriend, are you trying to ignore me?" David asked, lightly pushing Damien's shoulder.

Damien turned around, "Of course not, Chocolate. Now what's on yo' mind?"

David fell back on the couch, obviously frustrated. "Come on, Damien. What's going on in *your* mind? I've known you five years, and you've never been the one lost for words. Are you nervous about the news I shared with you?" David prodded.

Damien sighed. "News? Child, that was not news. Between your news, dating hell, trouble at the salon, Dominique's domestic squabbles, my needing a good foot scrub, and of course this husband of yours gallivanting around town with his piece, bitch has enough news to start my own station."

Stephen walked in, rubbing his hands together and grinning wildly. "I think this is going to turn out pretty nice, guys," he said, face covered in ash. "Jamal would be so proud to see me cooking. I only wish he didn't have to work today."

"Cooking? Boy, those are only ribs. We haven't even got you to a stove yet to be talking about impressing someone," Damien said, with a roll of his eyes.

"Stove? Can't I just install a grill at home?"

"You are not about to be cooking that child grilled meals twenty-four-seven. Babe, the grill is your starter kit. But don't worry, Momma's gonna hold your hand all the way," Damien said.

"You are so good to me."

"Whatever. You can suck my tit after dinner, okay?"

"Also, David, when do you plan on getting some of your stuff out of that place? I got a storage room in El Segundo ready for you," Stephen said, waving a piece of chicken on a fork at him.

David looked at Stephen uncertainly, as if the thought hadn't crossed his mind until that very moment. "Oh, I don't know,

Stephen. I guess Friday would be a good day, considering Allen goes to the health club in the afternoon, and then to the Annex for a drink with his buddies."

"Well, Friday is a bit shaky for me, but I'll see if I can finish up early at the office, then we can head over there together," Stephen said.

"You don't have to trouble yourself. I'm a big kid now," David replied.

"You are not going over there by yourself."

"I don't have that much stuff over there, Stephen," David remarked.

"Then it shouldn't take us long."

There was suddenly a knock at the door. Damien rushed to answer it, while Stephen took a place on the couch. The knocking became more frantic. "Now just wait a minute!" Damien shouted. He looked through the peephole, and quickly opened the door.

Once opened, Dominique came charging into the room, her fists fluttering in the air. "That bitch!" she shouted, stomping toward the sofa.

"Girl, you bring more drama to this place than mail to my door. Now what's got your eggs bursting that you have to come in here charging like—" Damien asked, closing the door.

"She's gone! Sarafina has up and gone!"

"Damn, girlfriend, what happen?" Damien asked, grabbing a chair beside the nearby wall, and carting it over to the group.

Dominique looked at Stephen and David on the sofa, and then waved her hand. "Come on, baby. One of you has got to move. I can't stand much longer with all this frustration going to my head," she announced, flopping down between the two men, shoulder to shoulder.

"All right, Ms. Devaroe. You are gonna have to buy Damien a bigger sofa if you keep this up," Stephen said, moving to the sofa's arm. "Now what do you mean, Sarafina left you?"

"She's gone to San Francisco to be with that rich bitch she was involved with before. I thought she was just out for the evening when we came back from the hospital last night, and I'd decided to talk with her before doing anything rash, but this morning I discovered the plane ticket was gone, and then I realized some of her clothes were missing, and ... oh, fuck her!"

"I tells you, sometimes it's jus' better to be by yourself," Damien said.

"Well, I'm not shedding a tear for her, no way, no how. If she wants that millionaire Madame, then fuck them. I don't need it, and I sure don't need her."

"I'm sorry, Dominique," David sympathized, stroking Dominique's back gently.

"Yeah ... thanks. I just can't understand this, that's all. I guess this is just one of those thangs."

"And it ain't over yet, Dominique," Stephen said, scratching his head nervously.

She looked up at him curiously. "What do you mean by that?"

"I think David should be the one to tell you," Stephen said.

Dominique looked at David, and watched the expression of the rest of her friends, and her stomach did a quick turn. She knew that whatever this news was, it was certain to be one thing: not good.

– II –

It was the night of Memorial Day, and the last thing Sarafina thought she would be doing was taking a flight to San Francisco to meet with her ex, Gerri. She also didn't expect there to be a limo waiting for her at the terminal. She had forgotten how hard it was to surprise Gerri; it was like sneaking up on a bull with bells on.

There was a feeling of melancholy as the plane touched down on the runway. It had been almost two years since she'd experienced this city. She didn't realize how much she had missed it. The chauffeur guided her through the old neighborhoods and instantly she recognized the surroundings as they pulled up to Gerri's home. The sun was setting, and activity was plentiful.

Music fell softly to Sarafina's ears as the driver entered the steel gates and rounded the driveway to the front of the home. There were dozens of cars parked about, and Sarafina wondered whether she was at the correct residence. Gerri was never big on parties, and this one was grandiose. Lights were blazing in every room, and she could see many shadows moving behind the sheer curtains. The sound of laughter was meshing with that of reggae tunes floating on the air. A white woman emerged from the home, martini in hand, smile on her face. She glided down the stairs in a most stunning sequined mini dress, black high heels, and an amazing across-the-shoulder, mohair sweater. The heels never lost their gazelle-like stride, nor the martini its liquid as she trotted along the driveway. No mistaking, it was Gerri.

"Sarafina, darling!" exclaimed Gerri as she ran to the car, flinging open the door to reach for Sarafina's wrist. "I hope you had a nice flight," she said, pulling Sarafina into her open arms, squeezing her tightly; not a drop spilled from her glass.

"It was all right," Sarafina replied, her arms at her side like baseball bats on a string, she was not sure this was a celebratory event; it wasn't as if two years ago she had stepped out only to get a loaf of bread. But Gerri was treating her as if that were all she had done.

"Good," Gerri said, taking a sip from her glass. "I'm glad to hear that. Now come on in here and enjoy yourself. I just thought I would throw a little something for the holiday," she said.

Sarafina let Gerri pull her through the door, and she was stunned to see such a massive crowd.

"Sarafina," said a tall black woman, hair weaved high atop her head and huge diamonds hanging from her lobes. She had a wide grin and an even wider overbite she found no shame in brandishing to its fullest. She extended her hand, the fingers thin, the wrist covered in gold bracelets. "Gerri has told me so much about you. It is a joy to finally meet with you."

"Yeah, it's good to meet you too," Sarafina replied, unsure of who this woman might be.

These unexpected greetings continued as Gerri took her around the room—greetings where her name was already known. It was rather unnerving. The main room was festooned with pink and blue balloons, tiki torches, huge African masks hanging on the walls, a strobe light bouncing rainbow colors across the ceiling, and bamboo shoots were staged throughout the house as if she were reenacting a scene from *The Jungle Book*. A tall black woman covered in a leopard-print bikini strolled toward Sarafina carrying a tray of champagne flutes. "Would you like a refresher?" she offered.

Gerri graciously plucked one of the glasses from the tray to hand to Sarafina. "Thank you, Kittana," she replied, waving the girl off.

"When did you start throwing pussy parties?" Sarafina asked, taking a sip from her glass. The bubbles tickled her nose.

Gerri led Sarafina to a long table covered in banana leaves, flanked on either end by huge ice sculptures in a replica of Venus de Milo, chilling everything from caviar to canapés. "It's a special occasion," Gerri said, placing a cold hors d'oeuvre into her rose-colored mouth.

"Memorial Day?"

"No, silly," Gerri assured, as she swung her hand toward a far wall. "Something a little more special."

Sarafina looked up to see her name spread out on a banner, with the words WELCOME HOME emblazoned underneath. "Um, Gerri, I think we need to have a little talk."

"We'll talk later, but first I have a surprise," she announced, snapping her fingers. Within seconds another tall woman, walnut complexion, hair pulled back into a glittering ponytail, appeared in front of them, holding a filled long-stemmed champagne glass on a marble serving tray. There was a single rose lying there; around the stem of the glass, a silk red bow. The young lady offered a closer look at the glass, and to Sarafina's surprise, inside rested a cherry, pushed into the circular band of a stunning diamond ring. "It's for you, baby. I'm just so glad to finally see you back home where you belong," Gerri said, stepping forward and wrapping her arms around Sarafina in a tearful exhibit of emotion. Sarafina stood, frozen, the knot in her throat nearly choking her.

—III—

David stormed into the apartment, slamming the door so hard he could hear the bolts rattle. "Fuck!" he yelled across the room. "I knew I should've stayed here, but nooo, I had to drag my ass to the Catch One. Shit!"

Malcolm walked in next. He opened the door cautiously, standing at the doorway observing David. "Are you okay, David?"

David continued to talk, oblivious of Malcolm. "And look at me. My face is still swollen; I can feel it. I'm sure everyone was laughing at me. Especially that damn Allen! I look like hell warmed over. I must've been a damn fool to have agreed to go out to that crowded-assed club!"

"Would you calm down?" Malcolm said, walking into the living room and gently closing the door behind him. "No one could see anything. You look fine."

"That man is gonna drive me crazy long before thoughts of this disease will!"

"What was that?"

At that moment David realized Malcolm was in the room and he was speaking aloud. "Could you get me a glass of lemonade from the fridge, Malcolm? I made it fresh this morning."

"Sure, and you sit down and take it easy. I'm really sorry about the evening," Malcolm expressed, as he walked to the kitchen.

David fell on the couch, pounding his fists into the pillows. "It's not your fault," Malcolm offered. David's mind was reeling. Why did he have to go out tonight? The club was much too crowded; the wait in line was two hours. Two hours! For a price of ten dollars! This wasn't fuckin' New York, where that price got you greater atmosphere and a last call that began at six o'clock in the morning. The Catch closed when the drinks were finally starting to hit you. There was no room to dance, to talk, to breathe; taking a fuckin' piss was a major trek. Then to see Allen there hugged up with some man. Allen saw him and just rolled his eyes. That bastard! If not for Malcolm offering to drive, David would have walked the ten miles it took to get back to Damien's place.

"Here you go," Malcolm said, returning with two glasses.

"Thanks, Malcolm. I'm sorry about my attitude, but I knew I shouldn't have gone to that club in the first place," David concluded, propping his feet on the glass coffee table.

"Well, who knew your ex would be there?"

"Shit, I should've known something. It's Memorial Day. Every queen in the nation is trying to find a kingdom and catch a king. I bet Allen is crowning somebody in our bed right now," David said, gulping down a mouthful of liquid.

"If someone else is in there, then it wasn't your bed from the beginning. You should've stayed home from the start."

"Home? You mean here? My name isn't on the door. My name isn't on *any* door. I had what I thought was home taken from me," David said, leaning back on the sofa.

Malcolm placed a warm hand on David's shoulder. "It's only four walls and a ceiling, David. Your friends will make sure you get another. I'm here for you too if you're in need."

David smiled. "Thanks for that, Malcolm."

"A relationship is work, David. Allen just doesn't want to work on it as hard as you, and you can't be the only one clocking in overtime. It wears you down."

"It would be nice to meet someone on the same level, express a level of emotion that didn't coincide with a thread count."

"Most men are territorial, always trying to run shit. Allen is like many of them, trying to show he is better than others. He is territorial, and you are emotional. He goes to the gym, you go to the kitchen. He expresses strength, you express creativity. He spends so much time proving he is a man, he forgets he has a dick in his mouth half the time."

That quip made David laugh. "So many men are like that, as I saw at the club tonight. I wonder if there are any men out there that actually care about the man they are with instead of the man they are in."

Malcolm began to rub the back of David's neck. "They're out there, believe me. You never know…one could be sitting right under your nose."

Then there was a moment of silence, as David felt Malcolm's icy fingers began to soothe his neck. He turned to look at Malcolm, and saw something deep in his eyes—something he had not seen before.

Malcolm's lips parted, and he was about to speak when suddenly the door opened, and Damien and Stephen walked into the room.

"Honey, what kinda' fever you givin' tonight?" Damien said as he walked toward the couch, hands waving in the air.

"Leaving the club like that. I didn't figure it out until I saw Allen there." Damien stood above the two and noticed Malcolm's hand retreating from David's neck. "What's going on here?"

David looked at Malcolm then back at Damien. "Nothing. . . I just had to get out of there, Damien," he said, purposefully ignoring the true question of Damien's curiosity.

"You know I would've left with you, David," Stephen added, stepping toward the sofa.

"It was too packed in there to gather up the posse."

Dominique walked into the room now and headed toward the sofa. She grabbed David's hands. "Honey, that asshole! I say fuck him and the air he breathes." She plopped down on the sofa between David and Malcolm.

David inched back. "Girl, you gonna get enough of squeezing those big hips on this couch."

"Keep those claws retracted," Dominique spoke. "I'll give you two a little room. I was just concerned about my little brother, that's all."

Malcolm attempted to stand. "That's all right, Dominique. I need to be leaving anyway. I have to be up early to take care of some errands. It was nice meeting all of you."

Damien helped Malcolm to his feet. "It was good meeting you too. I want to thank you for driving my sista home, 'cause she ain't above walkin' if she don't have a ride."

"Oh, it was no problem. David is someone worth helping," Malcolm replied, his eyes moving toward David.

"Well, thanks Malcolm," David replied. "I'll speak with you later." "Sure," he answered, walking toward the door.

Damien closed the door behind him. He turned to look at David. "Okay, what the hell went on here? And I don't want to hear you say it was nothing."

– III –

Sarafina rose from the bed very drowsy. She rubbed her eyes and lips; her mouth felt pasty, dry. She looked around and could tell that she was in Gerri's room.

If only she knew how she got there.

Hearing a noise, she looked toward the door, and could see Gerri slowly closing it. "What happened?" Sarafina asked, her voice strained, as if out of breath.

Gerri turned, Sarafina's voice seeming to startle her. "Oh, you're up. I thought you had blacked out as I carried you up the stairs. How are you feeling, Sara?"

It had been a long time since Gerri had called her by that name, Sara. What was she talking about, blacked out? Had she drank that many glasses of wine? It had to have been only three or four.

"Excuse me? Blacked out?"

"I think you may have had a few too many. You were never able to handle more than four glasses of wine. But six, Sara? I think even you need to watch your liquor as you get older."

Six! Sarafina let her head fall back on the pillow; she could still hear the calypso music being played downstairs. How did she get caught up in this? This was supposed to be a simple, quick meeting. She sat up and looked around the room. "Where are my bags?"

Don't worry about those things," Gerri reassured, standing over Sarafina. She placed a hand on Sarafina's thigh.

Sarafina pulled her leg back. "What's going on here?" she asked, staring at Gerri's hand.

Gerri folded her arms. "Well, I simply thought I would bring you up here so you could rest. With the way you were looking downstairs, I had hoped you would be just a little more grateful. Maybe I made a mistake by offering you my bed."

Sarafina needed to think. Gerri had been very congenial since her arrival, and somehow this situation didn't seem right.

"I'm sorry, Gerri. I just can't think straight right now. Maybe I can think with a clear head in the morning," Sarafina said, her head suddenly throbbing.

"That would be the best thing for you," Gerri replied, heading toward the closet. "Why don't you put on something a little more respectable for the bedroom? I don't exactly cotton to having khakis on my bed as sleepwear," she said, pulling a piece of clothing from the closet.

Sarafina could feel silk hit her face like a cool cloud brushing across her nose. "You want me to change into this?" she asked, holding up the light garment.

"What else? Now get up," Gerri said, motioning beside Sarafina, pulling her up to a sitting posture. "I will not have you falling asleep in those clothes. Now get this blouse off," Gerri suggested, reaching for the buttons on Sarafina's shirt.

"I can undress myself," Sarafina said, pushing Gerri's hands away.

Gerri slapped them back, and Sarafina felt too weak to resist. "I know you can, baby, but I'm not getting any younger, and you're taking too long."

Sleepily, Sarafina responded, "You know I'm still with Dominique."

The grip on her blouse suddenly became tighter, and there was an expression on Gerri's face of pure rage. Then quickly, it was gone. "Sure, I know that, but she's in Los Angeles and you're here."

"I came here to…I can't think right now," Sarafina said, holding her head, and resting back against the pillow again.

Gerri placed a finger on Sarafina's mouth, as she pulled her arm free from one of the sleeves. Sarafina allowed it, suddenly feeling powerless. Her need to sleep was overwhelming. "We both know why you're here, Sara. Don't we?" Gerri cooed into her ear.

"But I have to discuss the things you sent to Dominique and the—"

"Shhhhh! None of that matters now. You're home. Dominique has no hold on you any longer. You never belonged to her anyway. You never belonged to her touch. Not like you belong to this one," Gerri said, as she ran her smooth nails across Sarafina's belly, resting one finger in her navel.

"Gerri, stop this," Sarafina demanded weakly. The muscles in her face felt like soft dough. Her body lay limp, and she lost the will to move, to push Gerri away, to run. There was a comforting breeze that eagerly hit her crotch, and she could sense her knees rising. She knew what was happening—or was she dreaming? In this dream her pants were sliding from her hips, and a pair of hands ran along the seam of her panties, pulling at the tough hairs that trailed to her womanhood. She found herself getting wet, her nipples hard within her bra, her libido becoming aroused . . . and her conscious mind falling into a shadow of darkness.

Then she remembered something that had happened when she was downstairs with a drink in her hand. She'd asked for water and some aspirin. She could feel a headache surfacing. Gerri had obliged and handed her a glass. She had dropped two tiny aspirins into the water and stirred it with her finger. Sarafina remarked on how small the pills looked. How fast they dissolved. How eager Gerri was for her to take them...how handy they had been. "Drink," she had commanded, like some scene from *Alice in Wonderland.* And so she drank.

But the headache had remained.

"What are you thinking about?" Gerri asked, unhooking Sarafina's bra and pushing it aside from her breasts, kissing her dark areolas.

"Nothing," she replied, her eyes gazing off. She wasn't here right now. She was still at that party. Even as she felt her panties being pulled from her ankles and something small and wet probe her inner thigh, resting within her muff, for a second-a split second before her world went blank—she thought it felt rather nice.

Chapter 12

— I —

David pulled into the driveway, shut off the engine, and waited for his nerves to settle. He hadn't been to this house in almost a week, but it felt like a lifetime. He only needed a few things. He would rush into the house, fill his small suitcase, and rush out. It was Friday afternoon, and with any luck at all, he would not run into Allen. He was either at work, with his boy-bitch, or at the gym.

Inside, David was stunned to see the house in utter disarray: unwashed clothes scattered about the living room, newspapers stuffed between the cushions of the sofa, dirty plates stacked under the coffee table, crushed cigarettes laying haphazardly on the television. *When did he start that habit again?* David wondered. He began to pull the discarded sections of newspaper from the seams of the sofa and stack them on the table, when suddenly he stopped himself. This wasn't his mess to clean up.

His old habits would be hard to break.

He walked toward the bedroom, thinking about what possessions he would need. He would map out his plan, get his items, and stop at the bathroom for a few toiletries. As he reached the bedroom door, he could hear something to his right, where the bathroom door stood closed. He listened again. Nothing. It was only his nerves. With a quick push, he opened the bedroom door and stared in shock at what lay there.

A naked form exposed; dark in color, lean in form, skin smooth, reflective, its position flat, resting on its stomach. A small flap of the bed sheet lay lightly across its slender legs. Then it spoke: "Allen, why don't you give me a back rub real quick-like. You got me aching after last night." David said nothing. "You mighty quiet. Did you hear me?" asked the young man, as he turned his head across the large pillows, his bright eyes began to question before the whites of them revealed themselves fully. He let out a short scream before David could duck back into the hallway, closing the door.

He fell back against the opposite door that led to the guest room. His breath came out heavy, lungs tight. He angrily stomped his foot against the floor.

The door to the bathroom suddenly opened. Allen stepped out, wearing nothing more than a terry towel wrapped across his waist. "What's with the noise around—" he stared at David. "David! What're you doing here?"

Too shocked for words, David began to head for the front door, his legs moving of their own will. This situation was feeling unreal.

"What's he doing here?" said the faint sound of the stranger's voice; an angry voice.

"Quiet, Percy! Go back in the bedroom for a minute," Allen said, his voice crass, ugly. Why hadn't David ever noticed that before?

David tried pulling the door open, but it was a struggle. He pulled again, and again, sweat running down his forehead. A cold yet familiar hand gripped his arm. "Get away from me," he demanded.

"Damn! Can't you wait a minute?" Allen questioned, placing his palm on the door.

"Move your hand from the door, okay? I need to get out of here. I never should've come. I thought you would be at work."

"I was. They let me go home early today," Allen explained. "Now, what are you doing here? I thought you had moved in with your sissy friend."

"I needed a few things, but I'll come back when you're less busy."

"Come on, David. I'm glad you're here. I want to talk to you. Don't you think it's time that we talked?" Allen said, placing a hand on David's shoulder.

David jerked his shoulder back. "I don't think so. I don't think we have anything to talk about. Now move so I can leave."

Allen yanked his hand down. "Well fine! Since you're here, why don't you just get your things and go back to your life with Lucy."

"Won't your boyfriend object?"

"My boy—? That's not my boyfriend. Besides, your clothes aren't in there. I put them in the guest room."

"What?" David mumbled. He couldn't believe what he'd just heard. In one week he had been moved out and exchanged for some tall black bitch with a hairy ass. One week. "Got my replacement already, huh? You sure do move fast."

Allen turned away from David, adjusting the towel on his waist. "Whatever, David. You came to get your things, so I suggest that's what you do. I don't want you walking into any more surprises."

"I guess not," David uttered, marching past Allen, picking up his pace. He flung open the door to guest bedroom, stepped in, and slammed it back. He looked around the small room. All his belongings were stacked neatly against the far wall. His CD collection, computer desk, photo albums, books, two table lamps, stacks of clothes, and other personal items. David stared absently at his possessions. He told Damien that he could do this alone, that he had to do it alone, that he was strong enough....and was assured that no one would be home. He was wrong. This pain went deeper than he ever imagined.

"So, when you coming back?" came a filtered voice on the air.

David turned to see Allen easing into the room, and swiftly brushed away the angry tears at his cheeks. Allen had changed into a sweat shirt and pants, his hair was combed back into a wave of curly ribbons; their moistness coursed a trail down his neck "What did you say?" David asked.

"When are you coming back?"

"How can you ask me something like that when your boyfriend is sleeping in the next room?"

"He's not my boyfriend," Allen repeated.

David rolled his eyes to the ceiling, "Who the fuck cares what label you use? Fuck buddy, one-nighter, trade, piece, whatever! He's in your bed, and I'm not, and I think I like it that way." David turned back around and started to open the small suitcase he brought. *Have to get some underwear first,* he began thinking, ignoring Allen's presence.

"I want you back, David. I miss you. I love you."

David closed his eyes. His lungs felt tight again. "Why don't you go back in there and be with your new man, Allen. I have things to—"

"Fuck Percy! I love *you,* David. What did you expect me to do after you ran out of here, abstain? I have *needs* just like the next man."

David spun around, fists clenched. "What the hell is that supposed to mean? For one, I ran to save my own neck, and your *needs*…you've been fulfilling those needs on the cadaver of my flesh. I have some needs too, and one of them right now is to get the hell out of here, ASAP," he said, throwing clothes randomly into his bag from the selection on the floor. Then suddenly Allen's hand was on his shoulder – and while the touch was light – David flinched all the same.

"Listen, David. I know what I've done, but part of me had no choice. I've been scared. Ever since we both got the news about our health, I've been scared. I've been scared of dying, and I've been scared of losing you."

What!? Two years, and now he chooses to express the fear about this diagnosis. Two years of acting like some damn Macho-Muthafucka! Two years, and he had been as scared as David often was. David's walls were breaking – he could not even turn around to face this man, this coward, this...victim.

Allen continued. "Sometimes I want to forget about the pills that I am taking, about the disease that I have, about the time allotted to me. Being without you scares me. So I flirt a little, I drink more than usual; I have a man in our bed right now. It's crazy, I know, but it reminds me that I'm still alive. I'm sorry that I've hurt you, and maybe deep down I'm just an angry man putting all the blame on you. Maybe that's how I feel deep inside, because I would never intentionally hurt you. I love you too much for that." Allen fell unexpectantly silent, his hand slipping from David's trembling shoulder.

David, unmoved, continued to stare out the window before him. He looked beyond the curtains towards the tops of the telephone poles that lined the aqua sky above. Pigeons perched along the telephone lines, their brigade broken by a single discarded sock that swung between them; and for a moment David was hypnotized. He thought about nothing and everything all at the same time. He spoke, as if to the very sky itself. "I remember that we had promised to never hurt each other, Allen. I thought it was said in a dream, but I now realize it happened. Yes, it really happened. But you went back on that promise. You broke it slowly, every day you came home drunk, every time you yelled at me out of insanity, every time you hit me... I knew it, and continued to stay. Maybe I was scared too; scared of being alone. I'm still scared of that, but not as much anymore. When I saw you at the Catch One on Monday, your fag all hugged up on you, my heart broke into a thousand pieces." David turned to face Allen. "Does he know about your status?"

Allen was leaning against the door, arms folded. "That's none of your business, David."

"Humph. I didn't think he did. You still need him to make you feel disease free. I doubt you're even playing safely, but of course that's none of my business either."

Allen flinched, then moved forward, and quickly grasped David's fingers, squeezing them tenderly. "Let's forget about Percy, okay? What matters is right here and now. I want you here by my side. I want you bringing me a hot meal when I'm not feeling well. I want to know you'll come through my door or kick the covers off me at night or tell me you'll hold my hand when death finally claims me, 'cause believe it or not, I would hold yours. It can be like that, like we both want it to be, like it should be, forever."

Malcolm had been right; Allen could reach through his emotions, except now, all David wanted to do was slap a fistful of emotions upside head.

Allen stepped closer and placed a supple kiss on David's forehead. He stroked David's arm. The kisses continued across his cheek, and David could feel his resistance ebb, his mind pulling back, as if each kiss was laced with amnesia; causing him to forget why he came, and projecting reasons for why he should remain.

"And Percy said he wouldn't mind ..."

He pulled his head back. "What did you say?" David asked, taking a step back.

"Percy said he wouldn't mind being with both of us."

"Are you out of your mind?"

Allen looked dumbfounded. "What's wrong with that? I want you to be there. At least I wouldn't be doing it behind your back."

"No, you'll just be doing it in my face, and probably on my face. I must be crazy being here." David spun around and slammed his suitcase shut. This was insane! "I'm getting outta here. I've had enough," David announced, picking up his luggage and walking briskly toward the door.

Unexpectedly, Allen swung out his arm, knocking David's suitcase to the floor. "You're going nowhere! How can you just walk out on me like this? Can't you see that I want to be with you? You're in here," Allen said, pounding his fist against his heart. "And nothing can take that away."

David took a step back. He figured he could leap through the window if he needed to suddenly escape. "How can you say that? Your little fuck hole is right in the next room, and you say I'm in your heart. I don't need this, Allen. I don't need you and your games."

Allen reached out to take hold of David's belt, and then swiftly began to force his hands down his pants. "Come on, David. You know you want to, so stop this shit."

David seized Allen's wrists, plucking them from his pants. He looked down to see Allen's manhood at full attention. He couldn't believe this. This violence, this aggression, it excited him! And before David knew it, Allen was upon him, groping at him, his lips puckered, his gaze incensed, his fingers clawing. Then the fear overcame David. He began to remember. He re-envisioned the beatings, the abuse, the constant forced acts of sex, the rapes—why couldn't he just call them what they were? Rapes!

David reached back, taking a tight hold of his bag's handle, and heaved it into Allen's torso, knocking him aside. There was a low grunt as Allen doubled over, and David rushed for the door, pulling at the knob frantically. *How many times will I run from this house?* He thought. Sweat streamed down his face, and reminders of Stephen's warning echoed back to him: *One day that man is gonna kill you.*

A voice broke out beyond the door, catching both their attention with a sudden cry, "David, are you here?" It was Damien. David pulled open the door, leaning into the hallway, to see Damien standing at the end, looking around curiously.

"I decided to come help you gets a few things. I brought the—" he stopped speaking as he now saw Allen emerge from the room.

"Let's get out of here," David said, walking quickly in Damien's direction, until he was right upon him, and continued to march forward, pressing his hands into Damien's chest, forcing him back towards the door.

"What's Allen doing—" he was about to question – until he saw another figure emerge, from another room, with a most familiar face. "Oh my God!"

"What's that faggot doing in my house?" Allen shouted, while Percy looked on in confusion.

David quickly shoved Damien out the door, silencing him with a carefully placed finger across his lips. "Don't say a word. Just take your car and meet me at home, okay?" David warned.

Damien smiled, pleased at Allen's displeasure, his karma moment. Their eyes locked. "You're the cause of this shit, you fuckin' queer! You better stay out my life, you little shithole!" Allen roared, stomping towards the open door, angrily watching both men enter their separate cars – and only one of them continued to stare, to smile, to goad at him, and he began to hate Damien even more. Damien hated Allen too, and bided a farewell to him with a raised middle finger as he sped out the driveway, signing them in a band of skid marks – shaped like a smile.

– II –

Sarafina slammed the phone on its base, cursing the damned answering machine again. She had called Dominique every day since Monday, and here it was Friday, and the woman was not answering the phone. They had one conversation on Tuesday morning, and Dominique had basically told her, it was over, and to get her shit straight with Gerri once and for all, because there was no room in her life for two women, one of which was the bitch she now called her boss. Dominique finished by saying, that she would be staying at a hotel; calling would be futile.

That statement proved correct. Sarafina fought the urge to run back to L.A. because she knew that wouldn't solve anything. She had to talk to Gerri, which was proving difficult because Sarafina found herself falling back into her old habits. And the fact that Gerri had treated her to more of the world in four days than she had seen all her time in Los Angeles didn't help matters any. There was a day spent in New York to see a play, a day trip to Vegas to see Cëline Dion, and who knew what else was planned. Sarafina had to admit she had missed being spoiled this way.

Then there was the incident in the bedroom.

"Is there anything wrong, Ms. Chandler?"

Sarafina looked up to see Carlotta staring down at her. She was the only housekeeper of Gerri's to survive long term, or the only one she truly trusted. Carlotta twisted a rag in her hand as she observed Sarafina. "Would you like some lunch or something? You done slept through my breakfast this here mo'nin', so I thought I'd make a shrimp salad for you if you was hungry."

"Sure, I'll have it later. Thanks, Carlotta."

Carlotta stepped into the room. She placed her glasses on the rim of her nose, her wrinkled eyes squinting at Sarafina. Carlotta was at least seventy, her dark skin polished and flawless. Like the furniture, she had become a major part of this household.

"I also wanted to say it's been good seeing you, dear."

Sarafina smiled. "It's good seeing you too. Haven't spoken to you much since I arrived. Sorry about that."

Carlotta waved her rag at Sarafina. "Aw, don't think about that, child. You ain't been here but three days, and I don't ask that you cater to me. You be looking sad though, so I let you be."

"It's that obvious, huh?"

Carlotta shrugged. "Yeah, but I seen that look plenty of times, when you last lived here. You never did seem really happy, even when you really were."

Sarafina nodded. Carlotta knew her well. The evening of the party was still haunting her. She could remember bits and pieces of what had happened, but it all came to one conclusion: she and Gerri had had sex. She could remember each orgasm, each embrace, and each kiss. She remembered it like a game of three-card-monte; always catching a glimpse of the card, but never enough to guess correctly. It was like that, and Sarafina was afraid to confront Gerri with it—because in truth, she didn't want to be right.

"No, I guess being here was a bit too much for me. Trying to be happy isn't an easy thing sometimes. Oh, and I wanted to thank you for the hangover remedy that day. I guess Gerri's party kinda overwhelmed me."

"Don't mention it. Dat' remedy been in the family goin' on ten years now. I been through too many young folk to not get it right this time. Too many grandboys in the family not to have something handy like that."

"And where is Gerri? I can't believe she left the house without saying anything to me. We have some things to talk over."

"You know her," was all Carlotta could offer.

Sarafina looked at her hand and the diamond ring on it. Gerri had placed it there while she slept. It was typical of her to leave something material as a replacement for her physical presence. "Yeah, it's beginning to feel like old times."

"Well, child, you come in here and get your salad 'fore it get cold," Carlotta said jokingly, as she headed off into the kitchen.

Sarafina followed her, and sat at a wooden stool near the center island, where Carlotta had dinner preparations scattered on the Formica top. She was chopping onions into a pile. Sarafina reached over to pluck a chopped carrot from an adjacent stack. "Is that quail, Carlotta?" Sarafina asked, noticing the glass pan filled with the tender foul.

"Yes, baby. Don't they feed you L.A. folk? Of course this is quail, honey."

"I guess I don't go to those restaurants anymore. I've been living a different lifestyle these days. I sure do miss your cooking, though. This looks like a pretty big feast. Are we expecting company or something?" Sarafina asked, looking at the arrangement of six birds.

"No, not to recollection, but Ms. Moore likes to bring businesspeople over from time to time, and she likes to be able to grab something out of the kitchen. So I make a little extra on Fridays, bein' that I'm off till Monday."

Sarafina placed her elbow on the counter and leaned in a bit closer to Carlotta, smiling shyly. "So tell me, Carlotta. Who are Gerri's business partners these days?"

Carlotta grinned, looking at Sarafina over the rim of her glasses. "Hmm, I think it's a Miss None, most of the time," she answered. Sarafina looked puzzled. "A Miss None?" she repeated.

"Yeah, a Miss None of Your Business. You know I don't have an interest in the business of Ms. Moore. And you shouldn't either," Carlotta chastised, tapping Sarafina on the head with a wooden spoon.

"No need to get violent!"

Carlotta walked to the refrigerator, and pulled out a small bowl, then set it on the counter. "Here, you need to put your mind on other things than being in other folks' affairs."

Sarafina looked down at the bowl to discover it was the salad Carlotta had spoken about. "Oh, this looks good!" she exclaimed, digging at the leaves with her fingers.

"Girl! Didn't they teach you no manners in that L.A. place?" Carlotta spoke, tossing a salad fork her way.

Sarafina gladly took it and continued to devour her meal. "Thanks, again. You so good to me, ya know that."

Carlotta smiled. "Yeah, whatever child. You just concentrate on that," she kindly advised, pointing to the bowl. "By the way, how are you and that girl coming along that I heard you was seeing?"

Sarafina looked up from her meal. "You mean Dominique?" Carlotta nodded. "We having some problems, but we're okay."

"So I guess you not here to stay for a spell. This old house misses you sometimes," Carlotta said, returning to garnish her food with a touch of paprika.

Sarafina knew that message was coming from Carlotta herself. "I miss this old house myself sometimes. But I'm out here to discuss a little problem with your boss lady."

"Humph. I see your life be filled with problems since you done took root elsewhere. I guess it's no different than anyone being in a man and woman relationship. It look to me like it's all the same tree, just the leaves be different."

"So tell me, Carlotta," Sarafina began, as she dabbed at her lips with a napkin; the salad gone. "Have you ever been with a woman?"

Carlotta slapped a rag from the thin air across Sarafina's forehead. "Boy, you sho' is full of vinegar and salt to be askin' me that. It's those folks from Beverly Hills that been teaching you to be so rude to an old lady," she announced, and she replaced the rag across her shoulder. "But no, baby. I leave that kind of stuff to you and Gerri. I don't have the taste for another woman. We all have to find our own ripple in the water of life, and mine just don't go that way."

"You don't know what you missin'," Sarafina said, reaching for another carrot.

"Baby, just let me cook the fish, and you eat it."

They both laughed.

Just then the phone rang, and Carlotta answered it. She spoke for a brief minute, then turned to Sarafina. "That was Gerri."

"It was? Where is she?"

Carlotta placed her hand on her hips. "Well, it looks like she outside this very door in the limo, she said get some clothes together and meet her in the car."

"Wha—? She's in a limo? What's going on, Carlotta? I know you know, so don't give me that moose face."

Carlotta bent forward, placing her hand on Sarafina's wrist. "You gonna be going to St. Kitts today, honey."

Sarafina was flabbergasted. "Another trip? What the hell is St. Kitts?"

"You have been away a bit, huh? It's an island in the Caribbean." Sarafina was silent. Carlotta asked, "You not in love with Ms. Moore anymore, are you?"

Sarafina could only shake her head.

"I figure as much. It's a shame though, 'cause Ms. Moore is a might confused on the issue. I think she want you back, although it ain't none of my business. She had never been so happy than the day she knew you were coming back to San Francisco."

Sarafina propped her elbows on the table, and rested her chin in her palms. "I kinda sensed that."

"Then why you stayin' here? If you ain't finding happiness here, then maybe it's time you packed your bag and head for high water," Carlotta advised.

"I don't know, Carlotta. I have an agenda I need to take care of with Gerri, but I guess all this royal treatment has made me procrastinate."

"Child, forget that royal treatment stuff. You need to get Gerri in this house and discuss what you got to discuss with her. The sooner the better," Carlotta warned.

"And miss my trip to the Caribbean? St. Kitts sounds like the stress reduction I'm in need of," Sarafina replied, enthused.

Carlotta didn't share her enthusiasm. She wiped from her brow a slight band of moisture, then spoke slowly to Sarafina.

"Girl, I'm tellin' you. This is a very dangerous game you play. Believe me."

Chapter 13

— I —

Felicia checked herself out in the mirror. Yes, the facial had done her a vast improvement. She looked and felt great. Six hours at the beautician had turned out to be well worth it. She touched up her lipstick, fanned out her foundation, and put a touch of powder along her neck. This was not a night for mistakes.

The timer chimed in the kitchen. Felicia dropped her lipstick into the basin and rushed to check on her roast. She brought out the oven rack and peeled back the aluminum foil to view the meat. It smelled and looked almost as good as she did. She smiled. Everything was going as planned. She went back to the living room and poured herself a glass of wine from the well-stocked host bar. She kicked off her slippers and looked around the apartment. Beautiful. She could not believe she was here, in Los Angeles, and in Stephen's apartment.

She could hear her mother now: "You're going where?! Have you lost your mind or something? Can't you just leave that man alone?" Felicia had shouted back no, she would not, could not, leave this man alone. He was, after all, *her* man! They shared a child together, for God's sake. They would soon share a life together.

Her best friend, Tammy, seized her by the shoulders, shaking her violently, saying, "Girl, you gots some serious hang-ups, if you gonna be takin' your dick-whipped ass out to see that pussy of a man that really don't care nothing about you." Felicia didn't hear a word. Was it them lying under cold sheets at night? Was it them going from one horrid dating experience to the next? Was it them catering to the constant needs of a two-year-old? No! No! Hell no! It wasn't. So who needed their opinion? None of them had a man or could keep a man, so how could they know about what a man wanted? They didn't.

Even as she had trudged off to the airport, they followed her until she stomped onto the jet bridge, her back facing them as she left; their voices overflowing with opposition fell to deaf ears. That was three days ago. She had been in a hotel for two days, calling Stephen, letting him think she was still at home in Chicago. She had to find out his schedule, when he would be home, when he would be away. Today was the day to act.

He was attending a photo shoot for an ad campaign. She knew that would take some time. She had to work fast to get her things together, use the keys he had given her in the event of an emergency (she'd convinced herself that this was indeed an emergency; saving her man from this ugly illusion, this strange lifestyle, he was tricked into belonging to), and fix a satisfying dinner. She knew this night would go perfectly. And if not, she had a backup plan.

As she relished in her own nirvana of thoughts, she could hear keys rattling near the door. Stephen was home! She listened, and the rattling stopped. She looked at the door in anticipation.

– II –

Stephen held his keys in the lock. Something was wrong. Crafty had not come scratching at the door. *That dog can't be that asleep,* thought Stephen. And the smell of food had permeated the air as he came up the stairs. He thought it was the downstairs neighbor, but he could swear that the scent was coming from his place. Odd. He hadn't smelled food coming from his place since Jamal had been over to make him breakfast, and Jamal happened to be in DC for the week visiting his father. Stephen knew he was hungry, but even when he imagined food on his hungriest day, it never smelled this good.

There was a terrible fear that seized him as he slowly opened the door. He scanned the room slowly, seeing that it was lit with candles made him think he was in the wrong apartment. Then he saw her! Felicia—smiling at him like she had pulled off a great heist.

"Hi, Stephen," she greeted very nonchalantly. "Glad to see you made it. I put your little pooch in the back room with—"

"Felicia!" Stephen interrupted, trying to ascertain the reality of this situation. He could hear Crafty scratching lightly at his bedroom door. "What are you doing here? How did you get in my house?"

Felicia casually placed her wine glass on the coffee table. "You sent me a key, silly," she reminded him, her grin now awkward, forced.

Stephen closed the door, dropping his portfolio bag. "That was only in the event of an emergency, like if I died or something. As you can see, I'm still here."

Felicia laughed uneasily. "I know that. I just decided to give you a little surprise visit. I thought I would give myself a little vacation, come out here to of sunny California, cook you a little dinner, bring our—"

"Arrrgh!" Stephen grunted in frustration, holding his palms to his ears. "I can't believe this. I come home from a shitty day at work to find that my house has been invaded—by my ex-girlfriend nonetheless—to discover that no one has died, no one is in the hospital, no one is doing anything, and she calls it an emergency."

Felicia remained silent. Her lips trembled as she spoke her next words. "I just missed you, Stephen. I just missed you." She was defeated, the grin gone.

Stephen felt defeated too. He looked at Felicia, and once again he was the bearer of ill tidings. He was the monster. Why did she have this power over him? What he saw before him was a little girl shaken and nervous. The shock of finding his home invaded and the fury that followed was now being replaced by feelings of guilt and contrition. She looked up at him with the softest eyes, and at that moment he was speechless, afraid to speak, lest he upset this delicate woman again.

"Why are you doing this, Felicia?" He loosened his tie. "I thought you understood everything that was happening between us. You know why I left Chicago and why I had to—"

Unexpectedly, Felicia leapt to her feet, and placed a finger over Stephen's lips. "Shhhh! I didn't say I came out here to change your lifestyle. I just came out here for a visit, not to offend you. Were you expecting someone else today? Your new man, perhaps?"

Stephen rolled his eyes. He knew she was being flippant, but he refused to reply. He, however, did think of Jamal, and was glad he was out of town at the moment. A visit from him now would truly become uncomfortable.

"Don't answer that," Felicia said, dropping her hand, and taking a step back. Once again Stephen became aware of Crafty's soft whimpering. "Besides, I'm also here for another reason. I know you've been busy at work, but it's Sunday, and you seem to have forgotten what today is."

Stephen watched as she opened his bedroom door, and out bolted his canine companion. He bent to his knees as the dog bounded into his arms. "Hey there, boy! Glad to be outta there, huh?" he said, accepting the onslaught of tender kisses from his best friend. He then looked up once again, about to comment on Felicia's treatment of his animal, when he saw something else emerge from his bedroom.

The young boy came from the room, pants wrinkled, tank top hanging out, and rubbing his eyes with the cutest little brown fists Stephen had ever seen. Felicia roughed the top of his head, which was cut into a fresh fade shaved close to his tiny scalp. In his other hand there was a white envelope, looking as big as a book, tucked between his fingers. He removed his hands from his eyes and his large pupils lit up, eyes blinking wildly as he adjusted to the lights. He smiled, and Stephen felt a chill rattle through him.

"Daddy!" said the boy, and he ran, his arms swinging erratically at his side for balance, as he headed toward Stephen.

"Hey, boy!" Stephen addressed, as the boy squeezed past Crafty to reach his father. He held the envelope out like a sword before him, and Stephen had to grab it as it came only inches from his nose. "What you got here?" he asked, staring happily into his boy's eyes.

"It for you, Daddy," Tumali said, putting his hands on his hips as if his father should already know this.

"Is that so?" Stephen said, as he opened the gift. He saw at once it was a card.

Felicia stood before him, and he would have remained unaware of her presence had she not spoken. "Happy Father's Day, Stephen," she said, as she looked at the smile on his face. She then was relieved; her ace in the hole was working.

—III—

Jamal knocked on the screen door, apprehension tying a taut knot in his throat. He always had this foreboding feeling whenever he visited his father. There was truly no reason to justify this sensation; the three-bedroom home, with its wood siding, was a lovely sight to behold at any angle. It had a beautiful tulip garden sprawled out in front, and the lawn was the neatest on the block. A huge oak tree stood boldly in the center, casting its cool shade across the front porch. It was quiet here, each time Jamal visited this pleasing residence nestled in the heart of Sterling, Virginia, just thirty minutes from Washington, DC. Still, he had this odd sensation of fear.

Jamal could see a line of sparrows clap their wings overhead across the blue of the sky, and a cool breeze licked at his face, followed by a rush of warmth letting him know that summer was indeed present. A kaleidoscope of memories pushed into his head, and he nearly jumped sky-high as the door to the house flew open, and the voice of Aunt Sylvia beckoned him.

"Jamal!" she yelled through the screen door, squinting her eyes tight, affirming her recognition of this young man. She took a quick step forward and began to fumble with the latch on the door. She pushed it out so fast that Jamal was barely able to keep it from slamming into his nose.

"Hey! Take it easy, Aunt Sylvia, before you break someone's face," he said with a welcome grin. "Now take these," he said, thrusting a dozen red roses toward her.

She smiled. Aunt Sylvia had one of those faces that made her appear younger when she grinned. Her bright cheeks were pulled tight across her wide face, her eyes seemed to gleam, her tiny double chin smoothed itself out, and her teeth lay perfectly behind her ruby-red lips. Streaks of gray hair and simple clothes, festooned with prints of sunflowers, covered her. She smelled of a combination of Glade air freshener and freshly cut flowers. She clutched the roses near her nose and beamed. "Thank you, baby," she commented politely, her voice choked with emotion.

A thin blanket of icy air surrounded Jamal as he entered the house; it felt good compared to the humidity that was festering outside. Jamal lifted his nose, his eyes darting around the room. "What's that you cooking in here, lady?" he asked. Aunt Sylvia was forever baking, and the house was never without the scent of food.

"Oh boy, you know that's my pear-apple pie cookin' for you. It's almost done. Now where your bags at? I got two pans of that pie comin' out that oven, and you gonna eat it all, so you better be staying a while. I know all you brought wasn't that box you hidin' in your other hand."

Jamal held out the present he was holding. "No, the bags are in the car. This is for Dad. It is Father's Day, you know."

Sylvia placed a heavy hand on Jamal's shoulder. "You know, that's right. I don't keep up much with those things, I guess. And I want to thank you for that lovely vase you sent me last month for Mother's Day. Prob'ly why you givin' me flowers now, so I can put something in there besides my imagination. I think I'll go do that right now, while you go say hi to your father."

"Where is he?" Jamal asked, that feeling hitting him again.

"Where else would he be?" Sylvia questioned, rolling her eyes in her head. "The Peanut Gallery, of course," she instructed, pointing a thin finger in the direction, and then headed off into the living room, nose buried in her well-received gift.

Unpredictability lived here. That was the fear welling up within Jamal. His father had entered a realm of unpredictability since his diagnosis of Alzheimer's. Jamal was never as comfortable with this condition as Aunt Sylvia seemed to be. There was no common structure to his father's personality. There were no set rules to his thinking or his actions. There was no sense of order, unless you deemed that order to be chaos.

Jamal stood in the doorway of the den, hearing the television blare news coverage across the room and being overcome by the pungent scent of Old Spice in the air. He could see his father's old recliner, the back facing him, and the top of the old man's head, his bald spot revealing to Jamal times yet to come for himself. There was an aged card table in one corner, one leg haphazardly held together by a thick band of masking tape, and a collection of cards spread across its dusty surface. A bookshelf stood directly to its right, its body leaning slightly, void of most of the books that once populated its shelves; it had now become a makeshift entertainment center. A potted ivy sat on top—Aunt Sylvia's meager attempt to bring life to this hovel. About the floor were crates filled with 45s and LPs. The room was rounded out with a worn leather sofa, two small end tables he'd gotten from a yard sale, a space heater, and a wicker basket of unwashed laundry.

And everywhere else, there were peanut shells.

Aunt Sylvia said that once his doctors had him quit smoking, Jamal's dad had found a new haven in roasted peanuts. He used to carry his habit throughout the house until Aunt Sylvia banned him to the den, thus christening it the Peanut Gallery.

"Come on in here, boy. No sense in you staring at the back of my head," said Terrance Warren.

How does he do that? Thought Jamal. The man must've been a Friend of Cleo to know he was standing here. There was a footstool next to his father's chair, a passed-down piece. Jamal chose to sit there. "Chair's holding up pretty good," Jamal said.

"Yeah, this here chair is gonna he around a good long time. It'll sure be here long after my departure," Terrance replied, a sense of impending doom in his voice.

Jamal hated when his father's voice was filled with such despair. "I'm sure that chair will outlast us all," he reassured, slapping the arm of the chair with his open palm.

Terrance looked away from the television, which was rebroadcasting news of a high-speed chase in Los Angeles, and smiled at Jamal. Eerie, that grin was, and much the opposite of the one displayed by Aunt Sylvia. His face looked older; the wrinkles around the eyes becoming more pronounced, the bags under them swelling to greater prominence. His eyebrows rose, and thick folds of flesh creased on his forehead. His lips were dry, and fragments of peanut shells dotted his mustache and sections of his jaw. The outward appearance was of a man that was giving up, of ceasing the fight he could never quite win. His failing memory was the greatest indication that things were getting worse. He would forget names, places, and even sections of a conversation. Some of it might not be noticed coming from anyone else, but this was Terrance Warren, a man who knew the names and birthdays of just about every relative that carried his family genes. His memory was his pride and joy—a joy he shared with his son in the form of stories and tales. Jamal hated the way the illness was stripping away the man he once knew and leaving in its place this shell, this *peanut shell*—of a man.

"Spoke with your mother," Terrance said, staring at the television.

Jamal continued to look at him as his father started to watch the news again. After a short silence, he asked, "Did she talk about me?"

"No," Terrance said quickly.

No surprise, thought Jamal. He knew that would be the answer. He knew she regarded him dead, and he did likewise. He learned of his stepfather's death a year back, and strangely, had felt nothing at the news; that a loss of life would cause him to feel such little remorse. But he did remember the name calling, the Faggots, the Queers, the Bitch, the Punk – and how his mother stood beside him, prodding him on like a love-struck cheerleader. He hated them both then, and wasn't surprised that she hadn't spoken of him, but she still communicated with Terrance "So, what did you two talk about? Why do you even bother with her?" he absently asked, just making conversation.

"It had been Mother's Day, Jamal."

"Oh," he replied, having long since regarded that holiday exclusively for Sylvia. "Aunt Sylvia is all the mother I need."

Terrance smiled, and he aged by ten years. "That she is…all the woman I've ever needed," he said happily.

"Well, you may want to need a maid while you're at it," said Aunt Sylvia, entering the room. "Somebody to clean up after your messy ass." She stopped behind Terrance's chair, wrapping her arms over his shoulder, and wiping at his mustache, clearing it of peanut shells. "I almost wish you were smoking again."

"No, you don't," Terrance replied, gently stroking Sylvia's hands as they lay locked across his chest.

"With all these peanut shells in here you'd think an elephant farted or something. I can't come in here without crunching under my feet."

"That's so I'll know you comin'. At least I give you the rest of the house to pretty up like you want, don't I?" He turned to look at Jamal. "Woman always complaining. Be glad you don't have to worry about this female species, son. They fickle."

Jamal smiled at his father's openness. "I'm a flight attendant, so I deal with women all day."

Terrance rubbed his son's knee. "Oh, the utter torture you must be *going* through." They all laughed. It were times as these that Jamal felt real family. "And so how is the love life, my boy? Any new beaus in your travels?"

Jamal was silent. He looked at his father quizzically. He looked up at Sylvia, who sported a sad grin and shrugged. Jamal had told Terrance countless times about his meeting Stephen and how he would like to get to know him better. A knot welled in his throat. His father was not only forgetting more, he was also remembering with less frequency. Jamal casually crossed his legs and took a deep breath, "Yeah, I've met a wonderful guy named Stephen."

"Stephen, you say?" Terrance questioned, as he reached into the breast pocket of his plaid shirt to pull out a handful of peanuts. "That name sounds familiar. How long you two been seeing each other?"

Jamal flipped his fingers in the air, counting in his head. "I would have to say it's been little over a month. Strange, it seems longer.

"If it seems longer, then that's good. Means you're making the most of your time together. Seems like I've known this old biddy forever," Terrance said, directing a thumb behind him.

Sylvia slapped his shoulder. "Watch it now, old man!" she warned, and looked at Jamal. "It must be hard being together, when you're always traveling."

"I have long stretches of days off, and we always talk on the phone. So it's been working out pretty good."

"So do I hear wedding bells?" Sylvia asked, clapping her hands excitedly.

Jamal held his hand out, fingers spread. "Not until I see a ring on this finger, and remember, I don't go for glass or the zirconia. Pure pressed coal goes on this finger. I'm talkin' diamonds."

"I hear ya, baby. Don't settle for anything else. And what's in the box, your tuxedo?" Aunt Sylvia said.

"Not quite," Jamal answered, reaching down to pick up the gift box he'd placed beside the footstool. "This is for you, Dad. It's not much, but I think you'll like it."

Terrance accepted the gift, his eyebrows cocked in great apprehension. He looked up at his son, then back at the gift. He wiped his lips with quick strokes of his fingers, and then brushed them against the arm of his chair. With the box resting gently on his lap, he began to open it.

Communication between Jamal and his father had become more and more strained as the years progressed. In early years his father was a well-traveled man, taking road trips across the country, and he would recall these stories to Jamal. When they attended those Fourth of July family reunions, many pictures were taken, and on their flights back within those wonderful DC 10s, Terrance would share those pictures, pointing out certain people, recounting who they were and sharing a small story about them.

Now, there were no more adventures for his father. He'd lost his interest in travel. He didn't speak much about his past any longer, and Jamal knew it was because of the frustration of reciting those destinations, trying to remember it all. Even the family reunions, all those photos, were now pictures containing a sea of lost names he could no longer remember. Jamal found it difficult to talk about his friends, because he found himself repeating certain events that he'd spoken of before. He hoped this gift would help.

Unwrapping the box, Terrance found it contained a large picture album, the texture a rich, soft brown leather with gold letters embossed on its front spelling the word REFLECTIONS (Diana Ross's tune ran through Jamal's mind). Terrance found himself rubbing his fingers along the edges of the book, slowly opening the cover.

The room was silent as Terrance looked at the first page, revealing a huge picture of himself in his Army uniform. He was very handsome with his smooth dark skin, his clean shaven face, and his bald head. His smile was beautiful, and there was such a resemblance to Jamal that all knew whose genes Jamal had expressed. On the bottom of the photograph was a handwritten message, reading:

My father, Terrance Gerald Warren.
A great man of this age and a great builder of ages past.
He is not only a man, he's my father,
and my love for him is everlasting.
From Jamal Warren, son

Terrance grinned at this, saying nothing, and turned the page. Following were pictures of other people gathered at a large cookout. Jamal had tracked down some of the relatives he'd been introduced to as a child. It took a lot of remembering on his part, a lot of phone calls, a lot of visits to people he hardly knew, prodding them of their photos—black folks held their photos dear. Many of the photos his father had owned were lost, and this was the only way to recover what Jamal knew his father had held close to his heart.

At the bottom of the photos were tiny handwritten explanations of what was going on, and the names of the people included. As his father turned the pages, Jamal noticed his face was as solid as stone. No emotions, excluding a deep swallow that registered through his large Adam's apple. Aunt Sylvia had her hand to her mouth and tears in her eyes.

Further into the album, the pictures changed to photos Jamal had taken of the places he'd visited since working for the airlines: New York, Chicago, Indiana, Hawaii, Guam, London, and many others. These too had explanations written at the bottoms of what great landmarks these pictures represented. These were followed by pictures of his close friends in Los Angeles, those he'd told his father about in their long conversations on the phone. Now he had faces to go with the names.

He had ended the album with a huge picture of himself in his airline uniform, posing in the same manner as his father in his Army uniform.

"That's wonderful, Jamal," Sylvia pronounced, chokingly, reaching out to place a hand on Jamal's shoulder.

"Thanks. I just thought it would be nice for Dad to have some knowledge of the people that have changed my life, the events that made me happy. It's all we ever talk about, it seems."

"I know that's the truth. I have the phone bills to prove it," Sylvia joked, dabbing a finger at the corner of her eyes.

Terrance remained silent, and Jamal had noticed he'd turned the album back a few pages, and was looking at a picture he'd taken with Stephen on the Santa Monica Pier, at one of the photo booths there. His lips were trembling, and his gaze was unmoved. He slowly placed a hand on his forehead and closed his eyes.

"Is there something wrong, Terrance?" Sylvia asked, as she walked around to face him. She bent down and slowly pulled the album from his shaking hands.

"So, that's Stephen, huh?" Terrance questioned. "Very handsome man."

"Thanks, but I think his mother and father had more to do with that than me," Jamal said, jesting, trying to relax the morose feelings that were manifesting within this room.

"You've told me about him before, haven't you?" he asked in a low voice.

Jamal paused before answering. "Um, I guess I could've mentioned him before."

"Yeah, you have, and here I am asking you about him again, as if you've never told me about this man. It's getting bad, isn't it?"

"What are you talking about now, Terrance?" Sylvia asked, placing the album on the top of the television.

Terrance looked up, his eyes tiny slits of anger. "You know what I'm talking about!"

Sylvia was taken aback by this outburst but quickly recovered, and she returned his gaze with one of her own. "Don't start with this craziness, Terrance Gerald Warren. This is no time to be thinking about—"

"Quiet!" Terrance shouted, slamming his hand on his chair. He turned to Jamal, confusion twisted into his features. "I'm sorry, son, but it's this damn shit that's eating away at my brain. I get like this sometimes. I remember we would talk about new things all the time on the phone, and now when we talk it's nothing really new, most of the time is spent trying to remember what was said in the last conversation. It's just difficult sometimes."

"I know it is, Dad, but it doesn't make you any less of a man, and I don't think any less of you. You have always been there for me, not that damn mother and father I grew up with. It was you all the time."

Terrance grabbed Jamal's thigh, shaking it. 'Thanks for the gift." He looked up at Sylvia. "And I'm sorry, Sylvia."

Sylvia brushed a hand at him. "Oh please. You don't scare me, old man. I better go check on my pies. I can almost smell them," she said, popping Terrance on the head with the back of her hand as she began to leave. "I'll be back to bring you guys something to drink."

"Thanks, Sylvia," Jamal said, as she blew him a warm kiss through the air.

"It really is hard sometimes, Jamal," Terrance said, as he picked up his remote control, and flipped the channel to another news station.

Jamal reached over to brush some debris from his father's jaw. "I know, but Happy Father's Day anyway."

Chapter 14

— I —

"It's time for me to get the hell out of here!" Sarafina yelled, her arms spread out in defeat.

Gerri approached her, reaching out to her, trying to calm her down. "Take it easy, Sara."

Sarafina grabbed her wrist, squeezing it. "Don't touch me, Gerri! How could you do this to me? I thought we were friends. Now you tell me that you sent that plane ticket to my house, knowing Dominique would be there to receive it. You wrote that letter to some Sara Fletcher, pretending to send it to my address by mistake. You also got our changed phone number from some hookup you have within the phone company. All this to try and get me here. How could you do that? How can you have the nerve to tell me all this and still expect me to stay here? How?"

"Stop that!" Gerri cried, snatching her bruised wrist away from Sarafina's stronghold. She rubbed her arm, easing away the sting of pain. "I was only trying to help you. I was only—"

"Help me?" Sarafina pounded her hands together. "Help me to do what? Get a quicker divorce? I thought you were on my side, Gerri. I thought we were friends."

"Of course we are, but we were lovers too," Gerri said, walking to close the bedroom door which was left ajar.

"But that's over with. I love Dominique, and now I wish I hadn't left L.A. to come here to talk with you. You're one crazy head case, Gerri."

Gerri sliced her hand through the air as if it were a whip. "Shut up with that talk! You left here to think about your life, to think about our relationship, and not to break up with me. I never thought you would *go* running off to Hollywood and go find somebody behind my back. You were supposed to come back. You were supposed to be with me."

Sarafina shook her shoulders violently, as if she were ridding her body of building tension. "You are trippin', I swear. You were the one that said I needed to grow, to be on my own, to leave here. You said if I never came back here, then perhaps we were not meant to be. We were not meant to be. Do you hear—?"

"But you are here," Gerri interrupted. "You are here. You are back with me!"

"By invitation only! And now I think this invitation is over. I'm never coming back here again."

Gerri looked visibly stunned. "You don't mean that. I know it," she managed to whisper.

Sarafina turned around, facing the canopy bed. She didn't want to look at that face. She didn't want to think that this was happening. How could a woman she would have trusted with her life betray her this way? She looked the same, her voice was the same, and through all this there was the sense that this silly woman still loved her. That motive weakened Sarafina. "I need to have my things, Gerri. I haven't seen my things since I got here. I've been letting you buy me all kinds of shit—shit I really don't need. I need my own identification, my own identity back. So get my stuff so I can get out of here."

Gerri remained silent.

Sarafina slowly turned to face Gerri again. *Perhaps she didn't hear my request,* she thought. "I said I want my things, Gerri."

Gerri seemed to ignore her and walked to the vanity mirror, her eyes looking blankly at Sarafina from the glass. The lights installed atop the dresser were on, and it shown brightly upon Gerri's face. The image was dismal. Finally she spoke, very calmly, with great reserve, yet the words were dynamite. "I'm not letting you go, Sarafina."

Sarafina shook her head. Was she actually hearing this? No. This was her imagination. "What did you say?"

"I'm not letting you go," Gerri repeated confidently. "You were not supposed to go to L.A. and meet someone. You were not supposed to fall in love."

Sarafina was confused. "It's been a year, Gerri. What do you think I've been doing in that time? I've told you about Dominique. You thought I was playing games? She's my lover."

"No! I'm your lover!" Gerri stated, pointing a stiff finger at herself. "I'm the one that loves you. I'm the one who gave you the money to get yourself grounded. I'm the one who bought you a new wardrobe, who set you up with your first apartment. Not the hovel I'm sure you're living in now, with that bitch that's done nothing for you!"

Sarafina stormed in Gerri's direction, and with one open palm pushed Gerri strongly in the chest, causing her to fall back against the vanity. "You have no right to talk about Dominique. I'll kick your white ass before I sit here and listen to you talk about her."

Gerri looked strongly at Sarafina. There was hurt in her eyes at what Sarafina had just uttered. Words she had never heard in the three years they had been together. "So I'm a color now. Didn't know I'd been living with a bigot all those years. You left me because I was white? All this time—"

"Shut up, Gerri. Quit trying to turn this around," Sarafina said, backing away. She couldn't believe she had spoken that way to Gerri herself. The color difference had never been an issue between them, and now for some reason Gerri had become "the Woman," just as for many males, there was "the Man." She was trying to exert power as she had always done. Sarafina could only look at Gerri as one of *those* people: Gerri's friends, business partners, employees, all of those who looked upon her with contempt, all those eyes that said she wasn't good enough. Gerri was the only one who had treated her with a little respect, and yet Sarafina had begun to wonder if that had been true at all. It didn't seem true now. Gerri had never respected her free will, her right to make her own decisions. Maybe there was an underlying prejudice that was never faced. Sarafina had never thought about it until she came back here and fell into the same routine as before, having Gerri take care of her. It had been so easy that Sarafina never saw it as a form of control, as a form of slavery. Perhaps Gerri never saw that truth too. It was, after all, an inbred reaction through society to relate gradations in color to gradations of power.

That was not the issue now, Sarafina concluded.

"Okay. I'm sorry, Sara. Is that what you want to hear?" Gerri said, lifting herself and walking past Sarafina. She sat on the bed.

"No, I'm the one that's sorry. I never knew you were this possessive. I've made a terrible mistake. Maybe I am a bigot, because right now I feel like the emancipation was just passed, and my owner doesn't want me to be free."

"I'm sorry you feel that way, but I've never seen our relationship as one of being black and white, only as one of committed love—of one that's not over."

"It is over, Gerri. I can't accept your kind of love anymore. I think I've overstayed my welcome," Sarafina said, crossing her arms.

"And how do you think you're going to *get* home, Sarafina? It's a long walk from here to Tinsel town."

Sarafina's eyebrows knitted together in bewilderment. "I expect to use the ticket that you sent to get me here."

"How can you do that when the ticket was only one-way? Hadn't you noticed that? Using that ticket meant you'd accepted the idea of being back here forever," Gerri declared, folding her arms across her chest.

"What? Are you serious?" Sarafina said, as her eyes began to roam, as she tried to remember the ticket and realized that she hadn't studied it closer. This was insane. "What are you trying to do, kidnap me or something? I'll pay for my own ticket if I have to."

"Without your bag that would be hard to do."

Sarafina dropped her arms to her side, clenching her fists. You mean to tell me that you are not going to give me my things? Is that what you're saying?"

Silence.

Who is *this woman?* Sarafina thought. She had once loved this person—a woman who had caused her to believe that despite all the racial and economic differences between them, love would prevail. And now this same woman was stark-raving mad. How could she have gotten so possessive, so self-centered, so wrong? Sarafina looked at Gerri and saw a stranger.

"You're sick, Gerri! I don't have to stay here. I'm going home, someway, somehow. I knew people before I left here; I'll just contact them. I have friends in L.A. that can help me out. You are not doing this to me, you hear?" Sarafina said, as she rushed for the door.

Gerri bolted from the bed, heading her off, barring her path. "Where do you think you're going?" she pleaded, her voice sounding almost childlike. "Come on, Sara, stay here. Stop all this running. This is your home. This is where you belong. I love you, baby."

"What the hell's wrong with you? I'm not in love with you anymore, Gerri! I'm not in love with you! I'm not in love with—"

The hand came across her cheek so fast that she didn't feel the sting of it till seconds later. Sarafina looked down at Gerri's still trembling palm, the fingers splayed apart, the inside a bright red from the sharp contact with her face. It was hard to fathom what had just happened: Gerri had struck her.

Gerri then attempted to speak, remorse registering on her face, but her words were quickly cut off as Sarafina lunged forward, grabbing the woman's neck between her thick hands. Sarafina could sense her muscles tighten; slick sweat began to pour from Gerri's neck across her fingers, the beat of her arteries tickled beneath Sarafina's palm. The fear in Gerri's eyes meant nothing at this point. The tears that hung at her lids only made Sarafina laugh inside. It would be so easy, so clean ... so unlike her.

She released her. "I've had enough!" Sarafina said, pushing Gerri aside and reaching for the knob on the door, violently swinging it open.

With one hand clutching her throat, Gerri reached for the door, reaching desperately for Sarafina. "No! Don't leave, Sara. We can work this out," she insisted, stopping at the doorway.

Sarafina ran down the staircase, gripping the handrail steadily as she lost her footing and nearly fell. During this, her mind was racing. She didn't know where her friends were in this city any longer. She had no one to call. She would have to try and contact her friends in L.A. and hope for the best. She had no idea where she would even sleep tonight. But she had to get out of this house. She had to get to that door and worry about the consequences later. She had to....

"Stop!" Gerri yelled to the top of her lungs, standing at the apex of the staircase. "Just wait a goddammed minute! I'll go get your bag," she said, defeated. This halted Sarafina as she watched Gerri return to the bedroom and seconds later returned with a manila envelope. She tossed it through the air in Sarafina's direction.

It landed at Sarafina's feet. She picked it up, the contents bulky, and the letter X was written in bold black ink on the front. "What's this?" she asked, raising the envelope above her head, shaking it at Gerri.

"Why don't you go in your room and find out? Then maybe we can talk," Gerri commanded, returning upstairs to her bedroom and slamming the door.

Sarafina was fuming. This whore was playing games with her. She ripped open the package and saw a video tape inside, unmarked, she trudged up the stairs and headed for her room, she looked at the tape more closely, trying to figure out what this charade was all about, and found nothing. She would have to play the tape. So she slid the object into the VCR and pulled a chair up close to the television. The picture came on very grainy and snow-like, which told her nothing. Then there was an image. Her first reaction was shock, as if all the air in the room had been sucked out. Sweat burst across her forehead. She looked at the television, extending her hand to touch its cold surface, trying not to believe what she was seeing. The image was of this very room—of the bed behind her—and her lying naked atop its sheets, eyes at half-mast in a drunken exhibition of helplessness. Her legs were spread wide; a grimace of a smile was on her face. Below her, between her thighs, hovered the tiny head of a woman, buried within her crotch, gripping her thighs. She steadily crawled upon her, resting on her tits. It was Gerri. They both appeared to be enjoying themselves, but Sarafina knew better.

She did drug me! Sarafina thought. *Oh my God! What has she done to me? What have I done?*

Suddenly the door to the room slowly opened and there stood Gerri, leaning against the frame. She had a look of joy and anger all combined into one frightening look. "Are you ready to talk now?" She asked. Sarafina had never been more afraid in all her life.

– II–

Dominique kicked open the door to the apartment, and allowed her heavy overnight bags to fall to the floor. She couldn't think of a better place to be after staying at the Hilton for the better part of a week. She thought a change in location would help ease her mind. She was wrong.

She had half hoped that perhaps Sarafina would be here when she returned, having come to her senses. She was wrong about that too.

All the messages on the answering machine sounded the same. It was Sarafina, declaring that she was only out in San Francisco to finish things up with Gerri. She felt it was best to do it in person and to do it right now. Sarafina had called her from all over the country, it seemed, as numbers from the caller ID displayed numbers from New York to some island in the Caribbean. Dominique laughed. It sounded like she was having the time of her life, gallivanting across the world. Dominique cursed herself for still missing the woman.

Walking to her bedroom, she fell upon the sheets, turning on her back to stare blankly at the ceiling. She listened to the silence. Every now and then it was interrupted by the rush of cars speeding past her apartment on the street below. The sounds of children's voices jingled in a cacophony of gleeful tones as the first weeks of summer vacation began. She sighed as she listened, because she actually missed being home. The Hilton was a nice escape, and it helped her concentrate on her work, but it was too sanitized; the sounds of neighboring guests roaming the hallways or the occasional knock from the maid to clean the room were the only distractions. This is where she was meant to be, but she never thought she would be here alone. She and Sarafina were to be here together ... forever.

She never thought forever would be so short-lived.

Dominique reached beneath her pillows. The bud was still there. She pulled it out and drew it under her nose, smelling the choked scent and smiling at its apparent freshness. This is what she needed tonight. She sat up and reached over to open the top drawer on the nightstand, taking out a box of wooden matches.

She took a hit and thought about their relationship. Where was it going now that Sarafina was in San Francisco? Should she bother trying to return those calls? Should she care? Sarafina was a grown woman and was making her own decisions at this point. Gerri was now Dominique's client, and soon they would meet.

Who knew what would happen at that confrontation? And yes, it was bound to be a confrontation. Dominique had no answers. As the joint drew her into a more relaxed mode, she decided not to worry about a woman who seemed to not worry about her.

— III —

David pulled the soiled garden gloves from his tense hands and reached for the lemonade that sat on the umbrella table. He let one of the thick ice cubes slide between his teeth, where he crunched loudly on it

"You know that's bad for your teeth," Mark said, sipping at his Evian bottle.

"Yeah, yeah, I know," he replied, quickly crunching the remainder and swallowing it. David gave Mark only a momentary glance, then casually smiled at him, his teeth as white as his skin was pale. They continued to stare out at the traffic as they sat along the curb, relaxing after a long afternoon of work. Mark was straight, and was getting married soon. He had just bought a three-bedroom home in Palos Verde, and David was helping him with the landscaping. He had worked on Mark's sister's place when he was freelancing at the beginning of his relationship with Allen. They had a good friendly rapport, but David had never told him or his sister of his sexual preference.

"If you crack a tooth, don't say that I didn't warn you," Mark chastised. "Unless, of course, a missing tooth is the style these days."

Mark leaned back in the lawn chair, his tank top drenched in sweat. He belly was starting to protrude, like so many straight men in their late thirties at the beginning of married life. He crossed his legs, thick ivory pieces of flesh with a hint of red hair, and David wondered where he was when it was announced that plaid shorts were back in style.

"Well, it seems to be the style according to these rappers that I see on television," David replied.

"Well, rap is surely not my style. I can't keep up with the words. It makes me feel older just listening to it."

"I feel the same way. I think you need a translator to understand that stuff."

"Don't we all?" Mark said. He leaned his head back, as if listening for something. David then noticed a ringing coming from inside the house. "That's the phone. It must be Cassidy calling me. I guess I should be getting ready to leave. We're having dinner tonight at Lawry's." He began to stand. "We can lay the sod for the lawn tomorrow if you want to?"

"Sure, Mark. It's been a long day. I have a friend who should be here soon for lunch. I'll just wait for him and see you tomorrow."

"Talk to you tomorrow then," Mark said, as he ran to the house.

David stood. He held his glass of lemonade and looked along the block at the rows of beautiful homes that lined the street. At the end of the block he noticed a white Honda Del Sol and an image of Allen flashed across his mind. The image was so strong that he could swear he smelled the liquor off his breath. Sometimes his mind was stronger than reality.

"Glad I could finally catch you alone, baby."

David spun around so fast that he dropped his glass, grateful it fell on a patch of grass. He looked up and saw Allen grinning wildly back at him - *drunk*. He was in shock. He wanted to run, but his legs felt fused to the concrete. "What are you doing here?" he spat from trembling lips.

Allen gazed at David, his features hideously macabre: hair tousled on his head in thick frayed clouds, his jaw covered in stubble, eyes glassy, inebriated. As he swayed slowly from side to side. He wore only a T-shirt and wrinkled jeans. He smiled at David.

"I just wanted to come and tell you that I'm not with Percy anymore. You can move back in."

David turned his back to Allen. *Maybe if I click my heels together three times then this will all turn out to be a dream. Maybe, maybe, maybe .... .*

He then swallowed, and spun back around – and the nightmare was still there. With one slow breath to calm him, he spoke, "I don't want to move back in Allen. Frankly, I think you need some help, but as for me, I need to help this nightmare we're going through, to end."

"Are you saying you won't come back home?"

Allen was not hearing him. He was a wreck, and David almost felt sorry for him. He didn't want to feel sorry for anyone any longer. This addiction with the bottle seemed to be taking over Allen's life, becoming his new lover, kissing his lips every night. "It's just too soon for me to decide on moving back in with you," David said.

Allen stepped closer, his feet dragging against the pavement. "But you will come back home, won't you? I love you, David," Allen said, his head cocked to one side like a confused puppy.

David chose not to answer. "I think I should call you a cab. I can't believe you drove up here in this state." He reached for Allen's arm.

With a rapid motion, Allen twisted his hand and quickly clutched David's wrist. "Come back home with me, David. Percy isn't there anymore. It'll just be me and you. I'm so sorry about all this bullshit I've caused." He pulled David closer.

"What're you doing, Allen?" David asked, as Allen placed his arm around David's waist.

"Why can't you hug me like you used to, David? Come on, hug me," Allen demanded, his actions becoming more forced. He pulled David closer.

David shoved him. "Allen, I'm not gonna stand here and hug your drunk ass in the middle of the street!"

"Fuck this street! I want you, David, and I know you want me. Why don't you just go home with me and let me fuck you all night—"

"Enough!" David wrestled himself away and stood back. He stood, catching his breath. He could see the anger in Allen's eyes and knew there was danger. He thought that this separation might have given Allen time to recognize his faults and give them a second chance. He was wrong. Allen talked with his hands and his dick - the former twisted into a knotted fist and the latter forming a developing impression within his pants. The most horrible realization for David was that he still cared for this man, still loved him.

"David! David, is that you?"

David turned at the faint voice coming from behind him. He turned to see someone running up the street. "Malcolm? Is that you?" He questioned, as he watched this muscular form jog in his direction, wearing black shorts and T-shirt. It was Malcolm, and there was a look of determination in his eyes.

He stopped in front of David, his eyes locked unto Allen. "Are you okay?"

David glanced back at Allen, who seemed to scowl, "I'm fine, Malcolm, um...I don't believe you've met Allen."

Malcolm's eyes never left the man. Malcolm stepped up and offered his hand. They said nothing to each other, but their gazes told a story that was loud enough to hear for miles. Their handshake, the tones a stark contrast - Malcolm's dark against Allen's light - the difference of night and day, fire and water, heaven and hell, reminded him of bulls locking horns before battle.

When the hands separated, it was as if a great chasm had split the earth.

"So how did you know I was here?" David asked Malcolm.

Malcolm turned to look down the street. "Your girlfriend brought me," he said, directing his finger to another approaching figure. It was Damien. "He said you guys were going to lunch, so I thought I'd kick it with you all, if that's cool with you."

"Well, seeing that my work was cut short, I think we can all leave together."

"That'll work. I'll just ride back with you," Malcolm suggested, his eyes darting at Allen's for reaction. There was none.

David placed his hand on Malcolm's shoulder. "Just wait a minute," he said. He turned to Allen, walking up close to him, looking him over. He couldn't let Allen drive home in this condition. Allen must have gotten drunk in the car while waiting for Mark to leave "You mind if I drive you home, Allen? Malcolm could take my car."

Allen grinned. "Sure, baby, you can come with me," he replied loudly, eyeing Malcolm.

David grimaced. He returned his attention to Malcolm, noticing that Damien had paused half a block away - he would not get any closer with Allen in view. His friend also looked concerned. There was only one conclusion David could think of at this point.

— IV —

David opened the passenger side of Allen's car, forcing him inside, his monumental build a challenge to negotiate. "Will you try and sit up straight?" David demanded, gripping Allen's shoulders and pushing him upright in the seat.

"Thanks, baby. I knew you still loved me," Allen said. It came out garbled, but David understood.

As the car pulled away, Allen rested his head against the window and mused over the idea of convincing David to return home. He was not going to allow this man to abandon him again. And that sissy friend of his—Mallard, Mason, Malcolm, whatever—wasn't going to stop him, He knew when a man was trying to move in on his territory. He reached his hand out to caress David's knee and could feel bare flesh. He pulled his hand back, realizing David hadn't been wearing shorts today.

"Don't try that shit again, brother! It's not that kinda party."

Allen shot up in his seat, his eyes fully open, and his high leveling off immediately. He turned to notice not David in the driver's seat, but Malcolm! "What the hell are you doing?" Allen shouted so loud his temples throbbed with each declaration.

Malcolm offered a single look in Allen's direction. He then returned his eyes to the road. "I'm dropping you off at your crib, that's what."

Allen reached for the steering wheel. "Why don't you just pull over?" he shouted, attempting to pry Malcolm's fingers from the steering column.

Malcolm pushed Allen's hands back, raising his own as a threat. "Chill that shit!" Malcolm voiced, never taking his eyes off the road

Allen withdrew and placed his hand on his sweaty forehead, feeling
the *thump, thump, thump* of his heart across his fingers. He rested his head against the cool headrest, and patiently asked, "Why isn't David driving the car?"

"I asked him to let me drive. He's following right behind us, and Damien is leading us."

Allen strained his eyes, looking ahead. Sure enough, there was that loud-ass yellow Mustang bouncing ahead, with Damien inside, bobbing his head to some dance tune he blared. Behind them Allen noticed David driving his own car. "What's going on here?"

"I need to talk to you. That's what's going on," Malcolm said.

"You need to talk to me? What've we got to talk about? Who the fuck are you?"

Malcolm snickered. "Good. I hope we can maintain that level of conversation in our relationship. I just wanted to tell you nicely to leave David alone. Simple."

Allen burst into laughter. "You want what! You got nerve sittin' in my car and trying to tell me what to do with my lover. You have got to be out of your mind. I know you have to be, Malcolm—is that right? May I call you Malcolm? I would rather call you a dead son of a—"

"You heard what I said!" Malcolm interrupted.

"And what the hell you gonna do? You catch me drunk with this bullshit. I can't believe this. David is mine, and I'll decide what we're going to do. He's my man and—"

"He *was* your man, but not now, homey. He don't belong to no one, but you haven't caught that bulletin lately, have you? I'm just here to remind you."

Allen lunged for the wheel again. "Get the hell out of my car!" he said, pulling at the wheel.

Malcolm swerved into the opposite lane of oncoming traffic. He forced the wheel back, prying Allen's fingers loose, and shoved him back against his seat with one powerful thrust. "Don't fuck with me, man!"

Allen caught his breath. "No, you don't fuck with me," Allen said, slamming his hand against the armrest. He hated himself for having drunk so much while waiting in his car for David to be alone. He was in no condition for this right now, especially in his own car. "You ain't Superman, brother. You don't know anything about me, and you trying to get into my shit. Fuck you!"

"Hey, I'm just warning you. David is trying to get his life together. You remember that? It's the one you fucked up. I know you like to beat your pieces, but I'm not one of your bitches, so don't try me, okay? I just want you to keep your fingers off my friend."

Allen could feel a wave of heat rush across his face. The traffic was going by his window at a blur, and his eyes were feeling heavier. Today he would let this fool have his moment. The next time they met, he wouldn't be so lucky.

— V —

Jamal stood at Terminal 4 of American Airlines, waiting curbside at the upper level of the LAX airport, holding his bags and two of Aunt Sylvia's famous pies. He was waiting for Stephen to pick him up, but for the last forty-five minutes none of the passing cars he watched, had paused to give him notice. *Where is that man?* Jamal thought. He'd left him a message saying what time his flight would be in. Stephen assured him that he would be there. 7 p.m. and there was no sign of him.

When he called his father's place, he said that Stephen had called. Aunt Sylvia had verified (she'd picked up the other line) that, although the connection was a little bad, it was short enough for Stephen to guarantee his arrival. Jamal had called several times earlier to confirm himself, but there was no answer at Stephen's place, and his cell phone had been off. And now even the answering machine wasn't taking messages – it either being full or having been turned off. He didn't understand.

Another gray Lexus streamed by…nope, not him. Jamal pulled his crew bag closer to sit upon, while adjusting his jacket against the chill in the air. He looked around at the bustling energy of the airport: the hustle of the many skycaps flagging down cars and retrieving passengers' bags, the growing line at the ticket counter, and the rumble of voices within the building each time the electronic doors slid open. Jamal began to think he'd become too trusting too soon, but of course it was his habit to trust the wrong people. Men were so full of shit sometimes. Promises made of tissue paper. He would give it another fifteen minutes then he'd catch a cab. That's what he would do if it came down to it.

And unfortunately, it did.

***

Stephen sat up with a start. He looked at Tumali bouncing playfully on his stomach as he lay on the sofa. The little man raised his nose in the air, sniffing loudly, then looked back at his father. "Good smells. Mommy makes good smells, mmm!" he exclaimed, speaking of his mother's cooking. He began to rub his belly. "It goan be good," he said, running his tongue across his lips.

Stephen nodded, lifting his son by the shoulders and placing him on the floor. "It sure is," he replied, turning the boy in the direction of the kitchen. "Why don't you go in there and see if you can help her?" He tapped Tumali lightly on the back of his jeans.

Tumali bounced high in the air, hopping all the way to the kitchen, and yelling, "Okay. Mommy, Mommy, I gonna help you. I gonna help you."

Stephen smiled as Tumali bounced into the kitchen. He swung his feet to the floor and picked up his watch from the end table. "Eight o'clock!" he whispered. He placed the watch back on the table. Jamal should have landed almost two hours ago. He said he would call to tell him what evening flight he would be on, but the phone hadn't rung all afternoon. "Felicia!" he called.

Felicia came trotting into the living room, a pair of tight jeans *hugging* her legs—the same style as Tumali's. There was a light smudge of flour on her cheeks, and her lips gleamed in the light. She strode toward Stephen at such a gait that he knew it was something left over from her modeling days. She wore one of Stephen's old T-shirts, which hung loosely on her slender shoulders. Her hands were wet, and she flicked her wet fingers as she approached. Tumali came in tow, a slice of orange gripped in his fist. The juice from it was smeared all over his face. "What's wrong, Stephen?" she asked kindly.

She was still a very beautiful woman; even after all the ugliness she'd been through. "Has the phone in the kitchen rung?" he asked.

"No. Haven't heard anything since I've been in the kitchen," she replied, turning on her heels and heading back. "Are you concerned about your friend, *Jay?*"

Stephen didn't reply. There was no bitterness in her voice. He'd expected with each mentioning of a friend (male in nature), that Felicia would blow up in a jealous rage. There had been none of that. She seemed so content at just being here that his lifestyle hadn't become an issue of late. It was turning out to be a great visit. Felicia's vibrant new attitude was very welcome. Ironically, it was also very scary.

Tumali, however, seemed to make all suspicions disappear. The child had such energy, such innocent wonder at the things around him, that it welled up a joy in Stephen that he could not describe. Work had even become better. However, he was yet to inform Jamal that his ex-girlfriend was staying with him. With so much attention spent at work and now at home with Tumali, he was running out of spare time for Jamal.

"You sure about the phone?" he yelled into the kitchen. "I'm sure," she replied.

Stephen reached down and picked up an X-Men action figure from the floor, and played with the arms while thinking, *surely he'd call sooner or later.*

Felicia could see Stephen through the space between the closed shutters that slid over the mini bar, next to the kitchen. She broke up the green leaves and placed them in the howl with the rest of the salad, watching Stephen. She reached for the salad oil and drizzled it sparingly over the food, tossing the vegetables as she did. Finally, concentrating on her meal preparations, she was able to relax her jaws and unclench her teeth. Jay, Jay, Jay! That named burned her brain. She wanted to scream, "Fuck Jay! I'm here goddammit!" But she remained cool, tranquil, and placid. She was on a mission.

Of course the phone hadn't rung; she'd turned it off. This was a war, and she was pulling no punches. The answering machine was off too. She wasn't going to have any faggot calling this house while she and her son were here—not if she could help it. She even managed to hide Stephen's cell phone. While Stephen was out with Tumali, that Jay fellow had left a message. Although he left no name, she knew it was him. He'd left a number in Washington where he could be reached, after giving information on his flight. Felicia called back, pretending to be Stephen, and confirmed with some old man about receiving the message, and that he would be at the airport to pick him up. Sneaky, yes. Wrong, perhaps. But this was a war, wasn't it? She was taking no prisoners.

She could hear her father's voice in her ear, "Damned faggots! Trying to take over the world—that's what they're up to. Someone should burn that closet they keep trying to step out of." She hadn't thought about her father in a long time, and she hadn't agreed with most of his skewed philosophies, but he was on the money when it came to these disgusting creatures. Stephen was being pulled farther into this world by his choice of friends. She couldn't just stand by and let that happen. He needed to be here with his son and not running around with men in tights. He just needed time to get back on the right track. He would; she was confident. She'd already picked out the delicious fourteen-karat diamond ring she had seen in the Sunday paper. She kept the page folded optimistically in her purse. One day Stephen would buy it for her. One day when she freed him.

– VI –

Jamal kicked the still-packed flight bag with his foot. "His fucking ex-girlfriend!" he yelled. He could not believe the conversation he'd just had. Stephen was still at home, waiting for his call. What kind of craziness was that? Jamal told Stephen that his father had received a call saying he would be at the airport at 6:15. Stephen stated he made no such call. "Bullshit!" Jamal had shouted. "The fool forgot. Why couldn't he just tell me that?"

Jamal said he left countless messages. Stephen declared he had received no messages. Then Jamal asked him to play his machine back, and POW! There they were - *six* glorious messages left by him. Stephen could only say that his son may have been playing with the machine. Whatever!

Jamal knew his anger stemmed from the fact that Stephen was not there at the airport, and it had cost him forty dollars to get home in a cab. Such a waste. He didn't know this woman, this ex-girlfriend Stephen spoke of, but something was going on. He knew sisters like her; he flew and worked beside them every day, talked with them as they plotted about their men, their baby's daddy, their ex-husbands; their never being able to let go. This ex of Stephen's didn't just bring her *son* to California; she brought him *and* herself - she was up to no good.

Jamal knelt down to pick up his bag. He would try to be civil. He and Stephen had only just begun dating. Stephen hadn't been in the lifestyle long enough to know that straight women and fags were not a good mix. Time would tell if he would have to cut that woman loose to show her who wore the real stockings in this relationship.

Chapter 15

– I –

Damien dug at the sand with the heel of David's shoe, making it a bit more comfortable.

"What are you doing?" David asked, rubbing goose pimples from his arms.

"Honey, you can't just sit on hot sand. The cool sand is always underneath," he replied, while pushing a mound to one side, creating a mock pillow. "And I needs to be comfy cause I will be checking out all the tushes 'round here." He spread out his blanket, and hunkered down on his makeshift bed.

"You don't need the sand to be any cooler on a day like this," David said, looking into the sky at the gray-hued film that covered it. "What happened to the sun?"

Damien shook his head. The sky was gray, and there was a breeze licking at his skin. Why was the weather like this almost every year that he attended the At The Beach Party? Blacks across the country would come here during this time around the Fourth of July holiday, here in the star city of Malibu, here on the sands of Zuma Beach…here to freeze their asses off. Well, at least the sights were always to be admired.

"I know one thing," Malcolm spoke from behind David. "It is packed out here today, cold or no cold."

David looked around and, sure enough, Malcolm was right. The Girls were out in vast numbers. Tents were erected along the sand like rows of Egyptian pyramids. Some of these were large enough to house a living room set...and some of them did. One tent housed an older couple, sitting on a futon, both of them in smoking jackets, drinking out of martini glasses. For $5 they would mix one for you.

Men and women alike were gathered here. The gym girls had been crowding the gyms for weeks for this moment to unveil their perfected pecs. The fem girls revealed their newest weaves and the men their newest silicone enhancement. The thugs carried thermal cups filled with liquor, and the freaks carried waist packs filled with condoms.

Skin tones: black, brown, light skinned, high yellow, copper, and even white to red. It was all there to celebrate a unity built upon color without prejudice.

Damien began rubbing lotion on his arms. "I just hope it starts to warm up soon," he said, looking up at the cloudy skies.

"Is that suntan lotion you puttin' on? There ain't no sun out here," Malcolm said.

Damien shook the tiny bottle in his direction. "See, that's why a mind is a terrible thing to waste. UV rays are worst when it is cloudy like this. Even your black ass can burn, baby. My Puerto Rican skin is sensitive, so I have to treat her with some love," Damien continued, shaking his head.

"So what do you think of your first black pride?" David asked. "I'm loving it so far. A lot of brothers here, both male and female, and I like to see that, and both types are fine."

"Amen for the brother type!" Darien proclaimed. "I know I should meet me a husband today."

"You always on the hunt for a husband," David said. "You should put that on your resume."

"It's already there, sweetheart. I need to be rewriting yours."

"No, thanks. I would rather he unemployed if I had to have your list of clients."

"I tell you what you really need to do, and that is to take Malcolm out there to bait you some real men. I am sure he would appreciate that too. He's not wearing those spandex for nothing."

David looked back at Malcolm. He had to agree with Damien; the man was looking rather good today. He had a beautiful body, and his package was putting on a display all on its own. He could easily compete with any of the Barbell Queens that littered the beach now.

"Does a stroll sound good to you, Malcolm?" David asked, standing and holding out his hand.

"Let's give these boys something to remember," he replied, grabbing David's hand.

Damien waved as his two friends walked off. "You two have fun. I'll be here guarding the food and waiting for Stephen to get here. Look out for Dominique too. She said she would try and make it."

"Don't eat us out of house and cooler," David said.

"Child, please ... I have other things to attend to," Damien said, as he reached in his bag and pulled out a pair of binoculars, a camera with zoom lens, a megaphone, a new phone book, and a rainbow flag, which he immediately stuck in the sand. He was ready.

"Keep the sand warm till we get back then," David said.

"Will you get out of here?" Damien said, raising his binoculars. "You are seriously blocking my view."

—**II**—

The horn blared and Jamal sat up instantly, rapidly blinking his eyes as he reached up to rub away the sleep he felt was caking the corners of his lids. Quickly he turned to take note of the time. 11:00! Stephen was late.

He quickly grabbed his windbreaker and sunglasses from atop his dining room table, and rushed out the door. He dashed down the three flights of stairs leading to his apartment—two steps at a time— and pushed open the smoked glass of the entrance. He quickly reached for his knees as a gust of cold wind lashed at his bare thighs and ran through his runner's shorts. He wore a pair of high-tops, thick sweat socks bunched around his ankles, a black FUBU tank top, and a G-string under his shorts. He threw his jacket across his shoulders while keeping his sunglasses clutched between his teeth, and focused on Stephen's Lexus. Stephen was casually waving to him as if they had all the time in the world.

Jamal caught his breath as he slid into the passenger-side seat and kept his eyes centered out the passenger window. He could feel Stephen's hand touch his thigh. "I'm sorry about being late, Jamal. I was reading to Tumali, and time slipped from me," Stephen explained.

Jamal shrugged his shoulders. "You don't have to explain to me."

"No," Stephen said, sensing Jamal's disturbing tone, "but I want to.

Jamal turned to face Stephen, a false grin on his face. "You don't exactly look dressed for the beach," Jamal commented, noticing Stephen's two-piece khaki outfit and sandals.

"It was rather cold this morning, so I thought I would play it safe. Besides, I don't feel like brandishing all that flesh this year."

"I guess," Jamal said, turning to face the road once more as they headed to the 405 freeway. "So, how long do you think it'll take for us to get there?"

"Hmm, I'd say about another hour n' a half. We should be there about twelve-thirty," Stephen answered. He looked at Jamal. "Is there something on your—"

"What's going on with you and Felicia, Stephen?" Jamal blurted. "What? Me and Felicia? Where did that come from?"

"It's a simple question," Jamal added.

"Nothing!" Stephen said swiftly, pushing the word from his mouth. "We just have a son together, that's all. You think we're sleeping together or something?"

"All I know is that this woman has come back into your life, when only a few weeks ago you told me you two were not even communicating. Has she suddenly changed and accepted your lifestyle?" Jamal challenged.

"I don't know if she has or hasn't. We haven't discussed that, Jamal. What we once had with each other is over now. If I wanted to be with her, then she would be in this car instead of you."

Jamal leaned his seat back a bit more, placing a hand behind his head as he stared at the roof of the car. "I think that woman is still in love with you no matter what your feelings may be. I have nothing against her, but—"

"You don't even know her," Stephen interjected calmly.

"True, but you don't have to be George Washington Carver to realize that she still wants to make peanut butter with you. She seems to be pushing aside a lot of feelings to be near you. And isn't it funny it's just at the time you started seeing someone else? All I'm saying is that you could be putting yourself in a dangerous position."

Stephen gripped the steering wheel tighter. "I think you're just jealous of Tumali."

Jamal quickly sat up. "Jealous! Don't be ridiculous. That's your son, Stephen. I haven't met him, but I'm sure he's the sweetest thing alive, and he has nothing to do with this."

"And you think Felicia has?"

Jamal leaned back again. "You think about it, Stephen. You used to call me every day. You used to be on time for your appointments. Felicia is preventing you from acting yourself, being yourself. There seems to be no room for me in all this activity. None at all."

"So, what are you saying, Jamal? Are you tired of dating this way? Are you ready to move on?" Stephen asked, anxiety mounting.

Jamal sighed. "That's not what I'm saying at all. All I'm saying is that I'm here for you, Stephen, but you're going to have to find some time for us, and not when you can fit it into an already full schedule. That's what this lack of punctuality is all about: you trying to find time for me. It shouldn't have to be that way. If it is, then you are obviously too busy."

Stephen remained silent, the white center divider of the freeway becoming his focus. He did have a few things to think about. Somehow Felicia had come back into his life without him realizing it. Somehow she brought a peace offering in the form of his son, and he forgot about the woman attached. He forgot about how she had been only weeks ago. "Can we talk about this some other time, Jamal?" Stephen surrendered.

"Sure. Let me know when you have the time."

—**III**—

Dominique shuffled through her CD collection and pulled out a few selections she wanted to take to the beach. She walked to the curtains and parted them, looking out at the overcast skies. "Damn! Still gloomy out there." She knew Damien would be there by now, but he was always the early bird. She looked down at the one-piece bathing suit she wore and adjusted the knitted shawl she had across her shoulders. She picked up her backpack, which contained a pair of sweatpants, thermal cooler, beach blanket, and other essentials. It was still rather light. Good. There was nothing worse than lugging a bunch of stuff up that bill leading to the beach. She slung the bag across her shoulder and dashed in the bathroom to check her grooming in the mirror, making sure her teeth were clean, all pimples eradicated. She pulled her hair back and set a baseball cap on her head. Cute.

She was determined to have a good time and stop thinking about Sarafina freakin' it up in San Francisco. She hadn't called today, which was strange, because the answering machine was always filled with her messages, her pleas for forgiveness, her excuses. If the girl had any sense, she would bring her ass back and face the consequences. She wasn't about to call her at that woman's house.

Suddenly, there were a series of light raps on the front door. This was a secure building, so Dominique knew it could only be a neighbor, and wondered who. But when she opened the door, she was surprised to see an Asian woman standing before her. She didn't know who this woman was. She was dressed in business attire, with a navy blue pin-striped jacket, matching skirt, and black heels. Her hair fell along her jawbone. She had no bangs; hair was simply parted down the center. Tiny pearls dotted the lobes of her ears, and her makeup was light, almost unseen. She clutched a small black handbag against her stomach. "Excuse me, but are you Dominique Devaroe?" the woman asked very cordially.

"Why, yes I am. I'm sorry, but have we met before?" Dominique replied, falling quickly into her business tone, despite her casual state of dress.

"No, I don't think we have. My name is Cyan Kai," she greeted, hesitant to extend her hand, because the rough part came next. "I'm a friend of Gerri Moore."

Dominique fought the impulse to close the door on this woman. It was only by the grace of God that her body seemed to immediately lock up her fingers digging into the edge of the door.

"Really?" she forced herself to ask, teeth clenched. "Has this anything to do with the Manchester site? Angela hadn't paged me. Is there a problem with—?"

"This isn't about the cosmetics firm," Cyan interrupted. "This is about Sarafina."

Dominique's mouth fell open. "Sarafina? What do you have to—" she stopped, thinking for a moment. "How did you get in this building? Who buzzed you through the gate?"

Cyan shifted her stance. This was done on purpose. She had to quickly establish some form of trust, and she could only do that by getting inside this woman's home. Cyan was playing on her sympathy. "Sarafina opened the gate for me. She's waiting in my car right now until I've finished speaking with you. We've traveled down from San Francisco this morning."

Dominique looked unsure. *What is this all about?* She wondered. "San Francisco? Is Gerri with her too? Are you coming to get her things?" she questioned, her heart racing, her palms becoming sweaty. Was this how it would end? Why was she still surprised after all that had happened?

"No," Cyan said quickly, seeing Dominique's reaction, feeling her concern. "Sarafina asked me to come and speak with you on her behalf." She shifted her feet once more, sighing heavily. Couldn't this woman see she was tired?

"Why? She's never been shy before," Dominique responded.

Cyan dropped her shoulders. She was getting nowhere in this hallway. "Do you mind if I come in, Ms. Devaroe? I can explain everything if you'll allow me a moment of your time."

Dominique waited, unsure. This was a strange woman, coming from a stranger city, a friend of the strangest woman of all. But even as these thoughts ran through her mind, she could feel herself inviting this woman inside her home, the scent of White Diamonds trailing after her.

"Thank you. I promise this will not take long," Cyan assured her.

Dominique turned to see this woman standing in the center of her room, obviously waiting to be directed to a seat. "You can have a place on the sofa," Dominique offered.

Cyan looked around the home as she sat. "I hope I wasn't interrupting anything."

Dominique slowly closed the door. "Why would you say that?"

"Well, you're not exactly dressed for a social affair," Cyan stated, taking note of the bathing outfit Dominique was sporting.

"True. I was on my way to a little beach gathering," Dominique responded.

"Some sort of family reunion?" Cyan asked.

Dominique smiled. "You can say that," she replied, taking a place on the chair adjacent the sofa. "But I believe you were going to tell me something about Sarafina." She had no time for this idle chatter.

Cyan eased forward, clasping her hands in her lap. She cleared her throat. "Yes, that's true. This might appear a bit strange and awkward for you—and believe me I feel the same—but Sarafina thought you'd believe what I had to say if it didn't come from her."

"Really? And you say you're a friend of Gerri's as well? I assume you know of the time Sarafina lived in San Francisco?"

Cyan nodded her head. "Yes, I did, and I'd met Sarafina on a number of occasions while she was involved with Ms. Moore."

"I will also assume you know what's been going on now between us and that woman," Dominique stated, tapping her foot against the floor nervously.

Cyan noticed the gesture, and knew she needed to get off this subject or she would get nowhere. "Yes, but only in parts. But I didn't come here to rehash the circumstances that led to this confusion."

"Confusion? Now that's a cute word, I must say. If you didn't come out here to sort out any of this *confusion,* then what exactly brings you here, Miss Kai?"

"Well, let me get to the point," Cyan said, rubbing her palms. "Yes, please do," Dominique retorted.

"Okay. You may not take this seriously, but Sarafina was more or less trapped in Gerri's home," Cyan said, waiting for a response.

Dominique raised her hand to her ear, her eyebrows wrought together in mystification. "I'm sorry, what did you say? Trapped? What are you talking about?" she asked, looking up at the clock on the wall. She had better things to do than play cat and mouse.

"Maybe *trapped* is too vague a word. Perhaps the word I'm looking for is *kidnapped,"* Cyan sucked through her teeth loudly, as if that word was too strong.

Dominique couldn't believe this woman. What was she saying? "Kidnapped? Is that what Sarafina told you?" she asked, her manners falling short now. "That woman hops on a plane of her own free will and decides to stay with another woman who, quite frankly, makes my stomach turn, and now she shows up at her own choosing, and you want me to believe she was kidnapped."

Cyan held up her hand. "Now please, hear me out. I've come a long way to help a person I hardly know, and I wouldn't have done so if not for good cause. Why don't I start by telling you how I became involved in this, and the story Sarafina told me?"

Dominique held her breath. She needed a good joint right now. "Okay, I'll give you the time to explain this to me,"

Dominique declared, rising from her seat. "Not that I think this will take long, but I would like to offer you a drink. I have juice, water, coffee—"

"I'll take the coffee. What kind do you have?"

Dominique showed a menacing grin as she headed for the kitchen. "Why, I have hazelnut cappuccino. I hear it's one of Gerri's favorites."

***

Fifteen minutes. That's how long it had taken Cyan to explain what was going on in San Francisco. That's how long Dominique sat in awe at the tale revealed to her. That's how long it took for time to stand still.

She'd been running the streets for hours—that's what Sarafina had told Cyan—before she happened upon Cyan's home on recollection alone. Cyan had barely recognized the stranger knocking on her door. She'd been panting heavily, the streetlights casting a hideous glow on her features. She'd lost touch with her friends in San Francisco. She had no money, no credit cards, no clothes; they were all in her bag—a bag Gerri refused to relinquish. Who needed those things when a wealthy woman was willing to buy you all you needed? She tried calling home, but the machine just beeped then hung up—a sign that the machine was full and her other messages were never received. She wanted to call others she knew in L.A.—names like Stephen, Damien, and David came to mind, but they were more Dominique's friends than hers. She didn't think she knew them well enough to ask for help. She was desperate. She was scared. She was angry.

Cyan was the only one she could remember. They knew each other through Gerri—not very well, but she thought well enough. Cyan said Sarafina had been ranting and raving about Gerri. The woman was a monster, a vixen, a bitch, 100 percent, no additives, she told of a woman that showered her with gifts, trips, the luxuries she'd long forgotten, long thought she'd never missed. She was wrong. It was nice in the beginning, so much so that she forgot her initial purpose: to tell this woman to get out of her life. When the time came for such an announcement, she was appalled at the discoveries, the plots that had been planned beforehand. Gerri had no intention of letting her go back to Los Angeles. She'd taken Sarafina's bag of possessions and refused to give it back to her. She'd sent Sarafina a one-way ticket; no return was possible, she'd threatened to fire Dominique, if she didn't stay a little longer. Sarafina said she never prostituted herself, never willingly gave her body to this woman, never! But it seemed that wasn't Gerri's main purpose. Gerri wanted Sarafina by any means necessary. .

Dominique stood, extending her arm toward Cyan. "Would you like some more coffee?" she asked.

"Yes, if you wouldn't mind," Cyan replied, reaching out to hand Dominique her empty cup.

"That's some story, Cyan. It stretches the imagination, you know what I mean?" Dominique asked, as she headed for the kitchen.

"I understand quite well, believe me. If not for Sarafina's desperate demeanor, I don't think I would have taken it as seriously as I did. I also know Gerri quite well, and this behavior, although quite disturbing, is not at all surprising, considering Gerri's possessive nature."

Dominique returned with two fresh cups, and handed one to Cyan. "The coffee is quite good, Ms. Devaroe."

"Thank you," Dominique replied, taking a sip from her cup. "So what does she want from me now? Am I to suddenly forgive her for this behavior?"

Cyan leaned back against the sofa, her eyes looking off in the distance. "I don't know the answer to that, Ms. Devaroe. What I do know is that Sarafina has been through a lot, a great portion I gather is surely her fault to begin with. She just wanted me to inform you about her experience and, in a sense, to let you know that she still wants you, no matter how her actions prove the contrary."

"Is that what she wants," said Dominique, rolling her eyes to the ceiling in disbelief. "She didn't seem to want that while she was galloping across the world. How do you explain that?"

"Well, honestly, I believe Sarafina has been keeping a secret link with Gerri because she has fooled herself into believing that she could live without the luxuries she'd left behind. Life with Gerri wasn't easy, and the money made for a nice case of amnesia. Her friendship was a cushion she used in the event something went awry with the two of you, and she felt safer knowing she could resume her relationship with Gerri. But soon her confidence in her relationship with you grew enough for her to trust it, and I think this trip was a way for her to prove that. She fell quickly into her normal routine of being the spoiled spouse, and she didn't know how to get out of it only because she never before had to. But you were in her life this time, so it gave her a reason to fight. She could no longer enjoy the wealth Gerri provided because she realized she was no longer in love with this woman. So when she tried to leave, Gerri refused. It brought her to an emotional end, because now she didn't know how Gerri would fit in her life, and the more she discovered what that woman was like, the more she realized they had never been friends to begin with."

Dominique looked upon Cyan with awe. "That was a rather detailed analysis. You should make that a profession," she suggested.

Cyan smiled. "As a matter of fact, I have. I'm a therapist by trade."

"Is that so? Well, all of this about Gerri and her behavior, and still you remain friends with her. Why?"

"We deal with each other differently than she does with the women in her life."

"And how does your friend feel about you helping Sarafina get here to me?"

Cyan smiled again as she paused to take another drink of the wonderful brew. "I don't have an answer to that ... because she doesn't know."

– IV –

David stood back a few paces, sizing Malcolm up in the viewfinder of the camera, before snapping his picture as he stood at the water's edge, striking an exaggerated bodybuilder's pose. He noticed that Malcolm had an attractive smile and a wonderful disposition. He was glad to have this man as a friend. In the short time they'd known each other, he felt this was a man he could trust. It also frightened him, because he often sensed Malcolm wanted more than just a casual friendship.

Malcolm strode out of the water toward David, his chestnut thighs seeming to swell with each step. "Aren't you gettin' in the water?" he asked.

"Hell no. And freeze my ass off?"

"Boy, you got to *have* ass in the first place," Malcolm replied, reaching out to pat David's rear.

David smacked his hands. "Get those fingers back! You're just mad 'cause these buns are tight, and all without a gym membership."

Malcolm stepped closer to David, wrapped his arms around him, and lifted him. "All that ego weighing you down, and you're still light as a feather."

David laughed. "You are out of your mind and crazy."

"Now how about a little swim?" Malcolm said, carrying David toward the shore.

"You better not. I'll scream rape."

"These sissies won't hear that."

"Then I'll scream, *straight man on the beach!*"

Malcolm nodded his head. "Yeah, that they might bum-rush me for," he said, carrying David back, away from the water. "You've got to learn to take some chances in life, David."

"I've been taking all sorts of chances in my lifetime, Malcolm," David said, wiggling his legs. "Now put me down, big boy."

Malcolm lowered David back to the sand. He looked into David's eyes. "You just need to take the right ones this time, David. Some chances can last a lifetime."

"And what sort of chances should I be taking? Stepping in that water is—"

"I'm not talking about the water," Malcolm interrupted, leaning his head closer to David, until their noses almost touched. "I think you know that."

Suddenly, David heard his name being called. He turned to see a pair of women galloping through the sand, hands interlocked. Beyond that he saw a group of men huddled around a barbecue pit. Then he saw the caller—Dominique.

"Hey, girl," David yelled, taking a pace forward, and stretching out his arms. Dominique came rushing to them. "Thought you'd never get down here," he said, as they exchanged a friendly kiss.

Dominique acknowledged Malcolm. "So, how you doin', hot stuff?"

Malcolm nodded to her, while eyeing her at the same time. "I'm doing pretty good, Dominique. You looking for Damien? He's over—" he started to point in the direction of where they came from.

"We'll take you to him," David interrupted, pulling her hand and leading the way.

As they walked, Dominique looked at Malcolm, and she could feel a chill in his stare. She had seen the same stare, although less intense, when she would look into the mirror and think of Gerri, as if she were a square peg intruding into a round hole.

– V–

"Ewww-wee! Lookit the big fish David done caught," Damien said, pointing at Dominique as she and David came closer.

Dominique kicked sand in Damien's direction. "Quiet. I thought the best tent contest was over, and here you are wearing one," she quipped, kneeling on a nearby blanket.

"You throw her back into the ocean, David. We don't need any Red Snapper fish around here."

"I know something I could snap," Dominique said, looking at Damien's crotch. He placed a hand over his open mouth. Looking around she noticed that Stephen and Jamal had arrived, and also Damien's friends Gary and Peter were seated there. "Hey there, Gary and Peter. Haven't seen you two since that Halloween party Damien gave last year. Anything new with any of you?"

Peter opened his mouth to respond, but Gary quickly cut in. "This child done got hooked up with a brother," Gary smiled.

Dominique reached over to touch Peter's knee. "A little salt n' pepper, huh?"

"Yeah, and one day I will be able to announce my own news," Peter said, glaring at Gary. He began to stand. "Speaking of which, I need to root for my new man as he plays volleyball over there. He's going to be in the Hot Body contest too later on, so I expect to hear you guys cheering the loudest."

"You're leaving? But I just got here," Dominique said, taking a place on the blanket. "Serves me right for being late."

Peter shook her hand, and waved to the others. "Still good to see you, Dominique. We'll talk later."

"Great. It would be good to see how black you like your coffee."

"Very, baby," Peter said. "Bye, everyone. And I'll call you tonight, Damien."

Damien pushed a wad of food to one side of his mouth as he answered, "All right, sweetheart. Kisses!" He watched as Peter walked away into a sea of dark flesh. Looking back at the group, he could see Jamal shaking his head. He had done that all while Peter was speaking about his relationship. He knew what that meant.

"I take it you're not into the *swirl*, Jamal."

"It's nothing against your friend," Jamal said. "I just can't see myself being with a white guy, and can't understand a brother's interest in one, either."

Gary sat up and reached in a nearby backpack. I say, to each his own," he said, pulling out a bag of chips.

"Doesn't it just seem like something is wrong with all this intermingling?"

"Child, there ain't nobody trying to procreate here," Damien said.

"I have to agree that I like to see brothers loving brothers, myself. But some men think that by dating or fucking white guys, they have somehow overcome. I think it's a cop-out when a black guy dates a white guy and say it's because they can't find a black man to do them right."

"Getting mighty deep over here," Damien said, taking a sip of his cola. "I tell you, I don't mind a little whipped cream in my cocoa. Gary can attest to that."

"Yeah, anyone who reads bathroom stalls can attest to that," Gary said.

"You lucky I left my cutlery at home," Damien said. "But everyone knows I am not prejudiced when it comes to bedroom activity."

Malcolm then spoke, "I know I would hate to be liked solely because of the color of my skin, without the respect that comes with it. We try to make ourselves equal to our white counterparts all the time, and it doesn't work. We begin to lose our identity I think—display a watered-down version of ourselves."

"So what do you think, Stephen? How do you feel about interracial relationships?" Jamal asked, while leaning on Stephen's shoulder.

"I don't think much about it, considering I have been on the other end of the sexual spectrum. I do have to agree with Malcolm about the social differences and the social expectations. Many blacks assume the white culture in an attempt to vanish into it. They call it ass kissing in the corporate arena."

"That it is," Malcolm continued. "We are too busy fighting each other, and ass kissing to ever attain our own piece of the pie. We have the buying power, but not the owning power."

David spoke up. "I don't think any of it matters, really," he directed his hand toward Stephen. "Stephen may prefer to date blacks occasionally. And Malcolm," he placed a hand on Malcolm's shoulder, "May want to date blacks only. Gary may like whites better than blacks, and my sister Damien may go for the best fuck regardless of color. So what? We are black men first, gay black men second, but we are all men. If I love a white guy, or a black guy, I'm still loving a man. Where does all that political bullshit come in when the lights are turned off? Blacks are always looking to blame someone else for their handed-down-through-the-generations ideology. Slavery has been over for two hundred years, and although we like to blame that for our black issues, I see it as the only time we were unified. If we had the togetherness that we had back then while running through the underground railroads, then we would have amassed something. I love my brothers, and I respect them. You don't have to sleep with a black man in order to love him. You don't have to sleep with a black man in order to fear one. You don't have to sleep with a black man in order to remain a black man. So who cares who you fuck and what color they are? Respect begins on the human level, not a melanin induced one."

"Damn, David! Sunday ain't until tomorrow preacher-man," Damien said, now turning to Dominique. "I'm afraid to even ask what you think, Dominique baby."

Dominique shrugged her shoulders. "Well, I ain't ever loved a white man, that's for sure," she laughed, and the others joined her. "So you testosterone-driven boys are on your own."

"Speaking of which, by the look of my watch, the Hard Body Contest will be starting in just a few minutes. I love you all, but shut the hell up. The real show is about to start."

– VI –

Sarafina sat nervously on the sofa, stroking Bootie's soft fur with the tips of her nails. She was so caught in her own thoughts that when she heard the latch to the door unlock, she nearly dug her nails deep into the cat's flesh, causing Bootie to flee to the kitchen.

She wished she could run off into the kitchen too, to find sanctuary, an escape. She could suddenly remember Cyan returning to the car, informing her that it was all explained and the rest was up to her. She could remember trudging up the stairway to the apartment, her pores bursting with moisture, her lungs growing smaller, her *feet* like marble slabs affixed to her ankles. She found the door ajar and lightly pressed it open with her knuckles. Inside, she could see Dominique bent over the love seat, snapping shut the clips to her backpack. She hauled the bag over her shoulder and marched past Sarafina. "Try being here when I return," was all she'd said before breezing out the door.

When Dominique returned, sand trailing her footfalls, her skin a few shades darker, and her arms released from the burden of her backpack, she let the door swing open, stopping for an instant at the door's entrance, looking blankly at Sarafina, as if she were either surprised to find her here or had simply forgotten she would be. Sarafina looked into her eyes but found the stare too intense and moved her gaze elsewhere.

Dominique looked so beautiful and so deadly at the same time. Sarafina had practiced saying "I'm sorry" a thousand times, but the words were now wedged somewhere within her. She knew she was wrong. Almost a whole month away, so what did she expect to happen?

Dominique said nothing as she entered the apartment, walking past Sarafina and into the bedroom. The shower came on full blast, then the sound of a dresser drawer being pulled open, then the television. Sarafina continued to stare into space, her vision blurred by her tears. She was guilty of so many things: guilty about leaving L.A. without a word spoken to Dominique, guilty about defending a woman she thought was her friend, guilty about answering that damn phone, from which this whole ordeal had started, guilty about actually having fun in the lap of luxury Gerri provided. Most of all, she was guilty about the tape—allowing herself to become caught in a menagerie of blackmail that forced her to remain with a woman whose purpose was selfish and unnatural. To come back home was risky. Gerri could send that tape to Dominique, but Sarafina had to take that chance. She forgot how much she loved this woman.

"We need to talk."

The voice came so smoothly to her ears that Sarafina thought it was a remnant from her half sleep. But it wasn't. Dominique stood before her at the edge of the sofa, her eyes downcast, the scent of weed in the air. She pushed her hands through her hair, threading her fingers between the long strands restlessly, looking off into the distance, unsure of her next action.

Sarafina sat up, her hands clasped together in her lap. She began to speak. "If you want me to move out, Dominique, I could just—"

"Let me speak," Dominique said, holding up her hand. Sarafina could see true anger in her pupils, threatening to rupture. "I just want to know what kind of relationship you think this is? You just said 'Fuck it!' to us, and you ran off to your bitch in San Francisco so—"

"I didn't just run off to—"

"I said I was talking here!" Dominique snapped, turning her vexed stare directly at Sarafina. "I don't think you have a damn thing to say at this point. You lay up in that woman's home, and then a full three weeks later you drag yourself back here, and you thought that bringing that woman, that friend of Gerri's, was going to make anything better? What kind of fool do you think I am?"

She's high, Sarafina thought, *and that makes her menacing.* She wanted to rise up and smack her, to calm her down, to make her just shut up and listen. She didn't have an excuse for her actions, but that didn't mean she didn't have an explanation.

"You know I've tried to call you. I tried to tell you what was going on. I did all I could. I had to find out what Gerri was up to, what she was trying to do, why she sent me that plane ticket, why—"

"I tell you what she was trying to do, and that was to continue to be a no-good cunt!" Dominique began to pace the floor. "I told you that in the beginning. But you had to go gallivanting off to see her to find that out the hard way and risk our relationship in the process."

Sarafina slammed her fist against her thigh. "I love you, dammit!" Sarafina said, more to her feet than to Dominique. She didn't know why she had suddenly said that, but she felt it was needed.

"That still doesn't excuse this, Sarafina."

Sarafina leaned forward, resting her elbows on her knees, placing her chin in her palms. So what is this, Dominique? What is it that you want to do? What are you thinking?"

"What do I think?" She looked to the ceiling. "Now she wants to know what I'm thinking. I'll tell you, Sarafina. I'm thinking it's going to be mighty hard living around here. It's going to be mighty hard to sleep in the same bed with you. It's going to be mighty hard doing my job and coming home, never being able to escape this situation. I'm not going to leave my apartment, not for this, and not right now, and if you want to leave, then that's your decision. You, my dear, will be sleeping on this couch tonight, and I will be placing the cot in the spare room tomorrow if I decide you should venture in there. Other than that, I don't know," Dominique finished, wiping a bead of sweat from her forehead.

"I'm sorry this has happened," Sarafina began. "I only wanted to see where me and Gerri stood. I thought she was my friend—I really did—but I was wrong. She spoiled me, and I guess I liked it for a second. I guess there were a lot of things we never discussed, a lot that was never finished."

"And this friend of yours, this woman you trusted who became your kidnapper, your enemy, most likely from the moment you entered that house, what else kept you there, Sarafina? What else pulled you into that whore's clutches so deeply that you neglected to remember to even respect me? What really went on in that house? Or should I say, what really went on in that bedroom? I know there was more than a locked room and gruel to eat that kept you there."

"It wasn't like that, Dominique. I wasn't locked away. I was just—"

"Then what was it? What was it?" Dominique shouted.

The videotape swiftly ran through Sarafina's mind. It was the reason she'd stayed as long as she did. She was afraid Gerri would send it to Dominique, and then where would she be? How could Dominique believe that Gerri drugged her, had taken advantage, then filmed the whole thing? It angered her. She shot up from her seat, and spun around to address Dominique. She was tired of this whole conversation. Extremely exhausted.

"Okay, Dominique! You can blame me for a lot of shit, but I had to go to San Francisco. I had to find out what Gerri was trying to do with her phone calls, her airline ticket, her letters. I was angry, and I had to face her in person. How could I know she would trip on me? How did I know she was plotting to steal me away? True, it was a marvelous plan—getting me there, treating me like a queen, planning trips, having Carlotta make me fabulous meals, all beginning with a great Memorial Day party. I slowly forgot what the hell I had gone there for. I began to feel like I had never left. The only difference was that I was no longer in love with Gerri. I was in love with you. But you never returned any of the phone calls I sent. I'm not a psychic. How did I know where this relationship stood if you didn't speak to me? Why should I rush home if there would be nothing for me to come back to?"

"Damn it's hot in here!" Dominique said, fanning herself with the neck of her robe. "And what brings you back here now, Sarafina? Did you think I would forgive this crap you had served? Did you think I would listen to this crazy explanation and just accept it? What did you think would happen when you came back here?"

"I thought you were still in love with me. I thought you would listen. I thought we still had a chance to fix this."

Dominique turned toward the bedroom. "You've done .a lot of thinking, Sarafina," she said, pulling her hair back again. "Perhaps you should do some more. I'm growing tired of this, Sarafina ... very tired." She walked back to their bedroom, closing the door.

Sarafina could not believe this. She gazed at the closed door, .wishing it would open again and she could start over. It didn't, and it was then that she realized the sofa would be her resting point, perhaps for many nights beyond this one. She looked up at the overhead fan. She would have sworn it had become a bit more stifling in this room, a bit more heated. She thought this room was in for many a stifling night.

Chapter 16

—I—

Damien walked into his apartment on the verge of a nervous breakdown. He could still feel his throat holding back his sorrows and his hands still clutched the tiny teddy bear to his chest. He placed the bear gently on the sofa and began to undo his tie, then he sat down on the sofa with such force it was as if his legs had given up the fight to sustain him any longer.

Then he cried.

Andrew Christenson had passed away four days ago. The funeral had been today. Damien had felt a bit of himself die too. He leaned back to peer through the vertical blinds out to the shiny rain-slicked streets below at David who was standing at the corner. The light had turned green twice. David said he wanted to take a walk despite the mist that permeated the air, creating light sprinkles. Right now he was just standing against the signpost, looking out across the empty streets. Damien knew what he was feeling and wouldn't blame him if he stood there for the rest of the evening.

Why does it always have to rain at funerals? Damien pondered. It was the same in San Diego, and for the two-hour drive back, as if a storm cloud had been constantly following them. The drive was the most silent one he'd ever taken with his friends on this unexpected getaway. Damien turned away from the window and redirected his attention back to the bear that sat crookedly on the couch next to him. He straightened Kisan, brushed at its chest, and leaned forward to kiss it on its dark jeweled eyes. Just a few weeks ago Andrew had been holding this wonderful animal, talking with glee about the child who had given it to him. Mrs. Christenson said Andrew wanted Damien to have it. He'd been too choked up to even say thank you.

The call had come on July 19, a Tuesday, rousing Damien from his sleep at four in the morning. He had just seen Andrew the previous Monday, with the visit being rather short and difficult. Andrew had not looked good at all, Damien noted, with his pains getting worse, and the drugs he'd been taking doing absolutely nothing for him now. His bedroom had the odor of being half sour, half air freshener. He was so doped up that he'd barely noticed that Damien had come to visit him. Damien cursed those drugs, which he thought were the one thing making him sick by lowering his body's defenses, allowing anything to kill him. He'd become such a victim to them that there was no turning back. The damage was done.

Once Mrs. Christenson had informed him of the time Andrew had passed away (2:30 a.m.), he had heard nothing else she said. His mind quickly shut off, and once he finished with the conversation he found himself stumbling to the kitchen to quench a new incredible thirst, but instead he had fallen against the refrigerator, fighting tears. That's when David had entered the kitchen, and upon hearing the news he too found composure difficult to maintain.

Andrew was gone. Taken away by a horribly selfish disease. He was only twenty-eight, Damien's own age. It was scary. It was scary to see Andrew wither away, coughing, spitting, high as a kite on pain relieving medication. It was scary listening to him talk about the clubs they'd gone to, the people they'd known, the men they'd hungered for. It was scary to see the closed-casket ceremony and know behind the grand flowers that covered the box there was a man who still retained his great smile and wonderful sense of humor until the end. He'd talked with Damien on the phone saying that he'd made his peace with God and that he was ready to go; his pain was that great. He'd been only renting this world, and the lease was finally up.

The Catholic school that the little boy who brought the bear was from said that the rose garden would be in bloom next year, and a bush would be named after Andrew. Then on the anniversary of his death everyone could go there and have fresh roses to remember him by. The school had a huge five-acre garden, and Andrew would not be alone in this botanical paradise. He'd always loved a gathering. A beautiful man named after a beautiful flower. They'd known each other since high school, and now he was gone. Friends, lovers, and roses; that's what life was all about, it seemed.

– II–

David hurriedly buttoned his shirt, skipping a few holes along the way. He shook his head, cursing himself for coming here. Standing on the street corner had made him realize how alone he was in this world, how much time he had, how little he had, and how terrible it all could become. It hadn't felt right going back to Damien's place, because that wasn't his home. For five years he'd been under Allen's roof, and for those years that had been his place of dwelling, his residence, his home too. He had just wanted to be someplace familiar, so he had driven to Allen's, the place he used to call home, and sat in the driveway, staring at the front door as rain splashed against his window.

***

Inside, David pushed his arm through the sleeve of his suit coat so fast he didn't realize it was on backward. He cursed himself again. Why had he sat in the driveway of this house? Why had he accepted Allen's invitation inside when he had rapped on his car window? He knew why. He simply wanted to forget. He wanted to forget a friend, for only a moment. He wanted to forget that Andrew's fate could have been anyone's, even his own. David was simply scared.

"What are you doing?"

David's neck stiffened as he heard Allen's voice, its tone rather soft. The man had given him a warm greeting of hugs and kisses only minutes ago. It felt nice, and maybe that was all he needed, but he was sure Allen wanted more. Allen always wanted more.

"I have to go, Allen. I'm sorry, but I just can't do this," David replied swiftly, his movements never faltering.

Allen stood in the center of the living room, wearing only a T-shirt and boxers, with cotton socks gathered at his ankles.

"Why? What's wrong?"

David could hear the anger hidden in his voice, and he tried to brace himself for the forthcoming confrontation. As he tucked his shirt into his pants, he could feel Allen approach.

Allen came as close as the coffee table, then tossed the contents of what he held in his hand onto the glass surface: a tube of lubricant and condoms. Yes, he was good for making one forget one's troubles.

"What is this, David? Are you now playing my games?"

David looked up at Allen, who stepped forward, towering over him. "No, Allen. I just can't do this right now."

Allen spun around, his hands in the air. "Damn! You lead me on and now you can't follow through. Damn!" he shouted more to the situation than to David. He walked to the reclining chair and crashed down upon it, stomping his feet against the floor. "Well, get the fuck out then! Just get the fuck out!"

David pulled his belt tighter. "What?" he asked, more out of surprise. He'd expected a verbal battle at least. This instant defeat was truly against Allen's nature.

Allen pointed his finger toward the door; his other hand was placed across his forehead. "You are giving me a headache with this shit. I don't understand why you just can't be with me, David. I am sorry to hear about your friend, but this should at least show you that we should be together."

"Why, because we're both HIV positive? That's nothing to base a relationship on. You need a little more than that, Allen," David explained, as he adjusted the jacket on his shoulders.

Allen waved a finger at David. "Well, the glue has to come from somewhere, David. I have been here for you, despite what I've done or who you think I've slept with or whatever drink I hid myself under to do it. Do you think someone else is gonna love you or understand you like I do? I am willing to be with you until the end, and most people would rather you die by yourself."

Dammit! David thought. It was as if Allen had been at that funeral reading his mind as he cried in his pew. He cried more for himself than for Andrew. When the casket was lowered into the ground, and a friend of his played Diana Ross's "Remember Me," David burst into uncontrollable tears, wondering who would remember him and who would be there to hold his hand. Andrew left no lover behind. David's parents were both dead, so that left friends and very distant relatives. Was that enough?

Allen stood and slowly walked toward David. "Do you think anyone else is going to find time for your needs? I can do that, David. I can be there for you even when I don't have the time. It's what I want to do. Don't waste time looking for love, David. We could spend the rest of our lives searching for *us.*"

Allen placed his warm arms around David's waist. There was no force, and his touch was so light that David could easily have taken a step back to free himself from the embrace. But he stood his ground. This was a sober Allen talking, and David found he wasn't used to that. He didn't know if these were words of wisdom or manipulation.

"Is this because of your new boyfriend?"

"Wha—?" David blurted, caught off guard. "What boyfriend?"

Allen stepped closer, squeezing him gently. "Marty, Max . . . something like that. He was at the beach party with you."

"Malcolm? He's not my boyfriend. Why would you say that? How did you know where we had been?"

"I was at the beach. I saw how you two acted. I saw him carrying you across the sand. He told me he was your man. I know what's going on, so-"

"What are you talking about? When did he say this?" David questioned.

"The day you drove me home when you were doing work on that man's house in Palos Verdes. He threatened my life if I didn't let him have you. The boy's hooked on you," Allen said, craning his neck slightly to kiss David on the forehead. David didn't even seem to notice.

Is Malcolm capable of doing something like that? David thought. They hadn't even gone into that kind of discussion to even allow for him to say such a thing. Maybe he was being protective, considering he knew what kind of hell Allen had put David through. Maybe Allen was lying. He could not believe this, and it stunned him so that he hadn't noticed Allen slipping kisses along his cheeks, his jaw, at the tips of his lips. Allen's sex was pressed against his hip, slowly pulsating to life. David closed his eyes, feeling himself fall back into old habits, back into old routines.

His walls were breaking.

"No, Allen!" David said sternly, shaking his head, and pushing Allen away. "I've got to get out of here, Allen. I'm sorry. Okay?"

Allen stepped back, repositioned his manhood, then slapped his hands against his large thighs. "Yeah, you're sorry all right. I feel sorry for you. You're gonna need me one day, David, and I'm not gonna be there. I'll have someone else in my life, and then who's gonna have time for your sorry ass? Nobody, that's who. Nobody."

David looked up at Allen. He was unable to move. Never had he heard such words come from this man's mouth. Suddenly he saw an image of himself in a hospital bed with the only sound coming from a flapping curtain held aloft by wind rustling through the window, He was alone. *No!* He told himself. *I'm not dead yet.* It was just one of Allen's old tricks.

"I've gotta go," David repeated, pressing his hand on the door-knob.

"I guess I'm gonna have to take care of that boyfriend of yours, for taking you away from me."

David turned to look at Allen standing with his fists clenched. He'd found another enemy to hate. "What are you saying, Allen? Malcolm is not my boyfriend."

Allen grinned. "Never mind. He just needs to learn to live up to his threats. . . because I do. I was drunk in the car, but I won't be the next time I see him."

"And what's that supposed—"

"Good-bye, David!" Allen said quickly. He turned on his heels, heading toward the back of the house. "Close the door on your way out, baby."

David watched as Allen walked away. It was the first time he'd done that without David paying a price. Now he was concerned about who would pay in his place.

– III –

Dominique strutted into the house and took one look in Sarafina's direction, as she sat upon the sofa doing a crossword puzzle, then continued to the bedroom. She kicked off her black heels and tossed her ebony handbag on the bed, then fell atop it herself, fully clothed, she sighed deeply.

After the funeral everyone had convened at Momma C's home to partake of food and drink. Dominique hadn't known there to be so many people involved in Andrew's life, she wasn't surprised, considering Andrew had such a wonderful air about him that seemed to lift people up, to free them from any bad moods they may have harbored. She had met him through Damien two years ago, when he was working at a little clothing shop in West Hollywood. He knew how to give fashion for your ass back then, and he chatted away as if he'd been her friend for years.

She wished she had known him better, but whenever they met it was always in the company of Damien. She had met his mother, Martha Christenson, a sweet woman with lovely gray streaks running through her silky black hair and cheeks that made you want to just reach out and pinch them. She carried an album filled with pictures of Andrew in the most exciting places— Europe, Alaska, Australia, Puerto Rico. Dominique hadn't known he had visited such wonderful lands. He must have had a ton of stories to tell. But she'd just never asked. It had been these thoughts that brought her to recollections of Sarafina. She too had been to wonderful places in her life with Gerri, but through raw stubbornness Dominique had never asked about them. She didn't want to think that Sarafina had a life before her, or a lover for that matter.

When they drove back from San Diego, Damien dropped her off at home, but instead of going up to her apartment she went to her car and drove off to Borders & Books, to sift through some magazines and enjoy a café mocha. Why hadn't she wanted to know about Sarafina's life with Gerri? It bothered her. Perhaps she felt she was always in competition. She could never give what Gerri was capable of, and that disturbed her to no end. It made her jealous and bitter. It showed now, as the two of them carried on around the house without a word being said, except for extremely dry conversations of *yes* and *no*.

She was grateful that work had become a means of escape. That escapism also kept her away from home. Such a paradox it had become; she escaped from the memories of Gerri at home, only to run into its reality at work.

"They're dealing with it, I guess. What else can you do? Damien is taking it hard, and David nearly fainted when they lowered the casket into the ground. I know I'm gonna really miss him. We all will."

"Well, I'm here for you, Dominique. I know you don't want to speak with me now, but I just want you to know that," Sarafina affirmed.

"I know. Thanks," Dominique said. It felt good to hear those words coming from someone who really meant them. Whatever Sarafina was, she was dedicated to her friends and her relationships; she proved that by being here, and going through what she had with Gerri.

"If I could change things, I would. And you know that," Sarafina continued. "I never meant for any of this to happen."

"Yeah, I know, Tina. So much has happened between us, and so much is going on with me. It's been hard taking it all in," Dominique said, closing her eyes.

"I wish I could make this all better, but somehow I think it's out of my hands now," Sarafina said, standing. "I guess you'll want to go to sleep now. It's getting late, so I'll just see you tomorrow."

"Tina, why don't you sleep in here tonight?"

Sarafina couldn't move. "Are you sure?" she whispered.

"Yeah, why not?" Dominique replied, her tone very tired.

Sarafina slid up behind her and reached out her arm to rest upon Dominique's waist. "I love you, Dominique," she whispered, afraid to say anymore.

Dominique inched back until their bodies touched. "I know."

— III —

Felicia poured the Bombay gin slowly over the ice and shook the glass carefully. She brought the whole creation to Stephen, who sat on the sofa, feet perched on the coffee table, dressed in nothing more than a robe and black silk dress socks. "So how was the shower?" Felicia asked, handing him the glass. "Did it do the trick?"

Stephen reached for the glass without ever taking his eyes away from the television. "Yeah, it's what I needed," he replied, nodding slightly.

Felicia sat on the arm of the sofa and reached out to the end table. "Good. You need to be relaxing a bit today," she said, sipping on her chamomile. Felicia placed a hand on Stephen's shoulder. "And how are you feeling inside, Stephen? Are you really okay?" she asked, rubbing his arm tenderly.

Stephen didn't answer. He didn't know how he was feeling beyond the boundaries of the gin he was drinking. He knew he felt something while talking to Andrew's mother just a few hours ago on the phone. He was choked with so much emotion that it was an impediment to his very breathing. Her demeanor was placid, and it was Martha who had soothed *his* nerves, when it should have been the other way around.

He sensed an overwhelming feeling of fear. How long before other friends, new friends, traveled the same route? How long before this became the norm—the funerals, the grief, the sickness? He thought often about the heterosexual lifestyle. Would he have been spared all this had he chosen that direction? Had there really been a choice? Was it destiny that exposed him to this lifestyle so filled with rejection, with death, with fear, or was that projection all in his mind, conditioned there by those who opposed him and the new lifestyle he had chosen—or the one that had chosen him?

But to be with Felicia, even though they were now getting along very well, was not a possibility; Stephen knew where his strongest sexual attractions lay. He would only hurt Felicia and his son if he decided to resume a bogus relationship that would only feed his visceral desires.

Stephen leaned his head back, listening to the tender silence dictating the room. He was grateful that Felicia was here. It brought a sense of family that he appreciated. *His family, his family, his family...* the thought was a pleasant one at times like this.

And where was Jamal during all this? That question too haunted him. They hadn't talked much since the beach party, and Stephen felt there was a distancing occurring. Jamal had seemed to back away, as if allowing him more time with Tumali. Stephen knew Jamal was incensed at the tardiness, his unreturned calls, Stephen's association with Felicia. Jamal said that he had called one day, was put on hold, yet in the background he heard him saying to Felicia, "Tell him I'm not at home ... Oh well, I'll answer it." Jamal had been very upset and had not called since. Stephen could not remember such .a thing ever happening.

Then he had accused Stephen of sleeping with Felicia. Stephen had known that argument was going to come, but he hadn't expected their bond to drift so that it was all Jamal thought about. He thought about staying a few nights at Jamal's place, but his son wasn't going to be here forever, and the child was such a warm cup of coffee in the morning. So he let Jamal stew in his own juices. There were many late nights he'd called, knowing Jamal was not working, and would get no answer, leaving messages that were returned a day or two later. Stephen wanted to work at this relationship he had with Jamal, because he genuinely cared for the man, but he hated to think that his son and ex-girlfriend were the daggers tearing it apart. If so, the knife would only get deeper, he felt, before they returned to Chicago.

"Are you finished with that?" Felicia asked, pulling Stephen's empty glass out of his hand.

"Oh, I didn't even see it was empty," he replied, allowing Felicia to take the glass.

"I'll make you another," Felicia offered, already at the bar pushing the tongs into the ice bucket.

Stephen held up a wavering open palm. "Maybe I shouldn't, Felicia. I'm getting tired and a bit tipsy."

Felicia smiled. "Nonsense. You need something to ease your mind. You don't have to go into the office tomorrow, so just give yourself what you deserve tonight. You have to take time for yourself at some point, Stephen," Felicia preached, pushing the liquor under Stephen's nose. "Don't have me feed it to you like I do with Tumali's milk, holding your nose and forcing it in."

Without thinking, Stephen reached for the drink. "Wouldn't want that. Would we?"

"I also want to thank you for reading that story to Tumali, even if it was my first attempt at writing," Felicia said, walking back to the kitchen to freshen up her cup of tea.

When she returned, Stephen playfully pushed her shoulder. "When did you begin this new talent as a writer?"

"Hmm, I don't know," Felicia answered, returning Stephen's spirited push with one of her own, as she blew lightly across the lip of her cup. "I just thought it would be nice to try."

"Well, I think you have some talent boiling in you. I liked the one I read to Tumali last week. It was something on telephone manners, right?"

Felicia held her tea out at arm's length. "This isn't warm enough," she said to herself, standing, and returning to the kitchen. "Yeah, that was the one, about talking to people on the phone. He seemed to like that one."

Stephen stood and followed her to the kitchen. He leaned on the bar, holding his drink. "I'm sure I could find you an illustrator if you want to pursue this on the side. I would do it myself, but this has been a busy year at the agency."

"I'll have to think about that, Stephen," Felicia said, placing her cup in the microwave.

"I'm serious, Felicia. It would give you a chance to get out of this temporary work you keep finding, and then you could stay home with Tumali."

Felicia turned and placed her heated cup on the bar, then reached out to brush her finger across Stephen's nose. "I know you're serious. I guess I'm still holding out to do my modeling again. I hadn't thought about an additional career, but I'm glad you brought it to my attention, and that you're thinking about me. It's cute."

"Hey, you deserve something better than job hopping, that's all I'm saying. I was just thinking it would be good for you to be home while Tumali is growing up."

Felicia wanted to respond by suggesting that Stephen live with them. How hard was that? Instead, she said, "I'm doing fine, Stephen. As long as I can count on you to be there as a friend," she said.

"Of course you can. Right now, however, I want to thank you for the dinner you made, the drinks, and the conversation. The funeral really drained me. How did you deal with the death of your brother?"

Felicia suddenly turned her back to Stephen and leaned against the bar, folding her arms. She hadn't thought about her brother's passing in years. She had been only twelve years old, and he was just a half-brother, if that made any difference in her feelings toward him. All she knew was that he'd been in a car accident, and that the concept of death had still been very foreign to her. Suddenly she could feel Stephen rubbing her back.

"Did I bring up some bad memories, Felicia?" he asked, sympathetically.

"No, not really. There's so much I don't remember about that situation, and a lot I don't want to remember," she replied, turning back to face Stephen. She reached over the counter and closed Stephen's robe a little more around his neck. "But maybe it's time for you to get some rest."

Stephen spun around to view the sofa. "Tumali's sleeping in my room, so maybe I'll crash on the sofa."

"Don't be crazy. This is your house. You can sleep in the guest room. I promise you I have no stockings or panties hangin' around. Then I can snooze on the sofa, and Tumali and Crafty can stay asleep in your bed. They look too cute in there to wake up."

"But I don't think it's right for you to be sleeping on the sofa. You can have my room tonight and—"

"Hush!" Felicia said, walking around to Stephen, lifting him from the stool. "You just get up and get in your own guest bedroom. Your eyes are drooping and you don't even know it," she said, pushing him in the back. She then began to softly tickle him.

He laughed in spite of himself. "Stop that!"

"Well, get in there and get some sleep, or I'll make it worse," she warned, running her fingers more rapidly across Stephen's midsection. She continued teasing him down the hallway until they reached the guest room, where he fell on the bed in a fit of laughter. Stephen began to get comfortable and close his eyes, ready for sleep.

Felicia leaned against the door, grinning widely before closing it. She rushed to the bathroom and locked the door. As long as Tumali slept soundly she would be able to accomplish her goal tonight. Turning to observe herself in the mirror, she ran her fingers through her long hair, trying to figure out what she needed to do with it. Opening the drawer beside the sink she examined its contents: lipstick, mascara, lip liner, blush, Paloma Picasso perfume. She had a lot of work to do. She turned to look at the terry cloth robe hanging behind the bathroom door. She pulled it back to reveal what she had hidden behind it: a Victoria's Secret silk nightgown. She glided her fingers across the smooth material, confident this would do the trick.

When she again opened the guest bedroom door, Stephen was already asleep. His robe lay open around him, and Felicia experienced a warmth ignite in her body just watching him sprawled out in nothing except a pair of silk boxers. His smooth chest rose and fell regularly as he breathed, his tight stomach accented with a thin trail of hair that formed a seductive path to the top of his shorts. Beyond lay the sweetest bulge she had ever seen.

She pressed her lips together and adjusted the straps on her nightgown, then neared the bed. His calves felt strong as she ran her freshly painted nails across them, traveling tenderly up his thighs.

It roused him.

"Wha—Felicia?" he questioned in his state of half sleep.

Felicia continued, knowing the liquor she'd given him would do its work and keep him drowsy. She wanted to laugh at his effort to open his eyes. He always slept deeply after drinking. "Yeah, it's me. Just relax," she cooed.

"I thought you would be going in my bedroom," he said, trying to prop himself up on his elbows.

Felicia placed her hand on his large chest, forcing him back upon the bed. "Shhh! I know, but Tumali is sleeping so good in there that I was afraid of waking him," she said, rubbing her knuckle across Stephen's nipple.

"Well, I'll give you this bed if you want to get some sleep," he suggested, attempting to slide to the edge of the bed.

Felicia zealously placed her hand on Stephen's sex, massaging it. "Don't be silly, Stephen. I'm not going to bite," she said, crawling catlike up him, moving her hands from his groin to his inner thigh, holding his legs still.

"No, Felicia! What're you doing?" Stephen said groggily, his actions too laggard to stop her advances.

She began kissing his chest, setting herself down on his thighs, gliding her womanhood forward until they met crotch to crotch. "Stephen, I know you want this. I know you do. I can feel your need. Little Stephen is talking to me," she spoke between kisses, feeling Stephen pulse beneath her.

He grabbed her shoulders, pushing her upward and away from him. "This is not what I want, Felicia—"

"Hush!" Felicia demanded, her tone frustrated, but instantly she composed herself, her tone becoming calm: "I know just what you want, baby." she then reached up to unstrap her gown, exposing her breasts, nipples hard. She could feel a bonfire growing within her groin, an itching that craved to be scratched.

She reached between his legs, plunging her hand into Stephen's shorts, drawing out his erection, gripping it tightly in her fingers. She could feel the tension in his legs weaken—he was too tired to fight her any longer. She then pulled up the bottom of her gown, twisting the silk in her hands until her womanhood was uncovered, its hungry being plump and thick, its heart soft and wet.

"Don't do this, Felicia," Stephen pleaded, as he shook his head upon the pillow, unsure what he should do. Her hands felt so good, so welcome upon his, that resistance was losing to pleasure. He then felt his sex become wrapped in a powerful feeling of heat, and he sighed into the air, his lips forming one final word, "No."

"I know what you want, Stephen," Felicia said, slipping him fully inside her, his hardness thrusting against her inner walls, the itch relieved. She continued to kiss him, caress his chest, love him...make love to him. .

It's all working according to plan, Felicia thought. Even her attempt to distance Stephen from that boyfriend of his, by making up a bedtime story, taping him reading it to Tumali, and playing back a certain phrase when that man called. *Tell him I'm not here...Oh well, I'll answer it.* That was a gem. She grinned till her face hurt, and lunged upon Little Stephen a bit more.

– IV–

The sound of the doorbell was like a slap to the side of Stephen's head. He could hear Crafty whimpering outside his door. With a hangover fighting him, it sounded more like a raging lion. He could hear the doorbell again, and then he remembered: He'd slept with Felicia! And as if to validate that reality, as he turned in the bed he saw Felicia lying next to him. He wanted to reach out, shake her, and shout, "What have you done?" But he could barely see her through his blurred and tired eyes, filled with the paste from a sleepless night. He slid himself from beneath Felicia's sprawled legs, reached back to grab his robe, and rushed out the door, nearly stepping on Crafty in the process.

From his grandfather clock, he could see that it was nearly 1:00 in the morning. In his haste, he opened the door without asking who it was.

Jamal stood at the door. He knew Stephen had been at the office of one of his good friends, and he was concerned. He'd left messages, but somehow knew Stephen might not have received any of them. He had to get past these feelings of jealousy, feelings of wanting to step out of this relationship, feelings that were only hurting him in the end.

But now those thoughts resurfaced as he stood at Stephen's door, chocolates in one hand, and violets in the other. Those thoughts went through his mind as he looked at Stephen, eyes closed to mere slits, a thick vein swollen and throbbing on his forehead; he was either drunk or hung-over. Those thoughts went through his mind as he noticed the smears of red lipstick on his exposed chest, cheeks, and corners of his lips. Those thoughts went through his mind as he noticed Stephen's manner of dress: a drag queen's delight.

Those thoughts also went through his mind as he noticed a naked woman emerge from a bedroom and head toward the bathroom, dressed in a robe distinctly Stephen's.

Jamal didn't even feel the flowers and chocolates slip from his fingers and plummet to the welcome mat. He backed away from the door, eyes looking away, wishing for his alarm clock to ring in hopes that he was in bed having a nightmare.

"Jamal, are you okay?" Stephen asked, stepping from his doorway.

"I think I should be leaving," Jamal said, beginning to turn.

"Wait!" Stephen called out, as he reached out to take hold of Jamal...but stopped. He noticed something strange about the sleeve of his robe; there was a ring of cotton surrounding its edge. He looked down at the rest of his attire, and was astonished to discover he was wearing Felicia's robe! He looked back up to see Jamal walking down the stairs, leaning heavily against the railing. "Don't go, Jamal. Thanks for the flowers," he said as an afterthought, as he reached down to pick up the fallen items.

Jamal suddenly stopped, then turned around to glare angrily at Stephen. "You didn't have to play me for the fool, Stephen. If you and your ex-girlfriend were getting back together at least you could've told me. At least you could've stopped wasting my time."

"Me and Felicia are not back together," Stephen explained, as he gathered the fallen flower petals into his hands.

Jamal held up his hand. "Whatever, Stephen! We aren't lovers, so you don't have to explain shit to me. Now I know why you seldom get my messages. My father truly didn't raise no fool."

"You know I care for you, Jamal. Why are you acting like this when—?"

"Care? Yeah, you seem to care about everybody. I should feel real lucky to have such a universal caregiver in my company," Jamal finished, waving his hand through the air, as he trotted down the steps two at a time.

Stephen said nothing. He could only hold the rumpled box of chocolates and broken stems against his chest. He always seemed to leave a trail of broken hearts, like petals scattered in the winds. He just wanted to remember what happened tonight. Was it his fault? Had he come on to her? Because if he had, he was sure Felicia would hardly resist. He didn't know. He just slowly closed the door and stood against it in silence. In the back of his beating head, he could have sworn he heard the muffled sounds of a woman laughing, but he dismissed it.

Chapter 17

– I –

"Can I have another mimosa, please?" Stephen asked of the attractive flight attendant.

"Sure," she replied, with the loveliest Latin accent. "Would you like anything else, Mr. Smith?" she asked, reaching for his empty wine glass.

"No, thank you. That will do me just fine," he responded, leaning back in his large seat and peering out the window at the clouds scattered below him.

Somehow he didn't think the mimosa was going to sustain him through this flight; his nerves were on edge. After his incident with Felicia, he'd been keeping his distance, and she in turn had become very attached. He still didn't know the full story concerning their liaison, but he did know they'd slept together, and Felicia was ever grateful. He tried to wash the whole event from his mind, but Felicia kept throwing in more laundry. She invited herself to his room so often that he eventually had to lock it whenever he went in. She talked about them being together as a full-time family, making premature plans for their future, her moving to L.A., then on a more personal basis, him buying a home, she religiously thanked him for that magical night, reminding him that she cared for him, she was so high on cloud nine, that it was hard to tell her that it was only low-lying fog.

Eventually he did, and of course, in came the drama. He told her that she had to leave and the sooner the better. He had to go on with his life, and that did not include any further relations with any woman of any kind, she was adamant on using their son as a tool, an instrument of glue holding them together. "Look at what you're doing to Tumali. He needs a father. How can you do this to us? You. . ." then came the name-calling, the accusations, the verbal bashing. The old Felicia had returned.

He thought of Jamal often. It had only been a little more than a week, and this had been the longest they'd gone without any communication. His phone was never answered, calls were never returned, and even when he'd visited his apartment, although the car was distinctly out front, there was no response to his knocking. Stephen couldn't blame him. Their trust had been obliterated.

So in the midst of his present turmoil and battling with Felicia about packing her bags ASAP, the phone call came. Her friend Tammy Fae Russle had called with the news that her mother, Margaret, was in the hospital after suffering a serious heart attack. She became frantic, and Stephen found himself transformed from the adversary to the availer.

"Here's your mimosa, Mr. Smith," said the attendant, placing a fresh silk napkin on his tray, followed by a new wine glass sparkling with a renewed drink.

He looked up at the kind woman, wavy auburn hair swept to the side of her face, exposing the lovely gold earring clipped to her lobe. He nodded. "Thank you very much." He took a polite sip of his drink and looked back up at the attendant, and the image of Jamal unexpectedly replaced hers. He shook his head, and she returned.

He reasoned it must be exhaustion. He had agreed to accompany Felicia to Chicago, but nothing else. And he had upgraded his own ticket to first class, while she had remained in coach. It would be almost three hours before they reached their destination, and he wanted his body washed free of all anxiety. The mimosa was just the soap he needed.

– II–

Gerri raised the videotape over her head, shaking it like a madwoman. "I'll show your ass!" she shouted to the ceiling, and stuffed the item in the manila envelope, sealing it with a swipe of her moist thumb across the glue flap.

She was one tired stud, she concluded, looking at herself in the vanity mirror, bangs falling flatly across her forehead, permed at the top, short on the sides, cut just below the ears—yikes! It was salon therapy she was looking for, but the results made her head take on the shape of the Liberty Bell. It looked great on the cover model in *Elle,* but what would her date think of this? She pulled open her top drawer and reached for her apple-rouge lipstick, she would have to compensate for her hairstyle with a makeup miracle. As she leaned over to slide the lipstick across her lips, her mind flashed on Sarafina. "Damn!" she shouted. The girl was actually gone from her life again, and the sleepless nights were destroying her.

She tried to apply the lip color again, and once more Sarafina projected across her mind, her likeness manifested in the mirror like a shadow sheathed in a deep fog. She pulled the lipstick away from her mouth. "Damn you, Sara!" she said, slashing a deep line of apple-rouge across the smooth surface of the mirror. "Damn you! Damn you! Damn you!" she repeated, each word emphasized by a greater swath of color.

The doorbell chimed, and Gerri glanced up at the clock on her wall. Five o'clock! What was Emily Dossner doing here damn near two hours early? She wasn't nearly ready to be seen by anyone, especially her first date with a white woman. This was all becoming a disaster.

There was the sound of frantic knocking coming from the door now, and Gerri dashed to the closet, recklessly snatching a pair of jeans from atop the door and quickly slipping them on. Her slip fell haphazardly from the back, but she trailed down the stairs anyway, skipping two at a time as the door rattled once again, its sound echoing throughout the empty house. "Hold on!" she bellowed, trying to catch her breath before reaching for the door.

She swung open the door, expecting Emily to be standing before her. But to her surprise, it was Cyan. She fumed, threatening to close the door, but Cyan raised her hand against it. Gerri stepped into the doorway. "What do you want, Cyan?" she asked. Her teeth gleamed like an angry animal.

Cyan folded her arms across her chest. "Carlotta called me last night. I thought this was between me and you. How could you fire that woman after all she's done for you?"

Gerri didn't reply. A week ago she had given that old crone specific instructions not to allow Sarafina out of the house. Carlotta had tried to honor that request, but when Sarafina expressed an interest in taking a jog around the block, Carlotta had no objection to it. Besides how could she stop her? She didn't return. Gerri was furious and sent Carlotta on a mandatory vacation.

The next night, during a conversation with Cyan, Gerri was promptly informed that she had driven Sarafina home. Gerri called Cyan everything but a child of God and cursed her for all eternity. After slamming the phone down, she called Carlotta, asking her had Sarafina mentioned anything about where Cyan lived. Carlotta mentioned that Sarafina had asked about Ms. Kai, and that she didn't know exactly what her address was, but she'd given Sarafina the general area of where she lived. The woman must have gone door to door! She wasted no time in giving Carlotta her walking papers for blatant disloyalty.

And now *her former* best friend was filling her door, and she felt the temptation to reach for this woman's neck and tackle her to the ground, but she knew better.

Cyan could almost feel the rage emitting from Gerri, and could feel her own body stiffen, on guard for any sudden confrontation; she knew there wouldn't be one, however. Cyan was skilled in the martial arts. She didn't want any form of altercation to arise—not because she could kill this girl with one hand, but because they had been friends for ten years and Cyan knew where this behavior was stemming from: pure obsession.

"What do you want, Cyan? I have no time to discuss anything with you," Gerri snapped. She stepped back into the house when she realized she was wearing a sheer slip, and it did little to hide her bare breasts underneath.

"I want to know what gives you the right to destroy Carlotta's life for something I did."

"That's none of your business, Cyan. You're always involving yourself in matters that do not concern you. Maybe that's why you're in the business of shrinking heads. Why don't you go get a life, sugar?"

"Why don't you just let me in and quit acting like a bitch and giving the whole neighborhood a free peep show?"

Gerri quickly clutched breasts, realizing their exposure. She exhaled a long growl and spun around. "Damn! I don't have time for this shit, Cyan. I've got a date coming over here in another hour or two, and I don't need you here," Gerri said, walking back into the house.

Cyan kept in step with her as she charged back up the stairs. "A date? That's great, Gerri. Who's it with? I'm glad to see you're starting to get out there and have fun. I thought you would never get—"

Gerri rapidly spun around. "Can't you just shut up! It's only Emily Dossner!"

Cyan stopped her ascent, shaking her head with overt disapproval. "The white girl?"

Gerri stopped at the top of the stairs, placing her hand dramatically on her hip. "You act as if I'm committing a deplorable crime. Have you forgotten? I'm a white girl!"

Cyan continued up the stairs. "You know what I'm getting at, Gerri. A white woman is not the type you're attracted to."

"What do you know about me?" Gerri retorted, walking into her bedroom and quickly stripping off her jeans, tossing them on the bed. She then fell to her knees to pull out a shoe box from beneath her bed. "Did you come over here to talk about my sexual interests? I'm still angry at you for driving Sarafina back to L.A.," she said, dragging out yet another shoe box.

"We don't want to discuss that, do we? You know you were wrong from the start, bringing that woman out here with no intentions of sending her back home. You refuse to give her her belongings, and you try and keep her a prisoner in your home. What were you thinking?"

Gerri held out a stiff finger toward Cyan, as she sat upon the bed in nothing more than a pair of silk panties and a slip. "There you go again, getting in someone's business. Why don't you just take yourself out of my room and drive down to see your new friend Sarafina, who you obviously like better than me."

"What? This is not about favoritism. I'm just worried about you, Gerri, because this has gotten out of hand. You can't seem to get over Sarafina, and I'm afraid what you may have planned next for her. She's trying to live her life. Don't you think it's about time that you stop this insanity?"

Gerri walked to her closet, pulling out a dark gray Donna Karan cashmere skirt, throwing a matching blouse over her shoulder. "Let me tell you something," she began, stepping into the skirt. "Sarafina is mine, and I don't care where she is. That femme, muffin-topped bitch is only a phase she's going through. It may sound crazy, you may even think I should be committed, but that's the fact. Keeping Sarafina here against her will may not have been the best tactic, but I had to think fast. I admit that it was wrong."

Cyan nodded. "Well, at least you've admitted something. I just hope that—" Cyan stopped. She noticed the vanity mirror, red slashes running across it like deep wounds on the glass. She then looked on Gerri's bed and saw an open travel bag, half filled with clothes, and a manila envelope sitting squarely on top. "You planning a trip?" The worry was back.

"As a matter of fact, I am," Gerri spoke, nonchalant. "I have some business to take care of in Los Angeles."

"What? Tell me you're not going down there to start some shit."

Gerri adjusted her blouse. "Who, me?" she asked innocently. "I do have a company to run out there, Cyan. My sales office will be out there and I must keep up on its development," she said, walking to the bed, picking up a pair of hose and holding it up as she ran her fingers across it.

"The only business you're gonna start out there is monkey business. Are you trying to tell me you're not going to try and contact Sarafina at any point while down there?"

"No, Cyan, of course I am not saying that. I told you I made a mistake by keeping Sarafina here, and my methods were all wrong. I have learned my lesson."

"And what is that supposed to mean? What have you learned?"

"That you have to start with the source, that's all."

Cyan looked at her friend curiously. "Source? What are you talking about? Does that mean you don't plan to visit Sarafina? If not, then what are you thinking of doing?"

Gerri smiled. "Why, I plan to visit Dominique."

—**II**—

Allen pressed PLAY on the answering machine and slid back into his easy chair, careful not to spill a drop of the brandy he was balancing. He reached over to the food tray near him, moving past the empty beer bottles and dirty ashtrays, to dip his hand in a half-filled bag of potato chips.

The answering machine beeped: *Hey Allen, Monique here. You've got to straighten yourself up, bud. Give me a call when you get this message.*

Monique was always the caring one. Three days ago Allen showed up to work drunk and was promptly sent home after yelling at a customer concerning late registration on his Bronco. Somehow the conversation became a racial issue with the white customer, and how O. J. Simpson's name entered the debate was still unknown, but after the fire died down in his manager's office he was quickly suspended for a week. The decision was still pending if he would indeed continue to have a job when he returned.

Allen, I received your request for vacation time to be paid to you during this, and I'm going to grant you that. Maybe a vacation is all you need to take care of this personal problem you seem to be having. We don't tolerate such behavior, and you are very lucky I didn't fire you on the spot.

Bruce Cowler. He was the supervisor who had discovered that Allen's breath reeked of alcohol, that his eyes were beet red. Out of concern, he had contacted the manager. Allen pulled off one of his slippers and tossed it at the machine. "Fuck you!" he yelled, spittle flying from the corners of his lips. He wasn't in any mood to hear that cocksucker's voice, especially in his house.

Hey, Allen. Yeah, it me, David. Just…um…oh… Just checking to make sure you're doing fine. Urn, okay, bye.

The machine beeped. No more messages.

Allen sat up and reached for the decanter of brandy and poured himself a fresh glass. He was feeling quite joyous; David had called, wishing him well. The boy was still hooked. He could picture David now, sitting somewhere in Damien's home, dwelling on the well-being of his lover. "I knew he still loved me," Allen said, as he brought the brandy glass to his lips. The slow burn of the liquor was a warm welcome to his empty belly.

Allen scratched at the stubbly hairs across his jaw with his dirty fingers. He looked around his home. My God. It was a mess! Newspaper was scattered across the room. Plates of half-eaten food covered the coffee table. Dust seemed to be mutating atop the television set and entertainment center. Clothes hung across the chairs surrounding the dining room table, and empty cases of beer were pushed into one corner of the room. How hadn't he seen all this before? Had his constant drinking brought on a new sense of awareness? How could he have David come back home to this? It was unthinkable.

He would have to clean it up...all of it. He would then have to go talk to David face to face. This whole ordeal had gone on long enough. Vacation time was over. He would just have to apologize again, although he'd done it so many times before.

There was only one problem. Malcolm.

He might have to confront that sissy boyfriend of David's. If it came to that, so be it. It was a name that cursed his every night and scorned his waking morning. He would also have to be sober when he met that fool once again. He could handle old Glamour Boy, just like he handled Percy. That was a mistake. He let a good piece of ass drag him away from the only man he loved. He let some tall chocolate drop take him on a sex-filled joy ride to orgasmic heavens. Dumb, dumb, dumb. He didn't feel one bit sorry about throwing that fag into the television set. If Percy had really cared for him, he would not have let that tiny temper tantrum upset him. He would have come back. David would have. David was man enough to take his shit.

That Malcolm was throwing silly and dangerous ideas into David's head. After Percy, there were many one-night stands, some he could only remember from the backs of their heads. He only worried that some of his escapades may have been unsafe in his inebriated state. He tried, but he couldn't remember using rubbers at all, which posed more of a danger to him with the advent of reinfection. But fuck it— the shit was good.

Yes, cleaning up was the first step. Right now, however, he had to attend to some stress-releasing exercises. He reached over toward the coffee table, pushing aside an empty bag of corn chips, to retrieve a bulky napkin underneath. He placed the thick cloth to his lips, kissing it, then unrolled the napkin in his lap.

Inside were twelve long darts, and he picked one up with shaky hands. He looked up, at the back of his door, and quickly tossed the sharp steel through the air, hearing the hollow thud of it as it embedded itself in the wood. He missed!

On the back of the door was pasted a sheet of paper that ran its width, its length was about a foot long. He threw another dart. Missed again! "Dammit!" he cursed, picking up another projectile, placing the tip across his tongue. He concentrated once more, focusing his vision, taking a deep breath. He filled his mind with David, of the life they had, of the future that could be robbed of them. He thought of the thief causing all this turmoil, his features coming into focus before his eyes, becoming clearer.

He threw the dart again!

It landed on its intended target. He grinned and poured a victory shot. On the paper was scrawled a name in bright red marker: *MALCOLM.* And from the center of the letter C hung the dart, still shaking from the impact. *Right in the center,* thought Allen. *Right in the heart.*

Chapter 18

—I—

Felicia walked through the halls of Chicago County General Hospital, oblivious to the other patrons occupying the floor, as she all but stepped over anyone that cast a shadow in her path. Stephen walked behind, Tumali in tow, apologizing to the victims that were unfortunate enough to have now been introduced to the human tornado called Felicia.

Stephen was not in the best of shape this morning, having slept uncomfortably on the sofa in Felicia's apartment. She insisted he sleep with her, but Stephen had refused. She was so angered by this that Stephen awoke to his overexcited son jumping squarely upon his belly and the scent of breakfast in the air—breakfast that had already been devoured by Tumali and Felicia as he slept. He had to settle for Cap'n Crunch and a piece of butt-end toast before being rushed out to bring the car around the front. He was also tired of being in hospitals. He felt he'd seen quite enough of them. The scent of death always lingered within these walls.

Quite frankly, if not for the urgency and unexpectedness of the situation, he would have allowed Felicia to go to the hospital alone. But for some reason he felt he had to come with her, and not just because Tumali would be there, but on the strange feeling that he *had* to be there, that something important was about to happen.

A small group of women were gathered outside Margaret's room on the fourth floor. Felicia ran to the cluster and was immediately smothered in a barrage of outstretched arms and well wishes. Stephen recognized only one of them: Tammy Fae Russle, Felicia's best friend. She clasped Felicia's neck in her massive arms, her thickly braided hair falling coarsely across Felicia's shoulder, and her overly long orange-colored nails gripping her head. The other two women were in their late forties, and Stephen guessed they were perhaps friends of Margaret or her sisters.

Leaning against the wall near the four women was a tall brother at least six feet four inches tall. His dress shirt was hanging from the front of his pants, his paisley tie was undone, and his sports coat was folded across one of his arms. He looked nonplused at the ladies before him talking in rushed tones. From this angle, Stephen didn't need anyone to tell him that this was Felicia's brother; he had that straight rim of a nose all the Jenkins family possessed.

He had tiny mouse eyes, thin eyebrows, high cheekbones, a protruding jaw, and thick lips that always appeared pursed forward, as if constantly kissing the very air he breathed. He could've made a career modeling, just as Felicia had done. The genes were lucky when they came from this family. From what Stephen could remember, he was very opinionated, very sure of himself. He cursed quite a bit and spat words without checking with his brain first. He was a difficult man. He was also a very protective individual when it came to his sister, an attribute Stephen assumed stemmed from the fact that their younger brother had died in that terrible car accident as a child. He knew there were scars in this family because of that.

Stephen also knew there was resentment because of *him*, and the fact that Felicia was devastated at their separation; in the Jenkins clan, he was the blame for all her grief. Of course, the real reason was because of his lifestyle choice, but he doubted Felicia explained that to her family.

"Uncle Leo!" Tumali suddenly shouted with glee as he dashed from behind Stephen to run ahead of him into the throng.

Stephen was surprised, but glad Tumali mentioned his name, because it had totally slipped his own mind. Leo spun around and a look of joy washed across his face. "Hey, little man! Where you come from?" he said, as Tumali halted in front of this huge shadow of a man to hold out his arms. Leo stooped forward to pluck him up with one arm, swooping him up on his broad shoulders.

Felicia turned at the sound. At seeing Tumali swinging his arms wildly, she swatted him lightly on the legs. "Stop all that craziness, boy," she chastised.

Tumali poked his bottom lip out. "Oh, he's only being a boy, Felicia," Leo said, kissing Tumali on the cheeks. "So who brought you up here?' he asked his nephew.

"I did," Stephen spoke, gathering the attention of all. "So how you doin', Leo? Been a long time."

Leo looked at Stephen, and even at his vain attempt at trying to conceal it, Stephen could feel the contempt in Leo's eyes. "Yeah, about two years, I believe, since Felicia introduced us. Seems longer somehow to me, but isn't it always like that; some things you can forget, while others just linger on."

Stephen sensed anger in that tone. "Yeah, I guess it's like that sometimes," Stephen responded. He turned to address Felicia's friend. "And how are you, Tammy?"

Tammy said nothing at first and continued to lock eyes with Stephen. In that brief moment, he knew that this woman had been told. She knew the truth.

"I'm doing fine," she said, forcing a smile that truly looked genuine in the right light. "Considering the circumstances today."

"Come on, Tumali, let's go see Grandma," Felicia said, reaching for her son's tiny hand and pulling him from Leo's embrace.

"And how's she doing?" Stephen asked, directing his eyes toward Margaret's room.

There was that look again. "Not too bad. She's hangin' in there. She's kinda sore on her left side, and she can't talk too well, but she'll he straight again soon," Tammy explained. "She'll be *straight*."

"I hope she'll stop smoking those damned cigarettes now and take better care of herself," Felicia spoke, shaking her head.

Stephen stepped forward, extending his hand to the shorter of the other two women standing near Felicia. "I'm sorry; I don't believe we've met. I'm Stephen."

"You're Tumali's father, correct?" she responded, cutting a curious gaze in Felicia's direction.

Felicia leaned over to slightly nudge this woman. "Of course he is, Aunt Ethel. There ain't no other Stephen you know, is there?" she said, rolling her eyes hack to Stephen. "Yeah, Stephen, this is my Aunt Ethel, my mom's older sister." She turned to face the other woman, who was tall and thin nosed; very regal. "And this is Laura, my mom's good friend."

"Hello, Stephen. I have heard so much about you," she said, rubbing her hands together before extending one. She shook his hands lightly.

Her handshake was more like a touch than a grip as Stephen held onto her delicate caramel fingertips. "Glad to meet you, Laura. I do hope for the best in this situation."

Laura smiled, her teeth shined, her lips gained color, and even her wrinkles faded back into her taunt skin. Stephen wished she'd smile forever, because she made mid-forties look good.

"Well, honey," began Ethel, directing her attention to Felicia. "You need to get in there, and see about your mother. Maybe you should let Stephen here take Tumali; she's pretty weak, and the child may take all the energy she has."

Felicia jerked Tumali back in her arms. "No! It's his grandmother, and I think he should see her. It's going to be fine," she spoke, taking a cautionary step toward her mother's room.

"Fine, fine," Ethel said, as she turned to Stephen. "Will you be going in too?"

Stephen looked up at Felicia. There was only a blank stare that said more than enough. "No. If Margaret asks for me, I'll gladly see her," he concluded.

"Come on then," Tammy said, stepping up to Felicia, wrapping her arm around her friend's waist. All three dispensed with any further conversation and walked slowly into Margaret's room. The door closed silently.

"I'm going downstairs for a cup of coffee. You want to join me?" Leo asked.

Stephen looked at him and responded reluctantly, "Sure."

"It was nice of you to come with Felicia. Hell, we all know California is a long way away," Leo said, as they walked toward the elevator. "Well, it's the least I could do in this situation. Besides, it's good seeing my son," Stephen replied. "And how are your kids, Leo?"

Leo sipped at his coffee, then looked up at Stephen, "Can we be real, Stephen?"

Stephen nodded. "Be as frank as you like."

Leo leaned hack, crossing his long legs at the knee, taking his time to respond. He seemed to be preparing himself for battle. The confrontation was about to begin. "I think what you did to Felicia was shitty, if I may be frank. If you're gonna screw around, then you should have had the decency to do it at the bitch's home, not hers."

Stephen flinched. That comment was meant to unnerve him, but he refused to let himself be rattled. It was obvious that Felicia hadn't told him the whole truth about their breakup. Leo thought he had slept with another woman. "That's in the past, Leo, and I was the one to make the decision to leave. I don't see what that has to do with anything now, or what business it is of yours."

Leo's grin widened, as if to mask his growing furor. "The fact that we fuckin' came out of the same womb makes it my business, Stephen. She called me on the phone almost every day after you two separated, crying in my damned ear, asking my advice, so she inadvertently made it my business. I may not know the full story, but Felicia never tells the full story. The pieces she gave me were enough."

"What's the point, Leo? It's not like we broke up yesterday. Do you want to vent some frustration now that you see me face to face, or do you have some valid focus to all of this?" Stephen asked, letting the warmth from his cup soothe his now cold hands.

"The point is, I just want you to be careful. Felicia is trying to get back with your ass, if you can't see that, and it can only mean more hurt. I don't want that shit happening. You need to just take care of your business and get back to Hollywood as soon as possible. She's going to try and use your son to some extent, and I don't know how strong you are at resisting her."

Stephen held up his hand. "Now wait. For one, I have no intention of getting snared by Felicia, no matter what her motives. Two, I will leave when I am ready. Three, all this has been discussed and was resolved long before you came into the picture. I know you feel you have to protect Felicia because of Brian's death, but you—"

"Brian? Who the hell is that?" Leo questioned, sitting up in his seat.

"Your younger brother. Felicia told me he died in a car accident."

"What? My little brother? I have no—" Leo stopped, looking far off as if he were thinking of other events in his mind. His eyes widened. "Oh my God! Felicia is still keeping with that story? She's truly taking my father's promise to her grave."

Stephen looked on, bewildered. "Promise? What are you talking about? Didn't your little brother die in a car accident?" he asked, almost afraid of what Leo's reply might be.

"I guess Felicia really *doesn't* tell the full story," Leo said to himself, then he looked up at Stephen. "No...well, yes, in a sense he did die. His name wasn't Brian either, but I guess Felicia had her reasons for telling you that."

Are you saying Felicia lied about having lost a brother? Why in the name—"

"Shit!" Leo suddenly blurted, quickly standing. "Speak of the devil."

Stephen turned around. He was dumbfounded. At the reception desk he saw a man asking for directions from the short woman manning the front. Stephen had no problem recognizing him. It was Jamal.

—**II**—

Dominique walked into Angela's office and stood by the door. Huge bay windows displayed prominently behind her oak desk exhibited a beautiful view of the Hollywood Hills, its majestic sign standing proudly as her backdrop. Dominique was staring at the back of the woman's chair, the top exposing a tall billow of her golden hair. "You may have a seat," Angela suggested.

Dominique looked around at the lavish surroundings and wondered if she should take the sofa at the far end of the room. Of course not. She would take the seat directly in front of Angela's desk, placed there just for her. Dominique could smell the strong brew wafting from the cappuccino machine and was at once dying for a cup. She could think of no reason why she would be summoned to this room, but it was known throughout the firm that to be summoned to Angela's office was not a good thing.

"You wanted to speak with me?" Dominique asked, easing her chair a few inches away from the desk.

Angela twisted around, her pale skin appearing brighter in contrast to the dark mahogany of the chair. Her hair could only be described as *big,* as it was pushed skyward. Her eye shadow was a hint too dark, blush was too pink, and lips had a hint too much gloss on them. She leaned forward on her desk, a tired ghostly image. She smiled at Dominique, and the sudden sense of fear placed a swift pang in her stomach.

"Yes," Angela began. "I just wanted to compliment you on the fine work you're doing."

"Thank you," Dominique replied cautiously. She could sense there was more to come.

"But I do have a problem with your display of tardiness yesterday. Charlotte informed me that she tried contacting you three separate times to inform you of our meeting."

Dominique leaned forward, her hands clutching her knees. "I do apologize for that, Angela. I had to take care of some personal duties at home and didn't check my messages." She hoped that answer sounded convincing. Sarafina had created a wonderful meal that afternoon and pleaded for no interruptions. So Dominique didn't answer her pager, cell phone, e-mail, or the answering machine. It proved a mistake, because Angela had set up an early morning meeting with the clients in charge of Gerri Cosmetics to discuss some contractual changes due to unexpected flooding in the parking lot area, as well as some interior modifications that needed to be done.

Angela plucked a pencil from her desk and twirled it in her fingers. "You need to take this a bit more seriously, Dominique, if you plan to get anywhere," she said, tapping the end of the pencil against her desktop. Dominique could smell the scent of Angela's perfume commanding the air, another reminder of her power within this firm.

"I do take this opportunity very seriously, Angela. Believe me. And the incident of the meeting—".

"Which you missed entirely."

"Yes, which I did miss—it's something that will never happen again. I do apologize for that."

"I'm sure it will not occur again. I need you to be in constant contact with this project until it is complete," Angela reminded, nodding her head, as if planning her next train of thought. "There is something else we need to discuss."

A nervous chill pulled at Dominique's skin. Angela was avoiding direct eye contact, and that meant some serious issues were about to come down. "Something else?" she echoed.

"The fabrics you ordered for the conference room—who was the vendor?"

It was a loaded question, giving her no time to think, but she answered regardless. "Nancy and McNeal."

Angela nodded, then leaned back in her chair, hand touching her chin. Typical boss pose. "Your research on the place—how much was there? The items seemed an extreme price to pay."

"Extreme? Their product is top of the line, and I got a great price for them," Dominique explained.

"Do you watch the evening news much, Dominique?"

That's out of left field, she thought. "I try to as often as I can, but I don't see how..."

"If you'd had paid more attention to the news this past year, you would have learned that Nancy and McNeal is in pending litigation over the accidental burning of a child. He was playing some superhero of some sort, and his cape caught a spark from a nearby stove where his mother was cooking. The cape was from his mother's linen closet, an old tablecloth I believe. It went up in flames within seconds, although the label clearly stated it was flame retardant. The child suffered second-degree burns over his back and scalp. He was only ten."

Dominique quickly placed a hand across her mouth. She had no idea.

"And I believe you had intended on using these as drapes for the conference rooms, as well as for lining the tables. There are smokers in that firm, you know. As far as I have been able to discover, the company has not changed its line. Too expensive, I hear. Nevertheless, it is something you should have known."

She was right. When she was a junior designer, she would pick up orders from Nancy and McNeal and had developed a relationship with them. She hadn't even bothered to go into their history. That whole office would have been a fire hazard! This was inexcusable.

"I don't hold you totally at fault, because I should have gone through your purchase order forms, but I was giving you full reign. My fault. But we'll discuss that later. Right now, the client is here, and she would like to speak with you."

"The client!" Dominique blurted out. She wasn't sure what Angela was saying, and yet she knew very well what the statement meant.

"Yes, the client. Gerri Moore is here, and she wants to speak with you personally."

It was at this point she wished she had a cup of that coffee. She needed it now more than ever.

— III —

Jamal stepped from the elevator, his mind reeling. He walked quickly down the corridor, the heels of his shoes clacking against the tile, the sound echoing off the walls. He adjusted the strap of his flight bag across his shoulder and pulled at the front of his uniform; he hadn't bothered to change after departing from his flight. His father had contacted him to inform him that Margaret had suffered a stroke. He didn't know what to feel upon hearing such news. It had been ten years since he'd heard that name. Ten years since he'd been rejected by that woman. He wanted to ignore the message, move on with his life, but how could he when this chapter was still unfinished? It had been ten years since he could remember this woman, and had called her Mother.

"Excuse me!" bellowed a deep voice behind him, followed by the loud slaps of shoes jogging. Jamal swiftly turned to see who could be in such a hurry and heading in his direction. This large man had just emerged from the Emergency Exit door, waving frantically. It wasn't until he was almost upon him, that Jamal was able to recognize this person as being Leo, his half-brother.

Leo smiled. He stopped and then slowly stepped back, eyes dissecting. "Well, I'll be damned! It *is* you. I didn't believe Mom when she said she contacted your father. I wouldn't have believed you would show up."

"Yeah, well, I almost didn't, but I'm here," Jamal said, pulling the strap of his bag securely up on his shoulder again. He had come here to see Margaret, and he hadn't thought twice about the fact that Leo would be here. He had nothing to say to this man, as the memories of his youth came flooding back upon him like a tidal wave. He turned on his heels, trying to recall the room number his mother was said to have been in. *423 ... I think that was it,* Jamal thought to himself as he returned down the corridor.

"Not even a hello, little brother? Don't I even deserve that after so many years?" Leo asked, spreading out his arms as if awaiting a hug.

Jamal halted for a moment, perplexed at this wall with limbs. Was he serious? He had tried like hell to establish a relationship with this family, but after endless returned letters, unreturned phone calls, and no communication whatsoever, Jamal had severed that part of his life. So in response to Leo's welcome, he continued to walk.

"I'm sorry, Jamal, but can we talk?" Leo spoke, his voice reaching a louder pitch, resounding in an angered tone.

Jamal turned to face him, as Leo walked right up to him. "What's up, Leo? I need to see Margaret, okay?" astounded at the charge his voice took. He just didn't feel like dealing in any mess right now.

Leo folded his arms. He too was surprised at Jamal's demanding timbre. "I would just hate to think you came out here for nothing."

"What are you talking about? Is there something I should know about Margaret?" he asked, his temper becoming unglued.

"Humph! And you don't even have the fuckin' respect to call her Mom," Leo said, shaking his head in pity. "Why don't you leave a number where you can be reached, and we'll let you know how she's doing. That way you can go home and not upset Mom any more than she already is."

"For your information, she requested that I be here. Why don't you go home and get some rest? You obviously need it."

Leo placed his hands on his hips, tapping his foot. "Yeah, I'm pretty fuckin' tired all right. I'm tired of all these confused bastards trying to fit where they don't belong."

Jamal swung his hand through the air as if warding off insects. "I don't have time for you, Leo. I should've known the bull in the family could only produce bullshit." Jamal continued to walk.

To Jamal's surprise, Leo dashed ahead of him, stood his ground, their bodies only a breath from each other. "Like I said, why don't you go home, Jamal? Mom's too wasted on painkillers to seriously think she wants you here. Just go back to your sissy friends, your sissy life, your sickening perversions."

"Fuck you, Leo. I am not here to see you."

"No, fuck you, and your intrusion into our family! You faggots always trying to steal real families just because you can't have one."

Jamal pulled his bag from his shoulder and swung it into Leo, slamming him aside. "Like I said, I am not here to see your stupid ass," he said, and began to step past Leo, who appeared stunned at the assault.

Leo reached out to grab Jamal's wrist. "Why, you little punk bitch!"

Jamal twisted his wrist free, and wound the strap of his bag around his wrist, readying himself for the unanticipated.

"Jamal!"

A female voice from down the corridor echoed. She stood among three other women, but it was she who shined. A child lay coddled in her arms—arms that were as thin and wiry as she. She was tall, with hair pushed into a bun atop as if it were only created minutes ago. She charred Jamal's soul with her stare.

Pamela? Jamal questioned. It had been so long since he'd seen her, so long since he remembered. "Is that you, Pamela?"

"My God, it is you!" she stated, handing the child to one of the ladies present, before marching forward. "I'm using my middle name now since I started modeling. It's Felicia. What're you doing here?"

"I think he was just leaving, Felicia," Leo interrupted, purposely brushing past Jamal to stand beside his sister.

Jamal stared menacingly at Leo. "I'm going nowhere. I have to see Margaret." He began to walk around Felicia, but she held out her hand, flush against his chest.

"Why, Jamal? I thought you were *going* to stay away. She's our mother, not yours. Can't you just go back to where you came from? I have my son here, and—"

"What has that got to do with anything?" he questioned, knowing precisely the answer. Homophobes, that's what it was all about. As if by his very presence he was going to make her son gay. Suddenly he realized that his past efforts at contacting these backward people had been a total waste of his time, energy, and life. "She is my family, or have you two forgotten that I actually came out of her loins too? It was also she that requested me, so please don't think that this is about you two. It never has been, and it never will be."

"And I suppose we are to just take it as fact that she actually requested your presence?" Leo said.

"Whatever. Now if you'll excuse me while I try and get this over with," Jamal said, reaching out to nudge Felicia against her shoulder, moving her aside.

Leo shoved Jamal harshly against the arm. "Don't you touch her!" he demanded, rolling his fist, ready for a confrontation.

Jamal dropped his bag. "You just want to start some 'shit, don't you? Well, fuck it, I'm ready too, if that's what you want," he roared.

"What's going on here?" bellowed another voice into the hallway.

Jamal turned to see another man charging down the hallway. He was frozen at who he saw: It was Stephen!

It took three cups of coffee, a silent meditation, two candy bars, and a small amount of pacing the floor before Stephen was able to get his head straight and think about what he could say, take the elevator to the third floor, and walk into an area where he suddenly felt very alone. Looking across the hallway at Jamal, standing between Felicia and Leo, did nothing to resolve this quandary. For some reason, Felicia had lied about the death of her brother, and somehow Jamal was connected—not only to that fact but to this family as well.

"Jamal? What are you doing here?" Stephen asked.

Hearing that question, Jamal's first reaction had been anger. Why was everyone so concerned with his presence here? Then he suddenly realized who was asking it. He looked back at the two ladies near Margaret's room, his mother's room, the older women having since departed, and noticed the child among them, being held up by some broad dark-skinned woman. He'd seen that child before. Then it quickly clicked in his brain. "Oh my God!" he said aloud, slapping his hand across his mouth. He turned to look at Stephen, then at Pamela…No! It was *Felicia* now - her modeling name, her alias, her pseudonym.

"Tumali," Jamal said to himself, hearing the name in his ears, echoing across the cavern in his skull, over and over again.

Stephen turned to Felicia. "What's going on here, Felicia? Do you know Jamal?"

She fell against Leo, catching her breath. "Jay! This is Jay, isn't it? You never called him Jamal until now. Jay, Jay, always Jay," she repeated like a deranged woman. "He's my brother, Stephen."

"I thought your brother was dead. What are you talking about? How can Jamal be your brother?"

"He's not dead. Can't you see that? What kind of man are you? He's right here, and I..." she looked up at Leo. "What am I to do?"

Leo hugged his sister closer, his eyes never wavering from Stephen's. "What have you done now?" he asked through clenched teeth. .

Tammy suddenly came forward, Felicia's child in her arms. Tumali began to reach out to his mother, while Tammy looked on, having a ready put everything together. She could sense the escalating drama. "I'm going to leave and take Tumali to the car. We'll wait there for you," she said, looking at Stephen and Jamal and slowly shaking her head in disgust.

"Why couldn't you just fuck someone else?" Felicia said, addressing Stephen. She was glad her aunts had already gone home so as not to witness this mess.

"What the hell's going on?" Leo asked.

"Let's go, Tammy. I can't stand this anymore."

"Are you saying these two know each other, Felicia?" Leo prodded, looking at the two men, his eyes darting back and forth between them.

Felicia nodded, as she pushed herself away from them, wiping her face. Tammy began walking along the hallway.

"You said your brother was dead," Stephen said.

Felicia didn't answer.

"Is that what this insane family has been calling me?" Jamal began. "Am I dead to you now?" Jamal only shook his head and began walking toward Margaret's door.

Leo continued to gaze at the two men until the pieces fell together. *"No!* Hell no! Fuckin' faggot country!" he said, grabbing Felicia's hand. "Let's get out of here before I start moppin' these niggas. I knew you were trouble," he said to Stephen.

Stephen watched as Felicia and Leo receded down the corridor and around the corner. He then looked back at Jamal. He felt he was caught in the middle, always hurting people. "What's going on, Jamal?"

"I've got to see my mother, Stephen. I don't have time to talk to you. Why don't you just go home? You don't belong here," Jamal stated, as he walked into the room, the door slowly closing behind him.

Stephen stood alone with his thoughts.

– IV –

Dominique walked into the meeting room, her eyes instantly locking with the woman behind the oak-and-steel desk. She noticed the sweep of the hair, pulled back on the sides with massive waves on top, light brown highlights. It was a smaller version of the new look Angela was sporting. Was this the new corporate hairstyle? The silk blouse and matching collarless jacket were clearly expensive items meant to give her stature, and the two dangling pearl earrings swinging down past her jaw were actually nice accents. A thin herringbone necklace lay against her neck. The makeup on her creamy white skin was flawless, but that goes without saying, considering she did own a cosmetics firm. But still, she couldn't conceal the emergence of crow's-feet pushing through her foundation and powder. She exuded power and control.

So this is Gerri Moore, thought Dominique.

"Please have a seat, Dominique," Gerri offered, watching Dominique carefully. This woman was tall, very pretty, quite young, and she emanated sexuality like steam from a baked potato. She understood the pull she had on Sarafina.

'Thank you," Dominique replied, taking the seat offered to her.

Gerri gathered some papers on her desk. She spoke while examining them. "I assume you spoke with Angela before being sent in here?"

"Yes, I did," Dominique said, crossing her legs nervously. This whole incident seemed unreal. Here she was, right across from the woman who had brought extreme turmoil to her private life and who just happened to be, in a sense, her boss. She knew a meeting such as this was inevitable, but the reality of it had never sunk in until this very moment.

"Then I take it you are aware of the problem we've recently had with Nancy and McNeal?" Gerri inquired, glancing at Dominique. She then pushed herself away from the desk, and pulled open one of the drawers. She brought out a small leather pad and Montblanc pen.

"Yes, I am now aware of the situation concerning Nancy and McNeal, and I do apologize," Dominique said, biting her tongue.

Gerri nodded as she began to open what was obviously a checkbook and proceeded to write into it. "Angela also tells me you're up for a promotion, and this was in essence your first solo project. Of course, that's no excuse for being so lax in your research."

"Of course not," she said reluctantly.

"Miss Devaroe, I do hope this sort of performance isn't indicative of the staffing within the Shelby's D'Zines firm. I'm sure this whole mishap was a slight oversight and perhaps a bit of inexperience on your part," Gerri stated, drumming her fingers on the desk.

Dominique could feel the acid in her stomach froth to a menacing burn. She twisted uneasily in her seat. "I do take full responsibility for this affair."

"Hmm, such the martyr you are, Miss Devaroe," Gerri said, a bit sarcastic in her tone. "I want you to do me a favor, however," she said, as she ripped out a page from her checkbook and handed the paper to Dominique.

Dominique took the check with great caution, perplexed at the action. She looked around and could feel her breath swiftly leave her lungs. Eighty thousand dollars! It was more than a year's salary, and it was made out to her. "A favor?" Dominique asked.

Gerri pulled up closer to the desk, resting her elbows atop the surface, her chin in the palms of her hands. Her look was calculating, as if she were waiting for Dominique to guess her intentions. She let the silence mount, and then spoke: "I simply want you to leave Sarafina."

Dominique could feel her mouth fall open. "Excuse me?"

Gerri leaned hack confidently in her seat. "I want you to leave Sarafina," she repeated, speaking slowly and clearly.

"You want me to leave Sarafina?" Dominique echoed. She looked at the check in her hand. And I suppose this is my motivation?"

Gerri shrugged her shoulders. "It's whatever you want it to be, Dominique," she said, speaking Dominique's first name, all formality gone.

"I thought we were here to discuss the interiors of your company. This is getting rather personal, Miss Moore."

Gerri waved her hand in the air. "Yeah, yeah, yeah ... Can we be serious, Dominique? You know what's been going on, and you couldn't really think that I came all the way down here from my choice surroundings in Pacific Heights to discuss designs with you. I hire other minions for that."

Dominique could feel her breathing suddenly stop. Perspiration was beginning to cascade from her armpits. This was very unusual. She was face to face with Gerri Moore: cosmetics queen of America! Dominique kept her stance, willing herself from throwing a chair at those smug red lips. "Well, Miss Moore, I think—"

"Please, call me Gerri. I think we've given each other that much respect now."

"Okay, *Miss* Gerri," Dominique continued. "I can't believe you came all the way down from your high tower to sit here and bribe me. That's pretty tacky, if you ask me."

Gerri smiled. "Oh, you act like my offer is offensive to you. This is a lot of good money, and you scoff at it? How noble. How heroic. How ridiculous. This is to help you through the grief, my sweet child. Sarafina is still in love with me, and when that reality hits you, this compensation may take some of the sting away."

"Your money wasn't able to keep Sarafina in the first place, and you think I'll be any different? Your phone calls, letters, plane tickets weren't enough either. It seems to me that reality hasn't hit *you* yet. Don't you think this has gone on long enough?"

"No, I don't," Gerri replied softly. However, her fists were tight with tension. "No, I don't think I have done nearly enough. You seem like a smart woman, Dominique. You know Sarafina needs to be away from you and this near poverty you've allowed her to wallow in. That's why she accepted that ticket to San Francisco. I'm only telling you this as a friend and—"

Dominique suddenly stood up. "We are not friends, Miss Moore! We only have a client/contractor relationship. Nothing more," she voiced, slamming the check on the desk. "Take this, please. I am desperately trying to keep from saying something I know I would regret. I think it would be better for me to leave, and when we meet again, I hope it's to discuss business agendas, not bullshit issues."

Gerri reached out to retrieve her check, crumpling it in her hand.

"Don't mess with me, Dominique. Maybe Angela needs to know what sort of amateur she has on her staff. If you want to stick to business, I can do that too. I have been watching your progress, and it looks to me like you graduated from the design center just a little too soon. You have made some costly mistakes on my project, and I've been very cordial about them, but perhaps that should end. I haven't decided as of yet. All I know now is that I want Sarafina back, and you're in the way."

"Excuse me, but Sarafina is a grown woman, not a bitch to be led around on your leash. She makes her own decisions. I am no bitch either, for you to be flashing money in my face like some bone. I think this meeting is over."

Gerri stood, eyes steadily gazing upon Dominique, mouth pressed tightly as if she were holding in words that pushed at the back of her lips. "Fine!" she blurted out, as she reached into one of the top drawers of her desk to pull out a bulky manila envelope and slam it on the desk. She nudged it forward with the tips of her fingers. "Why don't you take a look at the design changes I made at my office in New York? I want similar changes for my office here. The video is very thorough, so please pay attention. I doubt your skill is up to this level, but hell, might as well let you dig your own hole, since you insist on carrying the shovel. We'll discuss your ability to render these changes and continue to draw up a new contract. This will give you a chance to see how a professional does it."

Dominique looked at the envelope. She was insulted at the accusations this woman made. She snatched up the envelope, tucking it under her arm. "I'll be sure to take a look at them, Miss Moore, and thank you for your time," Dominique said, turning briskly to head for the door.

Gerri grinned, slowly easing back in her chair, her eyes fixed on the envelope in Dominique's possession. "Then I guess that will be all, Miss Devaroe. We'll meet again to discuss those designs."

"I'm sure we will," Dominique finished, as she stepped from the office, slamming the door behind her.

Gerri watched the door and wanted to burst into laughter. *Yes, Dominique,* she thought gleefully, *you watch that video, and see just how a professional does it.*

—IV—

Jamal stood at the door watching the woman across from him in the raised hospital bed. She paid him no attention. He stepped up to the center of the room, taking notice of the television, which was showing a rerun of *The Beverly Hillbillies.* Then he looked down at his mother— a term he used rather loosely. Her skin appeared pale and taut, and her hair was pushed to the side of her head in a disheveled ponytail that seemed to be coming out of her ear. You'd have thought someone would have combed those naps a long time ago. Her lips were chapped and dry at the edges, and her eyes were puffy—perhaps something to do with the medication she was taking. He inched closer to the bed.

"Hello, Jamal," Margaret said, her eyes still fixed upon the television.

She motioned her hand for him to come closer. He stood there watching her thin fingers and uneven nails beckoning him. He couldn't believe he was here. He was waiting for some emotion to surface, some form of anger, surprise, confusion, something. He felt nothing. Margaret was a stranger in his life. He walked up to the bed, placing his bag on the floor. He held on to the strap, afraid to let go, to release himself into her world and away from his reality.

Margaret cleared her throat and slowly tilted her head, staring at him for a moment as if trying to focus on his face, to remember who he was. "You look well, I see. Better than me, that's for sure," she said with a slight grin and a thinly veiled cough.

Jamal released the luggage strap and placed his hands in his pockets, fighting the urge to pat her on the hand. "I'm doing okay, I guess."

"And how's your father?" she asked, fishing under the covers of the bed, bringing out a remote control.

"He's okay. How are you?" he asked, feeling the awkwardness of the conversation.

"Just a bit tired, that's all. Imagine, having a stroke at my age," she said, flipping through the channels. "Who'd ever thought? My grandmother had one in her late forties too. The doctor said it could be genetic, skipping a generation," she said, clearing her throat once again.

Jamal saw a small stand next to her with a water pitcher and cup. "Would you like some water?" he asked reaching for the items, and pouring her a cup.

"Thank you, Jamal," she said. "I heard some shouting in the hallway. I guess you met your brother and sister. "She leaned forward as Jamal offered the cup. She took loud, drawn-out sips.

When she finished, he found an empty cup to pour himself a drink. "Yeah, I met them out there. It wasn't what I would call a welcome family reunion."

"I'm sorry about that," she apologized, stopping the television on *General Hospital, "I* had no idea they would react that way."

Jamal shook his head. He didn't know how to respond to this woman. This idle chitchat was unnerving. He did not travel all this way for small talk. "Why did you call me here, Margaret?" he asked, turning his back on this illusion of what was deemed to be his parent.

Suddenly the television went off, and only then did Jamal realize just how dark it was in the room. The thick curtains were barely open, and it cast the room in a gray darkness. Jamal could hear Margaret taking another sip. She spoke again, her eyes staring at the blankness of the television tube. "I wanted to say I was sorry, Jamal."

Jamal moved around to the foot of the bed and stood directly under the television, and yet Margaret refused to acknowledge his presence with her eyes. He found himself looking down at her sheets, following the creases and valleys like river veins. He couldn't look at her now either. "What are you sorry for?" he asked, knowing the answer.

"For treating my son like he was the stepchild, for allowing your siblings to continue to hate you until this day, for allowing your father to speak to you so badly."

"That was never my father!" Jamal said, feeling his temper rise at the mention of his stepfather. "My father is in DC, losing what's left of his mind, and still he's smarter than that other man could ever be."

"Well, I am very sorry for that."

"Are you also sorry for telling Pamela—I mean Felicia—and Leo that I am to remain dead to them?"

"That was your father's...I mean your stepfather's idea. I had nothing to—"

"Does that make it right, Margaret?"

"You can't even call me Mother, can you?" she said, easing her gaze down to look directly in Jamal's eyes.

"No, I guess I can't, not when she considers me dead, and this the advice from a madman. To think that you would listen to such a fool is beyond me. Such a maniac he was. I don't know why you left my father to get yourself caught up with that damned fool, and—

Margaret suddenly pounded her hand on the bed. "That was the man I loved, Jamal!"

Jamal hit the bed railing out of frustration. "Then I feel sorry for you." He walked away from the bed, stomping his foot on the floor. He couldn't believe he'd had so much resentment built up. "I feel sorry that you thought it was necessary to allow your husband to kick your child out of a place he called home. I feel sorry that you couldn't love me because I'm gay. I feel sorry that you had to poison your other children's minds to please your husband's homophobic attitude. You let him call me names, punish me, taunt me, and you sit there and tell me that even his last words were to be obeyed and to have the whole family treat me as if I were dead. I feel very sorry for you, Margaret." Jamal went back to the pitcher and poured himself another cup of water, downing it all in one swift gulp.

Margaret said nothing. Her eyes looked on at some imaginary point just beyond the television. Her eyes stung from the tears that swelled in them. She was thinking, that was apparent; her quivering lips told Jamal that. She then spoke, her voice was soft, very controlled, although it shook with extreme anxiety.

"Well, you just continue to feel sorry for me. It wasn't easy to do what I did. I didn't like the fact that you were gay myself. You, Jamal, my son, created from the loins of a man I really loved. It wasn't all your stepfather, it was me too. I couldn't deal with what you were bringing to my family. I didn't want to deal with it. I refused to deal with it. I just thought I would get used to it and ignored what your stepfather did. I had no idea he would drive you away."

"You thought I would take his abuse forever?" Jamal asked, standing near the door, leaning up against it. He could hardly stand to look at her now. .

"There was more than just *your* abuse going on in that house, Jamal. Everything was going fine when Leo was born, then Jason cheated on me and I left him for two years. I met Terrance, your father, and I thought I was in love forever, but I had never fallen out of love with your stepfather. I went back to him, pregnant with you. He accepted you at first, but soon the reality of who you were dawned on him; you were not his blood. Even after Pamela was born, you were a constant reminder I had been with another man. His anger became directed toward me."

Jamal raised his arms. "I know all this. He was very wrong for treating me and you the way he did, but—"

"No, that's wrong. When he found those nude books in your room, after you came out to him, he directed his anger toward you even more directly. But when you left to visit your father during the summer, he was the model husband and father. We went on trips we never told you about. He brought me flowers, gave the kids whatever they wanted."

"All poisoning them against me. Making it easier, even more welcome, when I decided to leave," he said, turning to face the door, leaning his head against it. "Damn, if only you knew what I went through." He closed his eyes, trying not to remember his life away from what he thought was his home.

He could remember taping the pages from those nude magazines on the walls of his room when he decided to leave; so his father would remember the fag that lived under his roof. He could remember then going over to Lawrence Oliver's home, a man in his thirties who he thought was a friend. That friendship turned into a sexual relationship. One year later, when Lawrence's taste changed, he was back out on the street. He then went from friend's home to friend's home, until he decided to try for his GED and obtain a diploma. He wrote his real father, Terrance, but never left a return address, afraid he would ask him to move back in with the Jenkins's. He then went to the employment offices and placed applications for hotels, restaurants, and airports. He was accepted by American Airlines, the happiest day of his life and the greatest change. He had gone through selling drugs, his own body, stealing, and just plain surviving for three years, all because a man and his wife couldn't deal with their son's homosexuality. And now come the apologies.

Jamal turned to look at Margaret. He owed her nothing, not even this visit. How could he ever call this woman his mother, when a real mother would swallow her own pride and stand up for her son? It took her this long to wake up. It took this near-death experience for her to realize that she'd left some things incomplete. It took her this long to realize that the wishes of a dead man weren't worth the dirt that buried him. She realized it was a shame to die a fool, and she was certainly on her way. But he was the fool today, just for being here.

He was tired of being the fool. He was tired of it all. Walking out of that hospital room was the best thing he'd done in all his life.

Chapter 19

—I—

Stephen pulled at Tumali's seat belt, checking its strength. Tumali looked up at his father, a thick yellow piece of *egg* hanging limply from his mouth. His mother had made him an egg-and-cheese sandwich before they left this morning. For Stephen, she had made nothing. He wasn't surprised. After all that had happened yesterday, he wasn't surprised by anything. "Now, look at yourself," Stephen said, reaching over to wipe Tumali's face. The child pulled his tiny hands back. Stephen smiled. "I don't want your sandwich, boy."

This morning, Felicia had gone to visit her mother, making it clear she didn't want Stephen to go with her. She suggested he take Tumali to see his grandparents. He was thrilled to do that, because he knew he had no patience to deal with Felicia all day. He hadn't last night either, as he decided to drive around town after leaving the hospital...after leaving that drama. He had stopped off at Martin's Den to have a drink, then come back to the apartment and dropped on the sofa into a swift and inviting sleep. He had awoken in the middle of the night to a sharp pain in the center of his forehead. He had looked down to see an unraveled cassette tape in the center of his chest. When he looked up he saw Felicia tossing a second tape his way; this one landed on his shoulder.

"What are you doing?" he demanded.

"I've decided to forgive you," she informed him. "They're your answering machine tapes," she said, letting out a deep throaty burp.

"What are you talking about?" he asked as he pushed up on his elbows trying to attempt to sit up. He squinted one of his eyes as a "Felicia headache" charged through his brain.

"I should've let Leo kick your butt. He wanted to, you know, but I stopped him. I had him drive me home," she informed, wiping spittle from the corner of her mouth with the side of her arm. She pushed herself away from the wall she was leaning against, and stumbled over to the stool near the kitchen bar.

Stephen could smell the vapor trail of liquor following her. "I think you should go to bed, Felicia. You're going to wake Tumali," he said, concerned.

Felicia slammed her palm against the countertop, shaking the row of photos that sat upon it. "Shit! Tumali ain't here, okay? He's with Tammy tonight."

Stephen swung his feet around to the floor to sit up. He looked at Felicia angrily. "What's he doing with her? You don't trust him around me now?"

Felicia began to laugh. "Why wouldn't I trust him around you? What harm could his second mother be? My mom was right; Tumali has two mothers. What a trip that is."

Stephen stood, tucking his wrinkled shirt in his pants, while adjusting his tie. "You're drunk. I don't have to be here listening to this crazy talk coming from you at damn near two in the morning."

Felicia pushed her long hair to the back of her head. She kept her eyes locked with Stephen's as if establishing a focal point, as if trying to keep her equilibrium. "So you leaving? You gonna play butt patrol with your boyfriend?"

Right then, Stephen could have slapped her right off that stool. He didn't know who this woman was, sitting in this apartment, balancing on a stool with her robe now falling open to reveal one round breast. He knew she did this on purpose. "What is it, Felicia? You have something against me fucking your brother? That would make me your brother-in-law, wouldn't it?" Stephen spit out.

Felicia's eyes were red hot, and she breathed loudly, then suddenly she swept her hand across the counter, knocking the pictures across the room. "You mutha'fucker! How could you do this to me? My brother. How could you bring that faggot back into my family?" She exhaled, raising her fists in the air.

"Funny, you told me the boy was dead. You told me your brother died in a car accident as a child. Now you tell me he's Jamal. Are you raising the dead now? Your lies are just coming back to you, that's all. Your whole family has brought this boy back with the lies you've all continued to tell."

Felicia covered her face with her hands, resting her elbows on the counter top. "He was dead," she bellowed. "My father hated him. He hated that damn faggot. When Jamal ran away from home, my father made us promise to never mention him again. We were to treat Jamal as if he were dead. If the neighbors asked where he'd gone, we'd just say he returned to his father back in DC. As time passed, we just said he'd died in a horrible accident. I was only twelve at the time—what did I know? We never went on trips, or got good Christmas gifts, or had nice meals when Jamal was there; Dad would say it was because we had to feed him *and* us. There was never any money left for nice things…until he went to visit his father during the summer, or when he went there on certain Christmases. Things were nice then.

"When he told Dad he was gay, that gave him even more reason to resent him, and that gave us reason to hate him too. Mom was just glad the old man wasn't focusing his anger on her any longer. It was wrong for her not to stand up for her own son, but it was wrong for us too. Dad never called him *Jamal* after that; it was always Queer, Homo, Faggot, Punk—the names were endless. Even after his departure at sixteen, Dad wouldn't allow Mom to fill out a missing person's report. Then Dad went on a cleaning spree, eliminating every bit of evidence that Jamal had ever existed, from gifts to photos. It was as if he had truly died. And after a while, we all believed it. I believe if Jamal had ever returned, Dad would have truly killed him."

Now Stephen understood her shock in the hospital. Sadness equaled Jamal. To see him back, after all the brainwashing their father had done, only brought back the pain he caused while in their family. Felicia must have nearly died to know that Jamal was sleeping with the man she loved. Her hate for homosexuality could only run deeper.

"Funny, I'd always wondered how Jamal was doing. He was, after all, my brother, and I also wanted to ask his forgiveness. But now too much has happened, and I could never think of Jamal as anything but a bad omen, a bad seed." She looked around to see Stephen standing behind her, as she slowly wiped the tears from her cheeks. "Tumali will be here in the morning, and I plan to go to the hospital. So why don't you take him to see your mom and dad. He'll enjoy the time with his grandparents."

Stephen had agreed. Felicia stood silently. She looked down and noticed her robe was open, bare breasts exposed. She was about to close it, took one look at Stephen, shrugged her shoulders, and allowed it to remain open. She walked into her bedroom. The conversation was over. She had to deal with her own ghosts now.

And so now Stephen was heading to his parents. He looked over at Tumali, fast asleep, bread crumbs smeared across his lips. Stephen reached across to brush them from his soft skin. *Two mothers,* he thought, *that is pretty funny.*

— II—

David spread the morning paper across the tiny dining table and ran his fingers down the columns. He had to find a steady job, and that was all there was to it. The landscaping at Mike's was good until the end of summer, but that was it. He'd been staying with Damien almost two months, and enough was enough. He had to get his own place. He was positive he had no intentions of moving back in with Allen, although they had been talking on the phone lately and surprisingly the conversations were pleasant. Malcolm, on the other hand, was acting a bit strange. He could sense that Malcolm wanted more than just a friendship with him and was becoming very possessive in the process. He questioned David on his whereabouts, who he was talking to on the phone, and made constant plans to do things when he returned from work. David was not ready for any kind of relationship, and he and Malcolm would have to sit down and have a little talk soon.

Meanwhile, David had other issues to contend with: He had to retrieve other items from Allen's. He had to get a job and an apartment. He had decided to attend a cheaper form of therapy—better known as church—and had been looking into attending a group session for HIV-positive men. The Minority AIDS Project wasn't very far from him, and an organization known as Shanti was offering a three-day workshop for those who were just now dealing with their status. He decided not to let this disease scare him and to dive headfirst into the information pool.

Retail sales, airlines, real estate, programmer, yadda, yadda, yadda…the job market wasn't looking too promising these days. It was Saturday, August 6, so tomorrow was Sunday; the ads would be better tomorrow. David slowly began to fold the paper as he heard a loud rapping at the door, startling him.

He went to the door, easing back the tiny curtain in the window beside it. He looked out, and could see that it was Allen, a broad smile on his face. "Who is it?" he asked anyway.

"Hey, it's me, Allen. Is that you, David?" he asked, easing his eye toward the peephole.

David didn't know how to answer. He had spoken with Allen on the phone, but they hadn't met since that night after Andrew's funeral. He gripped the doorknob, pushing back the fear he felt. He refused to be afraid of this man. Things were over between them, so why couldn't they just be friends? He had to stop running sometime. He slowly opened the door.

"It is you. Long time no see," Allen greeted cordially, his smile very extreme. "I was passing through and thought I would come by and see how you doin'."

David casually sniffed the air surrounding Allen—old habits were hard to break—and could only distinguish the scent of peppermint on his breath. Still, that could be a ruse to hide any trace of liquor. "I'm doing fine, Allen. Just finished looking through the paper to see if I can get a steady job."

Allen took a cautionary step forward, watching carefully as David opened the door a bit more, admitting him inside. He walked in to stand in the center of the living room. David closed the door behind him. "That's good, David. Having any luck?" he asked, while looking around.

"Not much," David replied, walking back to the table and his newspaper.

"I guess Damien is out doing his hair thang?" Allen questioned. "Yeah, he left early this morning," David responded, his eyes continuing to scan the paper.

"And how's your health? You looking pretty good."

David looked up at Allen curiously. *Now where is this leading?* he wondered. He answered cautiously. "I'm doing fine. I'm going to be starting some medication soon, been putting it off long enough. My T-cell count is still pretty high, so all is well."

"So you been to the doctor? Well, I don't listen to T-cells anyway, and I know how I feel, so I'm sure I'm doing good," he said, walking toward David, casually picking up a separate section of the newspaper, scanning through it. "I do miss you though," he muttered, keeping his eyes on the paper.

A chill pushed through David's spine. He didn't know how to respond to that blatant comment, so he didn't. "Let's see ... cashier? That sounds like *it* could work for me," he said, ignoring Allen's comment.

"So?" Allen questioned, putting the paper down.

"I'm sorry, what did you say?" David asked, turning his attention away from the paper.

"Do you miss me too?" Allen prodded.

David smiled. "I refuse to answer that on the grounds that it could incriminate me."

Allen leaned over the back of one of the wooden chairs near the table. "Seriously, David. Do you ever think about us living together again? Doing stuff like we used to?"

David pushed himself away from the table and stood up. "I'm thirsty, Allen. Do you want something to drink?" he asked, heading toward the kitchen.

"Yeah, sure. Anything would be fine," he replied, obviously miffed at being ignored.

"Good. I'll be right back," David said as he pushed the door to the kitchen open.

Allen strutted over to the sofa, resting himself on its plush cushions. *Maybe coming over was a mistake,* he thought. *Maybe I'm trying too hard and it's scaring David. Maybe there is something else keeping him away...perhaps even someone else, but who?*

There was a light tapping coming from the door. Allen instinctively went to answer it. Glancing through the peephole, he saw it was Malcolm. He'd found his answer. He slid the chain back then slowly opened the door. "Yes, may I help you?" Allen asked, keeping the door ajar.

Malcolm knew that eye and bright complexion anywhere. It was Allen answering the door. He wasn't sure how to respond. "Is David there?" he asked coolly.

"No," came the swift reply. No other response came from Allen, just a large brown eye sizing up Malcolm as if he were prey.

Malcolm was unmoved. If David wasn't there, then what business did Allen have being there? He and Damien weren't the best of friends. Before he opted to break down the door, he asked, "Do you know when he will he back?"

"I don't—" Allen was cut off by a distraction within the house. He looked behind himself, then back at Malcolm, then he shut the door.

Malcolm could hear voices from within, muffled but erratic. Then there was the scraping of a metal chain, and slowly the door opened. David stood standing in the threshold. "I'm sorry about that, Malcolm. Would you like to come in?'

Malcolm rushed into the apartment, immediately ready to confront Allen if he stood near. He didn't. Allen was on the sofa, legs crossed, sipping at a drink as if nothing was wrong. Malcolm then turned to David and whispered, "What's he doing here?"

David closed the door. "He just dropped by for a few minutes, that's all."

"Then why was he answering the door, telling me you weren't here?" Malcolm asked, very vexed.

"I don't know what that was all about. Don't worry about it. Okay?"

"This fool is straight up punkin' me, and I don't like his games, David. You know he's full of shit, David. Why'd you let him in here?"

David was taken aback. "Don't worry about that, Malcolm. I am a big boy now. I think you need a drink too. How about some iced tea or something?"

Malcolm took a deep breath. "I guess that'd be cool," he agreed. David nodded then returned to the kitchen. Malcolm strolled over to the sofa. He stopped just a few inches from Allen, looking him over.

"So what's up, Allen?" he questioned. Allen continued to enjoy his drink. Malcolm repeated himself.

"Are you tawkin' to me?" Allen responded, his worst imitation from *Taxi Driver*.

"Don't play me, Allen. I don't like having the door closed in my face."

"Why don't you just drop it?" Allen said, leaning back on the sofa. "Maybe I don't want to drop it," Malcolm replied.

Allen leaned his head back then swung his feet up on the coffee table. "I don't owe you anything."

"That's fine. I just don't want you to forget what I said in the car. David had better be fine. That's all I have to say."

"Or what?" Allen challenged. "What're you gonna do, Malcolm? I'm not drunk today, like I was when you told me that bullshit in the car.

"That wasn't bullshit, and you might as well be drunk, 'cause that peppermint I smelled at the door didn't fool anyone."

Allen sipped at his drink again. He wasn't going to let this boy get to him. Malcolm was no threat. So what if he'd had a few drinks before coming over? What business was it of his? If Malcolm wanted to start some shit, he was ready. "Why don't you go find a seat and keep outta my business."

"Your business is my business when you're around David. He doesn't need a threat like you."

And what are you, his savior? His hero? I don't think so. You're just dick-whipped and you ain't even had the dick. David doesn't want you, and you can't deal with it. That's what this is all about."

The muscles in Malcolm's face went rigid. This man was mocking him, taunting his feelings, exposing him. It was obvious now that Allen was his enemy.

David returned with Malcolm's drink and halted when he noticed the obvious tension between the two men. At once, he regretted opening his door for either of them. He stood in the background watching them.

"You're just ticked because nobody wants your tired ass!" Malcolm brewed, his anger becoming more apparent now.

"What's going on here?" David quickly interrupted, as he rushed between the two men, shoving the iced tea at Malcolm.

"Why don't you take this and have a seat over by the table?" David suggested.

"I don't feel so thirsty now," Malcolm said, his eyes fixed upon Allen.

David spun around to gaze at Allen. "What's all this about?" he demanded.

Allen stood and placed his hand on David's shoulder. "I think you should be asking lover boy over there. He has this idea that he's here to save you from me."

"You're gonna need to save yourself in a minute," Malcolm challenged.

"Malcolm! I don't need this today," David voiced, pushing Malcolm back with his palm. "Now please, go have a seat."

"Yeah, before you find yourself hurt," Allen prodded.

"Allen, quit adding your two cents! I don't—"

"Oh no, brother, I won't be the one hurt!" Malcolm said, as he grabbed the glass of iced tea from David's hand and threw its contents at Allen. The liquid splashed against Allen's face, cubes battering his shoulders, a lemon wedge stuck to his cotton pullover. "I warned you before!"

"You mutha'fucker!" Allen shouted, stepping forward, pushing David aside. David stumbled across the coffee table. Allen swung at Malcolm, his fist connecting with the side of Malcolm's jaw. Malcolm stumbled back, holding his face. The blow only grazed him, yet startled him all the same. "I'll kick your black ass," Allen voiced, wiping tea from his face.

Malcolm lunged in Allen's direction, butting his head into Allen's midriff. He fell on the sofa. David rolled out of the way, falling to the floor. David couldn't believe what he was seeing. Malcolm rushed Allen as he lay on the sofa. Pillows fell to the floor, drenched from the spilled drink. David could see fists, hear the thud of connecting flesh. Arms and legs flew everywhere.

"Break this shit up!" David yelled into the melee. He was about to step into the fray, but Allen kicked Malcolm back, and he stood...brandishing a butterfly knife.

"Now what, pretty boy?' Allen ranted. "You not such a bad ass now, are you?"

"What the hell are you doing, Allen?" David asked, keeping his distance.

"Quiet! I was talking to your savior!" Allen voiced, jabbing the air in Malcolm's direction. "You're not so heroic now, are you?"

Malcolm said nothing. The knife wasn't scaring him. He had grown up on the streets of Los Angeles and had seen the tip of many a knife. He was more angered that he hadn't thought of it himself.

"Oh, you've got nothing to say, is that it? You come between me and David, and you have nothing to say for yourself. You are a punk!"

"What?" David gasped. "How did he come between me and..."

"Shut up, dammit! I'm talking here," Allen barked, slamming his foot against the coffee table.

That look! David thought. *How similar to the old Allen. Has he really changed at all?*

"So what'cha gonna do, Allen?" Malcolm asked, his arms out-stretched, a taunting gesture. "You bad, you got the knife, you in control."

"You damn straight I am!" Allen said, slicing the air just inches from Malcolm's face. He reached out with his other hand to shove Malcolm in the chest, but he continued to stand his ground. "Maybe I should give you the same advice you tried to give me," Allen continued. "I want *you* to stay away from David. He doesn't love you. He loves me. Who do you think he came to see right after the funeral? That's right, brother: me."

Malcolm looked at David, and there was visible hurt his eyes. David could feel a knot wedge itself in his throat. He'd never told

Malcolm that, and he knew it was too late to explain it now. David looked at Allen. "We didn't do anything!"

"Hell, but you came over, and we almost did, David. You can't deny that. You thought of me first, and there you were knocking at my door." He turned toward Malcolm. "You hear that? He thought of me first, bitch!"

"Fuck you, Allen!" Malcolm fumed, holding up a stiff middle finger.

"Aww, are you a bit angry, baby?" Allen taunted. "Did you think you were the first to coddle poor old David?" Suddenly his tone became more aggressive. "Well, get used to it, Malcolm! Now why don't you just take your sorry ass right on out that door before I change my mind and slice your ass up right here and now!" Allen proceeded, stabbing the knife before him. "Now get the fuck out!"

Malcolm held up his hands in defeat, backing toward the door. "Is this what you want, David?" he asked, looking over his shoulder at David, who was standing back.

David was about to speak, but Allen quickly intervened. "Fuck that conversation bullshit! Just turn your ass around and head out the door. I'm not playing with you, Malcolm!"

Malcolm dropped his arms and slowly turned toward the door.

"This isn't over," he mumbled, cautiously looking over his shoulder. Allen ignored his reply, but he continued. "And you know your biggest problem, Allen?" he asked, reaching for the doorknob.

"And what's that, lover boy?" Allen questioned, as he began to pick his nails with the tip of his weapon, his eyes steadily on his enemy.

Suddenly Malcolm twisted around and was across the room in one bound. Allen swung his knife through the air on instinct, but Malcolm had swept under him, wrapped his arms around Allen's legs, and launched him into the sofa. Allen was caught off guard. Malcolm swiftly wrenched the loosely held knife from Allen's fingers and, with a twist of his wrist, held the steel instrument to Allen's throat, circling the tip against his Adam's apple.

"The next time you threaten someone, it's always a good idea to dispense with the chitchat and make good with the threat. You got that?" Malcolm said, sweat falling from his brow to Allen's chin.

"Oh, the hero returns," Allen said through clenched teeth.

"Yeah, I'm the mutha'fuckin' hero. I told you once about stickin' your shit in David's life, and it seems I may have to send some of my boys to your fancy house in Torrance for you to get the message," Malcolm said, pressing the tip of the knife so deep into Allen's flesh that a mere swallow would break the skin. "Don't try me, brother, 'cause you will always lose."

"Get the fuck up!" David shouted.

Malcolm turned to look up at David, and what he saw shocked him to the point that he pulled away from Allen immediately. Allen reared up, his every movement intent on retaliation against Malcolm, until he saw the glint of steel from the corner of his eye. He looked until he saw the glint of steel from the corner of his eye. He looked at David and was stilled with instant fright. They both peered at David and the trembling 9 mm in his hand.

"What are you doing?" Malcolm asked, his fear only escalating as he witnessed the quiver in David's grip. He knew the weapon was real, no doubt.

"Quiet!" David commanded, then turned his attention to Allen. "And you get your ass up off that couch and get out! I am tired of this shit!"

"David, what are you talking about? I haven't done anything," Allen pleaded.

"Just get out. You're always bringing unwanted drama in my life and I just don't need it."

Allen leaned forward, in obvious defiance of the threat before him. "Now stop this craziness, David. Is that Damien's gun? You need to put that thing away before—"

The sound came swiftly, crackling through the air like a muffled explosion of dynamite, and the cushion between the two men imploded as the bullet penetrated its cotton hide, exposing its feathered interior. Allen nearly fell to the floor, and Malcolm stood to his feet, his instinct to head for the door in a mad rush, but he remained grounded. And then abrupt silence filled the room, and the only sound they heard was a plane flying overhead, and the beat of hip-hop music from a passing car.

"Now get out! And this time stay away for a while. I am not your man anymore, Allen, and I don't need you walking up in here acting like you want to be friends and the first thing that comes from your mouth is when you expect us to get back together. I would never go back to your drinking and beatings. My father died a long time ago, but I never thought in my wildest dreams that I would've ended up in a relationship with him. Well, I am through with it. Don't they have enough punching bags at the gym without you wanting to get back with me? Now just get the hell out of here, dammit!" David stated, clenching the gun tighter.

Allen stood and took a cautionary step forward, but seeing the look in David's eyes he thought better of it and swiveled himself to face the front door. He headed toward it, Malcolm graciously stepping aside. He was too tired to continue with this battle. His face was sticky from the drink thrown at him, his shirt twisted and stained. His throat throbbed with tension, and he was now eye to eye with a raging stranger—one he still cared about. "I want you to know that I am sorry for everything I have done, David. I still love you, more than any man I have ever known," Allen said, and with that, he walked out the door. He took one glance at Malcolm, and whispered, "Fuck you." Then he left.

David rushed up to bolt the latch. "You're always sorry," he murmured. "I would never live to see the day that you weren't."

"Well, I'm glad you kicked him to the curb, David. He was screwing up your life. I think—"

"I want you to get out too," David said quickly, as he walked past Malcolm, then stopped, not bothering to turn around. Malcolm could only stare at his back.

"What?"

David turned, his hands still clutching the gun, which swung at his side. "I want you to leave, Malcolm."

"Why? I've done nothing. I'm your friend," Malcolm confided.

"You aren't a friend, Malcolm. What you are is falling in love with me," David revealed, as he watched Malcolm's mouth drop open. It was time to stop playing these games. "And I am not in love with you and may never be. I have never given you the impression that I was sexually attracted to you, but you have still kept this infatuation. I see it all the time, and I am in no mood for it. I don't need another obsessed lover in my life."

"Who said I was obsessive?"

"You held a knife to Allen's throat, and I believe you would have used it if provoked just a little further."

"It's because I care for you, David. Maybe I am falling for you, but you have to give it a chance before you up and say no," Malcolm said, folding his arms, defeated.

"Get out, Malcolm. I don't want to seem the bitch, but fuck it, I *need* to start sometime. I don't need the kind of friendship you're trying to give. I need to start living for myself, by myself...a good friend told me that once, rest his soul."

"I understand, but—"

"No buts, Malcolm. Just please close the door behind you," David said, as he turned his back on Malcolm again. And when you're ready to be a real friend, give me a call, okay?"

"I—",

"Goodbye, Malcolm," David said. "I just don't need the drama. I just don't need it."

There was a silence that lasted for a full minute, followed quietly by the door being unlocked then closed shut. David took a deep breath. He wished he could have Malcolm as a friend, because he sure needed one now. But he couldn't even trust Malcolm with his HIV status; they had just never reached that point. It was time he stopped living life for everyone else and started living it for him.

– II –

Dominique turned the tape over, observing its blank state. No labels on it anywhere, she noticed, she then pushed it into the VCR, then turned the television on. "So these will be the new designs she wants, as if my ideas aren't good enough," she mumbled. The television came on. She thought about that bribe as the VCR began to rewind. *The nerve to offer a check if I agreed to leave Sarafina. imagine! The whore had some nerve!* Dominique heard the whir of the machine as the tape finished its rewinding, she reached up to press PLAY...and waited.

The initial image was grainy as the tape began to play, then suddenly it cut to a bedroom setting; plush sheets laid across a canopy bed, low lighting, and there was a small band of white light that cut across the room, as if a door had stood ajar. 'What is this?" she questioned. Had Gerri given her the right tape?

There was a jangle of keys near the front door, and Dominique turned to see Sarafina entering the apartment, a bundle of grocery bags straddled in both her arms. "Hey there," she greeted, thrusting one foot out to hold the door.

"Hold on," Dominique said, as she stood to her feet. "Let me get one of those bags."

Dominique reached for one of the bags just as it began to fall from Sarafina's grip. Sarafina happened to look up and notice the television. She turned pale. "No!" she shouted, placing the remaining grocery bag on the floor and rushing to the television.

"What is it?" Dominique asked, as she watched Sarafina stab randomly at the buttons on the VCR. The picture suddenly went grainy again, and the cassette popped out.

"It's broken!" Sarafina said with more anxiety than called for. She appeared to calm herself as she clasped the video in her fingers.

"Damn! When did that old thing go haywire?" Dominique questioned.

Sarafina looked on nervously at Dominique. "I was trying to fix it this morning. Let me see if I can get this thing running while you put my Hagan Dazs in the freezer. You know how crazy I get without my daily cream supplement."

"Oh, we can't have you going crazy, can we?" Dominique chided, as she took one of the bags to the kitchen. "I'll just put these away first, okay?"

"That's cool. I'll bring in the other bag in a minute. Let me see if the machine is all right," Sarafina replied, as she watched Dominique stroll into the kitchen. There wasn't anything really wrong with the VCR—nothing that a good cleaning couldn't remedy. She was only startled by what she'd seen on the tape, an image that forced a barrage of memories. She had to make sure she had not been mistaken.

She hastily placed the tape back into the machine, and quickly pressed the FAST-FORWARD button, all the while focusing her attention on the kitchen door. She knew she only had a short time before Dominique returned. She stopped the tape and let it play. She watched intently as the moving images shocked her: She was naked, legs open, breasts exposed, nipples hard, a woman lay face down, eating at her crotch. That woman was Gerri, and this was definitely the tape that Gerri had shown to her, the tape she had threatened to use against her. How in God's name did it get here? How did it get in Dominique's hands? She was terrified. She stopped the VCR and pulled the video out, ripping at its back, tearing at its black strip of tape, and frantically stuffed it all back into the door of the recorder, just as Dominique opened the door to the kitchen.

"Hey! We could use the VCR in the bedroom if that one isn't working," Dominique suggested.

Slowly, Sarafina brought out the tape, looking as surprised as she could. "Dammit! Will you look at what this damned machine did to your tape," she said, her voice shaky. "I'm sorry about this, baby. Was it important?"

Dominique lowered her head. "Figures. It was some fucked-up project I was supposed to look at from the firm. That bitch gave it to me.

"Gerri?"

When Dominique nodded, Sarafina then understood how it was given to her. It was obvious she had no clue what was on it. "Maybe you can work something out when you get to work. I'll take this to the shop tomorrow," Sarafina suggested, as she wrapped the loose tape around the cassette.

Dominique smiled. "I'll see what I can do. I just don't even know if this project is worth the stress that woman is putting me through. She said some bold shit to me today."

"Oh really?"

"Yeah," Dominique said, taking up the last bag of groceries left beside the door. "It really blew me away."

Sarafina followed her, tossing the ruined tape into a kitchen drawer; she had plans for it later. "You have to tell me all about it." "Maybe you should sit down for this," Dominique suggested.

"Maybe I should," Sarafina agreed. As Dominique began to speak, she finally deduced a conclusion to her Gerri dilemma, once and for all.

Chapter 20

— I—

The phone rang loud enough to rouse David from his sleep then have him running from his bed and across the hallway to answer it before the third ring.

"Hello?" he whispered heavily into the receiver. He knew exactly who it was even before they spoke.

"Why won't you speak with me, David?" said the voice on the other end.

David pushed his tired eyes open to mere slits. Streetlights from an open window shined into his face. He looked down at the time displayed on the answering machine's surface: two o'clock in the morning!

"Allen, quit calling me here. This is not my phone. Just leave me alone," David said, rubbing the sleep from his eyes.

"How many times do I have to apologize? It wasn't my fault that your boyfriend went ballistic," Allen explained.

"You were the one with the knife, Allen."

"But he threw that drink in my face. He's just as guilty as I am." "Whatever, Allen! It's two o'clock in the morning, and I am tired. Why don't you just go to bed and quit calling me here."

"All right. Will you call me later?"

"Goodnight, Allen," David finished, abruptly hanging up the phone.

David rested his head in the palm of his hands. *How much longer will this go on?* Malcolm was the same; this constant calling had to cease. He had told Malcolm to quit calling him yesterday, and he hadn't heard from him all day. At least some people could get the message. It had been two days since the gun incident, and the phone had been ringing off the hook.

The phone rang again, and before David could reach for it, it was already swept up out of view. He looked up to see Damien, a polka-dotted rag wrapped around his head, answering the phone. "Hello!" Damien answered; his pitch irate. "Allen? Now listens here, you *puto* bitch! It's too goddamn early in the morning to be callin' anybody, 'specially on my phone. So cut this shit out and don't call here anymore!" He swiftly hung up the phone. He then turned to David, patting the side of his head and adjusting his scarf. "We has to talk, David," he stated, reaching over to turn on the lamp beside the end table.

"You know, I'm sorry about all this," David cited. "And maybe I could get my own line."

"And maybe you should gets your own place too," Damien issued.

David gripped one of the sofa cushions tightly. He looked at Damien, refusing to believe the words he'd just heard. Damien stood over him, dressed in little more than a bedshirt with the words ABSOLUTELY FABULIOUS written on it and a pair of thick white thermal socks on his wide feet; the right tapped against the floor. He was pissed. "What was that?" David asked.

"I said I think you should get yo' own place, and soon. I can't afford all this drama going on now."

"Now you know I've been looking, Damien. I was hoping to get a good paying job so I can do that."

"Honey, you lookin' for that gravy train, and right now is time to settle for the stage coach. I'm not saying get something minimum wage, but you has to get somethin'."

David was in no mood to argue. "You're right, Damien, okay? I'm sorry about all of this. I'll be out soon enough and—"

"Let's shoot for Labor Day, David," Damien interrupted.

"Labor Day? That's no time for me. I thought you were trying to be a friend by letting me stay here awhile, but I see—"

"I am being a friend, so don't even go there. If I didn't set a time limit, then you may never get busy. I am only—"

"Some friend you are," David said standing. "If it's Labor Day you want, then that's what you get." He then stormed past Damien and into his room, slamming the door.

Damien closed his eyes, trying to calm himself. This whole situation was stressful for them both. He turned around and went to his room to think, and ultimately sleep. Seconds later he heard the front door slam shut. He didn't ' move and only stared at the ceiling. He knew David had left. Where? He had no idea. He was a grown man that still needed to grow.

—II—

Gerri ordered another strawberry daiquiri while she waited for her shrimp cocktail. She hadn't been to Gladstone's in ages it seemed, and to think, she never knew about the one here in Universal Studios CityWalk. It wasn't often she visited Los Angeles, she supposed. It seemed a pleasant place, despite the obvious lower income patrons that frequented this establishment. The afternoon was pleasant and the outdoor eating area quaint.

The message this morning surprised her: Sarafina called and wished to have lunch. She was very cordial on the phone, and it seemed reconciliation was beginning. That conversation made this wretched trip all worth the effort. Dominique must have seen the video of her and Sarafina together by now, and Gerri was sure that its viewing caused quite a stir in their household. She would have paid a fortune to have seen Dominique's face. She would have paid anything to have that night again, when they made love, regardless of Sarafina's coherency at the time.

The shrimp cocktail arrived, and Gerri plucked a delicate crustacean from its bed of crushed ice and sucked at it tenderly, still tasting Sarafina's tit against her lips. It all was falling into place, and Gerri couldn't be any happier.

Sarafina could see the woman a mile away. She arrived fifteen minutes late so Gerri could have time to herself. She trudged briskly through the thick throng of people lining the boulevard, not bothering to apologize as she forced individuals from her unswerving path. Her gaze was focused, her vision clear, her destination apparent. She gripped the bulky envelope in her tense fist. Her arms swung at her sides, anger in the motion. She was resolute in her judgment that this connection with Gerri had reached its finale. To let that tape—not to mention its very existence—fall into Dominique's hands could only be the work of someone she wanted nothing to do with. She was appalled at what Dominique had told her about Gerri's bribe. Didn't the woman know that slavery auctions were over?

As Gerri saw Sarafina approach, she stood respectfully, looking rather pleased. The look on Sarafina's face, however, confused Gerri. It was an expression like none she'd expected. Something was in her hand as well, but the swiftness with which it swayed at her side hid its shape. Gerri thought perhaps it were a gift of some sort, and that idea alone brought serenity. Sarafina moved upon the table so fast that Gerri was at once put on guard. She was too late in realizing that Sarafina was not here to socialize.

She was very late indeed.

Sarafina's hand rose up so fast that Gerri didn't see it coming until she felt a sharp pain against her head that started her ears ringing and caused an immediate burning across her cheek. She let out a shriek. Onlookers turned in their seats.

"You bitch!" Sarafina fumed, her tone amazingly controlled. She threw the manila envelope on the table, toppling the shrimp dish in a shower of ice, seafood, and cocktail sauce, which splattered on Gerri's cream-colored skirt.

Gerri stepped back from the table, her hand against her cheek, feeling the sting subside. Her eyes darted around to the adjacent tables, the patrons along the sidewalk, the waiters within the restaurant, all eyes on her, all trying not to look at her, all attempting to stay uninvolved. She had never been this embarrassed in all her life, and it was this realization that angered her more than the blow she received.

"Fuck you, Sarafina," Gerri blurted, dabbing the sides of her lips with a napkin. She was all about regaining her composure at this point. "You'll regret that, believe me."

"Is there a problem?" asked a tall white man who had rushed to the table, an apron tied around his waist and a name pin denoting him as the manager.

"I can't believe what you tried to do, Gerri. I just can't believe it. Dominique told me everything. I don't want to ever see you again!" Sarafina declared, ignoring the presence of the manager.

"Oh, she told you everything. And I suppose you told her everything too? Maybe you need to tell her about her future at Shelby's D'Zines. Maybe you need to tell her that, Sara-fuck-you-Fina."

"I'm going to have to ask you to leave, miss," said the manager, as more staff began to rally behind him.

"Consider me already ghost," Sarafina said, turning to leave. "The smell of rotten fish is in the air."

"Yeah, why don't you go back to your little whore."

Sarafina stopped and slowly faced Gerri. She grinned. "No, baby, I left my whore back in San Francisco. Someday you're gonna learn that love is more than a new ring and an unlimited credit line. I am not the one to teach you. I will be the one to tell you to stay out of my life, Gerri. I don't want to ever have to tell you that again," she concluded, and walked away from the table.

"I don't need you! There are hundreds of *you* that I can have. And tell Dominique I want to see her in the morning. You tell her that for me.

Sarafina waved her hand, "Whatever, Gerri! Whatever!"

***

At home, Sarafina peered into the room that served as Dominique's office. She was hunched in front of her computer. Dominique stopped and slowly lifted her head, as if she could feel Sarafina's presence. "What's up?" she asked.

Sarafina remained in the doorway, wringing her hands nervously. "I spoke with Gerri this afternoon," she admitted.

Dominique wanted to cover her ears as those words burned her drums. Why had she ever been introduced to that hellish name? She found it hard to decipher what emotions Sarafina was attempting to elicit by watching her. Was the news good, urgent, bad, what? "Why did you see her?" Dominique asked, not really wanting to go through with this type of dialogue again.

"I called her. I had to see her, had to end things. Partly because of what she attempted to do at your meeting and another part concerning your design tape."

"My design tape? You went to get another one for me or something?'"

"No, not exactly. That tape had more on it than design ideas."

Dominique shook her head and closed her eyes. What was going on here? How did Sarafina know what was on a tape that had been destroyed? "What happened at the meeting, 'Fina?" Dominique asked, rather irritated.

"We had a bit of a scrap. I'll just put it that way."

Dominique slowly stood. "What happened? This is the woman I have to work for and—"

"She wants to see you tomorrow morning, Dominique. I'm sorry about this, but I brought her into our world, and whether it happened now or next year, I had to be the one to end this shit. So I did."

"Just talk, Sarafina. Talk to me," Dominique pleaded, as she felt her forehead, and its beating, its swelling, its aching. She couldn't blame Sarafina in anything she did concerning that woman. She just wished she had a joint to help her cope with what Sarafina was about to tell her, because she knew it wasn't going to be good.

– III –

Stephen waited patiently, as he sat in the lobby of the airport Marriott hotel in Chicago. He looked through the double glass doors at the valet attendants gathered in the front of the building, as they waited for the next shuttle bus bringing new patrons to the hotel. They were waiting for their next chance at tips. Stephen, however, was there for another reason.

Tumali was with his mother at home, and later they would be visiting Margaret. He was leaving tomorrow, and for him, this family emergency was over. He was also exhausted from all the drafts that Barbara had sent him for the finished designs for the Andes campaign. She was taking on the full brunt of the work and was finally down to completing the radio spots. Luckily he was able to go over the print ads and send over the final touches Barbara asked for. It would be ready for Gordon at the next meeting.

As the shuttle was pulling up, he hoped things would go as planned. Out stepped men and women in business attire. A small family of five also departed the vehicle, with a load of bags in their possession, and the busboys nearly attacked them. Then there came an old woman, being helped kindly by the driver, and a few teenagers with backpacks strapped to their shoulders. Then came the airline employees lining up to take a much needed rest as they finished their last leg and wandered to the front desk to claim their rooms for the night before continuing back to the airport tomorrow.

Jamal was among them.

Stephen realized he had to talk to Jamal, even though his calls were never returned and communication had somehow stopped. He knew Jamal was on a Chicago leg all this month. It was the perfect time to catch him. He watched as Jamal nearly ran into him. "Hi there, Jamal," he said, nearly stopping the full herd of workers.

Jamal stared at him for what seemed like hours. Finally, he turned to the attendants standing on either side of him, and flashed a quick smile. "I'll catch up with you guys later, okay?" They both nodded, keeping their eyes on Stephen, obviously knowing who he was and letting him know the news was not very good. Jamal gave them both a reassuring glance, and they slowly departed.

Jamal rolled his flight bag in front of himself, as if creating a barrier of safety. He leaned on the handle as he spoke. "What's up, Stephen?"

"I just wanted to speak with you, Jamal. You're a hard man to catch up to."

"Imagine that," he replied, slinging his bag back behind him, as he began to walk away and toward the elevator.

Stephen followed, keeping his pace even with Jamal's. "Could you stop, Jamal, so I can talk to you?"

He did. So suddenly in fact, that Stephen collided with him. "What is it, Stephen? I'm very tired and I want to go to my room and rest."

Stephen threw his hands in the air, frustrated. "I miss you, all right? There, I said it, and I just want to say so much more ... if onlyyou would give me the chance."

Jamal opened his mouth to comment, but his eyes locked with Stephen's, and he saw the desperation there. He dropped his head. "You make things so difficult, Stephen. How can you talk about missing someone with your wife in the same house as you?"

"Felicia has nothing to do with this," Stephen reminded.

"I know what I saw, okay? It was obvious what happened in that place, and it's really none of my business."

Stephen shook his fists in front of Jamal, teeth gritted, eyes pressed into thin horizontal windows. "Stop that! Felicia means nothing to me. I'm here, aren't I? I came to see you and—"

"Flying out here only means you have the money to do it, nothing else," Jamal interrupted.

Stephen took a deep breath. "Can I just show you something?" he asked, holding out his arm toward the elevator.

Jamal looked at the elevator. "What are you talking about?" "Let's just go to my room. I want to show you something." "Your room? What room do you have in here?"

"I'm in room 18-D," Stephen said.

"18-D? I'm in 18-B. You're right across the hall?"

Stephen couldn't hide his amusement. "Well, imagine that."

– IV–

Damien turned off the vacuum cleaner just as David entered. He tried to not look worried, considering David hadn't returned home last night. "Are you okay?" he asked.

David walked to the sofa and lay down upon it, his hand placed on his forehead. "I'm fine. I had to think, that's all," he replied.

"I just hope you understand I'm not trying to kick you out or anything," Damien said, wheeling the vacuum back into the closet.

"I know, I know. I was getting too comfortable here, and you just put me in my place. I guess I need to get a little uncomfortable."

"Uncomfortable?" Damien questioned.

"Yeah, I need to get a little uncomfortable. I've always had to depend on someone else in my life. Allen spoiled me a lot, I guess, and maybe that's what makes it so hard to get him out of my life."

"That's not good, David. You have to do things for yo'self, baby," Damien explained, as he took a rag from the back of his jeans and began to dust his end tables.

David was silent for a moment. "Have you ever been so scared of being alone that it haunts you day and night? I feel that way, and I guess my health makes it worse. I don't want to go through life alone. I thought about what I am losing without Allen in my life, including the house, love, money..."

"You never had any of that with him, baby. It was never yo' shit to begin with. It was never yo love he had," Damien said, as he stopped dusting.

But it made me feel comfortable. When I first found out about my status, the doctor took me to a separate room filled with posters about messages concerning AIDS, its prevention and its treatments. Right then I knew what he was about to tell me. When he did, I was frozen. After he said, `David, your blood has been exposed to the AIDS virus,' I heard nothing else, although his lips were still moving. I could just picture me in a hospital bed with tubes running from me, pain exploding all through my body. I was frightened, and then I thought of Allen, and how I was glad he would be there for me, making life comfortable for me. And now there's nothing. It scares me to think about my mortality, Damien. It scares me to death sometimes. Can you understand something like that?"

Damien sat on the edge of the end table, placing the used rag in his lap. "Yeah, David, I get scared too. I had plenty of friends that have died too young. The new medications made it better to hide, but not always better to forget. The ads out there let me know that it isn't over, and since it isn't in my face, I worry that it is in my bed. I worry that someday it will surprise me with a phone call from someone I may have made a mistake with, or someone I may have wanted to make a mistake with. But here I am, living in this world, living this lifestyle, so all I can do is live."

"I don't know if life is worth it all," David said. "I don't know if I can survive."

"Don't think that, baby. Surviving your life means understanding it first, and you are used to living it by someone else's rules. It's hard living life, period. But a friend of mine once told me that with every bad day, there's a good one. We seem to travel around in a circle of living, and sometimes we're on the top, and others on the bottom, but we never stop traveling."

David sat up on the sofa, staring at Damien. "Boy, haven't heard you talk that much all summer," David said. They both laughed. "One thing I realized is that I do need to get my own place, get away from that man, and get a little uncomfortable in my own life until I'm in control of it."

"Sounds to me like you are already there," Damien said.

"Maybe so," David said. He paused for a moment before speaking again. "And what are you doing with a gun in the house, baby? You dating those hood rats again?"

Damien looked at the ceiling, as if contemplating his answer. He looked back at David, very intensely. "Well David, *mi amigo,* once upon a time I was scared. So scared that I too thought about going to a better place . . . I never quite made it though."

David felt a lump in his throat. "So do you ever think you will?" Damien grinned. "No, I don't think I will. Not in that way."

– V –

Stephen walked toward the dresser and stopped after seeing Jamal's reflection standing near the open door. "Would you please come in and have a seat on the bed or something, and relax? I'm not trying to pull you into a web of seduction or anything."

Jamal stepped forward, surveying the room. "What, no penthouse suite?" he asked, sarcastically. He pushed the handle of his bag down and sat upon it.

"I don't always have to spend the money I have," Stephen answered. "And I do have chairs in here." He swung his arms out to the small dining table and chairs.

Jamal ignored his offer. "So, what's up, Stephen? You did say you wanted to talk to me. I just got back from three legs, and I am a bit tired," Jamal said, crossing his arms.

Stephen appeared ready to comment but decided against it, and instead opened one of the top drawers in the dresser. He pulled out a few plastic objects, turned to face Jamal, and walked over to hand them to him. "I do want to talk to you. I want to say how sorry I am about all that's happened. I want to apologize about taking you for granted and taking advantage of our time together. I want to apologize for all the circumstances that involved Felicia, because none of it should've happened."

Jamal looked down to notice a few cassette tapes in his lap. He picked them up, turned them over, trying to figure out what they were, but couldn't. "Are these answering machine tapes or something?"

"Yes, that's right. They all have the messages you left me that I didn't get. When Felicia was home, she would let the machine take messages but claim it was broken. She'd take the tapes with messages out and replace them with blanks, trying to make it look as if the machine was erasing them. Just too much drama."

"And there you were thinking Tumali was messing with the machine."

Stephen sat on the bed. "Yeah, blaming my little boy for something his mother was doing. That was foolish of me. That night after the funeral she did a number on me too, which I would rather not go into right now, but one I am sure you could guess. Then she went crazy after seeing you in the hospital. If not for my son, I would've kicked her out as soon as I saw her in my house, but I think she knew that."

"You don't have to explain any more to me, Stephen. I knew that woman was trouble from the start. I knew she was still in love with you. You just needed convincing of that, and me being there was not going to help you see that."

Stephen stood, walked toward Jamal, and slowly reached out for his hand. Jamal allowed him, with a look of curiosity on his face. "I know I took you through a lot for someone you haven't known very long. But I want to start things over. I like you, Jamal. I can't lie about that. And I like spending time with you. I want it to continue somehow, and I hope you do too."

Jamal dropped his head. "That's a hard thing to ask for, Stephen. I've been through so many fuckin' disappointments in my life. You met one of them in a cold hospital room, a woman calling herself my mother, and then the men who used me as their boy toy, and street faggots trying to rob me, and my stepfather from the beginning. It makes trusting someone, anyone, really hard, and seemingly worthless."

Stephen *reached* down to take hold of Jamal's remaining hand. He held both against his stomach, and Jamal could feel the beat of his heart through his clothes. "I know about trust too, Jamal. I thought I could trust Felicia, but I was greatly disappointed. It just told me that people earn trust, and you have to know just how far you can extend it. I know to trust Felicia with my son's well-being, but not my own. I'm just asking that we communicate about what we want from each other. And you know how communication starts, don't you?"

"How does it?" Jamal inquired.

Stephen bent forward. "With the lips, of course," he replied, as he began to kiss Jamal gently on the lips.

When he pulled back, Jamal peered at him, holding back a smile. "That can always be a good first step."

Stephen tugged at Jamal's hands, pulling him up. "There are many more steps than that," he said, leading him away from his luggage and in the direction of the bathroom.

"And where are these steps leading me now?" he asked, watching as Stephen pushed the bathroom door open with his foot.

The smell of wax and roses hit Jamal's nose. The sunlight had gone, and darkness prevailed. Inside, Jamal noticed the bathroom window covered with a blanket. "What's this?" Jamal responded, seeing small reflections of light dance across the ceiling; candles stood around the floor, and there were even a few floating in the toilet.

"You did say you just finished three legs, quick turns I'm sure, and I thought you might want to freshen up. I happen to give wonderful sponge baths."

Jamal glanced at the bathtub, seeing the cloudiness of soap bubbles glistening atop, lined with candles and incense. A small stand had been placed in one corner, containing an assortment of grapes, chocolate-dipped strawberries, and tiny cheeses, with a small tray holding glass toothpicks. On the bubbles in the tub were numerous rose petals scattered about and also on the tub's rim. Under the stand Jamal could vaguely see two wine bottles and two flute glasses.

"Don't worry. The bottles contain sparkling spiced apple cider. And when you go, please take these with you," Stephen said, directing his arms toward the bathroom sink, which held a dozen long-stemmed roses standing up in the drain.

Jamal found it hard to speak. Stephen had done it again. "This is just too much, Stephen. How are—"

"I know it's a bit too much for someone that hasn't married me yet, but if it ends soon, at least the memories will last."

"How long have you planned this one?"

"Don't worry about it."

"I thought you said you weren't going to seduce me, Stephen." Stephen appeared shocked.

"Is that what you think I'm doing?" he replied with a smile of deceit.

"I don't know. James Bond, is it?"

Stephen placed a finger along Jamal's lips. "Why don't you stop with all the questions, and show me a little communication? You do know how communication starts, don't you?"

Jamal smiled. He knew.

Chanter 21

—I—

Jamal opened his eyes to see Stephen propped up on one elbow, head in hand, staring at him. "Now what are you up to?' Jamal asked, rubbing the sleep from his eyes.

"Just looking at you, that's all. No law against that, is there?" Stephen asked.

"Not right now, but next time there will be a fee. So what's on your mind?"

"Oh, I was just wondering where the chainsaw was coming from, and I turned to see it was your snoring."

"Snoring! I know I don't snore," Jamal said, snatching the pillow from beneath Stephen and hitting him over the head with it.

"Okay, okay," Stephen pleaded. "I was just kidding."

Jamal ceased his attack. "I thought you were."

They both smiled at each other. Last night had been wonderful. Stephen had ordered a fabulous meal after giving Jamal a soothing sponge bath. Stephen closed his eyes for a moment and could still feel Jamal's dark skin against his. He could still taste his warm flesh against his lips, his arms caressing his back, his manhood pressed firm against his belly. He opened his eyes and reached out toward this chocolate dream to run the tips of his fingers along the thin mat of hair that ran over Jamal's protruding chest.

Jamal looked into Stephen's yearning eyes. "So, what'cha thinking about?" he asked while taking hold of Stephen's hand.

Stephen smiled. "I was thinking how funny fate is. If I had decided to remain in Chicago and continued to be with Felicia, I would have still met you at the hospital, but I never would have known what I was missing." Stephen turned on his back, and stared at the ceiling, "And if you had remained on the street who knows what sort of man I would have met at the hospital."

"I could've been strung out on drugs, been hustling, been dead, or just remained a boy toy to some sugar daddy. Seems that fate has a funny way of bringing us to our destiny. My destiny had to do with not trusting men in the first place, which moved me from situation to situation."

"So when do you think you will ever start trusting people again, taking that chance to stop fighting destiny and find one you are comfortable with?" Stephen asked, sliding over to place his head in the cradle of Jamal's arm.

. "I think I already have, Stephen."

—II—

Dominique popped a Tylenol in her mouth and began to chew on the dry pill before remembering to wash it down with water. The morning was already starting out badly, and it was only ten o'clock! Yesterday Sarafina was going to explain about the contents of the videotape, after describing her quarrel with Gerri, but halfway into it, Dominique couldn't hear anymore. She didn't want to know the details of the tape, because somehow it just didn't matter. She could not let that device, that tool, become the reality Gerri had created.

Then this morning the *bitch* had called: "So you think you've won," she said in a slurred voice that indicated she had been drinking. Dominique had first questioned the caller, not quite recognizing the voice. "You know who the hell this is!" she'd blurted out. And when Dominique realized it, she wanted to burst out laughing, imagining this woman at the time Sarafina smacked the shit out of her. If only she had been there just for that. Gerri continued her outcry, reminding Dominique that the offer still stood, and if she cared anything about her employment with Shelby's D'Zines then she would take the money and run. She knew Angela, her boss, quite well.

Dominique kindly told her to stay out of her life and to take her money and to fuck herself.

She then contacted her at work through her private line; the whore had some major connections. "I meant what I said!" she yelled before Dominique could slam the phone back on its base. Heads popped up from their separate cubicles to look in her direction. And no sooner had her ear cooled from the phone than Angela e-mailed her, requesting to see her in her office in one hour. .

That's when the Tylenol came into play.

Dominique had to admire Gerri's tenacity, and could only conjecture what had been said between the two. There had been no grounds to dismiss her from the company, yet there were delays due to weather and zoning laws, and obtaining the permits required. Then there was the fabric purchasing fiasco with Nancy and McNeal. No, this meeting could only mean bad news. And as the clock ticked, Dominique found herself unable to work even what could be her last hour in this company. She needed to see Angela now; the anticipation was not to her liking. After all, this was her career.

***

Dominique slowly opened the door, and stood in the threshold as Angela continued to peck at her computer. "Please, have a seat," she offered as she continued to stare at the screen.

Dominique stepped forward, closing the door behind her, and stepped to the awaiting chair in front of Angela's desk. Angela continued with her work, as if barely aware of Dominique's presence.

"How are you doing today, Dominique?" Angela asked suddenly, almost startling her. She ceased typing and spun around to face Dominique, very attentively.

She feigned a smile. "I'm doing well, Angela."

Angela craned back in her seat, crossed her legs. She extended a hand across her desk to pull a crystal clock closer to her. "Hmm, I see you've arrived a bit early for our meeting." Dominique opened her mouth to respond, but Angela continued. "Just as well. I have a lunch appointment very soon. We'll make this expeditious."

"That's fine. I still have a few purchase orders to look over for the office furniture," Dominique replied timidly, unable to break her lock with Angela's piercing stare, trying in vain to read her emotions.

"Which brings me to the focus of this meeting. Shall I get straight to the point, Dominique?"

"By all means, please," Dominique responded, holding her breath.

"Yes, by all means," Angela agreed, as she reached over to the side of her computer monitor to collect a coffee cup. She sipped at its steaming rim as if she had all the time in the world. "I'm taking you off the Gerri contract, and I've decided to handle it directly myself."

Dominique felt a surge, as if all the blood in her body had rushed to her brain. She was voiceless. It was akin to the sensation of falling in a dream but never reaching the ground. She was caught in a frightful vertigo. "I see," was all she could utter.

Angela placed her elbows on the desk, trying to remain sympathetic. "Now, please don't think this is in any way a reflection of your performance in handling the—"

"What else am I to think, Angela?" Dominique blurted out, surprised at even herself. It came across as a statement more from frustration than anger. But it came out nonetheless, and she'd cut off Angela in the process. She'd never done that.

"Excuse me, Dominique?" Angela queried - her tone neutral.

She inhaled silently, then continued in a more restrained tone. "I assume that you've spoken to Gerri about this?"

Angela took another sip of her coffee. "Would you like some coffee, Dominique, before we continue?" she suggested.

"No, thank you."

"Very well then. Yes, I did speak to Gerri, and I assured her—"

"And I assume you are basing this decision on some conversation you two had about me?"

"In part, yes, but that—"

Dominique placed a hand on Angela's desk. "I'm sorry, Angela, but I think this is rather unfair. I'm not sure what transpired in the conversation you two had, but you have to know that Gerri and I knew of each other prior to her becoming a client with this firm. She's had a great resentment of me, and her personal bias should not be indicative of my work performance. You know I do good work, and I don't think you should have to listen to—"

Angela cleared her throat boldly, getting Dominique's immediate attention. "Please, Dominique! I didn't bring you in here to reveal what private matters Gerri and I discussed, nor to have you question my decisions. Yes, I spoke to Gerri, and she did express her displeasure with the way this project was being handled. I explained to her that this contract was being handled by the both of us, and that you were still under my tutelage. I told her that I would take care of it. Gerri has had a good working relationship with Shelby's D'Zines, and I want that partnership to continue, but it can't if things start to get personal. She brings a lot of money into this firm, and if she is having personal problems with an employee of mine, then it is my responsibility to handle the matter in a way I think fair for both parties."

"I don't see the fairness of it at all, Angela. I think the whole thing is a bit lame."

"What was that?" Angela asked, a bit shaken.

"I feel I shouldn't have to lose my chance at a promotion because of the personal opinions of a woman who keeps our stocks high."

"Who said anything about losing a promotion?"

Dominique looked at Angela, puzzled. "You're taking me off a project that would eventually lead to a position as senior designer. That sounds like a demotion, or at least a lack of promotion, to me."

Angela shook her head, as she indulged in her drink once again. She then reached around to the side of her computer once more, bringing out two Cifuentes cigars. She tossed one of the Jamaican Lonsdales at Dominique. "It has a woodsy taste, but I think you'll like it," Angela said.

"What's this for?" Dominique questioned, while twirling the cigar in her fingers.

"My dear, this meeting is in honor of your promotion, not demotion. Starting tomorrow, you will be in charge of the Thomas Sounds Studio account. They're remodeling their West Coast facility, and I want you to have entire reign of the project. You are familiar with Thomas Sounds, aren't you?"

Dominique knew exactly who they were. She was unaware of any bidding for this contract, but she knew they were one of the fastest growing sound and engineering studios in the United States, catering both to television, movies, and numerous commercials. She knew they were worth more in millions than Gerri Cosmetics could ever hope to attain. She continued to look at Angela in awe, who in turn grinned in pleasure at bearing such good news.

"You ready to go?" came a voice from behind Dominique. Someone else had entered the room, and for some reason the voice sounded familiar.

Angela looked up, the dark brown cigar hanging form her lips, "Just a moment. I was congratulating Dominique on her promotion."

"Oh, wonderful. I gather you've told her everything," said the mysterious voice as it approached closer to the back of Dominique's chair. There was a reassuring hand placed momentarily on her shoulder. This woman came into the room to stand next to Angela and proceeded to sit on the corner of the desk; her back was facing Dominique.

"No, not quite," Angela replied to this thin framed female in a beautiful silk skirt, hair cut short to the nape of her neck.

"Don't you think you should, before we have our lunch?" the woman asked, as she began to do something quite unexpected: She leaned forward just as Angela tilted her head upward to exchange a kiss!

Dominique was floored! The thin woman then turned to face Dominique and, to her surprise, it was . . . "Ms. Kai!" she said, shocked. Cyan Kai, Gerri's friend from San Francisco. The woman who had driven Sarafina back home. Angela was lesbian! Where was the Tylenol when she needed it?

Cyan stood and swung around, the tail of her skirt twisted around her thighs. "Hello, Dominique. I guess we meet again, full circle. Funny how life is sometimes," she said, placing her hands on her hips.

Dominique couldn't find the voice to say anything. All questions seemed to retreat from her throat and into her belly, where they festered.

Angela placed her hands on her desk, slapped her palms together, and rotated her thumbs. She too seemed at a loss for words, but spoke regardless. "You see, Cyan and I have been together for almost a good year now, so it stands to reason that I've been quite aware of this triangle you've been caught in for quite some time. I was uncomfortable giving you the Gerri account, but it was a good project, regardless of who had controlling interest. When Gerri called me this morning, her conversation had unexpectedly strayed from business, so much in fact that I knew I had a problem on my hands. It was in the best interest of all involved that you be moved to another contract and that I finish the Gerri Cosmetics one myself. We have a meeting with our new clients in four days, which will give you enough time to research the company, and I'll be able to get some blueprints of the building on disk. Today, however, will be spent on catching me up on the Gerri account. But that's later. How do you feel right now, Dominique? I know this all comes as a blow to you."

"So this means I'm a senior designer?" Dominique asked, her mind still caught in limbo.

Angela and Cyan looked at each other, both amused at Dominique's awe. "Of course it does. We'll talk about it more tomorrow."

"Well, I don't know what to say, except thank you. I want to say thank you too," Dominique addressed Cyan. "You've been a great help, and I appreciate it."

"Don't think about it. I saw how unstable Gerri was becoming, and I didn't think it was fair she hurt you in the process. She's a powerful woman, but also a very disillusioned one, and she hurts a lot. I just couldn't witness her bringing someone else down into her pain.

"I appreciate that, Ms. Kai."

'Cyan, please. And you're welcome."

"Now are you ready for lunch? I am hungry," Angela reminded, poking Cyan in the stomach.

"You're always hungry," Cyan replied, tapping Angela playfully on the head.

"I guess I should be leaving. I presume that this meeting is over," Dominique spoke as she began to rise from her seat.

Angela quickly regained her composure. "Very well, Dominique. If you want, you can take the day off, and we'll take care of things tomorrow morning."

"I just might do that. It's been a trying day," Dominique replied.

"Oh," Cyan quickly interjected, "I was able to get Sarafina's things from Gerri's housekeeper, so I'll be bringing them to your home sometime this week. Her bag was untouched, so no need to worry about it."

"Thanks again, Ms. Kai."

"Cyan, please."

"Well, thank you very much, Cyan. I'll talk to..." Dominique watched the two engage in idle chitchat and knew she wasn't being heard. It didn't matter—it didn't matter at all.

– III –

"So, how's your mother doing?" Stephen asked, as he bounced Tumali on his knee.

Felicia appeared to intentionally avoid eye contact as she replied. "She's doing pretty well, despite her weakness, and they expect her to be good enough to come home within a week or so. I'll stay with her for a while until I'm sure she's all right.

"Good. She's a strong woman, and she'll bounce back, I'm certain," Stephen replied, as he looked around the terminal. The Chicago airport was so huge compared to that of LAX that it overwhelmed him. .

"Yeah, the Jenkins women are strong ones indeed," Felicia responded, as she glimpsed in Stephen's direction, then shot her attention elsewhere.

That quick glance was enough to let Stephen know that her feelings would take a long time to change too; she was still very much in love with him.

Jamal had gone to the hospital, but he was taking a flight later that would get him into Los Angeles by midnight. Dinner was to be served at Jamal's place, and Stephen would be the cook. Jamal jokingly said that perhaps it would be better to go out to Aunt Kizzy's to take a few notes first. Stephen wasn't really a cook, but he desperately wanted to try what he knew, or at least what his mother had shown him while visiting, and that was soul food - hence the joke about Aunt Kizzy's.

"I'm sorry, Stephen," Felicia suddenly apologized.

Stephen looked away from his son, and into Felicia's eyes. The pain that registered there caused him to quickly look away. "I'm sorry, Felicia, what did you say?"

"Hey! I don't say that word very often, so listen up, okay?" she expressed, her lips pressed in mock anger. "I wanted to apologize to you for my foolishness in California. There is no excuse for my attitude, and I am deeply sorry for trying to ruin this lifestyle you're trying to enjoy."

"Everything's worked itself out, Felicia. I accept your apology, and I am sorry that we can't—"

"I just hope you take care of yourself," Felicia interrupted. She cleared her throat, as she continued. "And, how is…Jamal?"

"He's fine," Stephen replied.

Felicia lowered her head, then spoke very softly. "I wish we had gotten to know each other a little better. I've done little but think about him ever since seeing him at the hospital. My father's opinions still affects me, I guess."

"Yeah, the attitude of homophobia is very contagious."

Felicia was tempted to protest but held her tongue. She fell back in her seat at the truth of the statement. She was angry, angry at every faggot that graced her eyesight. Her father hated Jamal, hated him for coming out of the closet. He then took that hatred out on the family and consequently Felicia hated the source of that anger. To know that Stephen was gay and that he was in a relationship with her half-brother made the love or understanding of the gay lifestyle something she would never embrace. Yet Margaret was right in one thing: Stephen did have the good sense to leave; she unfortunately hadn't.

"But you never know, Felicia. Maybe you can talk with him," Stephen suggested.

"Maybe, Stephen, but that time is not now, for either of us, I believe."

"You could be right," Stephen agreed. There was an announcement over the loudspeakers, and Stephen realized that it referred to his flight. "Well, it seems they're calling the first-class passengers to board now," he said, lifting Tumai from his knee and placing him on the floor. The child spun around to grasp Stephen's leg, attempting to scale his father once again. "Daddy!" he cried, holding up his tiny arms.

Felicia reached down to nudge the child's shoulder. "Stop, Tumali. Daddy has to go."

Stephen stood, as he ran his fingers through his son's hair. "Yeah, Daddy has to go back to work, little man."

"No! No! No!" Tumali bellowed, stomping his feet, his attempt at being heard thwarted by the dense blue carpet underfoot.

Felicia eased from her seat, grabbed Tumali by his waist, and stood. "He's gonna miss you, Stephen," Felicia said, as they began to walk toward the boarding area and the jet bridge.

"I'm gonna miss him too," he replied, gently pinching Tumali's cheeks. He leaned forward to kiss him on his lips. Tumali lunged toward him to wrap his arms around his father's neck. Stephen accepted it for a moment until he felt a wave of emotion overcome him, and he pulled back, grabbing hold of Tumali's tiny fingers, kissing the tips. "Daddy will be back real soon," he promised, then looked up at Felicia. "I need you here to take care of your mother."

Felicia smiled. "I'm gonna miss you too, Stephen," she replied hesitantly.

Stephen placed a hand on her arm, squeezing it kindly. "Do me a favor, Felicia, and take care of yourself. And make sure Margaret gets better," he said, then leaned forward to kiss her tenderly on the forehead.

"I will," she replied, her eyes closed. When he stood back, she placed her fingers on her forehead, and could still feel the warmth of his lips there. She opened her eyes. "Yeah, I'll do that."

"Bye, Tumali. I'll be back around Labor Day to visit you. Your grandmother is gonna cook all of your favorites."

"Bye, Daddy," Tumali replied, as he watched his father retreat into the throng of people near the jet bridge.

Stephen could see them both waving as he fell into the crowd, watching his family retreat into the distance. As he did, he could see Felicia, and her lips form the words *I love you.*

—IV—

David walked along the boardwalk, looking at the herd of people around him also walking Venice Beach. His hands were stuffed into his pockets, as he stared down at the pavement, simply thinking.

"Girl! You knows this is funny, honey," Damien said as he came crashing into David's shoulder, trying to balance on his Rollerblades. "I don't see why you don't get some skates. It's gonna take you forever to get to Santa Monica Pier with me."

"I said on the way back. I just want to walk right now," David replied, as he pushed Damien away from his shoulder.

"Girlfriend, if you can't stand up on those wheels, you need to be walking yourself."

"And miss the chance for my husband to pick me up off the ground? I don't think so, sweetheart. Besides, too many damn men to see for me to be strolling on my feet and missing the eye candy. See you on the next go-round," Damien said, as he braced himself, and took off again along the boulevard.

David watched his friend speed off into the mass of people along the street. Diva was dressed in thick blue socks pushed down to the lips of his skates, spandex biker shorts, a midriff tank top, and a blue baseball cap set low on his head. He was spilling more tea than Lipton could soak up in a day. He should have just waved a gay flag and finished off the ensemble.

David was glad Damien invited him to the beach. It was a nice day, and the sands were crowded with all types of delicious-looking men. It was also a tranquil enough atmosphere to do a little soul searching. David felt as if he were reaching a turning point in his life. His living situation was surely on the verge of change. He needed a place of his own. The illusion of moving back in with Allen died when word came back as to what Malcolm had done to him: Allen had called him in a frenzy, claiming that he'd come home one day to find a pair of young thugs—dressed in oversized pants, high-tops, thick braids, an overabundance of gold jewelry, dark shades, and carrying guns—relaxing on his sofa. He'd never seen them before, as they calmly helped themselves to his bottled beer from the fridge. They smoothly threatened him, his house, and his car, if he were to ever mess with Malcolm or David. They then casually walked out the door. Allen had seen them from time to time since then following him. He'd become so paranoid that he was in the process of selling his home and moving.

David thought it was rather funny, and never confronted Malcolm with it. There were a few of his things still remaining at Allen's place, and he decided to allow Stephen and Dominique to go and retrieve them. It was just frightening to think of Allen being out of his life, out of his bed, out of his day-to-day routine. He was afraid of the loneliness—not from lack of friends, but from lack of friends that had gone through what he had been going through. He knew it would take time, but time was all he had. He'd been in denial for two years— both he and Allen had—and it was time that he stopped hiding from life, hiding from his status, hiding from his abuse, hiding from his fear. Life was waiting for him to live it.

He wasn't ready to see Malcolm yet. That was the hardest decision he had to make in his new life. Malcolm knew nothing about his status or his emotional state, and he wasn't prepared to share it with him either. Malcolm wasn't ready to become his friend. His actions showed his possessive nature. David had had enough of dealing with that.

He thanked God for his friends. They were there for him through it all. It was so hard to find true friends in a world of selfishness. Except for being a bit more motherly, they treated him no different. They would have to fill that gap left by Allen, and he knew they were willing to take on that minor chore.

Having to deal with Andrew's passing was the toughest exercise in mind control he'd ever had to accomplish. He could not get the picture of Andrew lying in that hospital bed, with his big head smiling and tiny body suffering, out of his thoughts. In dreams, David could see himself there, in that same bed, and he would wake terrified, in a cold sweat. He worried too much about situations that hadn't even transpired yet except in his own mind. He was too busy worrying about the colors without realizing he was looking at the rainbow.

David looked up and almost burst into laughter at seeing Damien sprawled upon a patch of grass, flat on his butt, perspiration across his forehead, as the wheels of his skates continued to spin, mocking him in his fall. "What happened?" he asked, as he neared his hapless companion.

"Baby," he said, panting heavily, "My ass is tired! Thighs hurtin' like I been workin' my kitty cat with some man or something. This Rollerblading shit is too much for a diva, girl."

You act like those thighs ain't used to some exercise," David commented, placing his hand on his hips.

"Horizontal, baby, horizontal! I don't do any vertical work. I don't stand on my feet too long without getting a paycheck, darling. Of course I could get one on the horizontal too, now that I think of it."

"Get your crazy butt up," David said, offering his hand. Damien reached out for it and David hoisted him up.

"Girl, I feel like some cotton candy!" Damien said, as he attempted to walk in his skates. "We're almost at the peer, so I guess I'll walk." Damien stopped and quickly slipped out of his skates. He then walked along the pavement with his socks on, grimacing with each step, holding his burning thighs. David thought it was amusing.

"You're gonna get your socks dirty, Damien. Why don't you take them off?"

Damien leaned in closer to David. "I didn't get my pedicure this week, child. No way these girls are gonna he talking about me in the morning."

"Yeah, I guess it's better than seeing you fall on your ass," David laughed. "And what's that smell?" David asked, sniffing the air. Damien raised his nose to the wind. "What?"

"Is that you excreting pussy juice again? You gonna have the men running over here in a stampede, if you don't learn to exude that a little more sparingly."

"Oh, shut up," Damien joked, wrapping his arms around David and punching him lightly on the jaw. "You need to quit it. And you leave my wet snatch alone."

David grinned. No comment. He just thought about his life and thought about how much more there was to live, and how eager he was to live it with the wonderful friends he had.

The End

ABOUT THE AUTHOR

Vernon Clay, a native of Chicago, Illinois, attended the prestigious Columbia College, where he studied creative writing. He has written short stories for *The Advocate* and *SBC Magazine*. This is his first published novel. He now lives in Chicago, Ill., where he is working on his second novel.